THE FRIENDS OF MEAGER FORTUNE

David Adams Richards is the author of *River of the Brokenhearted*, *Mercy Among the Children*, which won the 2000 Giller Prize and was nominated for the Governor General's Award and the Trillium Award, and *The Bay of Love and Sorrows*, which has been made into a feature film.

ALSO BY DAVID ADAMS RICHARDS

Fiction

The Coming of Winter

Blood Ties

Dancers at Night: Stories

Lives of Short Duration

Road to the Stilt House

Nights Below Station Street

Evening Snow Will Bring Such Peace

For Those Who Hunt the Wounded Down

Hope in the Desperate Hour

The Bay of Love and Sorrows

Mercy Among the Children

River of the Brokenhearted

Non-fiction

Hockey Dreams

Lines on the Water

DAVID ADAMS RICHARDS

The Friends of Meager Fortune

VINTAGE BOOKS
London

Published by Vintage 2008

2 4 6 8 10 9 7 5 3 1

First published in Great Britain in 2006 by Jonathan Cape

Vintage
Random House, 20 Vauxhall Bridge Road,
London SW1V 2SA

www.vintage-books.co.uk

Addresses for companies within The Random House Group Limited can be found at: www.randomhouse.co.uk/offices.htm

The Random House Group Limited Reg. No. 954009

A CIP catalogue record for this book is available from the British Library

ISBN 9780099499183

The Random House Group Limited supports The Forest Stewardship Council (FSC), the leading international forest certification organisation. All our titles that are printed on Greenpeace approved FSC certified paper carry the FSC logo. Our paper procurement policy can be found at www.rbooks.co.uk/environment

Printed and bound in Great Britain by
CPI Bookmarque, Croydon, CR0 4TD

For my friends

Brian Bartlett, Wayne Curtis, Jack Hodgins, Doug Underhill

And for my sons

John and Anton

With love

THE FRIENDS OF MEAGER FORTUNE

PART I

ONE

I had to walk up the back way, through a wall of dark winter nettles, to see the ferocious old house from this vantage point. A black night and snow falling, the four turrets rising into the fleeing clouds above me. A house already ninety years old and with more history than most in town.

His name was Will Jameson.

His family was in lumber, or was Lumber, and because of his father's death he left school when just a boy and took over the reins of the industry when he was not yet sixteen. He would wake at dawn, and deal with men, sitting in offices in his rustic suit or out on a cruise walking twenty miles on snowshoes, be in camp for supper and direct men twice as old as he.

By the time he was seventeen he was known as the great Will Jameson of the great Bartibog—an appendage as whimsical as it was grandiose, and some say self-imposed.

As a child I saw the map of the large region he owned—dots for his camps, and Xs for his saws. I saw his picture at the end of the hallway—under the cold moon that played on the chairs and tables covered in white sheets, the shadow of his young, ever youthful face; an idea that he had not quite escaped the games of childhood before he needed gamesmanship.

If we Canadians are called hewers of wood and drawers of water, and balk, young Will Jameson did not mind this assumption, did not mind the crass biblical analogy, or perhaps did not know or care it was one, and leapt toward it in youthful pride, as through a burning ring. The strength of all moneyed families is their ignorance of or indifference to chaff. And it was this indifference to jealousy and spite that created the destiny Jameson believed in (never minding the Jamesian insult toward it), which made him prosperous, at a place near the end of the world.

When he was about to be born his mother went on the bay and stayed with the Micmac man Paul Francis and his wife. She lived there five months while her husband, Byron Jameson, was working as an ordinary axman in the camps, through a winter and spring.

In local legend the wife of Paul Francis was said to have the gift of prophecy when inspired by drink, and when Mary Jameson insisted her fortune be read with a pack of playing cards, she was told that her first-born would be a powerful man and have much respect—but his brother would be even greater, yet destroy the legacy by rashness, and the Jameson dynasty not go beyond that second boy.

Mrs. Francis warned that the prophecy would not be heeded, and therefore happen. It would happen in a senseless way, but of such a route as to look ordinary. Therefore the reading became instead of fun or games a very solemn reading that dark spring night, long ago, as the Francis woman sat in her chair rocking from one side to the other, and looking at the cards through half-closed eyelids.

"Then there is a choice," Mary Jameson said, still trying to make light of its weight.

"If wrong action is avoided—but be careful to know what wrong action is."

"In work?"

"In life," said Mrs. Francis, picking the cards up and placing them away in a motion that attested to her qualifications.

Mary Jameson had the boy christened Will, and had Paul and Joanna Francis as his godparents. During the baptism, the sun which had not shone all day began to do so, through the stained glass. Mary decided she would keep this prophecy to herself. But she told her husband, who as the youngster grew became more affluent, and spoiled solemnity by speaking of the prophecy as a joke.

Soon the prophecy was known by others, and over time translated in a variety of ways.

It was true Mary forgot about it until the second boy, Owen, was born, so sickly he almost died.

She forgot about it again, until her husband was killed in a simple, almost absurd accident on the Gum Creek Road, coming out to inspect his mill on a rain-soaked day in April.

Mary thinking that it was a strange way for her husband to be taken from her. She almost a grandmother's age with two small boys. Worse, she had asked her husband to come out on that spring day—frightened that he would take to the drive and be injured, and he was killed by a fall on a road.

Mary and her brother Buckler took over the mill until Will came into his own, which was soon enough, and seemingly too soon for his competition.

It is a common misconception that people are as bright as their knowledge. Will Jameson was a boy far brighter than what he knew, which is an ordinary problem in a country like ours, partly in bondage to winter, where snow is a great blessing on the land. His father had started with nothing but a crippled roan horse—and Will now had camps and horses and men, and a sawmill he had to take care of.

He left school because of his father's death, and said leaving school was the least thing he ever regretted.

"Holding him is like holding a current itself," Old Estabrook said of the young man.

Yet his mother, Mary, warned him, he had his faults, could be cruel or uncaring, and laughed at his mother's sentiment and superstition. These traits came gradually. That is, he believed, because it was what society believed, what his father had believed, that a stiff presence at church service was what constituted good behavior, and jokes were meant to be manly and told in private. He thought, even at seventeen, of children as a woman's responsibility and a man's ignorance of the offspring showed a healthy character.

"She'll be wantin' me to believe in saints soon enough," he said of Mary. "Some darn old statues with damn wings."

But even as a boy there was never a person, or a nation that person was from, that he deliberately insulted, knowing how things were held against his father for no apparent reason. Nor could there be talk against the Indian, Brit, French, Scot, or Irish, or any other at supper, without him leaving the table and saying: "Besides us all needing a horsewhip, each nation is the same."

It was true he had a brother. The younger boy Owen he himself deemed "too sensitive" and "too weak" for the industry their family owned.

The second son Mary looked upon in secret, and decided over time there was nothing in him that could be mettle for greatness.

As time passed Will, who ran the house like a patriarch, decided this younger boy take what lessons his own leadership offered. He did not proffer this; it simply seemed the way things would be. Once a month he would come to his brother and speak about what Owen might do with his life. These lectures were impersonal ramblings, caught up in ideas of what a man should say to a boy. They were an embarrassment to Owen, who saw through them but loved his brother enough not to say so.

Will decided he would give the younger boy something—dentistry, he supposed. He decided this when he himself had a toothache.

"Goddamn thing," he said, staring at Owen and coming to that conclusion. Of course his mother wanted it too—that is, dentistry for the boy—because it would be nice to have at least one dentist in the family. In all her life she had not known a relative who had gone to school. In fact, if truth be told, she had not known a relative. Being younger by two years, Owen would have to do what Will said, for Will's temperament was iron, and he held the reins in a society which at that time demanded leadership from the first-born son.

Will was like his dead father, with a shrewd mind and fists to match, when required.

The younger son, however, was fanciful and into fairness.

Will hated fancy, and could not fathom fairness. That is, fairness could never be parceled, and he shunned those who thought so.

The poetry of the woods he himself sang, and was known to have penned a song or two. Still he frowned upon his brother's ideals, and all those books brought to the upstairs shelves were like slights toward Will, whose proudest moment was to state he would earn a million and never read a book.

In 1936 *Ulysses* was brought into the house by Owen Jameson—the Joyce that destroyed the Irish, Will said (because he had asked someone who Joyce was). He threw it into the stove. Mary, if she disapproved, condoned this action by silence.

This was the bowing and scraping to a propriety that men of Will Jameson's ilk believed they never bowed or scraped to. It was also the despotic teaching of mother, of school, of school principal, of pastor, of pastor's maid, of the maid's toady, of toady's boy, and of almost every twat on the street—all strangled by that propriety embracing tyranny, from university dorm down, that Will had by such independent measure escaped, and now unknowingly, unwittingly embraced, because power allowed him to. This then was Will's ultimate sin. One he never admitted, and therefore could not correct.

"I do not need no learning from no fuggin' book like that there," Will said proudly.

"He lives in poverty and great want," Owen said of Joyce.

"I'll feed him but I won't read him," said Will, showing his measure of charity and justice.

This was serious for Owen—for he was in all ways under his older brother's talons, and knew enough to realize he had, at that moment, no say. Or at least no say in the open. He decided, therefore, to leave the house, but got no farther than a street in Moncton when he decided to come home. It was three days later, but the very supper he had left was sitting at the table waiting.

Will was in all these household promotions and demotions his own man, even before his father died. Saying himself with a look of consternation when he was fourteen: "There is nothing to be done with Owen—he ain't sharp," and spitting a head of snot into the straw of the barn in youthful bravado at the contempt untested youth holds for weakness.

Therefore put him "out in the world," which meant for some reason, for Will, "not the world I know."

"It'll be a dentist's work for that boy," Will would tell his budding friends on a three-day moose hunt in late September, with the smell of moose hide and sperm and blood mingling with the fall's early budget, the huge carcass of the animal hanging down from spruce tripod, next to the white tent in the sunny and somehow muted clearing.

Reggie Glidden, Will's best friend, would caution him not to be rash with Owen.

"No—its dentistry for the youngster," Will said in fancy of a grown man, when he was in the camp taking a beaker of water. Yes, a somewhat practical profession, this dentistry business, and not given to the world of fancy, like *Ulysses*, which in truth disturbed Will more than it had his mother. Nor allow him, this Owen, the raw world or the tough world or the untamed world, our world where we must live and wrestle to protect those boys like Owen from their fuggin' selves.

Did Will know that he himself lived in a world of fancy, of guns and hides and treks into unknown wilds that Ulysses proper would approve of? Mary herself sometimes wondered it when she sat home knitting of a night. But if not, there was no time for a man of action to mope about and find out. He was the product himself of rebellion, his mother and father married at seventeen, when everyone thought his father would be a failure, nothing more than another of the thousands who used an ax. His father had begun their prosperity, Will made it fivefold by taking chances and dealing blows to the two great mills on the river—Estabrook and Sloan—making two rivals, who whispered rumors about him in grave ignorance and envy, hoping to stop him up.

They spoke about it to the twaddle on the street and hoped loyalty, envy, and common despair would allow others to take up their cause against this whelp. Others did take it up in the famine of their lives to impart disgrace on the Jameson name.

So Will became a target of many, too proud to say so and too young to know the consequences over time.

Will, after a fight at a dance with a Sloan man, wanted to carry a pistol, and though kind enough longed to shoot at least one man in the head, hearing that his father had once done the same at a quarry during a fight over a stone.

"The Sloans' men are bastards and will cause trouble to prove it—they have terrorized their own and so will terrorize others."

To prove to Owen that dentistry was easy, he took pliers and hauled from his own mouth a rotted shard of a tooth, spitting blood before him as he walked. "There you go, boy," he said, "don't be flinchin' at the sight of no blood."

Will would not see his mother or younger brother for weeks on end. And when he passed Owen on the back stair steps coming from the pantry, he would nod in taciturn embarrassment at the boy's eagerness to please. The dark eyes, the blond hair, the frame weak and not large, but the voice and temperament somewhat inspired—like his mother perhaps, who doted more upon him.

The year after Will took over the entire Jameson tract, Owen fell in love with a whimsical, emotional girl named Lula Brower. She had a father, Angus Brower, the prosecutor, who might be said to have disliked Byron Jameson, and she had airs of refinement, airs of fairness, her grandfather being a preacher. And if she liked Owen, which some say in hindsight she did, her father did not—did not like the Jameson family—Owen's father having, it was said, cut Brower's father out of a certain spot of land. So our Mr. Brower had nothing good to say, and Lula as his child seemed to catch this in fleeting moments herself. For she could be undeniably cruel to the boy. Most of it was done in simple naïveté and from the idea that what she heard from her own father—who kept much from her, and organized her life—must be true.

Owen would walk up to her lane in the drowsy summer and stand near her property, the small barren house with its tiny porch and insignificant maple tree in the yard. Her father, as town prosecutor, did not like lumbermen especially. They fought and caroused far too much for his liking. He brought too many to court for his liking. He had sent enough to jail. Besides, his daughter had been singled out as "the most talented girl" by our local adjudicator, and he wanted for her more than a common life.

There was another girl at this house on George Street, this solid mass of solid, uninspired people Owen wanted to impress. Her name was Camellia. There was a dark side to her story. Lula's father had prosecuted the girl's father, put him to death for murdering the girl's mother in Winch's Cave some years before.

There was no reason for her not to be an ordinary girl—except the profound realization that the entire town knew her father had hanged, her mother murdered, and already she was the object of what bedeviled so many: scandal and gossip. People said she would ruin a life or two herself, and watched for some signal that this would happen.

Lula kept tabs on her, and had her friends, the Steadfast Few, as she called them, observe Camellia as well. "For signs," as they said.

It was as if Camellia was put into a corner and told not to move when music spilled out of the air. Finally a toe would move. And the scandal came easily—off the tongues of those girls, those Steadfast Few. For rumors against woebegone boys could be true. And the Steadfast Few, as small-town, lower-middle-income girls, loved rumor the best.

Owen's father, Byron, they decided that summer, must have been Camellia's mother's "love." And now this Owen was "sneaking about again." All this speculation went on in the rinse and tide of that sunny little porch, where little Lula Brower sat holding little court.

"Oh dear and here he comes again," she would hear.

Owen Jameson had decided he loved Lula because she read, and because her uncle was a professor, named Professor Stoppard, who wrote poems. Poems that rhyme and don't lie, Lula said.

Owen, wise on many fronts, was gullible here. And he paid little attention to that other girl then, or to the gloomy self-righteous stares of the Steadfast Few.

So one day he told Lula he read books, like her uncle, Professor Stoppard. She showed no interest, even when he talked very well about these books. She ignored him, and rolled her eyes as he spoke. Then, as a last resort, a few days before it was thrown to the fire, he brought *Ulysses* to her. There, in the heart of that little house, with those very wise people, he read a part aloud.

After this, Lula and the girls decided Owen couldn't come back. She had talked it over with her friends. The reading, to them, was from a "horrible thing" that was not at all "acceptable."

And they were to protect Camellia if no one else.

So Owen was told to leave, while his rival Solomon Hickey looked on from the other side of Lula's porch door.

This was only a week or two in his life, in the middle of a drowsy summer, in the middle of adolescence, and would have ebbed away and been forgotten except for events later to take place.

Owen went home, and lovesickness overcame him. He didn't eat. He would not go outside. They lived in a large house on the edge of unkept fields at a place called the last outskirt. They were a family in the lumbering trade, and stared down over the town. Blocks and tackles and chains surrounded their muddy doors.

They had children and folks from broken lives for charity. And two old sleds (two giant sleds attached on which horses hauled the great trees from the woods) and log pits and broken tack, attended them in silence. Mary dressed in finery to go out, often had her shoes covered by manure when leaving the yard. The police were known to have come there to settle teamsters' disputes, over everything from horses to plug tobacco.

Jokes grew up about them, about poor unkempt Mary Jameson, her dotty brother, and her two wild boys. In the yard and paddocks, the great broad-backed draft horses that hauled the two sleds prodded and cantered. All weighed over half a ton. The toughest and smallest was the Belgium, which still could weigh twelve hundred pounds. It was most compact and most relied upon. Slightly bigger were the Clydesdales with their beautiful manes and soft-haired feet. These were the drafts the Jamesons relied upon themselves. Then there were the Percherons—a hand taller than the Clydesdales but more gangly in the legs. All were able to haul thousands of pounds of timber.

These Jamesons did not turn toward the town to work, with its shops and post office tower and giddy Grand Theatre. They turned toward the vast expanse behind them—beyond them, where men likened to soldiers lived and died. It was here that the prosecutor tried them on three occasions, hoping to lay a charge against this Will—not to ruin him but to instill in him respect for a law he assumed did not apply to free men like himself. Once over a stolen horse, once over the disposition of landings (last year's logs washed up or left on a skid pile) on the shore, once over an "episode" in town.

They were a house and a people solitary and much talked about and often discussed, especially now that Will Jameson, only eighteen, had to manage a lumber industry of upwards of ten million board feet, walked in and out of camps collecting pay sheets and staring down grown men when he had to.

This was the house, at the top of the town, where Will Jameson came from. This was the dark, brooding, unkempt, windy, solitary place gray-haired Mary Jameson tried to keep going.

They were dynasts growing up under the sword of Damocles. And if they were damned by it, both of them damned it, for both boys were solitary from "living in a half-wild state." Even Owen was wild enough to make one mother "just cringe to see his apelike amble."

And this is why Lula didn't like him. For all her ideas of education what was and was not acceptable to others was the litmus test she herself must constantly pass, for her father evoked it in her. He told her what she needed to know about people, and nothing more. So she did not know people—except to know that, at least for now, all of them liked her.

"Be with the best part of our town, not the worst," her father often said at supper, holding up his fork and smiling.

If there had been social workers in those days, the social workers would have returned Will to school and Owen to the protection of the province. And the world, of course, would be far the less for both actions.

Still Will did not have time to worry. He and his best friend and Push, Reggie Glidden, a little older than he was, off to claim some property across the dead of winter, at minus thirty-four and a gale both exclusively and happily death-defying in every pilgrimage they took, walking thirty miles on "shoes" (snowshoes) and making it somewhere "homey" by nightfall, where ninety-nine percent of humanity would think the desolate end of the earth, staying warm, cut off from the world and in the middle of a blizzard, and Will still being able to bring a kettle to boil in one minute.

This is how over two years Will Jameson mapped out, claimed, and completed the Jameson tract, the seventeen hundred square miles of timber that would be his family's claim. He did it for the honor of his father, and marked it off as Jameson's for him alone.

He was envied, loved, despised, and held in awe. He was hated by Sonny Estabrook for his looks and by the Sloans for his money. He was disliked by the prosecutor for his freedom, and by others for his prowess.

His mother tried to warn him about the prophecy, but it hung upon him in ambivalence, light as dust.

Yet once, after he had broken the jaw of a man ten years older than him with one punch, because wood had been stolen from a sled as a protest, and the sled burned, he drinking a pint of rum straight down said to his brother in boyish exuberance, "What prophecy can fuck me." His eyes were narrowed and filled with light as he tossed the empty pint aside into the snowpit at the end of the barn, and the wind howled through, and the house seemed far away and dim on a winter's day.

Not knowing that in his smile was visible all the boyish tragedy he had already managed to compile. Like the Athenians heading toward Syracuse, not knowing there would be no way back.

With Will I will give a starting point—like finding the beginning of the tail of a fast-moving comet. Now and then a woodsman

Dan Auger would work for Will Jameson, cutting and making roads, as a portager or axman—dependable in his work but not his loyalty. He would come one week, be gone the next, then show up again at the end of the third. He would be for Sloan on the Tabusintac as much as for Jameson on the Bartibog. Which is what infuriated Will Jameson when he was a boy of seventeen.

"If he works he has to be loyal—he can't come today and go tomorrow."

"He has lived his life that way. He hurts no one and I trust him and I like him," Mary said. "Your father always said leave him be—and your father knew men."

"And I don't?" Will smiled indulgently at the old woman, who having both born late was already approaching fifty. "He is in league with Sloan and Estabrook—who will never say I own this tract I am cruising—even as a lease."

"They may say that—but Auger is not in league with anyone," Mary advised.

"Well I won't have him in my camp—I know he's a good man on the drive, but I won't have him. I am working for our future—this tract is yours, Mary," he said, calling his mother by her first name, which he had done now for over a year.

"Don't be an arse, making enemies of tough people is never a smart thing!" she said with that whimsical disassociation, as if she was always thinking of something beyond them.

It was in 1937 that Will, out of school and away from the schoolmarms who were piteously ignorant and twice as domesticating, had decided to go north to the main camp and see how they were cutting, and if the scaler had come in to rod the yards.

At eighteen Will was a Jameson and as strong as a grown man, and could read the woods well enough. Besides, he would trust no one else with the pay orders, or orders at large. Will was loyal to his father's memory to the point of obsession. Though the Tote Road trailed off and was covered by crust a foot down, almost impossible to see, and the wood path he finally followed was not the Tote Road the portager used, but an old one the Jamesons' first horses once hauled a supply sled up, he still made it without rest, which many grown men could not do.

He attained the camp at dark. And after resting and looking into the smoke-filled faces of both young and old, all looking the same in the traces of camp light, all smelling of pine poles and socks, he got to the business at hand. He took the scaler's measures, and then the pay sheets. Seeing a discrepancy, he ordered the men about him.

"Dan Auger."

Auger looked at him.

"You've had three days out in the last fourteen, and so should be paid three days less."

"It comes at the end of the year—if he don't make it up on the drive, which he always do," Reggie Glidden said. "So I put in now—it will turn on the same dime."

But Will showed fury at this, and told them of his obligation coming on the back of their neglected duty.

Saying simply: "Dan Auger, you're to go home."

Everyone laughed, more like a titter, and looked at one another. Reggie looked at Will curiously, but it was his best friend and he knew him well enough.

They stood about him, in hats and coats and boots that people much like Lula Brower said "were worn until they rotted off them." And they *would* rot, and many would die in them. Of course the pleasantries of minor middle-class life allowed this assessment.

There was not another man there who did not think Dan Auger was the best man in the woods that year. Worse, he had come in here out of the same respect for Will's father that Will himself had.

"Dan Auger, I said you are to go out—I will not be paying a man for six who worked three."

Will's task was finished. Abruptly, with no lies and no hesitation. He stood in the middle of grown men who were having their supper of pork and potatoes that those loyal Clydesdales had hauled in by the portager, and declined everything himself but tea. Glidden, to soften it, told Auger it was late, and asked him to stay until morning. But Auger, a man almost his father's age, fired a look of contempt at Will and left though the wind was howling at the door, saying: "Yer father was a man. No man questioned me before—no man does it now."

His person soon obliterated by the sound of snow.

"If he finds his track he will be okay," Reggie decided. Other men said nothing. It was a hard thing, the woods, and harder a boss who makes a mistake.

Will remained utterly calm. He sat by himself watching them. Except for Reggie he would not be their friend. Still, he admired them, and wanted to be like them—where no inclemency or danger could cow them. (A romantic view to be sure—many were terrified of the woods, and swallowed that terror because they needed money for their families.)

Still, Will had proved himself at danger before. He knew there was not a man among them who could not be a hero, and he knew in his wild heart he was to be as great as any.

He drank the dregs of the tea and went to sleep.

Reggie sat alone that night at the camp table, silent and worried that this act would cause something against them.

But the next morning, without sleep himself, he was the first to get the men up for work.

Back in town, Will took the pay sheets to his mother—spoke of the greatness of the teamsters they had and told an off-color joke.

"Mom, did you hear about the queer bear?"

"What?"

"He laid his pa on the table."

Without a word his mother listened, smiled at the joke, and then told him to wash up for supper. Without a word the clock ticked and the snow started to fall out of an iron-gray sky.

It was on that winter night, long past supper hour, when a knock came at the door and they heard from dutiful Eric Glidden, Reggie's father, that Dan Auger had gone through on a patch of ice while trying to cross to his little stretch of land, at the talons below Good Friday Mountain, and though as a man of great courage and tenacity he managed to break ice for an hour, had drowned only fifteen feet from shore.

Will remembered how seemingly innocuous the moment was when he turned and told Auger to grab his kit and go. Now it seemed a deliberate settling of a score that could never warrant any man's death. He still a boy might have given a man a death sentence because of pettiness or fierce loyalty his family did not need. The next three days the Jamesons tried to make restitution to Auger's daughter Cora. Though only a girl of fourteen, she refused any clemency. She was as silent and as stern as stone. She listened with incomparable dignity to their offer and turned away.

Will went to the wake and walked behind the hearse and did his duty.

But that night his mother said, "You should never have questioned a man as fine as Dan Auger."

But she knew this was a wrong thing to say, and gave the boy's heart more trouble. Besides, nothing could be done about it now. Nothing, too, could be done about the way the town turned against him. The prosecutor sent the RCMP to investigate the death in the camp, and was rumored to be considering charges. Or wanting charges. This was the rumor flying in the air. Scandal was always meat to the famished.

After a while it died away.

Yet no one saw the signs of change in Will that Owen saw. Owen tried for the first time to protect his older brother from needless exhibition. And so did Glidden.

There were men waiting for him on every corner. Owen was skinny and woebegone and not quite five-eight. Will was five-eleven and strong as a young bull. It was somehow incongruous to see the younger brother try to protect the older. But the older boy could not be protected. His fights at dances became legendary within nine months, and he sat in jail many a weekend.

"Your brother's in jail again," Lula once said to Owen, who had run to catch up with her after school. "What will your family do, being ruined by your awful brother—that's what my father asks—so we pray."

Such was her mode of fairness. To explain the failings of others to themselves.

Solomon Hickey, the thin, dark-haired barber's son, looked at him with sadness, the kind seen so often in university.

Owen stupidly trailed along behind them. Lula spoke about her uncle, Professor Stoppard: "The smartest man I've ever met, writes poems as fresh as daisies."

Owen decided to ask her what it was like to have a professor as an uncle, but was interrupted by: "Solomon, you know him, don't you? You met him at my house."

Solomon Hickey, the only male member of the Steadfast Few.

Will was prosecuted twice, twice he received thirty days.

Twice the displeasure of the town came down upon his head. Twice police had him in court. And his bedroom, where his bed remained unslept in, cast a shadow over the lives of those in the house.

After each exhibition, each stint in jail, came terrible remorse, and he would sit in the barn, alone on a three-legged stool. The men who came at him, as Owen saw, were never man enough to be sober, never brave enough to be alone. Reggie Glidden was Will's only confidant and source of strength.

"You have to get back to the woods—we have a drive you know I need you in—not in jail—we have landings on three shores, and a loss of six drivers."

But he left it to Reggie and when he himself showed up at camp he seemed restless and changed.

One night he asked his mother about his father, who starting out was known to be tough.

"What about killing a man?" Will asked.

"He never done so," Mary said, "and except for shaking a man or two he never acted out." She stared at him, hoping it would register.

She did not realize that of all conversations with the boy this was the definitive moment, the one question and answer the boy needed—that in all the hard living, the miles of woods and swamp, their love for each other, this was the one answer with which she failed her oldest child, who had sent Dan Auger out, not on her bequest but on her behalf. The answer, in a secret way, left him broken. He remained so for a year and a half.

In May of 1939, Will, sober for a month, took to the spring drive. They had cut the winter logs free of their block and chains into the water, and after a good day's run, found they had a jam at the fork of one of the great turns in the river where the water is swift. It happened in the night when they decided to run the landings (last year's logs left on the bank) down into a river already full, and this crammed the logs together at the turn.

There was much cursing and blame, and the turn was blocked solid by morning. A few of Jameson's men were out on the jam trying to pry the timber, with a man in a scow to rescue them if those timbers gave. They decided by ten a.m. that if a charge was laid, the four timbers holding back the logs behind would split and allow the drive to continue.

"Who can set a charge?" Will asked his friend Reggie Glidden.

"The best one is not here," Reggie said.

"Who is the best one?" Will asked, inspecting the great timbers like mixed and matched toothpicks, and jumping surely from one log to the other like a flea.

"Dan Auger."

Dan Auger was the best. And there was no one else to lay a charge. Will's father would have done it, but he was gone. So Will reasoned he must replace Dan Auger and his father as well. He reasoned it was his duty.

"We can get Harold Dunn to come over," Reggie Glidden said, "or I could do it easy enough—"

"It's not a problem, Reg—and Dunn is angry at me, so bring the charges forward and I will do it meself," Will said.

The dynamite was brought forward after one o'clock on a 1918 Pope L-18 motorcycle, a V twin with crank case cast from aluminum alloy.

"There ya go, me young lad—she's all yours now," a toothless, grinning fellow said, tapping the box behind him.

The occupants in the houses upon the far bank were

informed. And Reggie Glidden went with his friend to set the charges—on the three main logs to bust through the one hunkered underneath.

"Take the cedar and the princess pine, and unnerneath will move," Glidden said, looking into the black, frothing, bark-filled water.

"And the whole world will be one great stick," Will answered, looking behind him into the gray wall of wood.

They set the dynamite almost at water level on the three logs, taped them secure and twined the fuses together, then hopped back to the shore with the long wick. Reggie, with a look of professional aloofness, lighted the fuse with a Player's cigarette, and the men watched it wind its way above the stalled timbers, like trying to follow a scattering snake. For a second the fuse disappeared. Then, without warning, it blew and the three cedars bogging down the run flew into the air, a great groan and foam threw itself into the rainbow the parting water made. Then logs started inching forward to the cheers of wood-hardened men. And then everything went still. There seemed to be a slight sideways canter to the whole drive—and everything stopped.

They waited a minute in the silence.

"It didn't go," Will said.

"Bring the Clydesdales—and attach them on the other bank," Reg said. That seemed to be the best idea—the Clydesdales could put the jammed logs right. That might work. But the Clydes were seven miles upriver, and would take a good two hours to get here. Nor was there another team, except at Brennan's farm. All they had to do was ask. But Brennan had the jaw that Will's temperament broke. And so he could not go ask for those horses, even if Reggie pleaded.

"No boy—I take no source from a Brennan."

"So what to do," Reggie said.

Will thought a moment. At nineteen, all eyes were on him. Thinking it his responsibility, without hesitating, he started out to the jam once more.

Reggie Glidden started after him, but Will ordered him back.

"I am just going to look," he said. "I thought I placed the sticks right on—I have to try it again."

"I want to go with you."

"No."

"Well let me bring up the scow—and wait on you—"

"If the jam goes, the scow goes—you're a sittin' duck—"

Will turned and, looking back at his friend longingly—as if there was a gulf between them the latter could not imagine—suddenly asked: "Do you remember that song my father taught us—when we were young?"

"Which one?"

And Will answered slowly:

No mortal on earth is as happy as we
Ah me dearie dearie, hey dearie down
Give the shanty boys whiskey and nothin' goes wrong!

He laughed, and with that turned away. He walked out to the logs and stood looking down in some pose, questioning the universe, as if he in his youthful pride and boast had never questioned the universe before. Then he looked behind him. Before another sound came, the log he had placed the largest charge upon gave way, and in that second the logs behind, the thousands of tons of wood, moved toward him like an avalanche. As they moved Will jumped backward and turned to the shore. He was sure-footed and had never fallen from a log his feet planted on.

"He'll be scamperin' now," someone said.

He jumped one log to the next with this wall at his back. And as he moved the logs themselves grew up over him. But even then, his brother heard later, he managed to dodge the first volley of logs that fell almost on him. He made a giant Hail Mary leap, when the logs as loud as a crack in the center of the earth swallowed him whole.

There was silence; after a minute or two everything settled, and then it seemed peaceful—the air alive with the smell of fresh wood.

Reggie, even before the logs settled, ran toward him. And was the first to him. Reggie found him jammed down under a massive timber, with his left arm twisted sideways, his right arm missing, and his back crushed. There was a smell of spring smoke, and a little boy far down the shore trying to fish eels.

When they moved Will they found his backbone exposed. Yet he lived for a while.

He was taken to Dan Auger's camp—it being closer—and in a life that seemed to have so much promise, he died that evening, amid the smell of earliest spring and spring chickadees, within the sight of swinging lanterns, the shadows of muscled and muted men, agitated as men are in the presence of death, and the enclosed forest in which he and they had lived. The doctor fetched by Simon Terri came too late, and could have done nothing anyway. His own mother did not get to him before he died.

The mother had lost her oldest—and wept for days; Reggie, who loved him more, did not cry, but brought back the shirt the boy was wearing, torn and bloodied, and lay it across a table for the three days of the wake. The boy was waked in the house, the town and the province's forestry men coming out in support of a great family grieving, to mourn and act as pallbearers.

Owen, looking on from the back of the room in crumpled suit, knew his place was not at the front of the mourners. Will's best friend, Reginald Glidden, came over to Owen, in parting held Owen's hand with the power of a vice.

"Thank you for coming—Will would be honored."

"You get some meat on yer bones, boy—yer momma needs you now," Reggie said.

Later, after everyone had gone, and the trees tapped against the house, Owen felt pity for the memory of Will's boyish, intemperate laughter. Will's great matter-of-fact principles did not matter; everything the family held on to had been solid while now it was transported to the netherworld of prayer and the elusive shadow of metaphysics, even in the white mold of the dead boy's face, that like all the dead held a warning and a meaning not comprehended by living man. Owen was angered by himself—for the first time, he saw his brother. All that morning while Will, only nineteen, was trying to open a jam he had been writing matrics and looking like a proper student, a "fuggin' lord." And why?—because Lula's friends told him she wanted a man who worked in a suit.

His mother sat in a stupor in the kitchen, talking aloud to her dead husband.

That night, all having left and being alone with the dead Owen told himself that he would offer what he had. He would put his plans "down" to become a dentist or a businessman, and remain at home. His plans, in the remote agony of youth, had been to please a girl.

He stood and opened up the coffin to say goodbye. Strange his whole life had taken a back seat to this boy with the parlor light shining on his puffed and white face. Owen shivered slightly, closed the coffin lid, and in the faint dreary smell of flowers switched off the parlor light. He walked up to the third floor and there, amid his two hundred books, wondered what to do. Even now the town was dismissing them. He hated to see his family in this plight.

He knew Estabrook, in a very friendly way, would try over the next few years to put his family out of business. What would happen to Mary's holdings if Estabrook had the best bids? It was what Will had concerned himself over, what he had worried about on his dead father's behalf. That was Will's life: obedient and loyal to the death. Loyalty to his own dead father made him send Dan Auger out. Will was a young prince doomed with his family under siege.

Owen, realizing this, seeing his brother suddenly in a new light, as this young prince struggling, loved him until a cry came from his throat.

So he would offer what he had to his family: himself. He could do this for he had other traits, and one of these traits—the kind that never minded those who laughed—was a certainty in his own genius. Tonight, for the first time, he saw them all, that is all those men he had once admired, as having been plied like children, made whole by being men and women of parts who scrambled to put parts together and act out sentiment like others.

Though he had waited ironically and terribly in his room one whole day for impressionable Lula to show up and offer her hand in sympathy, she had not. She seemed in the larger part of town, getting ready for her own bright-as-a-glitter future, wearing the clothes of a young coed and having her faithful Solomon Hickey drive her to the train for a visit to her uncle Stoppard. Once when there was a knock on the door he, certain it must be her, rushed down the stairs and into the hall, only to see it was men bringing in Will Jameson's trunk from camp.

They put it away in Will's room, and left it unopened.

The meeting between the mother and the younger son happened the day after the funeral. The friends from town and from the forestry industry across the province had now left, and the parlor except for some cups and china had returned to solitude and a rather traditional naked emptiness. The light from the sun told all. The family was left with this "other" boy, who was nothing like Will. The family was left with this second lad, the one Will's godmother—the Micmac woman—said would play havoc with the business.

They sat at opposite sides of the study, an empty leather couch (the place Will often slept when he was home) between them, and a picture of Will on the wall, holding a salmon taken from Grey Rock pool. What struck Owen was his own attitude to his older brother, which he now knew was one of intellectual snobbery. And Will, up nights worrying on behalf of his family, always making sure Owen had spending money and school supplies, did not deserve this.

Owen told his mom he would be willing to do something else with his life.

"Willing to what?"

"Help," Owen said, "and become more like Will."

Mary smiled at such a ludicrous idea and then nodded, for the sentiment was noble. She also admired that Owen spoke directly, as had her husband and oldest.

Owen in fact had gotten into more trouble than Will—but it was always something you couldn't put your finger on. It was always very opened. But it was indirect. When his mind took to something, he did it. Like getting drunk before his provincial matrics and making eighties. Or once protecting the young girl who lived at the Browers from teasing. Or bringing a boy home that was being beaten by his father, a LeBlanc man who lived in Injun town. It was long ago—an almost forgotten incident—but it did spell something. It meant that he would do something unexpected, and it would be startling.

"You will not hit me as you hit your boy," Owen had said to this man. Mary and Will heard about it. Mary embarrassed and Will condemned it, saying: "Sometimes a cuff is a proper thing—especially for a LeBlanc."

Yet Owen did not ask their opinion. Nor would he when he brought in *Ulysses.* Owen, with his blond curly hair and shiny eyes; his shirt buttons askew, just a little; his pants baggy, just a tad; his fingernails dirty, just a pinch; his hair oily, just a touch—and in all of this was a character, an extreme character—but of what? Not a fellow who was spoiled, like most in town thought, but a child who had been left alone, because of the death of his father. Will had, without knowing it, deserted this boy, and Owen had protected a beaten child because he would never desert him.

Mary said she did not want wood for her younger son. Nor any part of wood, any measure or drift of wood or the complex commitment of it, or of the men who made their living in the pitiless world associated with it. For it was a pitiless world—for animals, horses, men, it was every bit as pitiless as the sea.

She told him of their troubles when young—of the heroics of her dead husband, who had seen his fine draft horses fall through the ice and teamsters with tears frozen on their faces trying to get the doomed horses up.

She told her boy that it was not for him. And she said Owen

should study and become the man books wanted him to be. Here she smiled as if delighted at herself.

"There will be no one like Will," Mary said.

"That's true," Owen corrected himself. "He would have been a great man—I'm afraid God does not intend man to be that great, and let him die too soon."

"Well then no matter—men are what they are."

Owen sitting in his suit was the extension of, the personification of, the family pain, which was suffering through something it did not quite understand. A suit, worn as prop for tragedy, can show the lack of knowledge explicitly about that very tragedy, the unknown sadness with which we as men and women are forced to live and breathe.

Men now said the Jamesons were unlucky. And now, so suddenly it scalded her, people were turning away, leaving them devoid of friendship and alone. Would she sell her mill? Well, perhaps she would. But not at the moment, and not to Estabrook or Sloan.

She looked at Owen in a new and terrible light, but just for a second. In this terrible light she decided that this boy was no weakling, and his understanding came from sadness. That is, by neglect unintended, perhaps Mary herself was the main instigator of a prophecy she now fought against, at the same time as she reeled in the philosophical certainty of its apparent absurdity. That is, perhaps for argument's sake, prophecy given in storm to all, all form prophecy against themselves—this thought transfigured her, made her face wise and troubled.

She decided she would put the second boy far away from the woods, and have no cause to worry about him again. She would not allow him near the camps, near the saws, or in any way on a cut.

"No—you must have another life," Mary said to Owen.

"You're better off away from this—if I can't allow one son to have a life easier than my own husband's, then I have done nothing good at all."

Both sons had.

Reggie Glidden took the second boy under his wing, for a great loneliness swept over him that came and went like a draft of wind in a cold barn. He did this not only for himself, but because Mary asked him to. He was now main Push for Jameson, overseer of the properties of his friend. He was wild, cumbersome, and happy-go-lucky—all traits that brought men to him, and ensured Mary men to work her drives. For without a good Push the bosses were done. And Reggie was known to prance draft horses across lake ice when ice was going, to find the felled logs left on a far shore, or to take men and cut across the wilderness in the middle of a January storm.

"Worry only kills you faster," he would tell his sometimes frightened charges. "I learned that from the greatest man I ever knew—young Will Jameson hisself."

But Owen was not the same type of person as Will Jameson. There was, as Reggie said, "no funny bone in him." Not the carefree laughter at danger which youth always seek and Will had in abundance. Or at least this is what was said, and Reggie as an ordinary man believed much of what was said. That is, he accepted what the town said about its citizens, and had long ago realized the town did not wish greatness from its citizens. It secretly wished mediocrity.

Reggie knew very well this was how the animosity toward Will grew. Will took over the reins of a business at sixteen and the town had not wanted greatness for him.

Reggie understood this and though he did not approve of envy, he did nothing to deride it. It was part of the world. The resentment toward Will was always just under the surface, and Will was strong enough to hold it under and keep it there. But a man like Reggie wouldn't be that strong. His likes and dislikes must be known to be ordinary, for although he was as brave a man, he had no inner strength to fight scandal or speculation.

So Reggie, conscious of including Owen, was also conscious of trying to discover any quality that matched this older brother, who already had become a towering mythic figure among the province's woodsmen. There seemed to be none at all.

It was, in fact, a study of the younger boy—as a scientist would study a specimen. And this is how most looked at it. How do you study a specimen? Put him outside his environment and see then how he might react, how he might "get on" in the great world. And this is what Reggie did, and Owen reacted to this by being compliant. So, soon people were laughing at "Reggie's pet" as Reggie hauled him from dance to dance, drinking episode to drinking episode.

"I'm tryin' to teach you the great world," Reggie said one night.

Yet Reggie's great world Owen found was limited to these episodes in nondescript New Brunswick settings, and small dances where prideful boys stood drinking around buckboards and the dusty hoods of cars.

And Owen, standing with them, drinking also, let them think what they would about him. Hell, perhaps then he thought it too.

Yet one night they met Lula and Camellia downtown, and as luck would have it both Reggie and Owen were drunk.

"You see, Camellia—didn't Solomon and I tell you so—we told you this is how he would behave," Lula said, for she had all the manufactured clarity of the modern girl.

TWO

When the Second World War started, his mother never tried to keep Owen out of service.

Still, there were those in town who believed the old woman had tried and failed to keep the boy near her.

Mary did go to Owen and say that if he stayed home, no one would think the worse.

"Of course they will," Owen smiled, while looking through his shelf of books.

She might have been asking this, because she had worried that a desire to prove prophecy wrong might propel her to ask him to join a battalion and have his ears blown off. This was her worry in the fading light that seemed to slowly disintegrate against the shelves and curtains in his room.

So she used reverse psychology on her own desire and managed to want him home.

But Owen Jameson was resolute. Life had never been so good as to be addicted to, and gossip against him was nothing new. He sought out only one person to speak with—of his hopes and fears, one person to tell what might happen to him—and how he had cared for her since he was a boy. How he loved to walk up the lane just because she lived on it. How he applauded her knowledge of books, and secretly hoped to write one someday. Just like her uncle.

Lula was sitting on her veranda, on a swing that squeaked in the middle of a hot sultry afternoon, with fresh pavement on the street and the smell of impending rain.

She was a very small-town girl, at the very apex of her popularity now. What, then, could Owen ever offer her—when a greater woodsman family, the Estabrooks, had been over to see her, and the boy Sonny had asked her to a dance? The one lumbering family that her father had approved of.

Owen stumbled over what he had to say.

He said that he didn't know if he would live—but if he did, and he came back, and she wasn't yet betrothed, could she then see her way, possibly, and he did not want to impose, but if there was a chance she might marry him then—well, he had a brooch to give her and—here he handed her the brooch.

But just then Sonny Estabrook came up in a Ford car in the doomed heat of afternoon, the sultry moment just when Owen's present was being offered, and marriage being asked, in seemingly the poorest timing of Owen's life. She waved the car on, to circle the block again.

"Oh, it's Sonny," she said.

And turning to him said in the same magnificent breath: "I'm sorry so many of the boys have to go—I just pray everyone will be okay."

Owen nodded.

She smiled at this false emotion, as she always smiled at false emotion, and continued.

"You'll be okay," she said with sudden calculation. "Your family is important enough Old Mary will have you somewhere safe—or have Reggie Glidden to protect you day and night—just like he does when you're drinking downtown—but I am sorry for how I treated others who will have to fight all our battles for us." Her eyes welled with tears. "Do you think I am AWFUL—?"

She looked at his present, looked up at him and smiled, as the great Ford car came around again, with Sonny Estabrook's fine white skin and slicked back hair. She nodded out at him, in the joyous, dismissive selectiveness youth have for those around them.

It was fortuitous, this last look of hers, for Owen in a millisecond understood what he hadn't for so long. Her face was suddenly egotistical, shallow and vain. Owen's face went blank, and a sudden fear came over her—for the first time she recognized that he caught something of which she herself was unaware.

"I am not that fond of Sonny Estabrook," he said, "and someday the world will know why."

She was startled by this, and startled more that he left so suddenly, so soon, and didn't look back at the end of the yard.

Owen joined the North Shore, trained, decided to be killed in action, and left for Europe in 1941.

THREE

At first there was no word from him, nor indication that the ship carrying him off to war had managed to dock anyplace close to the fray. Buckler, his mother's brother, an old man who kept the mill going, tried to make inquiries but could not "get hold of him for love or money," as he told Owen's distraught mother.

Often Mary, losing the reins of the business, when keeping the reins meant so much, had to bail her men out of jail in order to get them into the woods. Trethewey often went with her, to roust out the men and get them to camp. Still, there was ennui and disinterest among her employees, which her brother and she tried to address with appeals that left the workers unmoved. There were also many fights between the teamsters of the various mills, and dances were often brawls.

Her brother tried to do what Will had done so successfully: move the men to action. But more than half were in Europe and he remained incapable of inspiring the others; and there were so many landings and unyarded fells from the Jameson crews that people said two new mills could be kept busy.

The cutters who cut the trees went in September, the teamsters who drove the horses that hauled those trees went in winter, and the drivers—those who worked the drives down the river—went in spring. Mostly it was commissioned military work, for Spitfires now—for much less pay—but it was Estabrook who handled most, Sloan who handled some.

And to keep any of her men sober was a challenge—especially with her husband and Will gone, and Buckler incompetent, and at certain points all these men were in the woods together—cutters, teamsters, and drivers all working, gambling. When they came out in May they spent their money, got drunk and locked up.

Mary often received calls to go and bail them out. Coming from that dark house on the hill, it seemed that all she knew and had ever known was men and horses, drives, saws, and axes. She looked like a little old lady with a toughened, sunburned face, and a gruff laugh, being as she was with men most of her life, and yet knowing only one.

Then, unexpectedly, on November 3, 1943, something tragic and peculiar happened. The young woman Lula Brower, just turned twenty-two, suffered a stroke in her home. Her condition filled the town for days. The young woman Brower had brought up, Camellia Dupuis, stayed at her side in the great gray hospital down in Saint John.

They said she would die, and her life it was said hung in the balance.

She recovered in Saint John, and learned to walk, but her face had suffered a paralysis on the right side. It took her looks away. Why had this happened? She didn't know. Nor did anyone else.

She was bitter and resentful. She told Camellia not to play the piano, she told her not to play the spoons. She told her not to dust her room because it made her cough. And when Camellia came in with a letter she was sending off to Owen Jameson overseas, Lula was too angry to sign it.

"Go away," she said, "I can't have you near me today—besides, he's probably dead already."

Lula wrote letters for war bonds, and did her best to overcome this affliction. But she realized soon, who could and could not be cruel.

The fact that her suitors had left was an unfortunate by-product not only of the war but of her injuries. The man in the Ford, the boy her father so approved of, Sonny Estabrook, did not hesitate to call her a crippled goat.

Solomon Hickey was at this time a constant figure in the background of her world, and so too Camellia, even though at her angriest moments Lula would make allusions to fathers who murdered mothers. Then, sorry for this, she would say, embittered: "I thought I had more friends."

The Steadfast Few, eager to know about the extent of her infirmities, visited her together and all at once, and then slowly drifted off, taking with them the well-defined tidbits and gossip about her private anguish. In this way they were able to show great solidarity with her to those townspeople greedy for information, while at the same time leaving Lula deserted. And the favorite line of the Steadfast Few, expostulated at times with tears?

"You just can't imagine how we feel."

FOUR

Still it was the war and there came news of death. Reggie, Owen, and the other boys had been in a terrible fray.

Eric Glidden, Reggie's father, heard of it first, and on an August day in 1944 walked from the prip-prop leanings to the *Leader* newspaper and said that he had been informed that his son Reggie had tried his best to save the young Jameson boy, and could not, in a fight outside of a French town. This made news across the province, in two columns on the first page: OWEN JAMESON KILLED IN ACTION—SECOND JAMESON SON TO DIE TRAGICALLY. SOME SAY JAMESON NAME DOOMED.

Eric was called to the Jameson house. He came into the front parlor, with its expensive vases showing scenes of wild horses and Arabian nights, and its crocheted rugs that displayed Mary's attempts at a domesticity no one had taught her. A scent of horse prevailed upon it, and scenes in gray pictures of men in heavy coats and cork boots.

"Tell me about me boy now," Mary asked, her hands shaking just slightly as she held a dishcloth—as if it could support her. Buckler stood behind his sister stoically, out of place.

"Reg did his bes— They got trapped in a field—it's that colonel always staying behind the lines and sending men out to their doom."

"You mean our Owen is dead?" Buckler asked.

"From what I hear, sir."

Eric went back to his house feeling he had accomplished some grave duty. He frowned at his grave duty. Now, instead of being a hanger-on with the Jamesons he had a position, and as he said to his cronies, "ran things over there."

The house turned inward in mourning all over again. The woman waited in silence for three more weeks, certain both boys were now gone.

Still, knowing that things had been left out of Eric Glidden's story—no one bothered to come to the Jameson house from the Department of War, and there had been no letter either—Buckler himself started to investigate the rumor. After almost a month, he discovered something. Owen was alive. The colonel who had reported the death had gotten the story completely backward, because he himself had not been in the field.

Within four weeks of Buckler's inquiries Owen's exploits became, as they say here, "half-assed legendary."

Owen turned out to be as tough as a night in jail and twice as mean. He fought with the Canadian First Army on the left flank of Monty for ten months. There were four occasions where he showed true bravery, though he himself rarely spoke of it. In August of 1944 he won the Victoria Cross for a series of actions and counteroffenses. The last of which, Owen carried to safety, through enemy fire he consistently returned, one man from his own platoon and his town—Reggie Glidden.

The local paper's front page:

ONCE GIVEN UP FOR DEAD,
OWEN JAMESON RECOMMENDED FOR VC.
REGGIE GLIDDEN FREEZES UNDER FIRE,
CARRIED TO SAFETY BY WOUNDED JAMESON.

The story went on to report how in the fog of war mistakes happen, and mistakes in stories happen.

He was, after all, what Mary saw: a prize.

After the war the soldiers drifted back in smaller company than which they left, on trains boarded in Halifax. The town expanded by their presence and many went back to working the woods or mills or small fishing villages. Or others drifted south into the cacophony of Saint John to labor for Irving in that industrial city. Lula was unhappy, and so too was Brower. They were unhappy that the men, when they called, did not call on Lula anymore.

It was during this time, in a stark moment, that Camellia realized Brower and Lula wanted her gone. That they had wanted her gone since the stroke had come, and had without her realizing it been pressuring her to go. That old Brower was bothered by a comparison that no one desired, yet no one could refrain from. Now she caught the anger in his eyes.

So Camellia consented to marry. To everyone who knew her, the man she picked was a rash pick—a man once considered brave, the town now ridiculed mercilessly. She married Reggie Glidden in late June of 1946. Some said this act alone saved him from suicide.

After this she went to work in the house of Mary Jameson, who it was said felt sorry for the two newlyweds.

FIVE

Alive or not, Owen Jameson did not come readily back to Canada after the war. He stayed away until October of 1946. He wanted the town and his mother to forget him.

He went to the museums, art galleries, and plays. He stayed in London, took a job at the Canadian barracks until that was closed. He became a nondescript citizen of the world, wearing a second-hand London Fog coat and reading George Orwell's essays. He drank dark bitter and had an affair or two of the heart.

No one seeing him would think his family had a million. So many millionaire Canadians did not affect a million. He disappeared into the great mystery of London fog, with little to keep body and soul.

He planned to write a book. He planned for a second or two to remain abroad like Hemingway, or claim British citizenship, but did not. There were a few months when he lived on the street. He took to drink, and liked it a lot. He went to Paris, and then to Marseilles. The book came to nothing—he found that though filled with ideas and events witnessed, he himself could not write. He was kind, he was good, but he had made no friends in the army, had little or none now.

Finally Europe bored him in the way only Europe can do—its history, even after a war, stifled, its art in excess, boasting of great people its own institutions had starved to death. So he turned his eyes toward Canada. The land of numbing promise which would come to nothing, he supposed, or be worse than Europe in the end.

When he came back in 1946 on a train going west he had no intention of stopping in town. He had built up a resentment toward his town in a way that was natural for a man who had proven himself so well, who felt he had been belittled or treated with a lesser hand then deserved.

He wired his mother from Halifax that he would continue on, and to post money to Montreal. No, he would not be a dentist, as Will had decided once. For him it was the university in Montreal and the study of law.

Owen was aboard the late afternoon train, on October 17, the one that did not stop.

As the train approached Newcastle, the town had it stopped (which showed for a brief, bright moment Owen's influence) and men boarded the train and brought Owen off. The men felt there should be a celebration over the fact that Owen had saved Reggie Glidden by crossing a field of withering machine-gun fire and taking two bullets for the trouble. It was said Camellia herself begged them to do this, hoping Owen would help Reggie gain his self-respect.

So in a display of affection Owen had never had before, and would not have again, the men got him as drunk as a condemned prisoner, and patches of cold grass at the corner of the buildings looked somehow brighter when the sun shone.

"Let his feet not touch the ground," they said, raising him up.

These were his brother's old crew, hard tough men who had little learning save the toughness they lived by—looking upon him now with unaccustomed grace and civility—looking upon him with new eyes, as Will's blood. They were men who could dance on a log in the middle of rapids strong enough to tear you apart, and were now smiling at him, as one of theirs, with affection as light as a feather in their hearts.

They finally set him down, on the platform, for the very first time among those townsmen who said he was their own.

They held up the old newspaper headline from 1944: OWEN JAMESON KILLED IN ACTION.

It was a proud moment for him. Family pride—and the feeling of certain townspeople that they had completely misjudged this second-born—necessitated this.

Lula Brower had sent a note she hoped would be delivered.

SIX

Reggie Glidden, home since the summer of 1945, had left the town on the Miramichi a day or so before Owen arrived.

For weeks after the war Reggie had gone every other day to the station, waiting for Owen Jameson.

Yet over time the talk from old friends about Jameson's bravery began to wear on him.

Before he married, he admitted to Camellia he felt he had lost part of himself.

"Well, we will get you all back together," she had smiled.

But there was something else as well. He felt he owed it to Will to keep Owen second. This was the boy who was looked upon by everyone in town as a failure.

As he saw respect for himself draining away, and Will's name relegated to the actions of a youth, he became bitter.

So over time Reggie Glidden's desire to celebrate Owen Jameson's bravery soured and became unnatural to him, while his own death and his young wife's freedom from him became more and more paramount. He suspected her, and others exacerbated suspicion.

"Oh, I know she loves me deep down in her heart," he said.

"Go on—the Browers wanted rid of her, and you would do," his acquaintance said.

Both were friendless now. Yet her pity for his friendlessness was new. And he could not stand this pity. Sometimes she would just stare at him, from across the room, and in that look he saw what he had not before, a disappointment at who he really was. She smiled at him and took his hand when they went out. But Reggie, plagued by the incident in the war, did nothing but drink by himself. Or if he had money he would drink with others, hoping to find his youth and his joy.

He got into fights like Will Jameson before him. And his young wife would often go in the middle of the night to bail him out with the little bit of money that they had. They were soon two forlorn creatures, and she, without one good skirt or slacks, walking two steps behind him while he cursed the world, imploring him not to make a scene.

Onward he would go, and onward he would curse, and onward she would implore—and onward he would curse her for imploring, and onward she would implore he not curse at her imploring.

Some wondered if their marriage was even consummated.

But drunk Reggie would lay with his face to the wall, wanting no one or nothing for days. "It wasn't like that—I didn't freeze in no battle—me gun jammed—and that was that—"

And though this was true, and though others knew it to be true, none cared at all.

The idea that failed men lose their wives is partially true—many drive them away, feeling unworthy.

They said he had frozen in the war—nothing more could be said.

He wanted to drive her away desperately because he saw how little she had and how much she had hoped for that day they were married, when everything seemed so artificial. And he had also seen the look on her face when she realized Owen Jameson was not staying in Europe but was coming home. It was not the elation in her look, as one might think, that disheartened him, but her eventual sadness—as something terrible began to sink into her consciousness. For hours she could say nothing.

She would go and clean for Mary Jameson, and earn fifteen dollars a week, her young body smelling of Lysol and clothes detergent. From that money she would try to put enough away for groceries and heat, and give a dollar to her uncle Sterling. But ashamed in his heart, Reggie would take the money to get drunk.

Once when drunk, he told a crowd of men that it was he who had saved Jameson—but because of Jameson's name, Owen got the credit. This was the worst lie he could imagine.

So here is what he did to pay himself back.

He had some men chain his left arm to a tying pole in the lumberyard, and he bet them that they could throw pulp sticks at him and he would bat them all down with his right hand. And if not one touched his head, they would owe him a bottle of wine, and if one did touch his head—well, he might be dead, mightn't he, and might he not be better off? He laughed at his own macabre joke.

It spread around town that this was what Reggie Glidden was doing, and a crowd gathered.

Reggie Glidden like an old bear, hunched over, waiting for the pulp sticks. Each one thrown in the late afternoon, he swatted away with his right arm. The men, at first reluctant, became more incensed at his prowess and threw them harder, and with better accuracy, as rain started to pelt down over the red muck, making it seem as if the world was being spotted with blood.

Still he batted them away, even as they came so close to his forehead that you would think he had to be hit, and he could feel the tiny scared bits of wood brush his temple.

But then, as men gathered, as people howled, with Reggie Glidden's right arm so battered and bloodied it would seem impossible for him to swat away another stick, Camellia jumped in front of him.

"Please," she said, "please, I beg you all—stop now please." Reggie insensible and grinning, the mad crowd howling in joy.

And Camellia took her man home as he lagged behind in the rainfall, accusing her of sabotaging his good name.

The next morning after he woke, so ashamed he blurted, "Leave me be, for I am damned," almost willing it to be, his right arm now scarred to the bone.

It was at this time Reggie told her he would not be Push for a Jameson.

"What do you mean?" she said, her eyes startled with tears, her heart pounding like that of a child.

"Nothing, only I have other things to do," he said.

Neighbors could hear them arguing for a day—the name Owen Jameson being mentioned as the dark, metallic fall night came on. Finally Reggie threw a lamp, smashed it against the wall, and left.

Glidden left town. He told a priest that he would annul the marriage if she wanted and say that he couldn't have children.

"When will you come back?" she begged. (For it was Camellia

who needed to prove to everyone that this marriage would work—if for nothing else for her own mother and father.)

"I will come back when I am myself," he said.

SEVEN

On the frozen platform, the hastily arranged celebration for Owen Jameson took place.

"There's the man who knows Pythagoras," his old math teacher yelled, and everyone laughed.

"We have defeated tyranny," someone else exclaimed, and none spoiled the moment by saying "no."

Owen was brought home in early evening. He was almost falling down drunk, his own mother reprimanding him.

It was a moment for the great barren house, and its people of the woods. A dozen of them stayed overnight.

After ten that night Owen was dragged upstairs to bed. There he saw a girl, the one who was once at Lula's house, and kissed her. The one who had written him a support letter during the war. She was a beautiful woman. He did not know that she was there late, only to give him the letter from Lula. He said: "You deserve a medal for your beauty, I'm going to marry you—what is it, Camellia?—ya, that's it—we'll get married tomorrow." When she began to protest he laughed and said, "I should have married you before the war—don't tell me you have someone else—well, we'll take care of him!"

He swept her hair back with his hand. Her dark eyes looked up at him, a mole on her cheek—her skin was soft brown.

He laughed and kissed her. She pushed him away in an instant, and told him he was drunk.

When he woke the next day a teamster said: "Camellia has something for you—" and winked. His intention was to look as if he was pleased for Owen's sake. A cold wind blew through the opened door, the hallway seemed to regale in morning light that suddenly ebbed by cloud.

"Who?"

"The little maid whose panties you was in—"

"That didn't happen," Owen said sternly.

Two other men looked at each other and laughed, and so did a man at the door, who had come selling apples in a crate.

It had already spread about the neighborhood, and to the town core—even to one of the town drunks, who happened to be Camellia's uncle. Two of the Steadfast Few, hearing of it that morning, rushed to tell others in their group. They could suppress neither their dismay nor their eagerness to share it. And what had they heard, which they hoped Lula had not—yet: Owen had said he was going to marry Camellia. Had kissed her, and laughed about it, saying he would "take care" of her husband.

Now Owen washed and went to see Camellia in the kitchen.

"You have something for me?" he asked.

She nodded and handed him the VC he had won, which he had pinned to her breast pocket. She told him to button his shirt and take care of his medal.

The rest of the day he tried to find out where she lived, and if he could ask her out, while others just stared at him.

"What about Lula Brower?" The Scot maid said.

"Oh—Lula—I thought she'd be married up to Sonny Estabrook by now."

When he was told what had happened to Lula he was sorry, but thought no more of it.

"Anyway," he said, with complete openness, "I was a damn fool not to see Camellia for what she was."

That night his mother brought him into her parlor, and with yards of knitting, which she had never learned to do, all around her said: "Camellia is Reggie Glidden's wife. They was married a few months ago—he took to her and Mr. Brower arranged it, so you leave them be."

Owen stared at her, blood leaving his face.

He simply said: "Why in Christ didn't someone tell me—I made a mistake."

He didn't say "a fool of myself," for he knew he had done more damage than that.

He limped across the parlor and went to his room. He sat rubbing his left leg, his eyes startled by pain.

"It will pain every day of your life—far more than you think now—and far more than the insults to you because of it," the doctor had told him in London. "And you must keep vigilant about it, or you will lose it, do you hear?"

Owen inquired about Glidden and said he wanted to see him. But it was all out what he wanted to do with Reggie's wife, and people did not take his inquiry seriously. Besides, Glidden had left town.

Camellia went home and, as fate would have it, washed the Lysol-stained skirt she had been wearing, and forgot Lula's letter to Owen in the inside pocket.

EIGHT

Owen had to go to the mill the next afternoon, even though he was preparing to leave town on a train to Montreal. He had his acceptance letter from McGill and found no reason now to stay here.

At the mill he saw his uncle Buckler sitting on a pile of sawdust peeling an apple and reading a magazine. Here he heard his first bad news: they had no good saws—and the cutters had just started a month or so behind.

"Well, when Reggie gets in—things will change around."

But the problem was Reggie's pride was hurt.

"He said he wouldn't be Push."

"That's nonsense," Owen said, "I'll talk to him."

Owen then took a cruise of the ground, and saw how they were handling everything. Everything at the mill and in the lumberyard was a mess. It spawned a thousand cannibalized parts to keep it going, and was in its death rattle at the edge of the water.

He came home, went into the office to see what their finances were, and became morbidly aware of the need to stay.

"Where was Reggie for the last year?" he said.

The idea was this: Reggie had not been himself—and Mary had paid him anyway.

After dark he sat out on the veranda smoking, until after the six o'clock train left.

Then he saw Lula. She had taken it upon herself to leave the house, something she seldom did. She was pushed into this by her father, concerned that Owen had not come to visit. The father worried all day thinking that someone—perhaps Camellia herself—had told him how disfigured and ugly Lula was. And so Lula was compelled by her father, who wanted the world for her from the time her mother died, to leave the house. She hadn't wanted to, and finally was bullied into it.

"You have to see your fiancé," Brower said.

If someone who had won a VC would marry his daughter, everything in his life would be fulfilled. That is, her stigma would not matter. She knew this is what he thought, and so did it for him.

She walked slowly up the great old lane at sunset, with the sun flaring in the naked alders on her right. Her red coat and flat blond hair could be seen almost specter-like in the distance. For some moments he did not know who she was. She was plain, and thin, and now walked with a cane. He rose then to meet her, and helped her to the veranda.

He had heard of the stroke and felt sorry for her. But he did not know her anymore. Long ago he assumed she had married. The only letter he had received from any one of those young girls had been from Camellia.

However, Lula was wearing the brooch he had given her. One of the Steadfast Few who had been at the house, had run and pinned it on.

"You've always been a greater charmer than Camellia, dear," she had said.

The air was cold, the trees were baring, and the ground was hard as frozen turnip at dawn. She sniffed as she spoke, her red woolen glove rubbing her face; there was a slight impediment, or slur, in her speech.

"Well—I've gotten hold of you—being a hero must take up your time—" she said. She found it difficult to look at him, as if guilty of something. He knew this and tried to put her at ease.

"Don't be silly, of course not—and I am not," he said.

"I wore your pin," she said. She smiled, a small red crease on her throat that followed up her right cheek. He was silent.

"Are ya staying?" she asked.

"I'm not sure."

"Ah well, the world is yours, I guess," she said. "Did you get the letter?"

"What—no—what letter? In the war, you mean—overseas?"

"No—I wrote you one the other day. I asked—anyway, never mind it—I just wanted to—I mean, Daddy and I, to congratulate you."

He looked at her now, could think of nothing to say except ask her if she was seeing a doctor.

She acted puzzled at his overall silence, lingered awhile to talk of the war dead, like Bennie and Bill and Donald and Sam, then quickly offered him a kiss, and left in the same shadows that held her cheek and hair, the elusive quality of both desire and despair.

The world was terrible, he thought. Terrible for her, and terrible for her father, and terrible for everyone else. He could see old Brower in this move—as in every move the poor woman made. That house he had once longed to enter a shapeless prison and nothing more.

Solomon Hickey was waiting at the edge of the property. Hickey looked back over his shoulder and nodded at something she said. Hickey, the little boy who was her confidant, little boy still.

She too looked back over her shoulder, which showed her paralyzed cheek captured in a desperate moment, as her perfume was caught in the flimsy late October night. Then Solomon took her arm.

If Owen had loved her once, that was gone. Her affliction

made it impossible for him to tell her this. He thought he wouldn't have to, for he would simply disappear again into some city where among the cacophony of engines and machines he could be alone.

NINE

The next night, going over certain papers about board feet and men, and equipment left inland after the spring run, he discovered there had been sabotage of a two sled, and a depot had burned the previous year. They suspected Cora Auger's fifteen men, brave and true—but no charges had been filed by the prosecutor.

"Where in fuck was Reggie?" he said angrily. He had pictured, perhaps a little too vainly, Reggie being completely loyal to his family now.

The thought of his mother and his well-meaning uncle trying to run things alone complicated matters.

"Tell me tomorrow what is going on here," he said to his mother.

"Oh—of course—I mean I thought I *had* been telling you."

He went to the third floor and lighted a cigarette in the drowsy, stilled air.

The hallway was dark, and portraits of Will and of his father and mother in a horse-drawn carriage on their wedding day hung on the wall. They sat mute and solid in the moment taken—forever in that split second of daylight and meaning no longer evident anywhere else.

It was then that he saw Camellia at the far end of the hall—for the first time in two days. Actually, he had avoided her.

But it was as if she was oblivious to the tensions already beginning to swirl about her and him. And two things enabled this. Her childlike faith, and her belief that Owen could help her and Reggie.

Even now there was something carefree about her—that didn't sit well with two other women, both part-time employees at the house.

The other women, who had babysat Owen as a boy—and who both disliked him, for he was not the man Will was—told her to come downstairs, and looked over at Owen as they said this in artificial obsequious deference.

"I want to speak to Mr. Jameson," she said. "I'll be down later, thank you."

"Mr. Jameson is far too busy a man—" one woman, a load of sheets in her arms, said.

Owen replied: "Don't be silly—I am not too busy for Mrs. Glidden."

There was a particular tightness when he said *Mrs.*

The woman nodded with some parental concern and left with the superiority a servant can have, talking to herself as she descended the steps.

"Come here and sit with me a while," Camellia said once they were alone, without the least worry, "and we will decide what to do about Reggie."

They sat in the dark on the third floor. The purpose of this clandestine meeting—her purpose, with the vague darkness between them and the sweetness of her perfume that seemed to wisp in her breath—was to ask a delightful favor—for Reggie. Reggie at this moment seemed her only concern. In a way she wanted to hotheadedly prove to Lula Brower, and to the Steadfast Few, and to the world at large, that Reggie was still a great man. So now she spoke, and he listened in silence as this new Reggie was revealed.

Reggie was not whole. And she needed him home. She, however, wanted him to be whole when he came home. He had married her when she had no one. And now she would help him.

"What's his problem?" Owen asked, puzzled. (It was true he had no idea.)

"You—or that day, or what they say about him—they have tormented him an awful lot. Well, some of the men—and he is too proud to act—I mean he doesn't fight back but takes it on himself to damage himself instead."

"That day could have easily gone the other way. Twice he ordered me to leave him—but I had more rank, and refused. That is twice he would have given his life for me," Owen said.

But Reggie's reaction somehow bothered him. He was saddened by it. He knew the reaction had come because of who he was. The smaller, supposedly inept brother was not supposed to save Reggie Glidden.

"He does not think I loved him when I married him—when he heard you were coming back—" she said rapidly.

"I see—"

They were silent. Owen again was confused by this. He felt it was a discredit to what he himself had managed to do, if the man was just going to destroy himself. Then she took his hand in hers as easily as she would a boyfriend and said: "Reggie is older and looks upon himself as your protector—because of Will—" (Here she paused.) "However, he believes he lost that quality in the war."

"Well then, you and I will get him back," he said, laughing suddenly.

"We—we will—"

"Of course."

"Oh thank you—sir—" She stumbled over the word, grabbing his hand with both of hers.

"Don't be silly—and it's Owen, not sir—"

Between them was only the flat, gray darkness of upstairs, where sheets covered the chairs Will had once sat on, tying flies or laboring over some algebraic problem he had no interest in solving. On those long ago nights everything in the world seemed possible, even happiness in the drudgery of high school arithmetic. Or perhaps giving more elation was the thought of what might have come after it. Which means the end of school and summer free to do what one wanted. Then, of course, he was pulled from school too soon, his father dead just before greatness claimed him, and Will dead just as greatness went away.

Thinking this, he blurted: "I will ask Mom to make him a better offer. We'll pay him more than the Push at Estabrook or Sloan—tell him that. He knows the woods, and every tree ever cut on an axman's pay."

"But—I don't know if—"

"So you tell him that—" he said, interrupting her, feeling suddenly that he was trying to sound like Will. But at any rate, he was himself again.

She jumped and started down the hall, turned, ran back, and in front of the old woman, kissed him. It was a strange kiss—for what would be forever between them alone—he tasted the inside of her lips. At that moment, without Reggie, she would love him and he her. Yet it was Reggie brought them together.

"My, my—haven't we expressed ourselves," the old lady said.

"Oh I'm sorry," Camellia said, laughing. "I always do—I mean I have before—" and here she ran downstairs laughing aloud again. "I'm phoning Reggie tonight!" she yelled.

At this moment he knew that if he was ever to be in love, it would be with her. Strangely it was the war that had taught him this. And he cursed again for not having recognized this before, and looked up guiltily at the maid.

TEN

At the same time, on the west side of Saint John, in an old house built before the middle of the nineteenth century that teetered on pillars overlooking the harbor, Reggie Glidden pondered his future. It was now to him a prospectless place of self-recrimination where an act he had no control over was a cedar he could not dislodge in a stream. He had become indebted to a man he once pitied. That was something he could not overcome. He had lied about that man's deed in order to save face with a cynical town. He could lie because he had once thought so little of Owen, and too much of himself.

Reggie tried to fathom where his downfall had started. It had not started in the war or in the trench or with the jammed rifle, or even in Owen's rushing with an extra clip of ammunition to the hole Reggie had dug. It had started when he had once tried to determine whether Owen was manly, and took him across the river to meet the drinking boys. This was a flaw not in Owen's character, but in Reggie's. Everything seemed to come from that.

Reggie's hope had rested on the well-known fact that Owen was off to dentistry if he lived through the war. The rather strange desire not to have Owen live through the war that had come to Reggie Glidden the closer the end of the war came was a silent problem Reggie could never speak about, for he was deathly guilty of this feeling, and thought of it as remarkably unnatural and unmanly. Yet if Owen had not lived through the war, Reggie could honor his memory and in some way control what was remembered. He could make the saving of his life more fantastic, and still seem a hero himself. But now Owen had come home. His thoughts were torn between feeling desperately grateful and terribly angry about the same circumstance.

He went to Saint John so he would not have to talk about it, and worked this past week loading ships on the dock. In his pocket he had an offer from Estabrook.

He told his cousin, whose house he was staying at, of his fears. He told him about Camellia one night when he was drinking. He thought he might find sympathy with a man he had known, and protected, as a child.

"She is working at the house Owen lives," he said. "Owen is a hero to everyone and, well, you know how impressionable young girls are! I married her perhaps in haste, but I do love her with all my heart—she is so like a child—and that I suppose is a bad thing—when you consider it—"

The cousin listened to him, felt privy to knowledge that was a silent cancer in Reggie's heart.

"Well," he said, as he held a cigarette in front of his face and smiled corruptly through the smoke, "any man who saves your life might have a go banging your wife and take it as good payment. Hell, she probably thinks that too. For sometimes women act innocent just to get men between the sheets. Just once or twice."

He was no longer that shy child Reggie had cared about but just another man motivated by his own wounds to wound as well.

Reggie said nothing to this blunt, provocative statement.

"I have no loyalty to the Jamesons except for Will," he said, feeling the note in his pocket that Sonny Estabrook had sent him.

That very night (the same night she spoke to Owen), Reggie received a long-distance phone call from Camellia. She sounded so joyous, it was as if he had suspected another person, in another world.

It was also a luxury to phone Saint John, and she cherished the moment.

She told him to come home. She told him Owen Jameson needed him back, never to mind the townspeople or what they said. It would all be good again.

"You will be foreman."

"I will be foreman anywhere, it's my job," Reggie said.

"Well, Mr. Jameson says he needs you with him—for Buckler is old and his mom is—well, a little dizzy," Camellia said. He could hear her voice hesitate because she wanted so much to convince him. He could tell she thought this much greater news than he himself did.

"Please come home," she whispered.

There was a long and desperate pause over the line. He wanted her to say, "Because I love you." But for some reason she did not.

"So you saw Owen—is he still there and you still working there?"

"Of course, but—well, that's why I'm phoning."

"And Owen—will Owen be staying?" he said.

"Yes."

He sat silent in the chair. For he knew something about himself now. He was frightened. He was not the same man he had been, and that was simply because people no longer respected him as they once had. And he already knew that

Jameson was forced to cut on Good Friday Mountain—the one place more than any in the province he and Will feared. This was where they wanted him to be foreman, and he didn't know if he could do it.

When he hung up, his face had turned ashen, his lips looked bloodless.

"Bad news, eh?" His frivolous young cousin smiled, hearing only Reggie's questions about Owen.

"Eh?" he answered, deep in thought. "No—good news all around."

ELEVEN

The next night Mary Jameson and her brother Buckler showed Owen the letter they had kept from him.

It was the final decision on the stumpage bid on the thousands of acres they had wanted to cut, discovered by Will all those years ago.

The letter told them what they had known for three months. The Jameson bid had not been accepted. The reason was simple. The initial bid had been delayed, until another bid had come in and made it moot.

Why the bid had been delayed until moot was ancient history. But it had taken this long for the timber Will had scouted to mature.

Now that the time had come, now that Buckler had ordered new saws, the government had accepted another bid. This letter told Mary and her brother it was no longer their timber.

This decision cut their board feet down by two-thirds. The men had built camp and hovel and store, and for what? They were by this letter soon to cross into an illegitimate cut. That is, it was now Sonny Estabrook's cut. They could have what wood they had yarded, but they must leave now. Mary left most of this up to the men she hired, and some were unscrupulously taking advantage of her—some were stealing her wood and selling it over to Estabrook, who pretended he did not know where it had come from. Buckler himself tried to figure this out but could never catch them. Their mill was in desperate shape.

The section that Will had found in the middle of Northumberland and claimed when juvenile would reap a great harvest of wood for the great Estabrook mill now.

Mary Jameson felt that she had been cheated out of this timber that the family felt always belonged to Will.

She had told Camellia about this just before they heard Owen was coming home.

That was one reason why Camellia asked the men to bring Owen from the train. This, in fact, was how those wheels had stopped. She wanted Owen back to save the mill, to save her husband, and her husband to save the wood.

She did not know Reggie would leave.

Owen also realized this year was life or death. How ordinary that was: life and death in a man's life's work. No one seemed to mind when it wasn't their own life. He would have to go into the woods himself and leave Buckler in charge of the mill—new saws had to be bought, and the wood already in the yard had to been sawed. The landings would have to be collected in a half-dozen places. He would do it for Will; he owed that much.

Yet the government decision meant Owen would have to have his men go further up river, past where anyone had gone before, and cut out of the wilderness once again his batch houses and his horse hovels, make his claim for the timber. So Owen decided the only chance to save the mill was going to cut on Good Friday Mountain, called Buckler's Mountain by some. None had gone there before. He would go there now. He did not know that Buckler had decided the same a month before.

Buckler believed it was his fault they had lost the holdings Will had struggled so hard to bid on. All that lumber that Will had mapped out—perhaps forty-five million board feet at maturity—what he thought of as Will's greatest legacy would be turned over to other mills.

"Tell me why that is," Owen said.

It was very simple to understand once Owen saw the date that bid had opened. It was years ago. The day after Will was killed. In the hidden fury that is grief, no one reminded Mary to make the bid that day. Buckler now blamed himself. He said that he had failed Mary's husband, failed Mary's son, and now failed Mary.

"Don't be silly," Owen said. "How could you have known?"

By the time they realized this oversight, Will's intention had been discovered by Estabrook and contested. Now that the wood had matured, the government had changed and all bids were reopened. Europe needed to rebuild.

Now that the stand was ready, it was no longer theirs.

If Will had not died that day, the bid would have been made the very next evening. The first evening of the wake.

But how had Estabrook found out about this? It took Buckler a while to understand how simply fate had played out its hand against them. Estabrook Sr. and Jr. were, along with knowledgeable timber men from the government, pallbearers at Will's funeral.

Fred Bots, an underling in the forestry department, had let it be known to the Estabrooks that the timber was found but the bid not made, because Will had died.

Estabrook Jr. (called Sonny) realized their chance and translated *non-bid* as *non-desire*. "The family probably doesn't want to bid on it after this," Sonny told his father. "Most of it's not going to be prime for ten years anyways—let's you and I go take a look ourselves—we have to go over to the *Jensen*" (this was a Norwegian ship that had come up from New England, and they had been asked aboard by the captain—they wanted to do business with his employer) "and then we can take a jaunt to see it—take the captain with us, to show him—how's that?"

"Ah—perhaps—Freddy, see what you can do to get us in a bid," Old Estabrook said.

Freddy Bots realized he had betrayed a man at his funeral out of stupidity, and a longing to impress. He was, however, too afraid of Old Estabrook to do much about it.

Buckler discovered this shortly after, but did not have the qualities that made Owen's father and brother so feared. He could do nothing.

It was using Will's death that mattered most to Owen. A stand that was no longer theirs, because of human grief and death. He also realized that Estabrook Jr. could easily have paid Bots a kickback for this lot. Of course, nothing like that could be proven.

It was in this moment that Owen decided he could not leave, for the memory of Will demanded that he stay.

"I'm staying here until you get straightened about—and that's an end to it," Owen said. "Tell the men to go up on Good Friday."

"I already have," Mary said.

Now Owen coming home was a great blessing. Buckler grabbed his hand and shook it, tears in his eyes. And it was on the tip of his tongue to call Owen, Will—but he stopped himself before that.

TWELVE

The woods are much changed, and how a good man lived then would try the best men now.

The next day Owen went out on the Tote Road with a team, packing in canned peaches and flour, pork and beef, and a barrel of doughnuts, to the camp far up on Good Friday Mountain. It took hours to get there, and so he slept the first night under the moon. By the time he reached higher ground, snow had fallen.

The next morning, in the crisp snow-filled air, he saw Good Friday Mount, and knew the teamsters would be hard pressed to get down a load. And on every foot up that mountain, he saw in his mind's eye the horses stumble, and the loads come down upon their backs.

"Poor fuckin' horses," he thought, for unlike Will he had always thought a little more of horses than men—which even he considered a weakness. And Will would consider unforgivable.

Any qualms or weakness here would soon be known by men who cherished strength.

He reviewed his site—knew which teams of horses would come in, the men, the cutting they had done at the top of the hill where they would start in a week or so to haul it by horse to the riverbank, to block and chain it up until the spring drive. He needed dams built so the runoff would be great enough to carry the timber, and that very morning he ordered his men down to do it. He also ordered a road straight down over an embankment—the only place on the face of the mountain where one could possibly do it—and to have a bridge constructed at the bottom. They did what he said.

Still, even the loyal ones knew it was a harsh place.

"I know it is a harsh place," Jameson said, "so go now if you need to."

None did.

It was widely thought in the last week or two that Jameson would give over their holdings and sell out to Estabrook. And that Owen had come home as a war hero to get the best price.

Owen made it clear that this was not the case.

They would continue to cut upon Good Friday, and they would bring the wood to the mill in the spring.

Later that day he walked down into the shine and told the fellers that he knew it was a hard place—but they had been in hard spots before, hadn't they. The way they would fashion the run down to Arron Brook would be the most dangerous run in the province. He told them this point blank.

One of the teamsters who had come in early, Gravellier, said there might be another way around. He asked Owen if he knew that.

"Yes I do," Owen, who had looked at a map of the area, said, "but there is no time to trim another road so far away."

They asked Owen if he had run out a team.

"Yes I have," he said, "once or twice. I won't lie, I am not a great teamster—but I will rely upon great teamsters here!"

They stood about him in the year's first snow, with axes, draft horses, and chains, the "shine" they had cut looking like a tunnel into the future, bright with the bark-scalped trees and dark with the shadow of trees ready to be felled, some of the men like ghosts scattered here and there, wearing thick woolen shirts, Humphrey pants, and old coats, their beards scrapped with tree chips, ice, and snot, they breathed in the dense wood, the only world they knew—while the world at that moment in Toronto, New York, or London knew nothing or cared little for the millions of board feet these men had cut, skewered out of the earth for the benefit of those cities and city dwellers, who would think of them, if at all, as savages.

Owen sat that night in the smoky camp—where things were not much different than what he had seen as a boy. He saw the socks and woolen underwear sacked up to dry on poles above the stove, the arms and muscled backs of men making ready for the night in the sweet acrid smell of burning wood. He understood it was the last of the lumber baron years, and of his family's operation (although he pretended not to). New companies as far away as the States would come in and create a new market, for tissue and toilet paper, for boxes to put trifles in. For commodities they did not even now know existed. They would haul by truck and not horse, they would cut by chainsaw and not ax, they would load by harvester and not hand—they would rid the world of the very woods they depended on. Owen could glimpse this future more than some others here, but it was an erstwhile glimpse, a glimpse he himself did not fully understand.

In twenty years this life, these men of almost two centuries, would be no more. They would be like Yeats' dissatisfied ones. Unable, many of them, to exist in the world now—at this time, what would happen—what would happen to dreams still soft in the night air?

A man like many here would not live in the world to come. They would fight it—would fight the new world unto death.

But the world would not lose. Just like the First People before them, these men, these tough, kind-hearted men, would lose. For that was the way of the world, and Owen knew it. That was why he was full of sadness when he saw these men scattered about the trees and imagined them ghosts, with their bodies still strong and hearts innocent. He knew if he told any of them to walk fifty miles into the wilderness they would turn and go, so anxious they were to prove themselves to those they worked and bled for. Already there was a great road being hacked out of the middle of the province by companies ready to use truck instead of horse and river, so in ten years horse and river would become obsolete, and truck and gas be the measure.

Owen's objection to the world changing might be the objection of a good man—but what did that matter? Ten thousand good men could object and still the battle of Stalingrad happen.

He looked at these men and sighed. He certainly had brought them to a tough place.

But for him was another tougher place, not yet seen.

The tougher place was the blossoming opinion of the town. In this opinion, of the old woman who had seen them, and drinking men on the corner, Owen had lied to the men who did not want to cut on a dangerous mountain, and was having relations with Reggie's wife—Reggie, who Owen had fired over a disagreement about this cut.

In the blossoming opinion of the town, which had so recently raised him up, "so not a foot touch the ground" Owen had snubbed his former sweetheart Lula, who had suffered a stroke and therefore suffered too much. This alone was the most disparaging rumor against him. He was obligated to marry her.

In the blossoming opinion of the town, Camellia was asking Reggie for a divorce, a very serious matter back then, especially for a Catholic girl.

This was the opinion of our town, which neither Owen nor Camellia had heard, but would have to face in the coming months.

PART II

ONE

Owen had been home three weeks, and much had changed in his relationship with people who had come to honor him. Some questioned him about Reggie Glidden and why he wasn't Push.

Others, the old maid at the house, told him to beware of Camellia.

"She's a gold digger," she whispered piously. "It's what I hear downtown at the cookie shop—I go for Mrs. Jameson and it's what I heard."

"I'll go tell her," he said.

"Don't you dare," she said.

"Well—let me see—what is she doing now?—ah, there she is—she is out playing hopscotch in the back lane with your granddaughter—a scurrilous thing. And she speaks to people as equals—young and old—a terrible thing—and she finds beauty almost anywhere—a maddening thing."

"Hopscotch can't fool me—or beauty—" the old lady mumbled (and rejoiced in her mumbling).

But hopscotch was not Camellia's only fault. Her hiking up her skirt as she did the floor was something too, which he had witnessed coming downstairs one morning. She looked up at him as he stared down at her almost-naked thighs.

"Oh God, ya saw my bloomers," she said, pulling her skirt down. "There is usually only women here this time a day." And she laughed, shrugged as if to shrug off embarrassment, both his and hers, and kept working.

More to the point, he was saddened by her being on her hands and knees, and told her he wished she didn't have to do it. She was so beautiful then that he caught his breath as he spoke.

"Oh, I don't mind nothin' like this," she said.

"What do you do?" he said, another time, seeing small bits of ribbon in her pockets.

"Oh dear," she laughed, "well, you caught me good for thievin'." She explained that the ribbons were off Mary's knitting baskets, and she was taking them to tie back three or four young girls' hair who lived in the neighborhood—and "who had little to make them look pretty."

"Then you take all you want," he said.

However, going into the woods, Owen felt things would straighten out, and he had a long, cold winter ahead.

Owen also knew it was great timber, but didn't exalt—for it was a hard, long way from the water, and no easy road down that great precipice. He was silent about such blessings. He had the letter of acquisition but knew Bots allowed him this quota on Good Friday Mount because he felt guilty about his slip of the tongue that day years ago.

After three weeks of preparation Owen went in to camp with the Clydesdales, Missy and Butch, Missy Butch's mother, to further the road and bring in supplies. All day he rode in behind them, on a two sled hauled over snowy gravel, with Innis the portager leading him on and cursing the horses at regular intervals, until Owen told him to stop, for the horses could not answer back and so it wasn't fair.

They stopped to rest along the flats beside Arron Stream, and could see the high ground rising up before them—already testing the horses to sweat—as they drank tea and ate a cold lunch. All along this flat in the coming months, they would have their timber yarded up on skids, waiting for the break in the weather. Owen pictured it all in his mind's eye, and for some unknown reason shuddered. Innis saw this shudder and Owen replied: "We better head up to it, or it'll be evening soon."

They arrived at evening and Owen went to the hovel, making well sure his horses were tended to. Smoke came from the camp stack, and lay serene in the icy air, which was thinner here, and made the cough of the horses distant, and the footfall of the men crack against the brittle ice. It grew suddenly dark among these sounds, and then the wind picked up as snow began to fall.

A week before (the first time he was in camp) he had had it out with his teamsters. At that time he went to Mr. Gravellier, a lead teamster, and asked if he would be able to move his Belgians, the smallest yet toughest of the big draft horses, down that steep grade that they had managed to make, cut out and cursed at, that plummeted from the top cut on the mountain to Arron Stream.

"The devil's back," one swamper called it. And the name stuck.

Owen wanted to know if he had the right teamsters to go down such a decline. It was a sheer drop to the river, with a wild turn to the right to cross the Bailey Bridge.

From the first, this cut up on Good Friday was considered a terrible place—and it was not just those teamsters who thought so, but ordinary people.

Mr. Gravellier had been subcontracted to hire his own teamsters—and he had done this, and Owen knew some of the men but not all. Gravellier was in the hovel, in a black coat and red braces, smoking a pipe, when Owen arrived, and soon left to go back toward the cut, looking over his shoulder at the boss.

People everywhere were giving Owen advice on who and who not to hire, each person having their own prejudices and dislikes. Owen had waited for Reggie, but Reggie had not come. So now Owen himself acted Push.

Gravellier's teamsters, their names nailed to the wall, were Colson, Davies, Stretch (Tomcat) Tomkins, and Lloyd.

Owen had chosen Curtis and Trethewey to come in when their teams were ready. He chose Richardson and Nolan, who were already there.

"How far up is we past the Arron Brook proper?" Gravellier had asked that day a week ago. He had a gaze that implied a continual questioning of the one he spoke to, as if the one he spoke to was suspected of something dishonest. The gaze did not diminish when one was answering him, but fastened to the man's face as if trying to discover lie or weakness. Nor did he ever agree with anything that anyone said. The closest Gravellier came to accommodation was not to disagree. If he disagreed, he would disappear into the woods and sit with his horses, or cause a mutiny—that it was too dangerous, or poor, or cold, or whatnot—and would connive to convince those with him to leave.

He had done so on other sites and Owen knew this, but had no choice. He was starting late as it was. There was talk about him already as it was.

But that day a week ago, Owen answered Gravellier with the same querulous, quizzical look he gave: "Twenty-seven miles—from that bridge to the proper brook—hard and rough all the way. I will say it won't be a light time for any of your men or your horses—any inexperienced teamster better hold off. The horses will be worked, no doubt about that—but I want to know if you can go down that grade. We have dammed the stream and plan to use it to float out to the brook—and from there to the river—"

"Down where?" Gravellier asked.

"Why, down here, sir—right here," Owen said, throwing over a stick.

Gravellier asked to speak with his men. They held a conference standing along the skid road. The wind so strong that it blew the men's pant legs like they were standing before the propeller of a plane.

After a time Gravellier came back: "What my men is thinking is we can go around—meet it from the other end—have a longer road."

"We could if we had two years," Owen said, turning away and holding the bridle on the little roan named Dixie, who had gone skittery in the gale. "We wouldn't get half the wood yarded. The men will have to go down here—" and he pointed down, into a narrow path between shale rock and cliff, where the snow swirled up in tormented circles, called the devil's belly.

Owen's hair was cut short, his eyes as penetrating as any Gravellier.

"That might be impossible," Gravellier said.

"If you think it is impossible, I will hire the teamsters who don't. You'll all have bonus in the end! But it has to be down here—the boys made time making this road and the bridge, and I'm not going to waste it by not believing in ourselves. Buckler oversaw it, and he knows something about this mountain. We are already a good two weeks behind Estabrook, three behind Sloan—"

Gravellier did not think Owen would know he would balk. But Owen had known from the moment he first spoke to him.

"How much is bonus?"

"Bonus is two hundred," Owen said calmly. This was a great deal of extra money for a teamster then.

"I'll see," Gravellier said, and he went to sit in the woods with his horses, not confiding in anyone, not even Colson. Colson didn't know who to agree with. Sometimes he agreed with Gravellier, sometimes with Owen—and sometimes he stood between the two, nodding his head at whatever anyone said.

Now he shook his head at the idea of going over such a hill as that.

The next day when Nolan and Richardson arrived, they said they would go over the hill to the brook.

"And drink a pint on the fuckin' way down," Nolan said.

It would save hours on every trip. It would therefore save money, and the horses as well.

Colson and Tomkins (speaking for Gravellier, who chose not to) said no horse should go where Richardson and Nolan decided—and tried to talk them out of it by appealing to their knowledge of horses and loads—something they felt Owen, as green Push, did not know. But Nolan said it could be done, and had to be done, and once the horses got used to it, it would be no problem at all.

"In fact, it must be done," he said. "And the long road around would tear the horses up in the end, just slower."

This had been the standoff, the men on both sides blaming each other for bad husbandry, and calling each other names like children standing in a schoolyard—ferocious and hard—while the sun bled through the naked trees and lighted slimly on the one-paned window of the forlorn camp.

Owen knew that whatever he decided would harm his relations with half his teamsters. He couldn't help but think that a wrong decision here would cause a terrible blow later.

"What would Reggie decide?" he thought. But he cursed himself for this and decided thus: "Nolan—take the first load over with Miss Maggie Wade and Mr. Stewart and see if you can make it across the bridge without losing your load. If you make it across without losing a stick, I'll buy you some good plug."

Gravellier muttered something out of the corner of his mouth to the men gathered about him shaking their heads. He broke wind for spite. Tomkins shook his head for spite. Colson shrugged for spite.

Then Gravellier turned and walked back into the hovel while his teamsters looked back at Owen, and then followed Gravellier. The clouds covered the sky and it began to rain in heavy pellets, against their already half-washed-out downhill.

The two sled was loaded in the freezing rain late that afternoon, by Pitman and Fraser, and before suppertime Nolan, a short man with broad arms who had a face like an owl, climbed onto the two sled over the first load of timber, and at twilight of November 19, with the waif of smoke coming from the cookstove, mingling harsh smoke with the smell of dying leaves, the smell of wet tin and bark in the air, Nolan looked down at a drop that seemed to plummet into the void.

"Let's see, here—I go from his mouth to his guts—to his arse—very best."

The other teamsters came out from the evening shadows and walked to the edge to watch, like children looking down a great hill.

"Don't make a wrong turn in his guts," Richardson advised.

Once Nolan climbed the timber, sticking his boots between the logs as if he was climbing a mountain, he was, even with this small load, almost six feet above the horses' ears, and the timber though sound would tip in an instant if not hauled right, even with the tie-down chains. He calmed his horses, especially Miss Maggie Wade, by whistling to them, and then whispering something no one else ever heard. These two Belgians, tough as nails with short broad legs, had hauled his great loads for the masters for six years.

Nolan knew if the sled slid off to the right on the way down, he would lose his entire load over the cliff. He seemed to think of this at the exact same time as Owen did. He walked the load to check it, then came to the front again and stared down the precipice while he kicked at the chains.

"I'll be on my way, boys," he said. "No snow in the quiff's belly will slow me—"

Owen paced back and forth with his wounded leg paining.

He knew some, like Stretch Tomkins and Colson, would want Nolan to lose this load, and perhaps his life, to prove that they should go around. He had noticed what type of men they were. Gravellier would then have accomplished a good deal, and his name would be heard of in town, as having advised an inexperienced boss, named Owen Jameson, the VC winner. He knew Nolan was doing this for him, without knowing him and with a shrug of his shoulders, because of his name and Will's. That, on this mean scowl of a day, was faith.

It was a desolate place, this mountain. An article written in the *Leader* in October of 1946 states this implicitly. It also states that the entire town was watching them—to see if they would be able to work there. Estabrook, the main rival, was watching most closely.

At first the town had championed Owen Jameson's pluck—but now it was more reticent about what might happen.

Even in the summer the heat never seemed to ripen the adolescent blueberries that grew on the mountain's side ledges. Five men had lost their lives here since 1903—which was the talk of our newspaper editor, a man not from here.

The trees however were of a stronger stuff, bent and gnarled they rose upwards, passed all obstacles and still towered above the heads of the axmen, who had to crawl over mountains of felled logs like ants, day in and out, covered in snow—and already twice this year falling into the dens of bears.

"Small bears," the axman who killed both said.

Owen felt sudden aching sadness in the wind now, through to his soul, the carcasses of those bears pinned to the wall behind him, like forlorn and graceful reminders of man's inherent thoughtlessness.

He could not tell the men he disapproved of those furiously sad pelts. They would mock him as weak.

He stifled this, as he would stifle much.

He grabbed a switch and looked up at Nolan, who continually chewed on his plug. What was so sad about Nolan's smile is that he couldn't help it. Owen thought briefly that the way Nolan's cheeks and mouth were formed, he would smile even as he went to his death.

Owen buckled the switch.

"Right down the devil's back, Mr. Nolan," Owen said.

"Shove it right down the devil's throat," Nolan said.

That brought a hush.

Miss Maggie Wade's front hooves slid just slightly and she backed away as Nolan broke the whip above the horses' heads.

In an instant he was gone, the horses running at a gallop down the incline. There was the snap of the whip as Nolan reached the "swallow," the narrow point between shale cliff and sheer drop. One of the runners seemed to slip toward the very edge, and a chunk of snow fell forty feet onto a wet ledge.

No one spoke.

The two sled had gone almost sideways, the hind rivets and planks twisting under the weight of the load as the tie-down chains tried to hold them. Owen could see the head of Miss Maggie Wade turned almost backward by the reins as Nolan tried to keep the sled on track, all through the belly toward the bottom turn.

Mr. Davies turned about and pretended to look for something in the snow, so he wouldn't have to watch what was happening below. He had always been a brave man at dinner.

Richardson yelled at them all to be still, and ran to the edge, brushing past Tomkins as he did.

"Hey," Tomkins said, "do you know who I am?"

"Ya—yer a fuckin' lying cunt," Richardson said matter-of-factly.

Nolan made the bottom and the sharp turn and galloped the horses across the narrow makeshift bridge they had constructed with a loud clatter, all the timbers straining and squeaking, and the sled runners making the green floor buckle.

There was silence as the horses came to a sudden halt on the far side of the bridge.

The sled had carried the first load, November 19, 1946.

The teamsters said nothing, just looked at each other. Then a loud "Hey, my lads!" from Nolan. "She's quite the little scamper right there now, boys—but don't let fear stop ya—fer coming down will save us twenty-four hours!"

The teamsters all roared with laughter.

"Too steep, Mr. Gravellier?" Owen asked, picking up the black switch again.

"Well—it is very steep."

"Yes—but is it too steep? Tell me now one way or the other."

"Going around might be safer—certainly it is a bit longer," Gravellier said. "So I guess we will put it over here."

"Good, good," Owen said, holding onto a gnarled spruce tree as he looked over the precipice with darkness falling and the smell of frozen spruce gum on his blackened leather mittens.

"It'll save the horses too," he said, as if to accommodate the man's bad temper. Gravellier stared straight ahead, chewing his plug in the black, furious night.

TWO

The whole camp was made in the roughest fashion of spruce and pine, small and low and cramped, with bunks on either side against the rough-hewn walls, but the food was good. The men were mostly half-illiterate, beggars of fortune in any other place. But with the whiff of smoke trailing against the trees, the smell of horses and tack, they were among their own, and could act accordingly.

There were men who worked and lived and died here who had never seen a provincial capital or knew an MP who claimed to work on their behalf, but who cut the wood that fashioned that man's oak desk, and the cedar that had made his sauna at Sugar Loaf Resort. Men who worked here would be laughed at with such ignorance by people in Toronto, one would sometimes wonder who was actually primitive. For those who believed that acquisition of things made you understand the world would always mistake these men as less than themselves until the time they had to rely upon them, either in kindness or in battle.

Just after dark Owen walked out to the side skids to set up oil lanterns that would, before dawn, guide the teamsters getting their first loads in the morning. The timber was ready along the side of the skid road—it had been piled up in the last five weeks, cut and hauled out to here by the men his uncle had first sent in. They were already down into the shine on both sides of the mountain, which simply meant the horses had to haul the loads up on a contraption called the devil's mount (which lifted the front of the log off the ground a foot) a few logs at a time to the rough skid road, where these logs were to be piled upon the two sled, and then driven over the hill, and over time for miles and miles along Arron Stream to Arron Brook, and to the great Bartibog River that Will at eighteen had made his own.

Owen wondered if his main faller might be able to drop the main trees in the new section tomorrow. The main faller Bartlett and his other axmen had divided the cut into twenty-two sections of woods. They were now at section four. A long winter.

Owen was hoping that six teams could work tomorrow, and since they did not have a long haul right away—because they were counting on a spring runoff from a dam they had built—they might each get three loads yarded.

Trethewey's team of large black Percherons, two hands taller than Owen's Clydes, Missy and Butch, would be in soon. So, six teams until the Percherons, he decided. In future days each haul would get longer. And Mr. Curtis, who was considered at twenty-two to be the best young teamster on the river and who they had just managed to hire, would be in toward Christmastime. Which would make eight teams. Owen had done his hiring relentlessly and ruthlessly, relying on his name and his new-found fame.

"Well, can I ask ya one thing?" Curtis said. "You be the VCer?"

"'Fraid so," Owen said.

"Then I'm for you on Good Friday," Curtis answered.

Mary knew he traded upon this, and did not wish him to. But, for his family, he would. Still, she thought it would bring bad luck. For everything in the woods was deemed lucky or unlucky.

This new thing between him and Reggie was certainly unlucky—so unlucky Owen did not speak about it. He had offered. He cared a lot for Reggie and knew he was a great man. The trouble was, Glidden had forgotten his greatness.

"I will cope," Owen told Mary on the day he left.

But Mary feared the unknown. She could not help it, with her pockets of money, her ability to handle thirty men, and her grade three education—which, as she said, she never felt compelled to brag about.

Most of the men were doing the only work they knew. Outside of this forest, these confines of somewhat brutal timber, they were no one and even nothing—in here, where death met life and stared it in the face every moment on a run down hill, they were some of the finest men who ever lived. Illiterate, unkempt, harsh on themselves and unforgiving of weakness in order to survive. Owen had known men who had stitched their own wounds in a hurry in order to save someone else.

In spite of the cold and the foul humanity he slept with, shared his life with, it was still a world of greatness. He did not say *greatness* easily—he did not say it about himself. He was silent with his men, most of the time. And most of the time they were wary to say anything to him. This was Owen Jameson—the second son, the one they didn't know. Even his bravery seemed different than the bravery of his brother. There was for some reason less fun to it. It was, in fact, more British uniform than fuggin' Irish whiskey.

"I don't like him," Tomkins whispered, seeing some kind of an advantage in not liking him. This would become more insistent as time went by, and as the days of winter came meaner and shorter.

"No one do," Gravellier answered, "but the fucker ain't paying us to like him—and he does much with one leg."

THREE

It was night when Owen decided who would be lead teamster for the morning, and a scowl of wind had come up over the black head tip of the trees and made him think, if he did think of God, which in honor of Will he had refused to, that God had acknowledged his problem. For this was a political decision as well. It would be either Nolan or Gravellier. He leaned toward Nolan, but Gravellier had assumed he would be the lead, and had been stung by their first argument—and he was far more political. Politics had swum in his blood all his life. Now he was for union, but when his daddy owned ground he wasn't. Still, Owen had to accommodate him, even if he didn't like to admit it.

So it would be Gravellier for now, which he knew would put Nolan out, for Nolan took the first load when none else would. He was trading on this, hoping Nolan would understand, for Nolan was less political and a better teamster.

Owen knew what Tolstoy said to be true—the more you did, the more was asked of you. And, Owen could add, the less you were thanked. Still, he knew Gravellier would give up the lead when times became tense.

So he was asking Nolan and Richardson at this moment to take a back seat to Gravellier and his men, even though Nolan and Richardson had done far more and complained far less.

Nor did he like it here—this mountain—already Owen felt a heavy hatred for it, and for those who worked upon it and who had whipped his horse and killed those bear. At this moment, too, came hatred for himself—for when Will burned *Ulysses* and bragged he would earn a million and never read a book, Owen bragged he would read a million books and never cut a tree.

And now the very wind caused his guts to ache.

But this was the sunless and stunted woods, and he was in it now. He had longed not to see it again. It was as if a nightmare had reappeared after a length of time, and he now must deal with it again.

Before they woke, Owen would be up. The black oil lanterns were now dimly lit—or as the men said, "dimmy"—to show the teamsters where their sleds would be loaded on the long, torturous skid road. They glowed and made the snow like fairy dust just in front of their oil bowls—like some impenetrable fairyland lost to modern man a century before. The winged earth was all about, and Owen tried to think of this winged earth, this bowl of green land incomprehensible to those in cities who without wood and quarry were fed by it. Still in the glowing light of lanterns of old traditions, Owen remembered his brother Will, and the great man beside him, Reggie Glidden, as they took him on a moose hunt in 1934—up beyond this place by nineteen miles. Yes, he remembered it now—and the moose a thirty-four-point bull, a picture of it still in Will's bedroom on a shelf. Where was this place—could he find it again, he wondered.

But the bowls of oil were for the morning. The tradition came from his father Byron and was simply a formality, for most of them knew where to go—and more importantly, half the horses knew exactly where to go, having hauled the wood up those hills in the last month. The wood, bark hanging like toffs of deadened skin, was enough in the end to make the horses mad. But a formality was very important here.

It was pitch black, except for those lanterns hung against poles, when Owen started back to camp. And it was snowing now, hitting him full in the face, with the grating trees making the sound: *Holdfast.*

He could not see the trees even four feet away—could only follow the path because it was the most open track. These were the gnarled and toughened trees. Like the men, they came to root in tough soil and could not be easily defeated. In fact, they were much like the men who cut them. They seemed benighted, but were magnificent, and made great wood.

The snow hurled down as if the world was in torment, and as if the torment was saying that this taking of trees was a wicked thing.

He had seen much death. He had also seen so much of the prophecy on Will's broken body that he still cried aloud. Would his body fill the glad maw of prophecy too? Even as an atheist, and somewhat of a modern calculated man, he still believed in—what? Well, whatever it was, he spoke to it every day.

Far away one lantern gleamed in the horse hovel where the young tend team Gibbs—a tend team was a boy hired to feed and keep the horses—was working with the Clydesdales and the Belgian teams. Finally seeing this small glimmer, Owen followed it in, half-blinded as he was by snow. But now he had first-hand knowledge of how easy it was to be lost.

He was freezing, his face and his arms, his wounded leg almost unable to move the last two hundred yards. He would not let the fuckers know this. For as always, not being Will, he was wary of these men. If they knew he was in pain, the weak ones would want to go around rather than down, and the weaker ones would try to challenge him in some way.

He came in, and the men looked at him silently. The teamsters nodded politely, and he nodded back, in taciturn accord and no more, as the profound jumbled-up wind blew and called.

He took a book to the bunk. Being one of the few men in the camp considered educated, this was looked upon as strange and spectacular, and not quite "manly" by the men moving around him, disjointed in their evening talk, muted because the new boss was in. In the days to come he would only be here periodically—for he had work to do at the mill. That's why having the right Push was so important. And he couldn't be here, he knew, for the woods would get to him—unlike his brother he didn't have the "feel" for it. But once this year was done, and with Reggie Glidden and perhaps next year Simon Terri in charge (Simon who had gone to get the doctor at Will's death, a man this year hired to Sloan with his Micmac friend Daniel Ward), he would propel himself into another life. Away from the torment of his past—for it did torment him—and away too from Camellia, who was a horrible temptress even if she did not know it. No wonder so many worried on her behalf.

"She has the bastard French," he heard the Scot maid say.

Tonight the men brought him a treat—to show they knew his stature—a white cloth napkin to wipe his face after he ate a piece of hot apple pie and drank a scalding cup of tea.

It was a lonely world, and this showed its loneliness, down deep. Small implements from home made it lonelier still. Great burly men became mothering to young swampers in their charge, and overcame embarrassment in doing so. Later, meeting on the roads in summer, they might not even acknowledge each other.

To the men, he looked peculiar—a small replica of the Jameson clan, yet an unknown quantity in their lives, a strange anomaly of substance they could not easily fathom.

A ladies' man, some said—too cute by half to lay into Glidden's wife.

He was a bookworm and had made the rank of major. He had been wounded, and yet didn't look like he could fight. They were silent in front of him, and as yet did not talk so much about him behind his back. They did not want to swear, though they had already heard him swear like a trooper.

The book he read was *Lear*, the play he had often returned to, trying at one time to fathom his brother's moods and whimsy and his mother's curious worry. It was an old tattered edition bought in London during the Blitz—a curious shopkeeper reminding him that bombs breaking overhead might mean more to an interpretation, and he answering that yes, and "so too my son our share of landings off a boom."

To which the shopkeeper replied: "You come from a land I have no knowledge of—what is it called?"

"Home," Owen said.

FOUR

The wind blew snow all night up against the outside walls, and far up against the trunks of trees they were to cut. Higher than the head of a man by dawn the snow had piled, the world outside frozen solid—with "an extra mountain of ice" on the mountain they were on. Each tree the fallers would cut today was boughed down with snow, and each tree trunk had to be freed from snow to be felled, and each felled tree had to be cut in two or three, and each section had to be hauled by grunting, overworked men and horses—both seeming to enlist each other's pain—leaning on and mocking it at the same time.

The world inside the camps was filled with the smell of smoke and meat and rank sweat. It was built in a hurry and was half a foot too low for many men. It was dark for the most part—and certain of the men feared theft from others. There were no rifles allowed in camp, though any man here could use a knife and throw an ax or hatchet well. One turn at forty feet and stick into a cedar tree. But a rifle was brought in by Owen himself and given to the cook, just in case.

"You might need this come sometime," was all he said.

Owen was up long before dawn. The first thing he had to do this morning was dig himself out of the camp, because the door never was free of the nightly drifts. The air was arctic and split his lip, so he tasted his blood a second before it froze. The trees stood in blackness and weighed down boughs, for miles, like muted solitary soldiers.

Meager Fortune coming through the door, snow falling down the back of his underwear, shook himself bare, picked up an ax, and cut some firewood for breakfast, the ax blade coming close to the fingers that held the birch chunk. He had been up in the night stoking, but the fire had gone down.

Owen had traveled with Meager in the war, and had hired him as a general camp keeper. He was up at 4:30 mending seven pairs of socks for the axmen and the teamsters, his little face having a childlike gaze when Owen awoke, *Lear* over his chest. Meager was considered simple-minded, but had fought all the way to Antwerp. He had been saved by a minister of the Lower Rapids in 1934 and baptized in the "full" dress—and he set an example because of it.

He was learning to cook, and learning to write, and had recipes hidden in his boots that he had copied from the cook to take home, as he told everyone, to his wife and little boy, Duncan. He called everyone *sir* and was looked upon by most, Tomkins especially, as a simpleton. Tomkins had already taken to teasing him, but Meager Fortune didn't seem to pay much attention to it.

Slightly ten minutes later, the acrid smell of burning birch and then hard rock maple drifted out over the camp's tin roof toward the sky that was just beginning to be shaded by gray. Along the sides of the hovel, where the horses started to clomp, the outline of boards and old sled parts loomed as the day dawned.

Gibbs, the number one tend team, was shaken awake, and came out in his Humphreys and long underwear to feed the horses oats.

The teamsters were the next to wake, an hour before the rest.

In the frozen snow, Gravellier and Nolan came out. A few of the two sleds were already loaded, a few weren't.

Owen helped harness the Clydesdales for Nolan. It took five men to dig his two sled free from a hard night's crust of snow and get it turned. The two sled weighed almost twelve hundred pounds before it was loaded, and it ran on slick runners with a great timber and block and chains in the middle. One of those chains could be wrapped about the crazy wheel, a contraption welded to a tree that would stop the sled on the downhill run if anything went wrong. Some of Gravellier's men used the crazy wheel. Nolan's men did not—but on the devil's back there was nothing to attach a wheel to.

"Who is lead teamster?" Gravellier said, throwing the question back over his shoulder, into the dark smelling now of back bacon and tea.

"You will be, if you don't mind," Owen said.

Nolan looked at his boss. His happy-go-lucky expression never wavered, though his eyes showed less mirth. Nolan was certain of his position and did not like being challenged. This was as true with his friends as his enemies—for anyone to tell him that his best friends Richardson and Trethewey were better teamsters was enough to make him mute for two days.

Owen was aware, and so were they, that any of these men could die, and that to haul for four to five months from this position, over a mountain, it was almost a certainty someone would be injured. And that further to this thought, they were already predicting calamity in town. So the bottles he had found last night in the bear hides he left to the designs of those who put them there, the beer hidden from him in the storeroom too.

After breakfast Richardson jumped aboard the Clydesdales heading out behind Gravellier and the Belgians. Miss Maggie Wade and Mr. Stewart teamed by Nolan. Then Colson and Davies and Choyce.

Two hours later, just as sunlight was flushing cold against the far ridges and flaring red on the one-paned window, the Belgians came back with the first load—six feet higher than the heads of the horses, which seemed dwarfed and puny—all big logs, placed vertically but flattened like an accordion squeezebox toward the base. That made it square and stable for the teamster and the horses to pull. The great two sleds almost disappeared under the weight of the wood. Each load was supported by heavy cross-chains.

This would be the best Jameson cut and haul since long before the war.

It was still just light and they moved past the hovels as silent as a nineteenth-century painting of some other place and time—heavy with logs and moving under a fresh snowfall, the very essence of romance those painted pictures seemed to illustrate.

They had to come off a mountain with these logs. It was what Will, when he was only fifteen and in argumentative fashion with his father, just before Byron died, said he would never allow his men to do. He would quit before he worked men on Good Friday Mountain, no matter how the trees grew up there.

The Jamesons now had no choice. So they sent this second son high, to do what the favorite son warned against a few years before he died.

With *Lear* tucked into his parka pocket and his chest still half bare, and the light from a lantern he carried lighting his shoulder bone as he swung it forward, Owen yelled, in a voice almost too shrill, as if he was giving something away about the hidden worry in his nature: "We have much to catch up with if we are to get our fuckin' pay!"

And he swung the lantern in the black air, as snow still came down on the exposed shoulder, and melted there against a patch of white skin. He walked forward swinging the lantern, as if at a runaway train. But this train was on eight sturdy legs, buckled by harness and twitching in the cold.

To get them down such a steep run, Owen ordered Stretch (Tomcat) Tomkins, along with some swampers, to get out with the shovels and sand and chaff the downhill as smooth as they could. In a minute Tomkins was running alongside his mentor Gravellier whispering, and in another moment Gravellier stopped his two sled and came back over. Both men reared out of the still half-dark like phantoms and stood before Owen, who was leaning heavy to get the stone to move better on the axes.

"What is this?" Gravellier said. "Trouble here—with Stretch—you know he came in as a teamster?"

"That's what I know," Owen said, holding Bartlett's double-bladed ax. "And he can go out today as a teamster, but he can't have a team of mine—can he have a team of yours, Huey?"

Gravellier was quiet. His lips twitched against the frozen morning and the side of his big, plump face. His eyes narrowed like many people saw when he spoke at union meetings. He shrugged his huge, round shoulders. He wouldn't take any of his men off to give a team to Tomkins, because he got a part commission on the load—and would not sacrifice one of his better teamsters. Yet if Tomkins took one of Owen's teams, he would get commissioned on that from Tomkins himself.

"That's settled then," Owen said. "We both know where we stand."

"Never mind—you go work here today," he said to Tomkins. "We'll have a grievance over this."

"A grievance, Gravellier?" Owen said, picking up a bucksaw and handing it to Pitman. "A grievance—in what way—let us have the cunt now, sir!" Owen shouted, shouldering an ax and putting his foot up on the stone. "This is not a union cut—and I'll have no fuggin' remarks about grievance this high up. For we all have a fucking grievance, sir—and it is this." And he swung the ax high against the snow.

Gravellier was too refined, and refused comment. He turned away and in the gloomy dawn was heading toward his load again, as paralytic snow wavered before the lantern's light.

Owen drove the ax down into a stump, and took another bucksaw and gave it to a youngster named Fraser.

Tomkins waited to see if there was any chance at all that people would protest. He then looked at Meager Fortune and said: "Meager, you couldn't have had all those kids by yourself." (He did not know how many kids Meager had but decided, because the man had almost no teeth, it must be seven or eight.) He smiled at this great joke. Meager simply looked at him curiously, like, Tomkins thought, the simpleton he was.

But with no more support, Tomkins turned and went down over the hill, muttering and carrying a bucket of hot sand, heated at one of three places along the downhill just that morning.

Owen heard the muttering trail off amid the sound of tin pans and coffee cups clinking against the side of the cabin wall, and what would be familiar for months, the squeaking of timbers and sleds moving together, with the hellish offsetting sound of wind.

FIVE

Soon after, the chaff was laid almost a half mile down—and across the hastily constructed bridge, then the Belgians came very slowly past Owen Jameson to the top of the great hill. And the larger Clydesdales that Richardson teamed, Missy and Butch, followed behind by a good two hundred yards; Nolan behind by the same mark. The Clydes would replace the Belgians as the lead within a week, seeing their strength on the downhill run. This would create tension between the two crews, even more than there was now. But by that time the loyal men would be ready for any show.

The horses breathed frozen air against the sharpening wind, their breath coming now like steam from a boiling pot, and icicles already forming under their mouths. Their great broadened backs seemed to shimmer, even in the gallant dawn, with muscle. They were animals who did not walk, but like the great giant moose that they themselves sometimes met on their journeys, they strode forward, the very purpose of their life cast in the symmetry between movement and power.

Richardson, with wisps of cold about his hairless, scarped face, looked down at the dog Nancy, and tossed it a sliver of bacon. Then the horses stopped up, waiting.

The horses did what they were told, in this age-old ritual, not because they were less smart than the men, but because they knew from experience they had no training to be as brutal.

There were very few horses—even Missy—who were not afraid of a load on the downhill. Sometimes, fearing the timber, they tried to halt the sled by stopping up. If that happened the logs would fall headlong into the animals, maiming or killing them. The Jamesons had lost four horses in the last twelve years from one calamity or another. Yet these were men as fond of horses as any animal rights activist, and knew them better.

A teamster got the horses going downhill by wiping them forward and not letting up. It looked harsh and it was (although few teamsters ever hit their horses, but rather snapped over them). It was to the animal's benefit—and that is what Gravellier, driving the Belgians, did as soon as he passed Owen.

Owen heard the snap of the ten-foot whip, heard the horses bolt down over the chaffed road, straight down into the valley in a wail of feet, clots of chaff and snow flying from their hooves.

It was at this moment the Clydesdales behind Gravellier were whipped forward by Richardson, and the same act occurred; and then a moment later Nolan's team went, the long, limber whip snapping above the horses' heads, and all the horses in gallop trying to keep their feet, with tons of logs behind them. Tomkins, dressed in black woolen coat and high V-shaped yellow suspenders, looked back over his shoulder at the frightening scene developing beneath him. Others ran to the edge to look, as the horses barreled down between the two shale walls as the first feeble rays of dawn came over the stark distant hills.

Within a week or so, the men would be so used to this headlong plunge that, taking a break and pissing over the embankment "into the devil's maw," they wouldn't even notice.

Each trip would get longer until they hit the south fork of Arron Brook itself—some twenty miles away. All this yarded wood would then be cut from its chains and tumble into the freshets of water come spring, and the men would stand upon it, ride it out to the mill, which was as dangerous or more as the job they were now doing.

At this moment Bartlett and seven other "fellers" were gone out to the shine, two at a tree, to cut. A good axman could fell a tree within an inch or two of where he said he would if the wind wasn't bad. Some made a mark with a spit of tobacco and had the tree fall upon it.

Two sawers could do a tree in less time than an axman, but some of the older men still used axes.

But with the wind coming through the mountain woods at noon hour and lasting all afternoon up at this height, it was hard to cut, or at least make a promise not to kill.

The trees would be sawed into two or three sections. The cedar were tallest, then the white pine, then the hemlock. Hooking chains to them, they were hauled to the side of the skid by roans or quarter horses if they had them—Belgians from the sleds, if not—to await loading on the two sled.

Then when tons of logs were loaded, sometimes three times higher than the horses' heads, the teamster would start his long journey, plodding the great horses out toward the stream they had recently dammed.

With Mr. Trethewey's Percherons and Mr. Curtis's Belgians arriving near Christmas, time was taken that afternoon to construct another hovel near the camp. It was dug out in the snow and cold, using barked spruce, rope, and nails.

Young Gibbs, Meager Fortune, and Nolan's boy worked at this all that day, in the freezing snowfall.

It was 1946—at the very twilight of the year, and the very twilight of this world—yet forty thousand horses still worked in the lumber industry in Canada. Missy and Butch were two. The four teams of little Belgians made eight more. The big Percherons were to come. Another team to follow. That made fourteen horses and thirty men that would cut and haul Jameson's wood. A feat of such character and strength that it is impossible to praise.

This first day there was another dispute between the two crews. Richardson and Nolan did not want the first loads put near the bridge.

"Take them down a mile," Nolan said.

"You're giving up a mile of space—for what?" Choyce asked. "This is insane—"

"You'll see how insane in weeks to come," Nolan said.

"Goddamn do as he fuckin' says!" Richardson demanded, his face already frozen. "You'll see why—if it storms too bad later, we can place them near."

Gravellier knew another reason why. And he said: "You are crazy boys, aren't you?" No one knew if the emphasis was on *crazy* or *boys*; Gravellier was too political to make it clear.

However, if time got short, these two and perhaps Curtis and Trethewey to come were going to run down loads in the dark. And they wanted space to drop their loads next to the bridge if they worked at night.

When they made the flat, one huge sled after the other was drawn by the horses, and the men shielding their faces from the wind would begin their sojourn over the flats and hills of snow.

Now and again they would yell back and forth to each other, and their voices would dissipate in the gusts.

This was the first full day—there were only 129 more to go.

SIX

Owen went out the next week to see Buckler at the mill.

Buckler and he decided they needed new saws, and Owen was to travel to Nova Scotia after Christmas to buy them. He was angry about this; feeling claustrophobic in the mill might have made him so. Feeling already the strain of overwork—which came because he had never taken to it like Will. He had never taken to firing men. Or to hiring them, for that matter. Besides, though he did not admit this, his leg was paining again.

"Will was a man for the woods, I am not," he said to Buckler.

That is, Will was a man for men, and Owen knew he was not that kind of man. He had been solitary and should remain such.

They needed new saws, new barker, new sluices—and if they were truthful, a new mill.

That night Owen did not get home until late. He ate supper with his mother and later went upstairs, where he drank Scotch to quell the pain in his leg. Then he undid his pants to look at the wound. It was now red raw again, and irritated from brushing against his Humphrey pants—and if not careful, he would run a fever from it.

He decided to clean it, which he did, and then lay down to sleep the night.

But at eight o'clock he heard some people come in. They had come to celebrate Mary's sixtieth birthday, and he was called to join them.

He walked down the stairs and around the corner to the room, with its high ceiling and pine walls, and saw in the corner, kneeling at the base of the tree, Camellia. She looked up at him, startled. Her face lighted up, and standing, she said: "Come with me—right now, Mr. Jameson, sir, and get your Christmas present."

"Go—where?"

"I don't want none of them to see it," she said.

She grabbed him by the hand and led him into the pantry and closed the door. It was dark, the pine wood smelled of earth and spices, and her hair fell in front of her face. This terribly compromised them. That she didn't know made him stay.

"A present—what for?"

She shrugged, took out a medal of something or someone, and lifted it over his neck.

"Saint Jude," she said, as she straightened the medal, "the saint of impossible cases. You have your VC, and I have this. I was going to up and leave it for you—I even wrapped it—but now I can put it on." She straightened it, and then put it under his collar.

"Who is he?" Owen asked.

"Saint—great saint—I promised long ago to pray every day for the intercession of Saint Jude." Then, seeing his incomprehensible look, she broke out giggling.

"So I'm impossible."

"No—but your job is—everyone is saying men will be killed—the paper has blasted you for being up there. That's why we need Reggie back," she said. "You save the mill, Reggie will get the wood."

"What about praying to God—instead?"

"God hears what one prays to Saint Jude."

"Well, I'm not Catholic."

"You don't need to be to have an impossible task ahead," she laughed, stroking his shoulder suddenly in delight.

He was startled by her beautiful troubled face and black eyes.

"Well, thank you," he said.

He had to move by her to open the door, pressing his body against hers and smelling—what?—some sweet candy on her breath, and they went back out into the living room.

Everyone had watched them leave. None watched them as they came back.

The idea that Owen had saved her husband only to have her cheat on him was one of the spokes in the wheel of rumor that now turned by her sweet breath against its hub. It was defaming, vulgar and in a way understandable, and was openly criticized and secretly applauded.

There was at about this same time a rumor started by a feeling of abandonment in that house on George Street, a rumor not so malicious or predatory as it was speculative, stating that Owen and Camellia had been seen together, not just at the house but in an embrace at a secluded place. It was speculative because Lula was so sure people were being dishonest with her, so frantic that they would not tell her the truth about these two, she took a dark and somewhat sardonic stab at what the truth might be—now that Owen had not come to visit after being home a month.

There was a place where lovers met as kids, and where the worst thing in Camellia's life had happened.

Lula was frantic to know how serious Camellia and Owen were. The Steadfast Few when they periodically visited suggested something terrible but declined specifics, to elicit Lula's awe and heighten suspicion. Then they left her to her imagination.

If she said Winch's cave—that dank, murky place of lost childhood and young girls' pregnancies—if she spoke of them being seen there, she would be able to tell instantly by a person's look if the rumors were true or false.

"Why won't anyone tell me? Because they are afraid to tell me—because it is more awful than I thought. And why did he give me a brooch and promise to marry me if he was going to do this, right in front of all my good friends?"

She did not know which person to tell, but needed someone who might tell her if what she believed to be true was indeed true.

So she told one person, the one who came late afternoon on December 22. It was the best person, for Solomon Hickey would know, and keep nothing from her—and if she mentioned it, she would be able to tell by his look what was going on.

So she told him that she had heard, and wasn't it just like Camellia?—hoping he would say he had or hadn't heard it himself. "I have heard from someone, I won't say who—and I heard Camellia is down there with him now—having sex on that old cot, planning their getaway—to go to Florida, mark my words—I can tell! There is an old cot back there to lie on and everything. Who knows where poor Reggie is, cheated on already, what everyone says, my word. And Owen with all his kind talk to me before he left to play hero, what was it for, tell me that!" She trembled and sounded angry and wounded.

Solomon only added that he himself was very heartsick about Camellia now, remembering all the nice things Lula's family had done for the girl.

Yet at that instant she knew it wasn't true, and just her imagination. She tried to lessen the import of what she had said, but Solomon left and didn't come back. She was awake most of the night. How could she just say this, without seeing or knowing anything about it—especially about Camellia? Because she had been alone and worried and her mind played tricks. But more important, she had always been able to say whatever she wanted about whoever she wanted to, without anyone saying a thing, or thinking less of her.

The following morning it was reported on the radio, which she constantly listened to for information about the town, that Owen had been in the woods for more than two weeks, taking provisions into Good Friday Mountain. Worse, Buckler himself phoned to ask her if she would like to see Owen over Christmas. She said she'd be delighted to. But then her heart sank. How could she, after what she had said? Certainly people would find out she had said something this mean.

So, thinking of her marriage to Owen in jeopardy, she had to stop the rumor.

She knew Solomon wouldn't keep it to himself, and to have told him was a very grave error. His loyalty to her would make him spread it—his anger make him embellish it.

She telephoned and asked him to forget it—she was

mistaken. That Owen was going to see her. She sounded like a lonely, frightened child.

"I have nothing to say about Owen Jameson," he said. "You can be nice to him if you want—and if you are going to see him, maybe you shouldn't see me!"

She knew by his tone she was too late.

Three days later her father came home agitated and wouldn't speak. Finally, using the very falsehood of her association with Owen that Mr. Brower himself had so promoted, Lula told him she had a right to know Owen's whereabouts, for Owen was her betrothed.

"Well, you will not be seeing him over Christmas—I know you planned to, and he invited you. But it's all show. So damn him," he said, unable to keep it from her any longer. "I thought she would have brains enough to honor her marriage and not go screwing on a cot." He had the sudden hysterical rage of a child.

"My God," she said. "Where did you hear?"

"It's all about town—never mind him—never mind that now—in the very cave her mother was murdered—that's the kind of woman she is," he said.

Lula had never seen him so furious on her behalf. To him, this upstanding Protestant man, it was an absolute betrayal of his life.

There was a phone call to her house later that afternoon from Owen himself—but her father said she was asleep.

"I don't think she wants to be hurt by you anymore," she heard her father say.

Lula now was trapped.

She must go listen to her records. She must do her exercises the physiotherapist gave her. She would listen to the snow fall down on the roof. Evening snow always brought such peace.

SEVEN

Reggie had left Saint John without telling anyone where he was going. And without notifying his wife.

Camellia had phoned to tell him the Jamesons needed him, but he knew unless he regained confidence he would have no chance up on Good Friday Mountain. That is, since the war Reggie had been worried that he wouldn't be able to do a dangerous job—and Good Friday Mountain was the most dangerous. That was the reason he hesitated in reporting to Owen Jameson. For if he could not be an asset, he did not want to be there. Men who used to respect him ignored him now, and he felt that this had happened because of Owen. So he must prove himself again in some way before he signed on. That is, he had every intention to go home to his bride, but he must be himself in order for her to have a happy life.

Still and all, he had to overcome certain things. He was a man who had never been laughed at before. That he blamed it on Owen wasn't fair, and yet he couldn't do anything else. He blamed it on his wife as well—why did she think he should be back doing this? That caused him pain. But anyone could see she did not look upon people with the same degree of mild intrigue that protected you. Her openness damaged her reputation, because she never thought in an underhanded or coercive way herself. Knowing this, he was still jealous and believed what men had said. That a woman as beautiful as she could not stay faithful.

When he came back to the Miramichi he stayed at Jameson's empty warehouse looking out over the dilapidated wharf poles of an abandoned mill (old Byron Jameson's first mill). He was only four blocks from the little house he and his wife shared, the small stone house he had grown up in. He had one suitcase, with two coats, and some cigarettes—a few dollars from the dock and not much more.

The first afternoon there, cloudy and swept with mild snowfall, he decided he would walk those poles, to see if he could keep his feet. And he would do this without anyone knowing. That meant he would have to do it at night. If he could keep to his feet, which he had easily been able to do as a young man, then he would be of help and a credit to the cut up on Good Friday. If not, he would take a job somewhere else. He still had the letter from Estabrook with his calculated offer.

But Reggie would challenge himself, and then see Owen after he did. He would survive this challenge and be better able to cope. He would apologize to Owen for having spread a falsehood in anger (this was still the most troublesome part) and he would be a credit to his dead father, who he felt had been ashamed of him.

Thinking this, he was calm, until the second development. Like so many things in life, happy or disastrous, it came unsolicited and without warning. It came in the morning, after he got to the river. It came in the guise of two men, one a young man his age and the other Camellia's reprobate uncle Sterling. They were drinking some muted Christmas cheer outside the warehouse doors. Sitting on old tarred pilings, her inebriated uncle spoke to the other, younger man about Gravellier seeing "first-hand" Owen kissing Camellia. But that wasn't all—Sterling said he himself saw them making love in a cave—last week. This came from the very rumor Lula had started, and was now trying to dampen out.

"He'll be havin' her now, because the husband's gone," Sterling giggled, and said he would go to her and get money.

"She'll have money now," he said, and he spoke to the other about this money and how they would be "set fer a while."

"I knew what she was like years ago—she knew the money she could find between her legs. You saw yerself how she is always hangin' off people—grabbin' them, giggling and such. That's the sign, boy—that's the sign. The first time she saw Owen she was giggling and grabbin' him—all fer her husband, eh!"

The young man wanted to know what she looked like, in the cave; if Sterling saw "it" all—or any of it, or what part—or which, and how long—and what way did they do it—

"A nice-looking cunt on her, I bet," the young lad said.

At first Reggie did not know they were speaking about his wife. It was said so profanely and with such cynical amusement that it took time to come as true revelation in the winter air about someone he loved, said by someone he thought loved her as well.

He was ready to burst through the doors and hit them, but something prevented him. They were both men who had once worked with Dan Auger, and at that time Auger had kept them straight.

That is, they were both men from the woods who'd become useless now.

And this is what the town did, it put the men from the woods to disgrace. They often wandered the streets in woods clothes like lost children, sanctified only by alcohol, teetering remnants of a world disappearing under their feet. What might have become of them if the great Dan Auger had lived? And how many times did Reggie try to help them find work?

He crept to the warehouse door and listened. They spoke for a while about his wife and Owen, and how his wife was out for money and Reggie was a stepping stone. And that Camellia had married Reggie but she was really in love with Jameson long ago.

"Who wrote him during the war? They had her marry Reggie to save the cripple bitch up the hill for Owen—who don't know that?—even the best of our town know that."

"Love finds a way," the young man giggled.

All of this as dismal as it was, Reggie believed in his own heart, so he could not refute it. He thought of Camellia and Owen when they were youngsters—and it suddenly came to him that all of this was true, and that he had looked at the world only in shadow until now. The world of shadows had disappeared. They had been in a cave together and he pictured them there. Then the terrible thought of her mother being murdered in that same place filled him with dread.

He listened in agony, and made no motion at all.

They stopped speaking.

For more than fifteen minutes Reggie waited for her uncle, a thin-chested man who had once worked for Owen's father before drink took over his life, to speak again. But he did not.

The younger man stood and pissed, wiped his mouth with the back of his woolen coat, the sleeve singed badly by a fire he had lighted the night before to keep warm.

Then he turned, pulled up his zipper, and asked if there was a chance at another bottle of wine.

The old man said there might be, down at the pilings (where old dealed up boards were piled in the lumberyard), and they could steal it if they were smart and old Ned McGowan was not nearby. Then they spoke about stealing being a justified "element" in their lives, because everyone had stolen from them, and not just a little, but a whole enormous amount.

"I'd have a million now if someone give me a break," the younger man said.

"Yes, yes," Sterling said, "they'd be fuggin' stealin' from us."

Then they talked about the jobs they had been offered and turned down, and how much money they could have made but were no one's slaves.

The idea of being no one's slaves seemed to prop them up, as they weaved in silence for a moment like two half-rotted hemlocks ready to go down.

There was that kind of hushed chink of a bottle in the snow, and both men tottered off, toward the little gray lumberyard, jostling one another and in the end almost coming to blows.

And Reggie thought: "Is this what will happen to me if I stay?"

EIGHT

That night Reggie walked through the numb, frozen yard, past the small intertwined houses of those who had come here on ships from Ireland more than a century before, to the house he and Camellia owned. Before they left Ireland, their respective families would gather to have a wake for them, for it was as if they were dying. Now, at this moment, Glidden wished his great-grandfather had died, so he wouldn't have to face what it was he had to face. He wouldn't suffer the pain of being human, of being only human and nothing more.

He moved round to the back—and saw Camellia sitting in front of the little Foley girl whose hair she was braiding. Reggie remembered her doing this even as a young girl with other children she sought out—out of kindness or loneliness. Or both. And she too told Reggie she wanted a child.

She had her housecoat on—the one he had bought her—and she took up a heavy lead comb and began to comb the child's hair to braid.

Then she jumped up and said: "Oh Vicki—your chocolate."

And he had to duck down.

But if she had wanted a child, she so often had backed away from his embrace, he thought. She had married him to escape Lula's father, he thought. (He had heard there had been an advance from Lula's father toward her one night.)

Reggie knew as well why she wanted a child. To make up for her own lost childhood—to be kind to children, for so few adults had been kind to her.

That this was exactly the way Owen saw his own childhood did not register.

But why then had they made love only five times?

This trumped all other reason, and with this, as if he was hit in the mouth with the fist of clarity, the clarity of rumor or scandal and the cave, he knew he must have another life.

"Leave her to herself, no matter," he thought. He was quite convinced now that she used men to gain her way, and that he was just one along the path of her destiny.

His one desire was to tell her off. To tell her to go to Owen when he was gone. But he knew at this moment he would not be able to be calm with her. And he had struck her once. So he decided to leave. It would be better—and he suspected more worrisome for her. That is, he wanted to cause her pain. If people thought he was dead for a little while, that might cause her the pain he desired.

He slipped back to the warehouse and spent the night. Twice remembering battles, he sat straight up swinging.

The next afternoon Reggie packed his cardboard suitcase and took the ferry across the river to a hotel on Water Street. There he stayed for a day under the name of his mother's brother, Antoine Savoir.

It was his intention now to leave forever. He was afraid if he did not he might injure himself or someone else. Owen especially. And that was the problem—that was the one person he couldn't harm. That and his feeling that to work for anyone else here would only exacerbate the feelings rising against him now.

When he went out on Friday evening along another part of the river, he stuck close to the buildings, his hat hiding his face. He noticed the strange looks of certain people who caught a glimpse of him. He believed they had all heard about his failures and all knew who he was, and why he was slouching against the dark gray buildings.

He did not know, Reggie Glidden, who had knowledge of so much, but not how to fight disgrace, that his disgrace was nothing to others beset by problems of their own, and that those who saw him this night had not much thought about him, not knowing who he was or caring what he had done, or that he was the soldier Owen Jameson had saved. That in so many ways each one of them wrestled in the vague, undetermined universe against their own fears.

He slipped out beyond the lights and houses and made his way silently across the river in the dark, to the poles lying above the old mill. They were the silent, great teetering of a structure never finished. Fifteen poles three feet apart and jousting eighteen feet above water that had just frozen, they stood like cannons, still and impotent, until the mind made of them what the mind would. They were put there by Will Jameson with the intent of constructing a great wharf for heavy ships, but had stayed mute and impotent since his death. They were part of Will Jameson's great soul.

Reggie decided to walk these poles or not live. To prove to himself that he was still what he once was.

There was silence from the streets above, and amid the winter gales he stood alone—blasted in the furnace of snow, seeming far removed and isolated from other people—even from humanity itself. He wore a black coat and his heavy bent workboots, his shirt opened and his chest hair damp with snow and sweat.

"They'll be slippery," he said, looking up at the pulsing sky.

Just as Owen had once decided he would not go home, Reggie decided if his task succeeded he would forever leave the river and its people. That their tormenting had destroyed what he had loved here. You cannot love the soil where your soul was mocked by lesser men. So he was here and now saying goodbye to Camellia Dupuis, that lively, kind-hearted girl who had married him almost without thinking on that gray day six months before, but who had warred for him because of it.

Still, how many times had they made love in their entire marriage? Five times, the last two nights before he went away.

Was he insane to think then of leaving her to others? Or to risk his life on the rod of logs above his head?

Perhaps, but good men are often their best when not hobbled by sanity. He looked up high.

He caught a glimmer of what was in store for him now. If he went back to work, no man would say a thing to him, and no man would forget what was said about him or his wife.

In a practical way, he must challenge the gods in order to have his humanity returned. He did not know great men wrestled the gods at all times, under all circumstances. That Will had as a boy of eighteen, and Owen had as a man running across a burned-over field.

He only knew two things. One was that he cared for Owen, and could not harm him. The other was that he was actually quite brave in the war. Even as brave as Owen. That he could have, if he had just enough reason to do so, told people he had been brave.

But he was ashamed of so much else.

He was alone, and no one could help him. Always men stood in the middle so as to have support. His support now gone, he remembered the dismissal of men who had once sought his advice. Smiling tauntingly at him. Before, and proudly, he had contempt for all of them. Perhaps humility is what God sought from us, perhaps it was the only thing required.

He walked down to the poles at midnight. He took off his heavy coat. It had bore the brunt of his fist against the wall, and had spots of blood upon it.

He braced himself in the pelting snow, to prove who he was, if only to himself.

He had promised he would take care of Owen in the war. And he had not. He did not at this moment think that a million people had hoped to take care of theirs in the war, mothers and fathers helpless and desperate, and had not been able to.

Taking a breath he walked straight up the tarred, blackened pole looking out over the great, dark river. If, as Will once said of him, he was a "prince of the forest," then he was a lost one, just as in those pages of *Lear* that Owen carried onto Good Friday. Or as Macbeth had heard, the forest would come to him, as it had so abruptly to Will. But having never heard of William Shakespeare, what did that matter?

He hated the logs that jutted into the open. He knew them too well. He, of course, had placed them there, fitted them when he was twenty. He walked right up to the tip of the first one, some twenty feet above the river ice. It swayed and teetered back and forth, he remembered now on what arc it swung.

"I'm for the fuckers now, Will," he said.

Here, into the black, sad sky, he jumped.

PART III

ONE

Owen Jameson and Camellia Dupuis would never know when this "energy," this "force" that alienated them from the town, started. Nor were they entirely sure at first that they both were targeted. Camellia had found a friend in Owen—and, since orphaned at seven, it was the first friend she had ever had. Still, she was too carefree to see that it was dangerous to have a male friend—a rich one, too, and one she could easily be seen to love.

She did not recognize this as others did, or even consider it as others did. Not with the man who had saved her husband.

Her character was such that if she didn't think disgrace, why should they?

Only a little later did she realize the much more volatile truth. She found this out when she went to ask a woman on her street why she forbade her child to see Camellia after school.

The woman came outside, closed the briny half-wrecked door, and coughing in the dark, cold air said: "Yer fuckin' him, arncha?" In such a hilarious anointing of blame that Camellia laughed.

Camellia was finally hit with the realization of how her own grace was treated by others.

"Tell yer child to come over anytime," she said, still managing a smile. "We get along so well—you see I'm not much more than a big kid myself."

There was a statuette at the house, bought by Will, of *The Kiss* by Rodin. It was from Dante's *Inferno*; adulterous lovers, Francesca and Paulo, kissing at the gates of hell. Though Will had not known what the statuette actually represented, Owen did. And he knew that he and Camellia were branded by a kiss.

It was a silly moment, his frivolous kiss.

From this kiss a liberty had been taken, not by them but by certain people in town who by December of 1946 wanted or needed them for scandal. It was such a lively thing after the war.

That Owen bore men up to the Good Friday without his Push Reggie Glidden, was all the town needed to feel rumor warranted.

That Reggie had married Camellia was looked upon as a crudity marrying a child. It was in fact hilarious, and showed the Browers for who they were.

Looking back, one might say who better than Camellia, who more than anyone else had tried to maintain her equilibrium despite her father and her mother. Who had tried to keep her uncle Sterling out of jail, and who had married Reggie hoping for a happy life, or at least a life without trouble.

Now people were turning their gaze upon her.

Almost every night that fall, Uncle Sterling would be waiting for money. She told him that Owen was her friend—and that Reggie would come home because she prayed for him to do so.

"Do you really pray?" Sterling would ask, "or do you just go up to church for show because of Les and Trudy?" (her father and mother).

"Oh yes—I tell you, I go to church—and I do pray—I say an Our Father and multiple Hail Marys—for I want my man back home safe."

"Ahhh—your man at home," Sterling would say, raising his eyes in false and cunning intrigue.

Over the dim, longing, guttered candles she prayed, as her great-grandmother had done in the same spot a century before, her head bowed, her hands folded like a child at confirmation, as the night crept silently on.

But after a while, she realized she couldn't say anything to Sterling because he was taking it wrong and telling people everything she said.

She became sickly looking and had weak spells after this. Her whole idea of what was happening changed.

So she tried then not to speak to Owen. But by mid-December things were bound in one direction.

The cave, one of Lula's Steadfast Few wrote her in a Christmas card. *It happened at the cave—you know certain women go there to wait for lovers—that is why her mother was killed, because of Byron Jameson—well, like mother like daughter. A certain soldier went there to wait for a woman—that that woman was your best friend and that you were betrothed to the soldier makes it all the more mean. And makes us all so angry.*

Every sentiment recorded in this letter was a lie, even the idea that Lula's friends, who no longer visited her, were angry. Yet Lula had nothing else to hold on to. And she believed it entirely at least for the moment, even though she herself had started it.

TWO

The day after Reggie in secret ran the top of those poles, a day overcast with sudden apprehensive squalls of snow, and the big tree being lighted in the square, there was a phone call to the house—the thirty-third day of the haul.

Camellia had arrived on this cold day, having walked up the hill in the soundlessness of early morning.

It had been almost three weeks since she had heard a word from him.

"He's probably run off," Sterling had said.

"Run off why?" she had replied.

"Oh, you know—he's probably heard all about it," Sterling had said, winking.

The phone call then concerned what she most feared in her life: Reggie's disappearance. No one knew where he was. He had been missing some while—four or five days now.

"Is he home?" his cousin from Saint John asked.

"No—he wouldn't come home—I have been waiting to hear from him."

"But he said he was going home," his cousin stated. "He said you wanted him to come home—he was going home to see you and be Push."

"But he said he wouldn't come—" Camellia said.

The cousin, Billy Monk, was silent for a moment, then added in a sterner voice: "Something is not right here, Camellia—I mean, why would he tell me you needed him home if he wasn't going there—?"

Before she could answer or even think of a possibility he had hung up.

A Detective Gaugin of the Saint John department then

phoned Camellia, first to ask if Reggie was at home, and then to tell her her husband, if not at home, was missing—unless he was on his way home.

There was no dispute on the dock, so then was there a domestic dispute? He asked all of this as if he was offering a prize for the correct answer—and he already knew all about her, this Mr. Gaugin. (For he had heard much from Billy Monk that he would not argue—first that she was the daughter of the "violent criminal" Les Dupuis who had killed his philandering wife in a domestic dispute.)

"There was no domestic dispute," Camellia said. It was the second time in her life she had heard the phrase "domestic dispute." Like the word *adultery*, another word she had not heard in many years, it would become more and more common to her as time passed. It would become almost riveted in her brain, like a teamster would rivet a runner to a birch pole.

"Then what was he doing in Saint John?"

Camellia did not answer. Not for her sake, but for Reggie's.

"Did you argue the last time you spoke to him?"

"I don't remember," she said, and though not wanting to, she started to cry.

"Well—try to remember," Detective Gaugin stated. "And try to stop blubbering," he cautioned.

Camellia ran to the large old office to see Owen, who was preparing to meet with Mr. Trethewey, the owner of the big black Percherons. He was coming north to help them even though he was an old man now. It was to be his last hurrah—Good Friday Mountain.

"Something has happened to my Reggie," was all Camellia said. Her face was frightened in a kind of surprised and reflective attitude, as if she expected Owen to tell her what was happening, that everything was a surprise for Christmas. She was ready to smile at this delusion if he allowed it. Again she looked like that child of seven who was left waiting for her father.

Owen phoned Saint John but got no answer at Reggie's cousin. Now Camellia was frantic—and it was the frantic, guilty state others were to notice and reflect upon her today.

"She's worried now," the older maid said, thinking this was unusual unless someone was unusually guilty. "All her kissing has done her in!"

Now the entire household was caught up in this event. It was the start of something that would last for months, seeping through the carpet and furniture like the smell of horses.

Sometime later a call came from the town police.

They had found Reggie Glidden's jacket at the conical poles near Jameson's old family warehouse, and Chief Crossman wondered what he had been doing there, and why Owen hadn't told them he was in town. Here Owen made his first mistake, angered by this disruption, worried for Camellia's sake, and feeling the pain in his leg he snapped: "I didn't know I had to inform you of him." Realizing this was not the best response, he added, "Besides, I don't know why he was there. Are you sure it is his jacket?"

"Yes—"

"How?"

"Well, it has his name stitched into it—maybe by Camellia herself," Crossman said, as if this act of domesticity was part of the proof of culpability. "But even so, she might come to identify it—and there is something else we found we might just talk to you about."

"Where is it again?" Owen asked, trying to fathom what was being said.

"Well it was on your property," Crossman stated, as if, since this was a revelation to him, it should in some way frighten Owen Jameson.

Owen made perhaps another fundamental mistake. He simply hung up.

"He might have gone to your place," Owen said. "Let's go there."

"But I have to wax the hallway floor here," she said.

The old maid smiled, taking this as a ruse.

"Not now," Owen answered angrily. This frightened her even more.

They went to Camellia and Reggie's small house. Clothes hung over the side grate, a piece of toast was half eaten that morning, but it was not Reggie's.

It was the first time that Camellia looked at the very house as an indictment against her. This old place of Eric Glidden's—a place that had been contested at his death by others from Injun town, her uncle Sterling being one, and claimed by Reggie as the only thing he had to give her. Now empty of him, it shot her through the heart.

THREE

Owen took Camellia in his Jeep, and traveled to his father's old mill. What a dreary nineteenth-century place, at the foot of Injun town—it was only used now to store dealed up board in the spring. The poles jutting out were the last leftover monument of Will Jameson's greatness. A greatness ended before he was twenty. Again Owen thought he was not the man for this—that some huge joke was being played upon him, and that for some reason Camellia was part of the con against him, even if she did not know.

Some of Reggie's former friends now feared Glidden dead, and the acts of ridicule against him after the war were heavy upon them. They knew these acts of ridicule and torment had gone exceedingly well against this man, and they had done so just to see how far they could go, and to fill up their own famine. That, in essence, is why they threw pulp sticks at his chained-up body.

They were, as they said later, "caught up in it." They even had bets on how long Camellia would stay faithful.

Now, all of this was creeping under their skin, in a kind of self-accusation.

Their attention turned to Owen, and all the terrible things they had said about Reggie dissipated among themselves and were blamed, or at least readjusted, upon he who they now focused on.

"I think there's somethin' up," Sterling said, shaking his head, as if he was telling a confidence that he didn't want to break.

Then the person he told this to would overhear Sterling ten minutes later saying to someone else: "I think there's somethin' up."

By this time there was across town a sudden speculation that Owen and Camellia would leave soon and not be back.

This came from someone's doorway at ten o'clock that morning. It was the principal opening in a gambit to make them both liable. Those who said it felt it to be true, and so told others in their circle. That is, as with so much rumor, one promotes the sin more than the blame.

It drifted back, this sin, over the gray afternoon toward the dock.

"What are you doing here?" Sterling asked Cora Auger. "This ain't no place for you, dear!"

"Just waiting," she said, "just waiting—union will come, and he will go." And she smiled, nodding toward Owen, her two front teeth just slightly rotted, and then frowned and looked back toward the water.

Cora wanted them (that is the constabulary) to know that she was here not for herself but for justice. She had a toff of fuzzy brown hair above her forehead that made her ears naked and small, plump legs and wore a tattered scarf. She was one of Camellia's enemies in school, for Camellia had been terrified of her and Cora had prided herself on having a murderer's daughter frightened.

She was also an enemy of the Jamesons. Why wouldn't she be? She was Dan Auger's daughter.

The police had this idea too, that Owen would try to spirit Camellia away, and decided to watch them. They had not leaned toward flight until others speculated, but managed to make it their own observation.

Yet where would they go?

They would take a ferry across the river and head down the coast of the United States to Florida. That this rumor had also started in the house on George Street more than a week before was lost at this moment.

So where this idea had come from no one knew, but it went from Pond to Pleasant to King George Highway in a matter of minutes.

Lula was informed by Solomon Hickey that this is what would happen.

"Be prepared for it," he said.

She cast her eyes downward, and said nothing at all.

People were informing everyone now, across the town.

All in the name of love.

"Of sex, you mean," an old woman blurted, laughing and sniffing. "Of dirty, stinkin', rotten, no good, humpin' sex—"

And a neighbor roared and laughed over the back fence, because she was such a wag.

FOUR

Camellia and Owen did not know they were off to Florida, and did not particularly want to go there. Nor had they ever been to the cave since they were boy and girl and had met there one day when swimming. Camellia was so outgoing and Owen was so shy that finally he ran up the cliff and hid in the grass.

Both remembered this, and neither spoke of it now.

In fact, there was a slight feeling Owen had, besides all the work and worry of Good Friday, of being put upon suddenly by Camellia. He did not want to react like this—it was selfish, he knew. There must be others to take care of her, Owen suddenly thought. That is, no matter how he was viewed, he still viewed himself as somewhat of an outsider in this episode, and thought, ironically, that the police would do the same. But how did his detached reaction come across?

With the men, it seemed quite natural—for they decided Owen had had her already in bed—and as men know with women they do not love, once had, fast gone. That is why he was aloof.

Sterling pointed this out to Cora Auger.

"Be like eternity staying with the skimpy bitch afterward— He's got hisself in a pot."

In fact, Owen discovered on this long, painful day that he was the only one on Camellia's side.

It dawned on him as he caught in the very corner of his eye that woman, who he did not know was Cora Auger, looking at him with a curious, distant stare.

This made no terrible or immediate impression upon him, but sometime later—before it all came crashing down—it would. Her look was intense, self-promoting, and hilarious, as if she had discovered in Camellia the large flaw she had always sought against the Jamesons themselves.

People stared at the poles, the river, the black pebbles glazed with ice and snow beneath their feet, and everywhere white snow that made the wet world dismal, that blocked out the view of the sun.

When Chief Crossman showed Camellia the coat, she burst out crying.

She explained the phone calls much differently than Reggie's cousin Billy, who said that Camellia was asking for a divorce (a very extreme thing in 1946), but Crossman, gruff and knowledgeable, inspecting the poles as she spoke, had some reservations about her story.

Crossman was absorbed in the idea of a man killing himself, and it seemed odd he would do so because someone offered him a job as foreman.

"So when you offered him this job," Crossman said, "did he seem confused or angry or somepun?"

"No, he did not sound confused," Camellia replied. Crossman shrugged, told her the poles were glazed with ice and no man would ever be able to walk them.

"Reggie would—he can waltz on a varr skid," Owen said (which meant he could waltz on a slick log in the middle of the river). But saying this brought no comfort to Owen, who was using one of Will's expressions. Men nearby knew this, and Owen, suddenly embarrassed, knew they did.

Then Crossman showed him the letter from Estabrook that was found in the coat pocket.

"Did you know anything about this?"

Owen was stunned and looked hurt. But this look might have come just as much because he was guilty.

He didn't answer, simply stared at Crossman and asked if a diver had been down.

"For fifteen minutes in a bell, but the current is too strong here—" Crossman said without looking his way, suddenly catching the mood of the crowd and being politic enough to use it.

Men crowded about Owen, looking at him as a curiosity, and his leg became inflamed. He felt pain shoot out, and grimaced. These men, some or many who for years drank near this warehouse, fought and squabbled, men who had been gassed in the first war, or psychologically destroyed, now simpered and smirked at him, as if they had caught him at something even more than they themselves had ever been caught at.

This was the most dreaded aspect of the crowd—their easy adjustment to vengeance and the blame of others.

He thought for the first of many times of Oscar Wilde led from court into the city street.

"This is what being a suspect will do," Owen said.

Crossman glanced up at him, and put Estabrook's letter away before it became too much of a curiosity.

Owen walked to the water. He stared down at the ice. He, too, saw some small spots of blood.

The idea that there was blood on the sleeve of the coat, as if Reggie had tried to defend himself, was a notable thing, though many there had thrown pulp sticks against that very same arm.

"Poor bastard," the young man drinking with Sterling said.

Owen turned away from them. He would have to get a diver. He saw Camellia standing hunched up along the side of the old warehouse. He remembered her father. He had been twelve at the time. It had seemed like a great adventure to hang someone then. He remembered a picture of her in the paper, standing with a bottle of nail polish (what her parents had gotten her that Christmas) on a side street smiling—as if it was an adventure for her as well. That picture was an enormous weight upon her. Kids made fun of her then for that little bottle. Yes—he himself if he wanted to admit it. So, she had startled them all and had risen a beauty.

How now to see her fallen.

Walking back from the water he saw a dozen men still staring at him.

"Do you have something to tell me?" he asked them.

They immediately turned their backs and left. As always, Owen was much more of a match than his physical appearance would indicate.

Owen walked with a cane—it was either walk with a cane or not walk. He was, in the dreary afternoon of pointed snow, somewhat of a caricature. Major Owen Jameson.

He bore little resemblance to his father, or his famous brother, but to someone of Mary's ancestry on another continent in another time, in fact a man who walked Ireland 134 years before.

Crossman hadn't liked Owen's famous brother, for he took too much for granted. Too many fights, and not enough prosecutions. Nor had the prosecutor Brower liked these people. It seemed now that events might come together so others would not like them either. However, Crossman for all his suspicion and gruffness did like Camellia.

Certain people came to talk to Owen, even if it was only about the rumor of death.

"God almighty—would he jump off at this time a year?" The idea being that if one were going to kill themselves they would at least do it when the weather was pleasant. Owen looked up in a heartbeat for the short, hard woman whose eyes had bore into him. He no longer saw her.

"I figure it murder," Sterling's young drinking companion said.

"We'll be back when the body comes up," Sterling added.

And soon all dissipated in fading sounds along the graying, snowy lanes.

FIVE

Camellia talked to Crossman when they went to the jail, for he wanted a missing person report filed.

Five-foot-ten with red hair, 160 pounds, last seen in Saint John, New Brunswick, wearing the coat now found. She asked for the coat back. Of course not. Crossman spoke to Estabrook by phone briefly, and kept the letter.

"It seems he was going to go work for Estabrook," Crossman

said. "Perhaps you should have told us that."

Owen listened to this—listened with what eagerness Camellia tried to say the right things—understood the way Crossman spoke to her, and became himself more aware of a noose tightening for no apparent reason. He could distance himself from her now, with one word. He still had the power to do so. But he must be very quick if he was to do it. He knew he couldn't. It would be deplorable.

He sat near the secretary, in the blank, cold outer room where she had her desk, and came in three times a week.

The secretary took an interest in Owen, just when he wanted to be unresponsive, and began asking him questions. He became aware of the unsettling propensity in her, too, for assumption, and understood that people assumed it their right to assume something between Camellia and he. That the sin was already monstrous and dark. To say that he was only trying to help Camellia seemed utterly ridiculous given what was perceived.

"It's too bad you couldn't a been there the other night—you might have saved him all over again," the secretary said, smiling quickly. She had no idea that this was a witty thing to say until she said it.

It was after six at night when they left the old jail and made their way through the winter dark, past certain dirty brick buildings, over to the center of town. The buildings hung in fog, the docks looked pitiless and silent. The old Miramichi Hotel, its lights gleaming in a shroud, winked out at them, saying: "We have overcome tyranny."

Other lights cast through curtains in back kitchens, where now and again a squalid shout erupted amid the cry of a town full of children, the age of baby boomers now beginning, being born—who would look back upon this age of their infancy as quaintly innocent, hybrid of hope and money.

But for these two there was a moment of startling awareness of the most innocuous shadow or movement or glance.

She nervously clutched her hands and tried to smile.

"I lost the letter," she said, looking through her pockets.

"What letter?" (For a moment he thought it was the one from Estabrook to Reggie.)

"I was supposed to give you a letter from Lula—I can't find it now. I just remembered it—was in this pocket—or maybe my dress pocket—if it were in my dress pocket, that means I washed it."

"It doesn't matter," he said. But he knew that everything mattered now, and thought of how Brower was so abrupt with him on the phone.

Camellia's idea was that if she did the right things, sooner or later everyone would see her to be worthy despite the love she held for a murderer, her own father, and for her uncle, who took much of the salary she earned at Mary Jameson's and who Reggie had once threatened in order to protect her. So, having forgotten about and then losing the letter was a greater matter to her than to others. She looked like an outcast. Her hands were red with cold and chapped from scrubbing floors, her stockings wrinkled and torn over the knees, and she kept blowing on her fingers and looking about. He was dressed in a warm long winter coat.

Then she looked at him a very brief moment, as she blew on her hands, and saw themselves in the eye of a storm.

Owen said: "Maybe he came back and for some reason doesn't want to be seen right away."

He knew that sounded patently absurd.

She was shivering with cold and he took his coat off and put it over her, not minding her protest or the stares of those down the street.

They turned in the direction of her house.

"What in God's name was the point of saving my husband in the war—only to see him destroy himself a year later because of you—if that is what he did?"

It is what many were asking, and it was not God they were accusing.

The next day Camellia put an appeal in the paper asking for information concerning the whereabouts of Reginald McDonald Glidden, veteran, missing since December 13, 1946, five-foot-ten, 160–165 pounds, hazel eyes, twenty-nine years old, last seen in port of Saint John, December 12, 3:30 in the afternoon.

She started going to mass each morning, and then made her way toward the great old Jameson house. After work, she took various routes home to her house on Pond Street because, though she never told anyone, some teenaged boys had begun to tease her. Boys she had played softball with in the back lots of town, now thinking she would be a better partner somewhere else.

Unfortunately the children she had loved no longer visited, even though she still stopped at the bakery to buy them squares.

Every night Sterling was waiting for her—trying to engage her in conversation. She did not know he was being paid by the police a dollar for each bit of information, and he took to his obligation with gusto. Because he was protecting his family name.

"Are you sure," Sterling would say, "that you didn't see him? God almighty, girl, he couldn't a just up and disappeared. You think the police have any information—what do you think they'd have to know in order to solve it? You know Owen was always a spoiled-up brat, that one—and the coat was found with a heap of blood spots—what d'ya think?"

She gave him money, as if a bribe, she had no idea what else to do. Then he would run to the police, understandably excited that he was involved, a conscientious member of our town, and tell the police that she was bribing him.

"I almost didn't take it," he said.

After supper once again she would brave the dark and cold, and walk up the long torturous lanes, visit the holy Catholic church, sit in the pew and stare at the gaudy brass crucifix, light a candle for five cents.

It was during these visits to the church that her home was entered almost at will by Sterling—though never ordered, he felt he had the sanction of the police to find out what he could. On one occasion he made away with coins and other things out of an old dress pocket. He stuffed them away, and with great ego walked about the house he took as his own.

He spent these coins—172 cents—on a bottle of loganberry wine. He looked at the colored glass from the dress pocket, not knowing it was her hopscotch glass, and threw it away.

He went to the cave and drank half of the wine by himself, blowing his nose and tossing what he took to be Kleenex from the dress, behind him, deeper into the cave.

Two days later, going back with a woman—High Bank Hilda—to lie down and drink the rest of the wine, he discovered the stained and torn letter from Lula Brower to Owen.

Insensible as to how it got there, it became Sterling's major find. It made him a hero in our town.

He took it to Mr. Brower himself, and shaking and sniffing handed it over, saying: "If I ever thought she'd act like that there—but to make a heap of fun of that fine crippled girl just turns me mean!"

That it was found in the cave was the most damning indictment of all.

For Lula, who had started this rumor, it made her realize that Sterling was a liar and almost none of the story was true.

SIX

Mary sat in the bedroom on her pale green rocker, staring through the white window at the snow falling and blotting up the roads and the white houses in the distance. It was a terrible world. On clear, cold days she could see down over the rails to where Will was buried with a massive tombstone—she had spared no expense and had his bust carved in the marble stone.

Here lies Will Conner Jameson. A great man.

He was, and yet she thought the very things the old Indian woman had spoken about in her soft, lilting accent were now coming true. What must she do to stop them?

After Owen came home that night from vainly searching for Reggie, she looked at him in apology. She was almost ready to tell him that it might be better if he left, and did go to Montreal, when he said: "I have to get the Percherons up the mountain—I'll have to see Trethewey—the world doesn't stop because Reggie fell off."

Mary followed him, on heavy slippers and tired legs, into the large, uncomfortable, and manly office once occupied by her husband and then by her oldest son. At one time she refused to come in here. Nothing, not a thing had changed since the moment of Will's death.

There was a picture taking up three-quarters of the far wall. It was almost surreal in its application of the unseen truth of the world—therefore a myth, therefore nothing at all. Owen looked at it, and Mary stood behind him.

It was a modern print of the painting, illustrating the great legend of the devil and the woodsmen; Will had picked it up when he was on the Penobscot in 1932, and had brought home to study. He ignored it for some time, until Dan Auger's death, and then he studied it for hours.

The story the painting told was this: Once upon a time a canoe filled with woodsmen out to see their children New Year's Day was transported through the night on the devil's back. Satan knew the world, and had appeared to a camp of lonely men, deep in some forlorn, lost wood, in the middle of the previous century. Knowing what they would give for the comfort of a look, he offered this proposition: They could see their loved ones if they would give up their simple, pedestrian souls.

So these woodsmen had to trick the devil in order to see their loved ones again and not be damned.

They did this at the last moment by touching the cross on top of the church steeple as the devil rode them to their houses.

Looking at Satan's smokelike form underneath the large canoe, the dark earth below, Owen remembered an old priest once telling him that the devil's greatest feat was to convince millions of men and women he did not exist.

He thought of this and shuddered at the predicament now forming like smoke about him.

And there was something he had not told Mary when he first went into the crowded camp a month ago. How startled he was, because of something he and Will had done as a joke when they were children.

On a summer day long ago in the 1920s they had stolen four of Estabrook's live beaver and had run away with them, when he was visiting their father at the old camp at Arron Brook. They were going to kill the beavers, but neither had the heart. Then they realized the trouble they would be in with their father if they got caught.

So they decided to put them somewhere they would never be found.

They trekked all day and late into that evening, and let the beavers go on a ledge up Good Friday. At that time, if Owen remembered, though the stand went long up the mountain, it was dry and hardly a tree was growing well. The place was called Good Friday because one cedar grew there in the shape of a cross higher than all the others.

That night they slept half inside a log, near the forks of Arron Brook by the south talons. The next day they told their frantic father they'd gotten lost.

"Did you see me beaver?" Old Estabrook asked.

"I saw them in the back of yer truck yesterday, sir," Will said, which was not a lie at all.

"Well, I am out the pelts, boy," Estabrook said, for some reason staring at Owen.

"All we can do is help you look," Will said, and he offered to go up toward Hackett Brook, which was in the opposite direction whence they came.

What Owen realized was this: the real possibility that the beaver they had released had by their own industry created the flood plain that nourished the very trees he was now harvesting.

If this was the case, Will himself was responsible for this abundance, which would save the industry he had died for.

This was startling destiny—but only if he believed it. Believing it allowed all kinds of silly notions, like Saint Jude. Or Hamlet's assertion: "There are more things in heaven and earth, Horatio, than are dreamt of in your philosophy."

Owen had believed Hamlet's assertion from the time he was fifteen, but had always equated the "more" as science. That is, he had thought of himself as Hamlet, not Horatio. Camellia, standing in his mind's eye, was telling him something vastly different with her silly Saint Jude medal. Something that went beyond every assertion he had made since he was a boy of fifteen, when he had first heard of Joyce and Hemingway and others.

And he did not like it one little bit. This new and terrible feeling that entered the room with Camellia. He had in fact wandered the world to rid himself of it. How could he be back here now, imbued by it? By superstition. By woodsmen and superstition. As if superstition was here alone, and not in every university his friends attended.

He turned to his mother and said emphatically that he would see this through. "For Will, and Buckler—and for you."

Still, what Practical Mary knew was this: she and Buckler had had an offer to sell to Sloan—and why hadn't they? They hadn't because of Owen. As strange as that was, it was true. And it was Camellia who had encouraged them, by convincing the men to stop the train so the Jamesons could keep their mill. She had been both happy and pleading, optimistic and sincere—all the things she was now suspect because of. It had been her great coup, this Camellia Dupuis.

"If Owen comes home he might get everything turned in the right direction," Camellia had said. Why had Mary trusted this vengeful and unstable daughter of Les Dupuis? The daughter of a murderer, killer, and sadist.

"She is a liar that one, for sure," Mary thought. She didn't like to think this, but her toughness allowed mistakes in her character, and one was rashness of temperament.

Everyone now was phoning Mary with advice, and she was trying to take this advice.

"Make damn sure the blood is not on his hands," they were telling her.

"The blood better not be," she said.

She began at almost every moment of the day to look at his hands.

Tonight, not seeing blood, she asked Owen did he regret having stopped.

"Of course not," he said.

She asked him if he regretted having been put to work on Good Friday Mountain.

"Well, I regret that more," he smiled.

Early the next morning Owen hired a diver, Matheson, a man he had known in the service, who came immediately and went down for thirty minutes in the river, under the ice. There was nothing to report when he came out. It was a useless and fruitless exercise, looked upon as theater by the two or three loud drunks now watching.

Matheson, too, thought it useless. He kept an eye on Camellia, wondering what she was like. He had been told that morning that she had thrown her husband over for this man. That she had planned it all along. That in fact she had convinced her husband to take a job in Saint John, and then had convinced Mary Jameson to stop the train. Reggie had come home and they'd had to get rid of him.

He had been told this by his neighbor, the older maid at the Jameson house.

"They'll come to no good," she said. "Like Will, like Owen—it will be done. She's a whore—knew it the first time she waggled her arse when she was sixteen. Puttin' on airs in front of us, you should see her hiking her skirt up to her bum when she does the floor!"

(He would like to, he thought.)

The rumor had a center and its apex was somewhere in Camellia's past, with her disgraced and hanged father, who was also a wife killer. A brutal sadist, and if you looked closely you could see it in Camellia—if, as the maid said, you looked at her closely.

The truth being that a good, decent family had taken her in as a child. A pedestrian, careful family, and look what had happened. She had mocked them now and had stolen that girl's man.

"She has Practical Mary bamboozled too," the old maid said. "Mary never had a girl and was all gushy when she come to the house—I said, I said to Mary—get rid of her, get rid of her now—what I said—"

Perhaps that is why Camellia was drawn and ill looking. What she had done was finally catching up to her. Matheson remembered her too as being utterly happy-go-lucky, and always having to be reined in by adults whenever she was out.

That, he knew, would work against her now.

"A body might be pulled out to the bay—" he told Owen.

Owen nodded and turned away. The difficulty for him was unmistakable—to save a man only to have him kill himself because in some way you made him think he was unworthy.

It was like a Greek tragedy. And how many ships might be launched? Matheson looked at Camellia, and beyond her agitation and tired face she was beautiful. She could launch quite a few.

SEVEN

Owen returned to the mountain, arriving sometime in the afternoon of the fiftieth day of the haul.

There was much cut since he had left; the wind for once had died. Far above, the sky was mute—incomprehensibly silent, as if the hundreds upon hundreds of dying trees needed requiem. It had not gone above minus nineteen in two weeks. The air was flattened and dead. Already two of the men had been injured, one by a widow-maker—a loose branch overhead—and the other by a glancing ax. One had stayed in work, but the other, a good faller, went out. It was poor conditions here, and Owen knew it. He had to keep the men happy or he would lose most of his teamsters.

There was, as anyone who has been in the true cold knows, a stilled, petrified feeling in the air, a lonely quiet within the camp when the men were on the job.

The cook's window—a luxury—was as clear as the great blue sky beyond the huge stove, and Owen could look out on the sled rails as slick and as effective in moving the big two sleds as electromagnetic force on a railway track. He finally saw a moose bird flitting here and there—and then a moment later, the great Clydesdales Missy and Butch, now driven in the lead. This was the team the other horses were to follow down. Richardson was atop the Clydes.

The horses stopped dead. They had to pass their hovel on the way to the precipice and stopped for a second, hoping they could trick the teamster into thinking it was night. Richardson only said, "Out," and onward they plodded.

Missy turned her head toward Butch and gave a snort filled with snot and mist.

Behind them came the Belgians, Hans and Gretel, with Gravellier; with their ornate buckled harness, making their big black chests look proud, and they too slowed up until they heard "out" and onward they went—towering tons of wood above them, some peeled of limb and bark and some of limb alone, but most with flecks of bark trailing off the timber like ghosts' arms, which is what the men called them, especially in the twilight snowfalls that happened here.

After Gravellier came Miss Maggie Wade and Mr. Stewart, which Nolan teamed, both squatter but with thicker legs than Hans and Gretel. Then five minutes later came something Owen had not expected, the huge Percherons. The outside one had red eyes, and he pranced sideways in his traces to give indication of both the immense strength in his legs and his independence from the horse he was teamed with. Although the Percherons were leaner, both were a head taller than the Clydesdales. They were known as Billy Budd and Outlaw Cole Younger, and upon them was Trethewey, a black man who was known to have knocked out three men with one swing of pulp. Unfortunately one of the men he had knocked out was Gravellier, who had kept him away from a job for no apparent reason—which to Trethewey meant it was because he was black. It was most unlikely it was because he was black, but because—black, brown, or white—he was not a paid member of Gravellier's circle.

Owen took a cup of tea and went back out into the frozen day, through a doorway covered in a sheet of ice, with dozens upon dozens of beer caps set in this ice, a splendid decoration of glazed art. He limped toward the loading skids, which stretched far down through the shine, punctuated here and there by a smell of horse shit and piss. Down he went into the solitary, silent wood, until he could hear the scrape of the peelers and the unmistakable crack of a tree coming down. There he saw the tips of a horse's ears sticking up innocently beyond an alder swale.

Curtis was in with his team, and was busy leaning against the grainier of his two off-colored Belgians while Gibbs, the young tend team, stood beside him holding some rein. The leather reins stayed limp in Gibbs' hand as Curtis leaning full weight looked half in a wrestling match with the hoof. Gibbs was by now so dirty Owen couldn't tell if the hair and smeared sweat over his clothes was his or the horse's, or the smell was horse or human. Or if the trees were any less human than those others.

No one bathed in here, there was no way to—you washed—at least some did. And for the most part, once the cold weather came you slept in your clothes.

Curtis, on his horses named Wildgreen and Duff Almighty, made a turn into the yard to pick up a load. In that time five trees had come down to ground, and the peelers began to limb.

They did five trees while Owen was there, each twice to three times the diameter of their bodies, while the wind picked up against them and the great trees began their swaying, like a top-heavy waltz in a crowded gym. The sky to Owen was almost morbidly blue above them with some distant, forlorn knocking. The unending cold had silenced almost the entire tract. Now and then a moose would come into the range of horses trying to get hay, and sometimes the men would take pity on its gnarled old back. Only the moose birds landed and flitted here and there during twelve o'clock break. Only Meager Fortune, as kind to the birds as the people, went into the shine each day with food and stories to tell not just the men but the birds themselves.

Owen looked at these men, all of them—and was saddened by their plight, and angered by his. In their great ignorance they would be the ones to build the world.

His leg ached now unremittingly throughout the day as he walked. And blood oozed out of the wound.

Two sawyers, Fraser and Pitman, sawed these trees through in a matter of minutes—depending on the length, either in two or in thirds. They were chained and hauled up to the skids, where they were loaded by men and chains onto the two sled, a very dangerous job as strong men got under the block and tackle to help and any slip would mean injury or death. They pitted day in and out their blood and bone against the solid wood that would be carved into beds where ladies dreamed.

Curtis waited standing between his horses as they loaded his two sled up.

"Get up out of there, you useless fucking son of a bitch," you could hear as someone beat a horse forward, hauling the logs on the devil's mount that had gotten stuck between stumps. They had to back the horse up and turn in another direction. Once in awhile you could see the problem down in the shine. Other times you couldn't until the Belgian broke through to the top of the skid road, plodding forward with limbs stuck in his tack, his eyes blazed by fear and anger, driven by the men who acted like minions behind him, the Belgian furious in expended strength as snow blasted about his face.

Men could become insensible in a second, thinking that the horses—straining every muscle and working from dawn till dark, fed too much and brought to their feet by Spanish fly or laudanum—were getting caught up just to spite them—that the wind and the smell of one another was the devil, that the devil's mount was the devil, that the stumps that impeded their progress were intentionally trying to, that God himself was doing this to make fun of them. And thinking of their brothers or sons at home, whiling away the afternoon, would make them furious with themselves. As their time in increased, so did their ability to become erratic.

"Up out of that, up out of that, you useless no good motherfucking cocksucking son of a whore," politely to the horses now straining to break free of everything in the world that had ever caused them pain.

The sound did not in any way stop until after pitch dark.

At supper Owen noticed Stretch (Tomcat) Tomkins staring at him and eating by himself. Stretch believed everyone in camp owed him an apology for an incident that had recently happened. The two crews had been at each other's throats over it, and it had sucked vitality away from the cut.

Today Owen had tried to mediate.

It had to do with the one-armed teamster Richardson. Tomkins felt that it was bad enough to be taken from horse. But Richardson, one-armed—how could he ever be given the Clydes? Tomkins believed he himself was entitled to them. Gravellier egged him on.

So, Tomkins had approached Owen about Richardson more than two weeks before. And he got Gravellier to approach him as well.

"Why is Richardson up on the Clydes?" Gravellier asked, hauling at his peaked hat as he spoke, his eyes squinting accusingly as snow, numb as a wound, fell against his peak and all around was gray.

"He is a good teamster," Owen said.

"But—but he only has one arm."

"Yes, and he has acquitted himself with one arm as well as most teamsters with two—"

"You mean he is as good as the others?"

"Every bit," Owen said.

"Better than I," Tomkins said, standing behind Gravellier and looking over the man's broad shoulders.

"Something he does not have to prove for this job," Owen said.

"If it was Will," Gravellier said.

"If it was Will my whore—if it was Will—kindly let me tell you if it was fuckin' Will—No one like Tomkins would be here—if, sir, it was Will. You speak of Will Jameson, you speak quietly and with reverence, and don't you ever suck life from me by saying, 'If it was Will.' And I will tell you this: Richardson is for me on Good Friday, hell or high water—and both hell and high water make you blanch."

He felt bad about this outburst and tried to make it up. Yet he knew something others did not. After Richardson had lost his arm, Will and Reggie had taken him on a moose hunt. It was there, after they had killed and quartered a twenty-four-point bull, Will being drunk said that Richardson lost the arm intentionally to get out of service if war came. Richardson pushed him against the wall, drew a knife from his boot, and put it against Will's throat.

"Cut," Will said, "and then I won't have to carry my quarter out."

It was to Richardson like drawing a knife against Alexander the Great, and he put it away. But it was Will who felt lessened by demeaning the man. So said to Owen: "Richardson is always to have a job with Jameson—until his death."

So it was.

Once Owen had gone back out after that initial conversation, tension had built as the cold came, and the days below on the flat where Tomkins watered the sled tracks, and chaffed on the downhill, were long and tedious. He'd not come to do this, not as a professional teamster. And now the rumor that Owen had gone out to fuck Glidden's wife was rampant in the air. So blaming him this, it was easy to blame the crew Owen admired.

The two crews—one supporting Tomkins, one Richardson—became more and more competitive. It was said that whips were used against one another. No one can say if this happened, because those alive will not say so now. Bartlett, it was said, ran between both camps explaining them to each other, while remaining out of the fray himself.

But this was a world unto itself and therefore the world, and people, hid envy and spite only so long. But envy and spite were there even among friends, like Curtis and Nolan, or Nolan and Richardson, and had to be tempered with wisdom.

This conflagration was normal for Stretch Tomkins to be involved in. Never was there a camp where he did not try to receive the tributes given others or take immeasurable credit for the slightest thing he himself did. After a time he became vociferous in his disrespect of Richardson—telling Gravellier that Richardson was formally Richard—French—and he had hidden his ancestry for shame. So Richardson would come on the cut and Gravellier would not speak to him.

"You'd not be in a union of mine," Gravellier would say.

"Who the fuck would ever want to?" Richardson would answer.

"I should take you down a peg or two of that load."

"Don't let fear stop you," Richardson answered.

It was told to me that Tomcat Tomkins (a man like ourselves) took to mimicking the way Richardson's empty shirt sleeve was looped in his belt as he hauled back on the reins, to get others to laugh. That is, Colson, and Choyce and Lloyd. Encouraged by this, Tomkins took to teasing the teamster at supper.

Like most targets, Richardson at first did not know he was one. Then he took to ignoring it. He prayed more with his bible at night. He prayed about what he should do. In any case, the torment Richardson was going through was visible to those who liked him.

"What are you praying for?" Tomkins said one day. "That'll not get you out of here alive."

Richardson looked down at his tormentor from the top of a load, its chains frozen across the backs of 108 logs, his eyes watering because of the vicious wind, his one strong hand black on the reins:

"No—no one gets out of here alive," Richardson said.

Tomkins turned and walked away, hauling up his Humphreys. He did not know, as he broke wind and took his chaffing pail, that he had made a fundamental mistake. To Richardson, he had challenged his right to exist.

Four days before Owen returned to camp, Richardson without any provocation picked up his hatchet from the side of his load, where he always stuck it, and threw it into a tree a foot over Tomkins' head as he was pulling up his Humphreys coming from the outhouse. Then he jumped from his logs, a good fifteen feet down, nonchalantly walked over and took the hatchet back.

"Don't be botherin' me no more, you lanky puke," he said.

"Right arm seems okay," Nolan said, shrugging.

The teasing was ended, but Richardson would not leave it even though men in his own crew told him to.

"Leave him be—you've proved yourself out."

"He'll get his now," he said, "even if I am fired."

He moved toward Tomkins whenever he saw him, once literally chasing him around the hovel.

"Go way—go way," Tomkins yelled.

Tomkins would not come back up from the skid roads until well after dark, and he would move not up the main bank but in through the trees, and come out behind the outhouse, and then make a dash for supper. Doing this he hurt his big toe and had to have it wrapped.

Tomkins sat alone and ate alone, and men on his crew, who had laughed with him as he teased the one-armed man, now left him to his own devices.

"Help me," Tomkins asked Choyce.

"Take care of yerself, boy," Choyce said, putting a pile of beans on his spoon with a slice of homemade crust. "You were man enough to tease a cripple, take care of yerself."

"Yous all laughed a' him yerselves."

"Nope—never did—" Choyce said defensively.

"What will I have to do?"

"Knowing what I know about Richardson—kill him."

"What have I done to you?" Tomkins asked one evening, smiling a plaintive, hopeful smile. "We have to live here together, don't we?"

"Not if I kill you, Stretch," Richardson reasoned. "I'll get you down on the flat someday—there is lots and lots of time—three more months—we'll just bide our time."

Why was Stretch there in the first place? One of the reasons was his father was scaler for Jameson. But that year his father was fired by Buckler for poor rods—saying it had been going on now for five years. Buckler was right.

However, there was no thanks for a scaler's job—he must measure how many board feet the camp was getting before it was cut into board feet. If he told the mill to make ready for seven million board feet he'd better not be shy. But the teamsters and cutters always said the scaler was "gypping" their load, for the scaler would rather be under the estimate given to the mill than over. However, because of his son, Mr. Tomkins had given Gravellier's crew too many "full counts" and Buckler was finally fed up with planning and paying for wood that did not come to the boom.

Knowing of this, Gravellier, who had brought Stretch (Tomcat) Tomkins with him as a teamster to placate the father who scaled, now did not need the man. And ignored him. Tomkins had no one left to fight for him.

When Owen arrived this time, Tomkins reported to him that a great crime had been committed, an attempted murder, and vowed to revenge this, even if he had to go to the sheriff. Owen did not want the sheriff knowing anything about this. So Tomkins became certain he had a good case.

In the end, Tomkins was talked out of this action by the other men who told him the crime started with the tormenting, and it would be difficult to live down if it was mentioned that he himself had baited a one-armed man, and then had pissed himself when the hatchet was thrown.

Tomkins demanded Richardson be taken from the team, and that team be given to him. For he was a teamster without a team, although he had been promised one.

Owen could not. Then Tomkins lessened his request. He demanded an apology and an extra day's wage.

Owen considered this but decided he would have done the same as Richardson, and could not ask him to apologize.

"If he can't take a teasing, he is not a man."

"I am sure he has taken many," Owen said, "for there are those who forget they are men."

Tomkins was more angry at this quip than at the attempted murder. So he petitioned Owen later that night. He waited in the dark, until half the men were asleep. Owen was reading, sitting on his bunk.

"You're the only one I can talk to—so, anyways, he tried to kill me—" he said, his voice frozen stiff in the air.

"If a man of Richardson's temperament decided to kill you, you would now be dead," Owen said turning a page and not looking up.

Then Tomkins brought up what he had always depended on to demean those he felt were targets. "He's a runt—just like Meager and some of the rest of them—as far as I'm concerned."

Owen paused and looked at him perplexed, for it was not in his own nature to think this way, or to question men's nature by their size, and he asked: "So how tall are you?"

"Six-foot-two," Tomkins said.

"That is what I guessed—some of the smallest men I ever met are over six feet tall."

Tomkins was furious with this as well. But Owen said this because he was not a large man himself, and knew the measure of Stretch (Tomcat) Tomkins.

The wind blew and moaned against the tin and timbers.

"It does not befit a boss," Tomkins began, over the sound of the wind.

"Do not presume to tell me what befits a fucking boss,"

Owen Jameson said, rubbing his face in exasperation. And Tomkins was silent.

However, Owen considered and said he would give Tomkins an extra day's wage.

Before dark the next night, after Richardson put Butch over to the tend team and was trying to straighten a harness with his one arm, Owen called to him. Richardson said he would turn over his team if Owen wanted. (His team and two others were owned by Jameson—one Tomkins thought should be his team.)

"It might be better all around if I went out," Richardson said. "I don't like Mr. Tomkins."

Richardson was ill tempered and did not take to slights. Still, Owen said no, that Richardson was for him on Good Friday.

"Go back to your team," he said, "and keep your fuckin' temper to yourself."

Richardson pondered, and said he would not throw his hatchet again.

As night came, Owen thought it was settled. Tomkins went over to his bunk and hauled the blankets up about him.

The next morning bright and early Tomkins was awake. And suddenly, as if inspired, he looked over at little Meager Fortune, who had lighted the fire and was now helping the cook.

"Meager," Tomkins said, winking and smiling at all the others, "how many kids have you given yer wife now?"

"Only one," Meager answered. "Duncan—he is a little boy—a lot like others, mischievous and full of fun—and he and I someday will take a trip—as I told him—"

"Ah well, she must have had all the others by me," Tomkins interrupted, and then guffawed at his own joke.

EIGHT

The next night, with Meager Fortune staying in with the horses and little camp scrounger Nancy, the men started out for Christmas all hearing of the great excitement now being talked about in town. But as far as Christmas Eve, it was quiet. There was a report of the search that Owen and Camellia had taken of all the haunts on the river trying to find poor Reggie Glidden.

They were followed by her uncle Sterling, who then informed the police.

One other bit of information was that she had gone to the doctor.

"Whadya think of that there," Sterling said, sniffing down a head of snot.

Yet on Christmas morning in 1946 a pivotal incident happened that would shape the events on Good Friday Mountain.

Tomkins met Sonny Estabrook at their church service about or shortly after eleven a.m. This was seen and later reported by their minister.

Although Estabrook rarely spoke to this man, seeing a chance at the side door he asked him how he was.

"How you'd expect, being up there," Stretch said and cast a cold eye in the snow. "They fired me daddy."

"I know that, boy," Sonny said, "a disgrace."

Sonny, in spontaneous enthusiasm, took Tomkins by the arm and led him to his car, asked him back to the house that afternoon for a drink. Stretch Tomkins looked baffled, his lips opened, and he tried to say something in reply—but even after the car drove off, he stood in the snow and bleating wind, astounded.

He was told, however, not to mention this to anyone. And he did not.

That afternoon as Tomkins sat in dignified embarrassment in the room that had entertained lords and ladies from bygone Britain, with its maps and giant woodland caribou rack on the walls, Sonny spoke of a great change coming to the woodlots. Tomkins, dressed even better than he had for church, looked dignified and humbled by turn—doing all he could to react the way he thought the great Sonny Estabrook would want him to. Finally, after Sonny spoke to him about golf—a game poor Tomkins had never before witnessed—he came to the point.

"What I need is a man up there to see if everyone is treated well—" Sonny said. As always, he said things sadly, as if he refused to believe in the duplicity of others. "He is not a good man, that lad—I liked his brother Will, and his dad was a champ—but he's now foolin' around with that woman—well, you knew Reggie?"

"Yes," Tomkins said, nodding his head, "yes—I knew Reggie—very best of a man."

"A champ," Sonny said. "He was going to come work for me—well, the police know—so that's the way it goes—a champ."

"Oh, a champ—work for you—good for him," Tomkins said. "A champ." He spied the enormous chandelier in the far room, cold and diligent and dead in the frozen epoch of afternoon, and looked quickly back in fearful timidity—wondering how he could act to make an impression.

He crossed his legs and then uncrossed them, he sat forward and then sat back. He picked up his hat and then put it down.

"But I feel—I mean, are you okay?" Sonny asked.

"I'm okay—but they—well, someone up there tried to kill me," Tomkins said, his face reddening and looking out at his host in sudden hysteria.

"Goddamn!" Sonny said. He was so outraged by this. As Tomkins knew anyone should be. He looked at his drink and said nothing more. He just shook his head.

However, Sonny had a proposition for him. It would allow bonus—more money than he would see in a year—if he did it. Sonny was taking a gamble here—and he was taking it simply because of the new situation Owen had found himself in with this woman. He felt he could rely upon the town to turn against his adversary.

And so he told Tomkins what he wanted.

Tomkins was a stamper on the skid road. That is, he marked the yarded timber after it was scaled with the Jameson stamp to separate it from all the other wood on the river.

Estabrook wanted Tomkins to mark Jameson's wood with an Estabrook stamp.

Tomkins stared at him, unable to breathe. He loosened his tie, which he had tied with such joy just a few hours before.

Sonny did not take his eyes off him. His face turned warm and compassionate. He reached out and touched Tomkins' knee. "They make you do the stamping, don't they?" he asked.

That is, he knew and had for two months who would be stamper of much of the wood at the lower end. Tomkins was so filled with awe he could not speak. He only wondered why Sonny would want him to do this.

"For the men," Sonny said, blaspheming without a trace of embarrassment, "for the union really—"

"I—see," Tomkins said, who didn't see a thing.

The truth, as always, was somewhere else. Sonny had discovered something terrible from his people. He had discovered that the wood he had fought the Jamesons for, for the last seven years, was no good. That did not mean an acre was bad, it meant the whole damn tract was not fit to put a scale to. For the last week he had been beside himself wondering how to save his year. He had phoned Bots in Fredericton and begged him to force Jameson to trade cuts. He would cut the great cedar trees on Good Friday.

Bots not only could not do this, he burst out laughing. It was the first time anyone had ever laughed at an Estabrook.

Why hadn't this been known before? The only thing he could think is that he had been made a dupe, the first year at the head of his family enterprise.

So this is the offer he made to lowly Tomkins in a very understated manner, with an indication that he would be well taken care of. And his father—the scaler who was fired just at the start of the season—would be paid for this year.

Sonny smiled, and waited for an answer.

"My dad will be paid?"

"Of course—he was determined to scale off Buckler's mountain—so I will pay him."

This subterfuge would not save Estabrook's entire year—but if the wood got to the water with his stamp, and then into the big communal boom where it was sorted, it was his wood, and therefore he would or might break even.

He took out an envelope with $350 and lay it on the table. Tomkins had his head down, his new tie, his new shiny boots, his hat in his hand.

After Christmas, the town itself shrank from winter, ice across the sidewalks like the backs of shells, and wind blowing the great oak trees, the sun a spot far away. Each day came darker and colder, the houses tighter and meaner unto themselves.

January appeared with a gale that blotted land and river in white; small sheds and shacks bravely looked out over the river upon a desert of snow.

Owen was forced to accept that he was here now, and even if his intention had been honorable, he was looked upon very differently. He saw Camellia infrequently, for he felt the town's scrutiny and realized that her position was compromised by him. She did not know this or care—she still told people, and the paper (a journalist came to speak to her on December 31, 1946), that Owen was her best friend. While before it had sounded innocent to him, now it was looked upon as much more insidious. Not a thing had changed, but, as Shakespeare warned, thinking makes it so. Still, he could not stay away, and twice walked by her house. The gaiety, warmth, and humor the people knew her for was now looked upon as wiles. Though more than a few supported her, the idea that she was uncommonly cruel was a by-product of the mystery.

So Owen, who wanted to keep her safe, and perhaps himself, tried his best not to succumb to an impulse to see her, and looked agitated when her name was mentioned. However, people knew he was agitated when her name was mentioned.

Therefore, many people thought that he and Camellia would turn on each other like guilty parties often do. That is, people had decided already on the sin, and on the retribution to come, without any compelling evidence to warrant either. That this was embellished in the small barbershop of Mr. Solomon Hickey should not be considered entirely Mr. Hickey's fault.

Still, what Owen was experiencing now—after his brief moment in the spotlight, in the warmth and adulation of people—was a turning against him, which is a common, almost universal occurrence.

Mackey, the coroner who had wanted to have dinner with him, now refused to look in his direction; Estabrook, who had phoned him to congratulate him, now shrank from him.

To offset this, they said it wasn't and couldn't be thought of as envy—for look how much they had admired Will, and how they cared for Reggie Glidden.

All were caught up in this scandal, all believed in the new position they had placed Owen and Camellia, as much as they had believed in him being a World War hero three months before.

Even Brower believed partly for himself and partly for Lula that he had always cared for Will, that he had tried his best with Reggie—but he said: "I have changed my opinion about Owen. I thought he was more like Will and Reggie, but I have been sorely mistaken."

Still, the idea that Owen had been Lula's betrothed gave Angus Brower certain feelings of perverse pleasure.

"Yes—I knew he would do this—" he told his friends at the courthouse. For their part, they were appalled that a man would so turn from a woman because she had so suffered.

PART IV

ONE

On the sixtieth day of the cut, Owen went to the camp to make sure of the provisions and the men.

None were ill, though some had not done as well as others.

Tomkins was stamping on the lower end of the skid road, so Owen thanked him for this, saying he knew Tomkins had come in as teamster and he was appreciative of that fact. He was thankful and reminded him of when they were children together.

Then he checked the stamp for his mark.

The stamp was simply a peavey with the company's indent or mark on the bottom to be stamped into the wood, and all looked a lot alike except for the mark itself.

With Jameson it was WJ, with Sloan it was an S, and with Estabrook it was an E in the shape of a bird in flight.

So Tomkins took the stamp after Owen inspected it and went down the road to do his job.

As far as the haul went, it did not get any easier now.

The men would check the two sleds, and make sure of the harnesses—then as the days got colder and more tedious, they wouldn't get back to the camp until almost midnight. They would fall into bed exhausted in their clothes, preparing to be up in five hours. They watched each other in wind and whiteout conditions, and often the bone-chilling fog. They were like specters on that hill, the snow coming off their backs in spray as they made their lunge—snow across their scarfs and faces so until you saw the horses, you could not tell one from the other. One lantern light to show that mankind still existed on this mountain. One beacon to call out that humanity in all its self-recriminations, falsity, and self-imposed foils was taking wood down to build houses in Europe and New York, Fredericton and Halifax. Even though they, these men, would never be welcome in any of those places, nor conceive of ever being so.

On their right was a shale drop to the water that descended from a height of 223 feet at a slant of about thirty-eight degrees. The turn at the bottom had to be made quickly or a teamster chanced running his load into the dammed and frozen pond in front of him.

Even the heaviest sled and the bravest horses were scuttled sideways because of the slickness of the ice, where no sand or chaff would hold, though the sand pails were kept heated at night under those desperate lanterns.

The bridge was small, and the runners on the sleds had just enough space to make the crossing. All of this with the teamster's hands frozen stiff, and his back aching. One slip and you were over the bank or, not turning quickly enough, into the dammed brook. The harder you worked, the harder it got.

But the men had reasoned it could be no other way down, and they could not construct the bridge anywhere else. Once these things were reasoned and done, and once the men began their harsh and frozen task, and once it was decided that the horses must do this and to hear the horses grunt out in agony had to be, no one was going to change.

Missy was designated to lead. And since the other horses only seemed to feel safe when in sight of the Clydes, they came off the hill very close behind. That is, they mimicked each other just as humans did.

This was a fantastic gamble, for the Belgians came behind her so close into the turn that one snout was almost up against the rear pole. When the snow blew thickest, it was a gamble just to see over the trackless slope, with tuffs of forlorn alders and hard clots of dung, windswept as any plain on earth.

Then, at night, they looked at each other, saying: "Don't you fuggin' fail me up in front," or "You keep her steady on my fuckin' tail."

Things were okay though—they roared and laughed, threw objects at each other's heads, and were silent only at dinner.

On the sixty-fourth night of the haul Owen was not in camp, and so the men were free to talk, for it had echoed up from the town that something was happening. These rumors came with the portager and were fed by the mail.

Tonight there was some talk of union, but most was talk about Reggie's wayward wife.

"The husband's not even known to be alive or dead," Gravellier said, holding up a letter from his wife. He read, holding his cigarette out and flicking the ashes into his turned-up cuff. "Fine piece of work this will be!" he said.

Then he would look down at the letter and shake his head. "They are looking for a body," he said, and he shook his head again, "I'll body her if she ever wiggles her bum at me," he said, looking up and winking, so Tomkins and others laughed.

Many said they were sorry for Reggie, that he was a brave man. That is, their idea of who Reggie Glidden was had changed completely again.

"Well that's what a woman can do to ya," Colson said.

Meager Fortune asked them to "give it time" and see if everything didn't "just work out." For he had known what rumor could do.

Then, after a while, Meager made his way to the hovel to be alone.

The snow whispered against the opened front, and hit him at the midsection.

It was his birthday—he was now twenty-seven years old. He remembered his funny ill-fitting suit with a missing shirt button on the day he was married. He had not told anyone, for he kept those recipes in his boots to take home, that his wife and child had died in a house fire sometime on June 5, 1944, and he could still not speak of them as gone.

Still, to celebrate this mischief called a birthday he had come to see the horses.

He placed his hands up on Missy's back, and listened to the wind whistle down though the wood, thinking and digesting all he had heard tonight about Camellia and Owen. His dark, rough hands were cut and chapped from the cold, his face almost as tough as leather and still as childlike as innocence itself.

He could be cut and bleed without knowing, and had been many times. He could stand cold that would kill many, and had been once caught up under the ice with a draft horse and survived.

And he would, like his father, have arthritis in ten years, be dead in twenty. That is what the world offered him. He knew no other life, and in fact was frightened of it. This other life, where men did not sweat or suffer the cold to half-frozen bodies. He had seen men prancing and preening at dances, in a world he did not belong to, where they all somehow looked and moved in the way of women. He cringed to think it might actually be that way in cities and places he would never go.

His life, then, was nothing. But he must stay and take care of the men. He was too kind to gossip and he didn't like them talking about the boss—so he came out here.

He was a tiny man, yet a man who could lift three hundred pounds on his back day in and day out. He looked at his leather gloves, his woolen jacket and thick woolen pants, and even here felt ashamed that he knew so little. If he had known enough to read and write—or enough to take a job on the railway—his wife would have lived. This is what he thought. He, through his splendid ignorance, had killed the woman he loved. Though no one else would ever think this.

He had cared for Missy as a filly. Now he moved the lantern forward and lighted it just enough to check her caramel-colored head and chestnut eyes. There were little flecks of hair missing along her back, small spots that the world had taken away from her.

"Hello, lady—it's me—Meager Fortune. I knew Will—the great Will Jameson—and arm-twisted him to a draw—way up at his camp on the Tabusintac. I also saved a mule in the war."

He set the lantern down and smiled without a tooth in his head.

Butch's right hind leg had been scraped raw by a loose piece of hemlock he had dragged to the yard, before he was harnessed on the two sled to haul over the bank and to the river skids. Which meant he and two of the Belgians were used all day long working either down in the cut or on the two sled. It just meant that his great heart would give out a year or two sooner, and he wouldn't stop working until it did. As soon as he felt the log on the devil's mount Butch would begin his ferocious stride up over the hill, cutting a swath through stumps and fallen wood that broke under his great strength but took each day more strength from him, as if he was saying to the man handling the reins behind his back: "You want me to do this—hook it on and watch how I alone will work my way to death."

Once, before the war, when the men were teasing a horse who would not work, Meager had tried to stop it. They had pushed him down, and he had fallen on his back. He looked up and saw Gravellier taking an ax to the horse's head.

Meager remembered the horse gave a sad grunt like a human being and fell down. "That'll teach ya, ya bald-arsed son of a whore," Gravellier said as blood spotted his heavy, angry face and the peak of his cap.

"No," Meager had pleaded.

But it did not matter if or when or how much he said no.

So he went away and sat by himself in the woods.

Meager Fortune knew there were many stories against Will Jameson—but he also knew who was kind to him, and who would not take an ax to a horse.

"Poor old Butch," Fortune said.

However, the teamsters were afraid of Butch.

Sometimes Butch would work so hard the teamsters could not back him up or stop him, and they would to a man marvel at his crazy lunges up the hill, or fear him.

"Get up out of that, you crazy Jameson son of a whore," Nolan would yell when Butch took it in his mind to do something on his own.

And all that wood, Meager thought. Where did it go? He had asked his wife Evelyn one night, and they had sat up late worrying about it. Neither of them were sure. So they went and asked her father, Ned, and he wasn't sure either.

"Goes down the river, don't it? Can't expect to know much more than that."

Maybe it built houses, or maybe it went to offices and buildings in cities he would never see. Some said the cedar hauled last year was used to make a sauna for a mob boss in New York. But wherever this great wood went, it came from these men. Meager knew that much.

Gibbs had not tended to Butch's cut right, so Meager found a way to poultice the animal using balm out of the old tack box at the end of the hovel and some mud mixed with straw. Butch stood in docile acceptance while Meager worked, sure that his own great and towering strength—given to him by the great horse Byron's Law and his mother, Missy—had sealed his fate to run those logs up the hundreds of yards through the stump-laden, snow-scowled cut and then down over the morbidly freezing mountain, slabs of ice that looked in the shimmer of distance like pale rock.

Knowing this, Meager whispered: "You take them down the slope, Butch. No one can do it but you—you have to do it, boy."

Butch once more stood furious and rigid, as if his plan, caught in the sinew of his blood and brain, was to kill a man before he took himself. Of course, that was giving human emotion to a beast, and Meager knew them so well as not to.

Then Missy dropped her head to the feed box, her breathing scattering a few cold oats before her. And this allowed little Meager a profound realization, that her years of work, years of being fed too much or too little, run too hard, brought to her feet with laudanum, had made her now forget him.

No longer was she the filly with the big clown shoes. Her massive strength had made her into something else entirely—an animal of such magnificent power she looked upon the universe of man with indifference. Her existence now was one of brutal work or death, and in the end both.

He patted her and smiled.

But now she stared into nothing.

It was strange, he thought, but didn't reflect on it too much—the peavey stamp Tomkins was using was sitting up against the side wall at the back of the hovel. But he was sure Tomkins had left his peavey stamp down on the skid road late today. He reflected upon this and thought he himself must be mistaken, and wasn't Tomkins a good lad anyway.

TWO

The men were still yelling in the camp, drinking and laughing—at the whore that had taken up with the boss. Meager had never partaken in talk like this. So he sat outside on a stump and whistled.

An argument was going on now in behind the walls of such a dreary place. He could hear them.

It seemed Gravellier wanted to force the young tend team Gibbs to go down into the shine and find a bit of tack that he said was missing.

Gibbs, as Gravellier and others well knew, was terribly frightened to be by himself in the woods. And this is why Gravellier had demanded it.

"Go now," he said, "and find that fuggin' tie-on, boy—"

"I can do it tomorrow—it is jus' an old piece of leather—"

"An ol' piece of leather to you—necessary to me to take down me load over that piece of mountain—" (This wasn't true, but to Gravellier—now in hysterics—it didn't matter.)

"Well then why did you take it off?" Gibbs said.

"Because I didn't think you'd be so foolish as to leave it behind—" Gravellier said, standing over the boy. "Go up out and get it now."

"He don't wanta get it," Trethewey said, "so leave him be."

"Are you gonna get it?" Gravellier said.

"No," Trethewey smiled, "I am not goin' down there to get nothing."

The problem was, Gibbs was Gravellier's tend team—though he worked Missy and Butch. And in fact this was the reason Gravellier wanted to show his authority.

"You go now—" he said.

The men listened to this wearily; Gibbs, though, could lose his job over this. And no one would say much.

Young Gibbs was staring up at Gravellier from his bed, his blankets up about him, as if being in bed would be enough to protect him from this unreasonable demand.

"Come on—go get it—and place it in the hovel where it's suppose to be," Gravellier said.

Young Gibbs reluctantly got out of bed and pulled on his Humphreys. "It's some black out, ain't it?" he asked.

No one answered.

"Anyone wants to come fer a walk?"

No one said a thing.

"Where is it?" he said, half smiling, hopefully. "Can anyone tell me?"

"Watch out fer the panthers," Tomkins said, grinning and hauling the blankets over himself, and laughing so much that those blankets shook.

But Gibbs reluctantly put on his hat, tied it about his chin like a child so that his cheeks suddenly became fatter.

"Can someone come with me?" he asked politely as he tied his hat on, and then hauled on his mittens. "I could get up early tomorrow," he said.

No one said a thing. The men were in for the night, and they decided it was his problem. Even if it was a harsh one.

"Take a lantern," Richardson said, "and you'll be okay. Its down by the last yard—that's where you lay it on that stump—it's a measly bit of leather that wouldn't fit over a gnat's twat—but Huey wants it. He could get it tomorrow on his load—but Huey wants it. He is the first to send you out and the last man to know the woods—but Huey wants it. He keeps talking about the Indians and how he knows how to live like them although he wouldn't last a day on his own on this here mountain—but then again, my little Gibbs, Huey wants it."

Gravellier ignored this challenge.

"It's on the goddamn stump!" someone else roared to shut Richardson up.

"Ah yes—that stump—well, that ain't so far, cold though," Gibbs said. "What's the reading?"

They could tell the reading through the window, for the thermometer was hooked to a branch just outside. And there was a cold moon over the camp.

Colson tried to read it through the ice and dark.

"I don' know—minus thirty-six, seems to say—Christ, could be minus forty-six fer all I can see—just go get it done."

Gibbs put on his boots as they turned down the lanterns in the camp. But he waited about five minutes, sitting on the edge of his bed, hoping Gravellier would go to sleep so he wouldn't have to leave.

"Yer takin' yer fuggin' time to leave," Gravellier grunted, as he rolled over and coughed.

Gibbs stood, buttoned his coat, and started toward the door about a foot at a time, slowly, as if he didn't want to disturb what his reluctance to do had already disturbed.

Now everyone was awake, watching him.

"Go go go—fer fuck sake go," they all said.

But just then Meager Fortune came in, and in his hand he held the leather in question.

"Look what I found down in that shine," he said, winking at Gibbs. "You get this into the hovel, boy, and get yerself ta bed."

Meager took off his boots, shook them out, and put them near the stove. Then he lay down and prayed as he did every night. He prayed for little Gibbs, and for Mr. Richardson with the one arm, and for old Trethewey and Mr. Tomkins who had no love. He prayed for Nolan who didn't believe, and Curtis who did.

It was his birthday and he thought of his little boy, Duncan.

The wind picked up so there was a smell of smoke backed up inside the camp. He pretended that's why the tears were in his eyes.

THREE

On the sixty-fifth day of the haul, Owen went by train to buy saws in Nova Scotia. He was ill. The wound in his leg by now periodically became inflamed, and he should have rested or seen a doctor. He had done neither. He had no time to rest and as with some men, even some very brave men, he had a childish fear of doctors.

He could not afford to leave the cut, though it infuriated him to have to deal with it and most of the men. The men had complaints—a steady complaint about the wind, and another petition by Tomkins to have his own team so, as he said, "I won't be marker—it would work out better for you."

It was at this point that Owen considered giving Stretch (Tomcat) Tomkins a team. He went into the barns of two men he knew to ask them about it. But really there were no teams to spare. Many people nowadays relying on half-told reports say he never once made an attempt. He did but he couldn't, for no one would give up a team to Good Friday. He wrote to Tomkins and pleaded with him to be patient.

But all the men complained secretly about each other. These secret petitions were in the "fun box" at the depot—and were given to Buckler every week or two. Everything from: "Colson don't smell the best when you are sleeping side by side—"

To: "I am not the man for fish stew—I will take a salmon and smelt and now and again a cod—but not a stew—I don't like the way it runs—"

To: "Gibbs don't smell at all human no more."

To: "Richardson don't know a horse from a bucksaw."

To: "Nolan thinks Gibbs grooms his horses—Nolan don't know his horses—you think he knows horses—neither do Gibbs. Why there ain't one man there who knows a horse—not a bit." Signed, *I know horses.*

To: "There ain't no pickles that I like."

To: "There is someone trying to touch my privates as I sleep—is gonna come missing his hand if he do it again." (This was serious, and Owen had a letter sent to post on a pole at the back of the camp.)

The train ride was an agony because of all this, because of his paining leg and the insipid nonchalant conversations of men he did not know.

In Nova Scotia they did not know Owen either. That is, they didn't know he was the same man so talked about now. Not this frail man with the wide eyes.

While there he heard the story of he and Camellia. It had misshapenly surfaced in this doleful little town. While names were not known, the circumstances were revived in giddy pathos.

It was now rumored, the men said, acknowledging each

other, that the two had killed Reggie after luring him back to Newcastle because he was going to expose their affair and work for Estabrook. They had stuffed the body in a trunk in a cave where they had their rendezvous, but it was about to be found by her uncle who suspected them, so they had thrown it off the Morrissey Bridge.

He stayed at a rooming house on King Street, and heard from a salesman who had been up to the Miramichi all of these goings-on as well. In the turbulent battered hat of the salesman, in his conical shaped face and rather pointed ears, he gave the impression of some hard backwoodsman escaped his heritage to try another, traveling on the rural road seeking an ambivalent destiny.

"The old woman caught them together—" the salesman said. "The younger son—he I heard killed the older boy in a barroom fight over her years before—when she was about sixteen. Her father was that wife killer there. I seen her myself—big buxom blonde—and I said to her, 'Hey, why are you doing this?' You know she looked at me with a sly smile and said: 'Get whatever I want—I got a million-dollar ass, so I may as well.' Cross my heart it's what she said. I coulda had her myself, I do suppose."

That's how you cheated someone: you changed their basic nature. So, to everyone she had become sadistic.

The clock ticked on.

He remembered visiting Brower's as a boy and seeing Camellia playing the piano—she had just "picked it up" without any lessons. She bounced all over the piano seat as she played, her face beaming in rays of childlike wonder, picking songs out of the air while Lula sat with her music sheet on her lap patiently waiting to play Mozart.

Why didn't he recognize how much he loved her then? Why, if he had, it might have been a different life—a life without famine in the soul. Were the angels she so believed in watching then? And if they were, why did they not do something about it then?

He arrived home on a freezing afternoon. First he went to the old warehouse to check something—and coming away from that, looking depressed and anxious and giving some money to Sterling who had caught up to him to ask, he went back to the mill, to check the wiring. He spoke to Buckler and they decided to ask Maufat McDurmot to rewire the mill along with Clinton Dulse, if he was sober.

But Owen blurted out what he had heard in Windsor about himself. He laughed as Will used to when men said they would destroy him. And Owen had stayed here, if for nothing else, for Will.

Buckler told him that it was assumed they had gotten rid of Reggie in some terrible way. This was because of Winch's cave, and the rendezvous that he and Camellia supposedly had had.

"What rendezvous?"

Buckler told him this was the rumor spread.

"From where was it spread?"

"From the barbershop," Buckler said.

"How do you know?"

"Because they stop talking when I go in."

"Who would have heard this rumor there—someone I might know?"

"Hutchings."

"Why in hell would Camellia phone Reggie and ask him to come if that's the case?"

"That's why they are saying Camellia is treacherous—like

Delilah. She convinced Reggie to come and protect her from your advances, and when he came—you dealt with him."

There was a long pause.

"I don't care what I hear about me, but if I hear of them laughing or taunting her—if I do—God help them," Owen said to Buckler. "She has had too tough a life—put on display before she was seven."

It was a cold day, with bright sunshine and the snow spraying in the wind. Children played hockey across the river on a homemade rink.

Owen wanted some lighter horses in to work the wood toward the skids where the Belgians and Percherons and Clydes could load. That would save Butch and Cole Younger for the longer, more demanding task on the two sled.

He went to discuss this with the horse trader Hutchings, who just by his evasion confirmed the rumors now in town that were known to almost everyone else. That is, looking at Hutchings' smile, and his nod, Owen realized that the rumors against someone are never told to them.

He felt strangely enraged by this obvious truth.

FOUR

That evening, with the lowering sun yellow across the back field of snow and alders, Owen went into the family barn to see the two-year-old Belgian, Ronald's Young. He walked quietly into the adjacent stall and patted it. White snow swept in at the main doors, and doleful rope twisted in the breeze.

Then he saw the stool Will used to sit on, and his heart was stirred. He looked toward the great old house, and thought of his life here.

Coming back to the house he asked Camellia, who for the first time in her life had not smiled and laughed that day, about these rumors and was annoyed when she turned eagerly and said, while backing away from him, almost like a specter toward the dimmer alcove at the back: "Wear your Saint Jude and never mind rumor—and we will see Reggie—he will come back and clear this all up."

"All of what up?" he said. "There is nothing in the world that is happening—what in Christ is happening?"

"All of whatever it is—never mind them—I am used to it."

She closed the door, to prevent him from saying anything else. He saw her look quickly away in the fading light. She had been called a bad girl downtown and she wanted to prevent people from saying this again. Closing the door was the only way she knew how.

And he sat in an old leather chair in the corner of the hall. He hadn't sat here since he was sixteen.

He decided that was the real problem—her being used to it. He remembered at school and other places, how she was treated. That is, she was treated very well by most people—but as always in every situation there was an element at the school who saw her as vulnerable, and treated her mercilessly. Perhaps that is why he didn't or wouldn't initiate anything with her when he was young. That and the story, fabricated by the Steadfast Few, that Byron had been her mother's lover. But if that was the case then everything that had happened to her since was in a way his doing.

He went to see Practical Mary—ostensibly to take her a receipt for the saws but more importantly to speak to her about whatever it was that was being said.

But Mary was in no mood. She had a difficult time not believing something had happened, and she didn't know Camellia would "act like that."

"Like what?" Owen said, surprised that supposition had infiltrated his own house.

"I don't know—I don't know," Mary said, "Everyone is saying poor Lula, and Camellia stole you away from her after her father gave her just about everything under the sun—and—"

"NONSENSE!" Owen shouted.

"Well, that's what I told them, but I'm an old woman—you know I'm sick—I'm running a temperature—my heart thumps, I have weak spells. But you were kissing her—and my friends have been telling me that. Why oh why would you go to Winch's cave—"

He left her, and walked back toward the front of the house. In the great darkness that invaded it this time of year, he had once spent his happiest hours, knowing that snowfall cut them off from everyone except themselves.

"Phantoms," he said.

There were two startling "past events," and some say that both of these events—or discoveries of past events—sent Owen to the bottle that had been prepared for him by the prophecy.

These silent notes from the past were laid away in Will's room in the old chest that had been brought from the camp at Talons. The trunk that had come on the day he had run downstairs to see if it was Lula paying a visit.

The night after he came home from Nova Scotia, he walked

into Will's room to see if he could find the company book on board feet and saw this trunk, just where it had been for years, and opened it with the key that lay on the old china plate on the windowsill.

In it he found a full bottle of Scotch unopened and a letter addressed to him, sitting on top of a red blanket beside this bottle. There with a hunting knife and a Remington pistol, a compass and a map of the Jameson tract.

He opened the letter slowly, and went under the light to read.

In this letter to Owen was fifteen hundred dollars tucked away—in fact, Will had put it there the night before he left for his last run, and no one had entered Will's room until Owen had returned from overseas.

"For your university," the letter said. "Take hold of the world, boy, and do better than me."

The letter was dated the day before Will had died.

Owen studied the letter for an hour, the handwriting, trying to determine where Will had been when he wrote this. He lay the letter down and picked up the copper-plated compass, looking at it for a long moment before noticing that the top of the red blanket had been pulled away. He took the bottle and set it beside him. Then he turned the blanket back.

Here Owen discovered something else none would ever have suspected: books. At first he thought they were his, mixed in with everything. But silently he became aware. They had been Will's—all purchased after the death of Dan Auger.

Owen picked these books out of this old trunk one at a time and brought them to the desk with Will's name whittled upon it, his face passive, his hands trembling.

Crime and Punishment.

Leaves of Grass.

Jude the Obscure.

Lord Jim.

Wuthering Heights.

And finally, and inevitably, *Ulysses* by James Joyce.

Each book had been read—whole passages of *Lord Jim* and *Jude the Obscure* underlined and referenced.

Owen took everything back to his own room and stayed there the next day, drinking from the bottle Will had left, staring at this letter—and these books.

The books, it was said, sent him to the bottle; the bottle sent him to prison. A simple enough prophecy any writer would understand.

Owen was required to go to the doctor for his hip but hadn't since he had come home. Now he fell into a fitful sleep, and woke up startled and thirsty just as it was growing dark. He was sure in his half-conscious state that Will was calling out to him from the doorway.

"You stay in here until I set things straight with Reggie," he heard him say.

He woke.

He had been out of uniform for a year and yet he had four letters from the army—two from Ottawa. He left them unopened.

He went downstairs seeing the light fade across the heavy carpets, lingering coldly on the brown windowsills of too many windows, and felt the heaviness one does after sleeping in the afternoon. Camellia was still at the house, cleaning a room off to the side of the living room that almost no one went in. Strangely, he saw her dusting the statuette of Rodin's *The Kiss* that Will, without knowing what mythology it spoke of, had brought home once upon a time.

And he noticed something else for the first time. A small wedding ring on her finger. He was dazzled by his understanding of how he had avoided her when he was young, just because others had, even though he could not take his eyes off her whenever she appeared. She turned and looked at him, and brushed a piece of hair back from her forehead. When it fell down again, she gave a quick smile and winked.

FIVE

Although she told him not to, Owen had been drinking and insisted he walk Camellia to her house. As they passed Solomon's barbershop he insisted she take his arm: "It is slippery, so be safe."

She took his arm knowing there was no safety in it.

On his way back home, passing Solomon's barbershop again, he saw the barber look out at him. It was nothing unusual, a momentary glance by a small, deft man who had always been on the right side when they were boys.

Then he thought of the rumor about the cave. Only a person from Newcastle would understand why he was so angry at the suggestion he had taken Camellia Dupuis there.

Solomon, he decided, had started it.

At home, as he drank one Scotch and then another, he knew why he was so bothered—but he didn't want to admit it to himself.

He had gotten used to being admired—even if it was just a little—and now he had returned from Windsor to the town's contempt. He put the glass down and sunk into contempt himself. He had killed twelve men in the war—one a boy of seventeen.

It bothered him now more than at any other time.

Later he went for a walk to see if the drugstore was open, to get something for the pain he was in (though the Scotch helped, his leg still burned).

The wind over flat, stark fields and the beautifully built two- and three-story houses as he approached the town seemed ambivalent to his crisis. The silence accompanying that clean cold of night seemed ambivalent as well. And in his heart was the idea that he might very easily have driven a man to his death.

He passed people who just two months ago had lifted him on their shoulders.

Owen nodded and people looked away. He smiled and spoke, but could not decide what was wrong. What was wrong was that the investigation, ongoing by the local police, was scientific. They had taken his and Camellia's fingerprints, and his mother's. They had given these fingerprints because they had done nothing wrong. But this science added to general suspicion. It had posed fruitful questions about him and Camellia and had already come to a conclusion based on what people conjectured was an obvious truth. The police themselves were mainly gossips, and told their families, who told others. Camellia especially, more and more as time went on, became sadistic and cruel in people's imagination—especially when she started to buy liver at the store.

The old mathematician who had risen to say, "There's the man who knows Pythagoras," did not shout his way now, but hurried down another laneway.

A feeling of disgust strengthened in Owen as he passed the barbershop where Solomon Hickey worked. Solomon, cutting Billy Pebble's hair, did not turn to look, but his mouth, as always, worked constantly.

"I will never mind it," he thought.

He thought of Camellia, and suddenly recognized how much he had to protect her from this scandal.

He wanted to board a train and go away. But, secretly, he wanted to leave with her. Then he thought again, if he had shown interest in her before the war—none of this would be happening now.

So why couldn't he change it for the better?

He turned the corner at Hanover Street and slipped on the ice. A shot of pain went through his leg and into his side. He grimaced and turned to make his way home, along the same avenues.

Owen was aware of the poor timing that now seemed insurmountable. Poor timing was everything—the moment when he turned on the landing and saw her—in another moment she would have been across the landing to the linen closet and upstairs bath. But he had stopped and kissed her—it had been pure braggart on his part—and some would say not because she was Camellia, but because she was a maid.

When people at the house had smiled knowingly at him the next morning, why hadn't he taken that for exactly what it was, the smile of gossips, and done something about it then?

Only Owen could tell you why—he had enjoyed the notoriety. He had enjoyed people assuming the worst. For in all of it, there was the idea that he had impressed other men who had once worked for his brother.

Now that he wanted the rumor to stop, it was no longer in his power to do so. For he as a participant in the scandal could twist and turn, but not so much as lessen it by a molecule. Denying fed it. He was as caught up in it as Camellia, and it must run its course.

He knew this now. It struck him like cold in his face—a bluster of sudden wind and snow. Now as he realized he cared for her deeply, he also realized what he himself had allowed to be thought. He and others had taken advantage because she was still childlike. To say that about a woman was to evoke all kinds of responses. But men like Meager Fortune he knew to be in this unconscious state as well.

He remembered Lula's tenth birthday party, the last one he and Will were invited to.

"A birthday party hurrah," Camellia had said. And everyone had laughed at her. But Will had not laughed. Thinking of this, Owen was sorry he had not seen her grace before.

No, he must take responsibility. He had used her fall from public grace to enliven himself, at first mischievously and without malice—but look what had become of it!

"If I allow for Nolan to be Push—and Buckler to oversee the mountain—then I can go away. In fact, I will leave tonight," he thought.

And he thought of something else, important but fleeting. What if it was not Buckler's kind or Nolan's kind or Trethewey's kind that came through in the end of things—what if it was much less than that? Solomon Hickey's kind of man, or Tomcat Tomkins', or Gravellier's? What if their kind would be the type to judge those men on the mountain who worked now on behalf of legions of houses, railways, and docks not yet built?

What if they were the ones who spoke out against him?

"Then their judgment won't matter," he thought. But he did not completely believe this.

There was a train at midnight, and he turned to the station. There in the dimly lit high-ceilinged building with its cement floor and its photo of a train going through the Rocky Mountains, he bought his ticket. The lone ticket, the teller told him, on the midnight train.

He nodded, put it in his overcoat pocket, and decided this: "I am not needed—when I go, Camellia will be better off—everything will die down—Reggie will see I am gone and come back to her."

Yet instead of going home, telling his mother, packing, or doing any of these things, he immediately turned toward the bottom row of houses, to let Camellia know. And all the way there he knew he wanted to see her more than anyone else in the world—and the strangest sensation overcame him. Camellia was free to go with him. Or to come later. That, in fact, is why he had bought the ticket.

He was plagued by this thought, as some are by thoughts they hate, and he shook his head, pulled his overcoat tighter, and made it to her street. Once there, he realized his thoughts about her were fleeting and not serious. Strangely, they would have been serious had he been sixteen and not twenty-six.

When she spoke to him on those walks to her house from his, she often spoke of Reggie. "A big kid," she said.

Owen saw them quite differently than anyone else in town. He saw them—Reggie especially—completely vulnerable and lost together in that little house, where they had tried to make a home, frightened of the world outside. Though he was angry at her for praying, he could at least understand why. Once, asking her what she wanted to do, offering to help in any way, she asked if someday he could see his way to write her a recommendation so she might get a job—a good job, at the five-and-ten.

SIX

At the front of Camellia's lane botched with snow gone blue in the night, Sterling—a kind of colossus in the town, his figure always apparent—stood watching the house. Owen went by him and knocked on her door.

"Come in," she said, and hurried him inside.

"What?" she said, turning and out of breath. "Have you seen my Reggie?"

He paused, secretly disappointed by her question. "No—what I want to know is—do you think you are in trouble?"

"No," she smiled, "people always say silly things—"

"Are you sure?" he said angrily.

"Yes," she said, taken aback, looking at him curiously.

"I'm leaving then. It is best I go—the boys on the mountain will be okay—they have done work like this all their lives—"

"Leaving?" A cloud came over her face. It was as if he could see her heart beating. She turned the radio down. As she did, she said softly: "Don't go yet—you're my only friend and we are going to find Reggie—and—"

He wanted to make her understand that he wasn't running away, but how could he after she said this?

"If I go tonight, I think everything might be okay—Reggie might come back—but if I don't, Camellia, what will happen—?"

"I'm not sure—" Camellia said, smiling slightly.

"If I go the rumors will stop."

"Yes," she nodded, "of course—yes. Would you like a sandwich—I have—I was—I mean I don't want you to go—" And then taking a breath as if steeling herself to hear information she didn't know, she sat down on the couch and stared at the corner of the room. "I don't know what to do."

Because she said this he suddenly took two hundred dollars and placed it in her hand.

"What is this for?" she asked. She stood, half-scared, dropping the money but looking beyond him.

"Just in case," he said, as confused by what he had done as she was. He bent, his body trembling, and picked the money up. As he stood up he kissed her. Suddenly, so she couldn't protest. She backed away as if he had burned her face.

"No," she said, tears in her eyes, "no, Owen." But she was staring beyond him now in panic.

He turned, and saw in the lower kitchen window Sterling looking in on them—his face almost beatific in its self-absorption. Owen ran outside, falling and picking himself up. But Sterling was gone, along the back lane and across a snowplowed track and over a crooked fence.

He went back to the house, where he calmed himself, leaning against the door.

"You keep the money—you must keep it."

After saying goodbye, but promising himself never again to touch her, he moved quickly back up the dreary snow-filled street.

This final kiss—the third—had actually determined everything. He could not go. He knew this as he walked. The kiss would be in every house, exaggerated. It hadn't been her doing. It had been his. Going wouldn't do anything but jeopardize her.

He determined not to speak to anyone. To ignore them and make his way home, and to get to the mountain as soon as possible. He now knew what he had been remembering when he had dreamed of Will at the door, saying: "Wait until I set things straight with Reggie."

It was a conversation he had had years ago after he had told Will how much he cared for Lula.

"Why?" Will had asked.

"I don't know—her uncle is a professor, she likes books—so do I, so you know—"

"That's nonsense—fool's gold. Camellia is the one who loves you," Will had said.

"Camellia," he said surprised.

"Reggie likes her—but wait until I set things straight with Reggie and you take her out. She's got no friends either very much—she would be safe with someone like you."

"Safe?" he had laughed.

"Yes," Will had said, "from all those who think of her as less than themselves. How you stood up for the LeBlanc boy proves it."

This had been Will at his best wisdom, and Owen hadn't seen it.

The very next day he had brought *Ulysses* over to Lula—ran to her with it, thinking she would be impressed.

He turned and followed his footsteps again, about the square.

And then, with some confusion, he realized what part of town he was in.

Solomon Hickey's barbershop was open on a Friday night, snow drifting down over the candy cane–colored sign, the victory over tyranny allowing this evening, the smell of fresh aftershave faint in the cold night air. The barbershop—called Antonio's after Solomon's boss, who was now retired—sat in a little nook on the street, pleasant and well looked after.

Owen paused for a long moment.

"Go home now," a voice told him.

But he had been drinking Scotch all day, and that voice was fleeting, in among the boys and girls coming down from the hockey game or over from the Grand Theatre. He must stop these rumors for her sake. (He might not have thought this if he hadn't been so foolish as to kiss her. Still and all, he had caused it.)

So he put his hand on the doorknob, took a deep breath, and walked inside, a bell tinkling.

"Did Sterling run in here?" he asked.

Solomon stopped sweeping and looked at him.

Owen smelled heavy cigarette smoke, hair lotion and shaving cream, and the warm scent of cut hair that had fallen like some deposed bandits to the floor.

Solomon Hickey had been watching Owen for the last five minutes, and did not know why he was anxiously standing outside or now coming in to ask about Sterling. He shrugged.

He, of course, had spread rumors, especially the one most damning—the one about the cave, and the letter found there. Still and all, they were just the rumors everyone else was spreading—they had circled about him too, and once started there was no starting point. In fact, by that point a rumor takes on validation. You could not blame Solomon Hickey more than anyone else in the world.

Owen heard the fizzle of the candy cane light go off. For some reason he never understood, this sound caused a terrible pain to sweep over him—it sounded like the beginning of a night before battle, with flares over the sky, and he found himself bathed in the half-dark light from the street, as if traces of flares were once again in the air over his head.

"I'm sorry, it's just that Sterling won't mind his own business," he said. He knew in a kind of daze that this was who he really wanted to speak to—Sterling.

Then, for some reason, he could hear himself apologizing. But it is not unusual to have very brave men apologize to very foolish ones.

He told Solomon he was leaving town (even though he was certain he would not), and if there were any hard feelings between them, he was sorry. He wished Lula only the best. If Solomon Hickey or Sterling or anyone thought there was anything between him and Camellia, they had the wrong impression. He then asked Solomon to help Camellia, a woman he knew from his time at Lula's all those years ago. Help him to help Camellia regain her reputation. Turn the tables in the barbershop.

"We have to help her," he said, and his lips trembled slightly. This caught Hickey by surprise. He seemed delighted.

Owen then said he was willing to clear her of any wrong impression, and apologized for this impression. Camellia loved Reggie and they were both trying to find him.

"And what about Lula—should we help her," Solomon Hickey asked, "or just leave her die in her room? She's had a stroke, you know—did you hear that?—and she has no one now—did you hear that?—no one but me!" Again he seemed delighted by this.

"Of course—well, yes," Owen said, "but—well, that was a long time ago—I mean, when I liked her."

"Yes, before her stroke," Solomon said. There were small scissors in one of his pockets and a heavy comb in the other, and his shoes were solid black, and hair spread on the white floor as he lay the broom aside. He looked piqued by Owen's gall.

"I didn't know the great Owen Jameson would want to apologize—and run away, my, my," he said as if speaking to someone else.

"It's not that—I just want to clear it up," Owen said.

His leg was paining. Why couldn't he think? Perhaps he had drunk too much. He decided to go home, turned to go, and then—though hearing Will's voice in his subconscious telling him to leave immediately—he turned and faced his accuser again. "Just tell me who it was spread these goddamn lies about us—that's all I want to know—was it you or Sterling?" he said, trying to be calm and taking out a cigarette to light. But his hands shook now from pain and drink.

Solomon thought he had gotten rid of his tormentor with a minimum of trouble. But now he had to readjust in the dark with certain night lights coming on. "No, it wasn't me," he said, averting his small dark eyes. "Why would it be me? Your filth has nothing to do with me—you have hurt a lot of people." He smiled in spite of what he said. "You hurt the Browers—after all that waiting for you that she done."

The room was in semi-darkness. And Owen remembered the seventeen-year-old boy he had killed in battle. Well, there was not a day when he didn't. He had come up to the German position—the day before the incident with Reggie—and seen the boy, helmet off, his blond hair tossing in the wind, heart blown away, freckles on his face.

Hickey opened the closet, closed it, and turning around to place the heavy comb on the counter, seemed surprised Owen was still there.

"I thought you were gone," he said. Suddenly he was ready to put the man out. "If you want to know who talks about you—everyone does. Everyone that comes in here does, every day—you're killing men up on Good Friday you are, and we know it. But that is not my fault. And everyone talks about Camellia, because she let you make her into used goods—but that's none of my fault."

"We have done nothing at all," Owen said.

Solomon decided not to answer. He just stood still with

his black coat on, waiting silently for the man to leave. Twice he sniffed, and softly touched his cheek because of a paining tooth.

Owen went toward the door thinking only that he would find Sterling and settle it with him. When he turned Solomon followed, motioning with his right hand, holding the heavy lead comb.

"Go," he kept saying, "you get on."

Owen thought he remembered this later, but was never sure if it was an actual memory.

At any rate, at that second, seven minutes after nine o'clock on a cold January night in 1947, came a heedless act. Solomon Hickey did something he had never in his life done before. Why, one might ask onward to doomsday, would he do it now?

Why Solomon Hickey jabbed the pointed end of the heavy lead comb hastily into Owen's side, when Owen had started to open the door, no one will ever know.

The point hit in the very spot where Owen had been shot, and where part of a German bullet was lodged against a nerve in his leg. Owen felt immense pain. And then this: He turned and swung his right elbow hard into Solomon's throat—the way he had done in action two years before. The little man crumpled without a sound, one leg twisted behind him. Others rushed in, and the cold entered as well. All was in semidarkness, and all the men entered like detectives.

Owen did not know what had happened. After he went outside the small, immaculately kept barbershop, he made his way home in a daze, but someone (the same woman he had seen for an instant at the wharf on the day he and Camellia were there) followed him at a distance to make sure he did not run away.

When he got to the steps of his house, she turned back toward town, hurrying along on her short plump legs in rubber boots—the action of her walk invigorated by what she had to tell. Her name was Cora Auger. All of this would help one thing—the lumbermen's union.

Owen had lost his gloves and scarf. He went back to look for them along the sidewalk, then realized he had set them down in the barbershop. He returned home, sat in the kitchen, and took a drink of beer. Then he went to his room and poured from the same bottle of Scotch a glass three-quarters full and drank it. The bottle was now empty, but he found another pint.

After about an hour, Camellia came into the house calling him. She came upstairs to ask him what had happened, walking straight into his room. He did not answer immediately. Then looked up at her in a stupor. She wore a white blouse and an old ragged coat of Reggie's and some high boots that didn't fit her—which meant she was in bed when someone had told her the news. (Sterling had gone to her door banging on it and calling her.)

"Why why?" she said, taking his face in her hands, as if she were his sister.

"Who spread the rumor about you and I?" he asked. "Who—so that's why—who did it—I wanted to find Sterling and tell him off—and found Hickey instead, that's why." It was as if he were blaming her.

"Oh my God, this for a stupid rumor—who knows how a rumor is started, or spread. I told you it would be—just as it happened—you have to go," she said, rushing about, trying to find him clothes. "You must go! Get on the train, please, I can't go through this again—"

"There is nowhere in the world to go," he said.

Then he snapped something from his neck and handed it to her. It was his Saint Jude medal.

It was 12:07 in the morning when they heard a knock on

the door. The two women stood in the small hallway between the kitchen and the pantry, waiting as Buckler answered.

Three men were at the door. They had come for Owen Jameson. Here to arrest him for the murder of Solomon Hickey.

SEVEN

It was easy to capture a mad criminal like Owen Jameson—for that criminal simply went home to sit on the bed and stare at the wall.

The crime was witnessed by various people, and by the time the news got about many who didn't witness it said they had. Buckler hurried on his arthritic legs about the town trying to discover what had happened.

At home, Mary, beside herself with worry and recrimination, was now certain of the prophecy. "Perhaps it is like original sin—perhaps it is what I was born with," she told Buckler. However, old Buckler was far more "politic." Prophecies and such had too much of the religious evangelist for this practical Protestant. So did things foretold.

"I was foretold," Practical Mary said, sitting in a stupor, "I was foretold, I was foretold."

Buckler, however, thought it was simple mechanics.

He had warned Owen, and now he was angry with himself for not recognizing Owen's emotional state, or worse, the physical pain working for them had exacerbated. He was not a woodsman like Will. In fact, the very woods would take a harrowing toll on Owen—though he understood it well enough.

"He cannot go nineteen hours a day like Will," Buckler said. "He cannot jump-start a fire in a minute, nor do he explode with happiness in snow."

But Mary, sitting in a stupor, told him that the old woman reading her fortune seemed like a second ago. So then the prophecy was just a second past as well.

"The earth is just a second past," Buckler said. "Everything in it and about it is just a second past."

"I can remember Joanna's eyes looking at me as she spoke—" Mary said.

Her major concern was Owen.

"What will they do with Owen," she whispered, "what will they do?"

The next day, the police finding the ticket to Montreal, hearing of Owen giving money to Camellia, refused him bail.

The two hundred dollars he had given Camellia was increased exponentially by gossip to twenty-four hundred by late afternoon. The kiss in Camellia's house was all that was spoken about, and never spoken about as just a kiss.

That night, Mary went to the jail where they had taken her son.

There Owen, in front of the old jailer, admitted striking the man.

"I must have," he said without emotion.

"But you didn't mean to kill him," Mary said.

"No—" Owen responded, "of course not."

It was not in Owen's nature to be disposed to easy violence. And if he had wanted to, there would have been a hundred ways to deal with Solomon Hickey—alone, so no one would trace it back. That is, if he had wanted to. However, people decided he had gone there to get the man who had spread rumors against him and Camellia. Once that idea became established, it was difficult to see any other motive. It also meant that the rumors were true. They were as true now for Cora Auger as they were for Camellia's uncle Sterling. The gossip had gone through a metamorphosis, from stage to stage, until it flowered into something—unrelenting, from the top of the town to the bottom.

"The scandal now has broke wide open—everywhere—across the province," Mary piped up. "They are searching the shore for Reggie Glidden—near the cave where you two met and planned it."

"Mom, we didn't plan it—and didn't meet in the cave."

But she simply shrugged. She looked at her son, and with her kind eyes on him asked: "You didn't have anything to do with Reggie, did you? You didn't bust him over the head too? I mean, kill one, kill two is what they are saying—it's kind of revved them all up."

Owen looked at her and smiled. "No," he said.

She left him discouraged at asking this, aware of her great duty to protect her family, and how Camellia's encouragement to take her son from the train had caused it all.

Mary now realized the prophecy was not neat and orderly, but was like sin, circuitous and involved, and in the end, deadly. It was a misshapen kind of animal that had attached itself to them all, a strange parasite that traveled on the breath from the mouth of gossip. Nothing could be done now to prove the prophecy real—it was mundanely and sufficiently incognito.

And all held together by some incalculable chance meeting last evening, which had caused what the old First Nations lady had said years before. It had caused "rashness by the second boy." This rashness was to turn and strike a man whose neck was soft. The strike was meant, without knowing how soft the neck was. The prophecy made before either was born. Still and all, it was rash, and took a life. The body went limp beside the strands of hair he had recently cut from the head of Billy Pebbles, who walked back into the store at that moment to retrieve his cigarette lighter, left on the barber chair.

Owen had looked at the body quickly—and then had made an enormously rash statement: "If you say anything, the same will happen to you."

Owen was later to state to his lawyer that he did not know Solomon was dead, and he was not telling Mr. Pebbles to not report it to the police—he was simply saying that Billy Pebbles should not make any statements about Camellia Glidden's virtue.

Owen was not silent about why this had happened. He told his mother that the comb's point—which was the prophecy refined to its finest insistency—must have driven into his side on the very wound that caused his nerves to burn and made it hard to walk. When this happened, he must have lost sight of any rationale. (Dr. Hennessey verified this a few days later, although Owen did not really remember it.)

"Mom," he called as she left.

"Yes."

"You wouldn't have a train you could carry me back out on, do you?"

He was in the same cell Camellia's father had been in seventeen years before.

People suddenly rejoiced at Owen's downfall.

"Yer son will hang, Mary—just like the whore's own dad," she heard as she walked through the town. She turned just in time to see an upstairs window closing over a grocery store.

Why had this woman come into their lives, Mary now thought. If she was smart even now, she would put her out into the street. She remembered when she first came, a tiny girl with an innocent smile. She tried so hard to please everyone, did her duty always, just in order to belong. Mary remembered being at the wedding. How tiny Camellia had looked beside Reggie. They said she did not really want to get married and was under unspoken, unseen pressure.

"If she didn't want to, she should have said no—it's that simple," Mary said, exonerating herself as people tend to do as soon as a crisis arrives.

A woman did as a woman did, or a "woman had her ways," and Mary knew this. "Women don't fool me," she said.

So, as she went home she thought of this. The idea that Camellia was playing games suddenly obsessed her. After all this time, how could she think this? Well, she thought it because others did, because she was in a bind, because Camellia had smiled and clapped her hands when she heard the train was to be stopped, and because it had been foretold.

Camellia had come to the family and Mary had taken her in. Her father was a murderer—now it had happened again! Camellia was a walking enticement to have sex and commit murder.

These were Mary's thoughts as she climbed the steps, and when she saw Camellia at the door waiting, twisting a Kleenex and looking as if in shock, she reacted:

"Please, you have done more than enough—bamboozling my son—please, please go away."

Camellia stepped back as if hit. She staggered a little.

"Mary I would never—I didn't," she said in her sad voice that still sounded like a child. This too, this voice like a child, was trickery—and her praying to the Virgin! What nonsense was that!

"You don't know what you would or would not do—" Mary said. "You don't know. You're the one I've always worried about," Mary continued, smiling a little self-consciously. "You're the carrier of the seed of destruction!"

Camellia went home. Every few steps she stopped in the middle of the sidewalk that was plowed down to ice and stone, and would stand petrified for minutes at a time. Then, as if wounded, she would take another few steps. But even at this most vulnerable moment she was seen by her uncle and looked upon as a charlatan—because he himself had always been one.

Sterling was standing alongside a huge snowdrift under a light, smoking.

"Oh," she said, "Uncle Sterling—can you help me?"

He, her uncle so used to taking from her, was only silent now, as if she had severely disappointed him. Sterling looked at his cigarette ash and commented, "Oh, have no fear—we'll figure it all out, girl—you just wait and see."

As for Mr. Brower, he was informed what the betrayal of his daughter had led to.

"Yes," he said, "I knew it would."

EIGHT

The men in the camp—on a mountain forty-five miles away—had hired on for one thing only this year. They were men, none of whom would be hired by Estabrook or Sloan. They had only one boss; they worked for Will Jameson—and now his brother, out of respect. They were themselves forsaken by others. They themselves did not know of the events happening in town.

Each day they did a job that would make most men turn pale. Each day each of them did what was expected without complaint. The morning Owen was taken to jail, the temperature on their hill had fallen to minus thirty-eight.

Trethewey, Richardson, Nolan, and Curtis were each up an hour before dawn.

Trethewey was a gray-haired black man who had come here from Nova Scotia. He had a picture on the wall of his daughter, whom he had not seen in years, drink or mischief had caused his white wife to flee back to Nova Scotia, so he stayed alone with his great Percherons up at a camp near the Dungarvan. He had by chance received a letter from his wife, a retired teacher at a normal school in Windsor, Nova Scotia. He opened it in excitement only to discover how she cursed him, accused him of terrible things.

"You will never see Milly again," the letter stated, referring to his daughter.

So he came to work for Jameson on Good Friday.

"You are too old to go up there," someone said. He had only shrugged.

He had with him a bowl, a cup, and a spoon that he had used since 1915. He did not know this would be his last year to need them.

Richardson had a picture on the wall. It was him as a young man, taken just the day before he lost his left arm. Though people said his right arm was as strong as two, and did the work of two, it was filled with pain now—his muscles torn and his elbow ruined from hitting the timbers when he lashed the whip forward. He had come in for one reason, to take the largest load down the hill and prove what he could do, though for the last four months he had had visions of his own death.

Nolan had a picture of his Belgians in gold harness at a show and a ribbon on their bridles, to say he had hauled the largest load ever hauled on the river. But that was years ago, in 1933. Now almost no one would hire him. Only Jameson on Good Friday.

Curtis had a map pinned where no picture stood. At twenty-two he was seemingly too young for pictures. He wanted to go down to California. He thought of stagecoach riding in the movies. He thought of himself and Clark Gable drinking in a bar.

"What could you say to Clark Gable?" Tomkins derided him.

"I'd like to know what Mr. Gable could ever say to me," Curtis replied.

The highest load here this year—one taken by Trethewey atop the Percherons—was about 260 logs, almost the same amount you would put on a skid near the river. It took the men six hours to load it well, and Trethewey went down over the hill almost at dark, and traveled the eight miles alone and then back, not coming to supper until long after lights out and the stove cold.

"You look like a white feller," they laughed. And he did—even his chest seemed white.

Richardson wanted to do better by fifty logs. He would do so just because he had one arm, and had been teased because of it. That was his single motivation now.

A one-armed rider with the largest load ever drawn across a cut, larger than Nolan's in 1933. That might make the papers. That might make him forget.

He was going to do it for the McCord girl, who had left him within a day of his losing his arm.

"Don't you understand—" Nolan said. "You don't need to haul down any fuckin' load to prove bravery to her—"

Richardson shrugged and spit his plug.

"No matter."

If Richardson succeeded, many would hear nothing about it—if he failed, they would only hear that he was dead.

And within ten years every tool they used with such pride would be obsolete, scattered in a forgotten forest, traces and tack and treats for horses, lost forever underfoot. Become the object of ruthless historians like myself.

The next day Stretch (Tomcat) Tomkins stayed out on the flats stamping the timber. His job was ostensibly to mark the timber as Jameson.

The days were lasting a bit longer and the men were working longer hours, and the teamsters were traveling farther. They would come back up the frozen mount, the two sleds white and ghostly with hoarfrost.

Tomkins stayed out until after dark stamping logs. Then he went back to the hovel, feeling quickly for his money and looking suspiciously about. He had money with him, for as a spy for Estabrook he would tell how far ahead or behind they were—how good the wood was, and when they would get it to the mill. He had been paid $350 extra to play Judas by stamping as many rods of cedar as he could with an E. He hid this stamp down on the flat, and traded the Jameson stamp for it when he got there. Each night walked back to the camp with the Jameson stamp—nothing more than a peavey with the company's name on the bottom. Each piece of wood he stamped would go to Estabrook's boom in the spring. But Tomkins was anxious about this—for if anyone caught him, he would be beaten to a pulp. It was perhaps the most deceitful thing to do.

"How would they ever know?" Estabrook had told him smiling, over Christmas holidays when he had invited Tomkins to his house with the caribou racks and the sensation of an old lumber baron's world having seen better times.

"Don't worry—just think of yourself as a teamster they treated poorly. And think of yer mom and dad—they should have something as well—"

"Of course," Tomkins said, "of course."

After supper he went about his business, looking at no one and thinking of his future. Three hundred and fifty extra dollars was a good amount; two hundred extra promised for his father and a promise in writing of being a teamster for the Estabrook cut next year.

The men played cards and sang—and listened to the horrible wind—until well after nine o'clock. Then slowly, their bodies aching, their entire lives dependent on those bodies, they struggled into bed, and the main lanterns were turned down.

Tomkins thought of porridge with dark brown sugar sprinkling down from the roof as he drifted off to sleep. He thought of his father always angry because he didn't measure up.

"Porridge," he thought, "porridge tomorrow morning!"

The trouble with porridge and brown sugar drifting you off to sleep, is sometimes, on occasion, it isn't brown sugar but flak from the ceiling, and a flue fire has caught in the eves because of the scowling northwest wind, sending those little pieces of flak down upon you. Then you are up and scrambling out the door into the cold arctic air, while men are trying to put out blue flames licking across the ceiling.

"Come, Mr. Tomkins, come," Meager Fortune was saying. He woke to the sound of hell all about him. Smoke and flame shot out of the bunk above him, and smoke billowed nearby.

Tomkins grabbed at his heavy coat, and lost half his money in the flames. (He had carried it all on him into camp like a child wanting to hide it from and impress the others.)

"My God," he said, "I have to go back."

"Never mind that now—what you lose isn't worth you life," Nolan said, giving him a cuff.

"How dare you?" Tomkins yelled. "How dare you—I don't need to take that."

Once outside he saw Fraser and Gibbs up on the roof kicking at the burning timbers, and Pitman hauling these timbers down into the snow. He sat by himself and watched the men kick and scramble to try to keep their lives intact.

Before twelve that night all of them were outside salvaging what they could, throwing water on the north side of the camp, hollering to bring the horses away from the hovel nearest them because of smoke. Two of the Belgians were blinded and frantic, but the Percherons were brought out without lead and simply ran down along the shine to the gully where they would be brought back at dawn. The other horses were fine, away to the north, and it was there the men took shelter. But Butch stood at the front of the hovel, his back smoldering, and the smell of burning horse hair powerful. The tend team Gibbs jumped from the cabin roof, ran through the snow with a bucket, and jumped aside a two sled in order to reach his back. The horse grunted when the ice-frozen water splashed over it, and reared, tossing the boy backward and knocking him cold—but the smoldering was done.

Trethewey rushed in to grab the picture of his daughter, and came out with his white hair singed and his huge black chest dotted with sparks that went out in the wind, like stars going out in the sky. Richardson had lost the only picture he had of himself with two good arms.

Tomkins sat on the ground in his bare feet, socks in hand, each foot almost entirely covered in snow, cursing and shivering, and worried.

They had managed to stop the fire—and had enough provisions in the storeroom to continue.

Besides, Innis the portager was supposed to be in with staples and mail this week.

The main thing was the boots—two of the cutters had lost theirs, and Tomkins had been sure his were gone as well, except Meager Fortune rescued them for him. They were singed and looked odd, but they fit.

"Did you get my money," he whispered, "did you get my money?"

"I didn't see any money."

Tomkins searched the snow with his bare hands, looking at Meager and saying, "You stole my money."

"No one stole your money," Trethewey said.

But Tomkins kept moving the snow back and forth, looking to see if it had made it out, his lips wet, his face frantic.

"Half of it's gone," he said, "I'm down by half."

And he looked at them all with a curious and weak kind of confiding, nodding first to one and then the other.

"Where would you get all that money?" Curtis asked.

The fire caused the four in Gravellier's crew to decide this was a sign of providence to go out. They spoke of ghosts and messages, and warnings and signs. They spoke of the death of Dan Auger and how it would haunt them.

"No man should work for Jameson after Auger," Gravellier said.

Colson, the spokesman for Gravellier's crew, said he had no reason to stay on a mountain without a place to sleep to bring heavy wood down a hill that would break the back of the horse that stumbled.

The other three with him said the same. Gravellier stood in the center of the black yard as if something or someone had just displeased him.

"I toldum," he said, "I toldum."

Then they all went back to the original argument: The road should have gone around. Any true teamster would have known this, and have been safe. It was as if they argued that not going around had caused the flue fire.

Well, the camp was built in a place that caused the flue fire because of the horror of constant wind. They should never have been on the mountain—or at least taken time to construct a safer camp.

Even as they spoke now, the wind blew their clothes and scattered burnt embers upward in a gale, like specters shooting upward out of a circle of hell.

Tomkins did not know what to do, whether to stay or go—though he knew he must stay, for he had taken money, and promised Estabrook he would stay.

He stood in the dark, alone, watching those about him, when a man yelled "yahoo" to them out of the gloom.

It was the portager, Mr. Innis, in on two roans in the dark with letters and provisions. The first they had seen in well over two weeks. Innis had not waited until tomorrow, but had left earlier in the day, for he must tell them of the trouble their boss was in.

As he approached from the long flat, he had seen the flames.

They stood under the tight flare of lantern light and listened to him, while some opened their mail, the horses that hauled him panting and drenched.

He was tall as a ghost with a bent back, and his hands swollen and blackened by years of holding on to the reins. He spoke in his stutter about a death, a murder—and for what—

"A piece of tail," Innis said.

"Who is with us now?" Colson hollered, feeling very much vindicated. Colson, a small man with a wizened face, always deferred to others about what might be right or wrong, and acted only when others were on his side.

Innis looked at the camp and shook his head. He had seen the flames and thought he might have to bring out some bodies.

"We are not dead yet," Trethewey said. "We will tie up tents to the cedar here" (he pointed to the old cedar shaped like a cross) "and bring the tarps across to the front of the camp, and work to get it back in order—we'll be cozy enough."

"I'm here to warn you," Innis advised, "I just heard it. You will have a bad blow up here—storm is coming in off St. Lawrence. It will close you down on this here mountain like never before—you might not get off it, and no one will be able to get in for you."

"No, we will stay," Nolan said, "we have worked in snow before."

"But if four are going out, how will you get half the wood

yarded?" Innis asked—for he was hoping not to have to make this terrible trip again.

But Nolan's four had decided they would stay.

So the axmen and the tend teams decided as much, and the cook brought out soup and they had it by two a.m., while the four going out—and two besides—made themselves a shelter near the storeroom, and shared the soup as well. Behind them, three cedar trees rose high up in a circumference of stumps and thrashed roots, logs and limbs, for miles.

Bartlett, being a practical and punctilious man, was already deciding how to fell the trees in the huge dark lot behind these—for this was the major cedar vale that would lead them down the far side of the mountain.

In this cedar vale stood Richardson after going to fetch Curtis's horses, which he had seen rush down. Here he was alone, staring at those huge trees that rose up from beneath him. He was thinking of 310 logs; 310 would be a championship load. Then the woman he had lost in Strathadam, the McCord woman who left him, would know his feat.

Innis had told them the rumor was that Estabrook's wood was no good. The cedar was filled with sand, hemlock tottering and rotted up to the branches, and worms in the spruce. No one knew how it was ruined, but Estabrook, happy to get it, never much decided to inspect it.

"It's as if a plague came to it the day Will died," Innis said. For ghosts and hyperbole went together in the dark.

Here it was much better. It was in fact the largest and best wood seen on this river since the great Miramichi fire.

Jameson's scaler had been in. The cedar had no sand, hemlock no rot—at least not too far up, and so if they stayed all would be well.

"It is bona fide," Nolan said, smiling.

Tomkins now knew why Estabrook, who could have had any lease he wanted, had Tomkins doing what he did.

The next morning Innis and the four teamsters left just after dawn. Meager Fortune had made them breakfast. The men staying were already working, and the tents they had in the storehouse were already set up, stretched down from that big cedar cross, comfortable enough but not a camp. Those staying reminded Meager of a dispatch of bedraggled soldiers. The one in the worst mood was Tomkins, who threw the cup of tea Meager had handed him.

But another cup was passed to Tomkins. He knew now that he could not escape. He had already taken $350—a fortune for him, though counting it up he had lost more than a hundred in the fire. He had been promised more if he stayed the course.

A glaze of frost sat on each two sled three inches thick, and pools of frozen black water had collected in all those places the men had danced the hootenanny two nights before, drinking off the last bottled beer.

Seeing Mr. Innis's portage sled teetering along on the flat, hauled by his skinny roans, made it seem to some of the youngsters too proud to say they wanted to go home as if humanity was leaving them in the figure of that tall, aloof, somewhat prurient man. They watched this man until his body became speck and then speck disappeared.

The wind called out hilariously at their expense, saying through the treetops: "*It will snow.*"

Tomcat Tomkins, more than any, wanted to be gone too.

PART V

ONE

Long before Owen had gone to the barbershop, long before he had seen this as anything troubling, long before that, friends had already warned Camellia not to "act up." At least a few, though generous themselves, had gotten caught up in it all themselves and needed for their own sake to come to her rescue. They needed once again, even though some were as stunned as doorknobs, to show her the way.

So the Steadfast Few, as Lula had dubbed them in happier days, led by the one who wrote Lula the letter about Owen and Camellia's affair, went to Camellia's house and knocked on the door. They had a long meeting at Susan Gladstone's house before they did this. And decided, all holding hands, that if one went down to that place near the docks then by God all of them would. So, all of them stood together on the doormat in the coming dark and knocked while Camellia, sick for days, felt now like a trapped animal.

"She is in danger of slipping back into that world," one said as they had walked in single file along the snow-filled pathway, teetering this way and that and holding their hats. What world were they referring to? Who knows, for they themselves did not.

They were as pained by her poor surroundings as by what they eventually had to say. They looked only to one another for comfort—doing this for her stepfamily, those illusively proud Browers.

"You're a married woman," one said, suddenly smiling corruptly. "And you know how we care for you. You have to try to behave yourself before people begin to talk."

"Who cares for me?" Camellia asked.

"Why, dear, all of us—yes—don't we, girls! And we were the ones who did so much for you when you were getting married—"

The idea that outrage comes with moral certitude and without self-interest is in itself the harbinger of self-interest.

"Go," she whispered.

"Pardon us, dear?"

"I said go—" Camellia said, going to the door. "Go the hell away. Goodbye—you are SUCH FRIENDS—Will Jameson was right—schoolmarms for schoolmarms, he said, and he was goddamn right!"

So the Steadfast Few went away waiting for the hammer to fall, and knowing happily it wouldn't fall on them. And three of them were in fact teachers, and schoolmarms well enough. They traipsed back up that narrow path toward the center of town in single file, holding on to their hats, tch-tching that woman and that desperate world.

But though Camellia would break out laughing in the night as one does at people's terrible suppositions about them, and how wrong supposition could be, she was still broken-hearted.

Yet now that it had happened, now that all this had occurred, her few acquaintances could take up the rod against her. Which is exactly what the scandal was for in the first place. And her laughing at them was even more disastrous for her. So why shouldn't they condemn her now—they saw very quickly it was to their advantage to do so.

Besides, anyone who did not join in their condemnation was now suspect of having no feeling toward Lula Brower, the jilted fiancée of Owen Jameson. And this was the main issue—their own feelings of disloyalty toward their friend Lula over the last few years. Camellia was a way to make it up.

"Look how Lula always tried to help her," Miss Donnehy said. And they hurried on into the dark, tottering over the slippery ice.

"We must stop the rumor," another said, "for Lula's sake." This being the rumor that Camellia was well knocked up by Owen Jameson that all of them had started a month before, for Lula's sake.

"Yes, yes, yes."

Lula had been kept in the dark for a long time about these rumors, too. She, they said, was too sensitive to know, and it would break her heart to know, for she loved Owen Jameson so much. And as they all said: "We thought he liked books—well, this just goes to show!"

Just as they had told her that Owen was coming back to marry her—just as they had said this was a certainty, now they let it slip over the next few days to this woman that Camellia was pregnant with Owen's child.

"Then if it is Owen's, I feel sorry for them," Lula said.

"Just never you mind, dear," the one who visited her said.

None tormented Lula more than those who were trying to protect her.

"Marriage to her is nothin'—not even a blessed sacrament—more like a snot rag, I figure," Sterling said about his niece, blowing his big red nose in the middle of the street and running to the priest. Ah, the priest caught shit over this later, but the priest must comfort those who call—and though there are bad priests, the best ones always have, even poor Sterling who now had the support of the entire town.

Camellia knew the rumor, and knew the rumor wasn't true. Yet for her to go to confession and not confess adultery would be seen as sacrilege. So she did not go, and did not confess, and was seen by old nuns and old parishioners not to have gone, and not to have confessed.

But on the seventy-seventh day of the haul, Camellia went to see Owen.

An old man, a neighbor who liked her, the grandfather of the Foley girl, told her she shouldn't visit if she wanted to keep perception of innocence. But she could not do this to Owen Jameson.

"Then go, girl," he said, "and never mind them."

Even before she got to Jail Street, a crowd spotted her.

"His lovebird has come—so hang her too—fer Reggie's sake," a woman shouted.

"She's got the devil right in her guts—" another yelled.

"Hang 'em back to back—the whore," one of the men said.

Crossman stood as soon as she came in, and walked toward her—quickly, as if to frighten her. But then he calmed himself; though the very look of her enraged others now, he was suddenly sorry for her. And so he smiled in spite of himself and asked how she was, asked if she was feeding herself for she looked sick—said he remembered she played the piano so well, did she play it now? Now, she said, she had no piano to play, but she could play and did play the spoons, at night by herself in her room. Then she laughed at this absurdity.

He looked at her old coat, her small hat, her ratty boots run down on the heels, and smiled again.

He was the one who had arrested her father, Les Dupuis, after he had killed his wife. It was a very strange day, that day seventeen years ago—how it clouded the town and the entire river. Dupuis had come home from work, gone to the cave and caught his wife waiting for someone. There in Winch's cave he pulled his knife and she was dead in a second. Not having wanted to kill her, seeing her plain drab face, worn down over the years by work, her small hands she held up to prevent him, he took the knife and stabbed himself. He bled on the stones but did not die.

Camellia was at home, waiting for them to come back, and bore the terrible knowledge of death at an early age. In school she was teased viciously by a few who wanted to lash out at the world.

"Who could make anything of such a disaster?" one reporter for the Halifax paper wrote at the time.

Well, in a certain way, Crossman knew, many people—even the reporter from the Halifax paper. Looking at her in her small hat and half-scared eyes, he realized this. That is, everyone involved had taken whatever they could from Camellia, to further their own ambition. He remembered her alone in a gale of wind, at the crossroads waiting to hear the sentence against her father. Everyone left the court jubilant at his death sentence. When she saw their jubilation, she thought he had been declared innocent and became jubilant too. This very picture of her was used against her father's appeal. YOUNG CAMELLIA, ORPHANED BY MURDER, REJOICES.

Before he was hanged Les Dupuis made an appeal to the town for someone to take in his daughter. Everyone at every juncture hesitated, and it seemed as if she would follow the road down to the orphanage of the Sisters of Charity. But Brower made the humane gesture, which was written about across the country. He who had sent Dupuis to his death would now care for the girl. It was a kind and noble thing he did.

Once they heard of Owen's greatness in battle, Brower completely changed his opinion about the boy, longed to see him again, and convinced Lula they were engaged because of that small brooch. Lula clutched this brooch like a drowning girl. There was, however, Camellia—who was not engaged, who was beautiful, and who had written Owen during the war.

"So get her married," Crossman said glibly.

"How?" Brower asked.

Crossman thought a moment.

"Well, I have a man in my cell. Reggie Glidden. Glidden always liked her—it might straighten them both out."

The idea that it would straighten them both out was appealing.

Brower told Camellia about Glidden that afternoon.

"Oh I know him, he's Owen's friend—just let him out of jail and tell him to come and see me," she said excitedly, thinking they wanted her to help a friend of Owen, for the interest Owen had shown in saving him.

Crossman let the man out. Brower bought him a suit. Glidden came to the house. He and Camellia sat together, and Glidden came back, and again came. Within a month everyone considered them betrothed. For certain, Brower did.

Camellia's kindness had done her in.

Mary Jameson then hired her—because she was betrothed to Reggie.

"I have a job," Camellia said, "can you imagine? I finally can earn some money—and won't be such a bother anymore!"

"You see how everything works out?" Lula smiled.

Secretly Camellia knew they wanted her gone. Her beauty too stark a reminder.

She went to her wedding night—a white dress second-hand, and a small complement of people she hardly knew. Brower giving her away with the stiff formality of a preacher.

A rainstorm came and made the ground murky. The reception was held in a little hall Mary Jameson had rented for them, where the lights over the center table had been burnt out. Reggie got drunk and was too frightened to make a speech. When he fell down, people started to titter.

"Off on the right foot!" someone yelled.

"Now she's settled," one of the Steadfast Few said to Lula, squeezing her hand in sudden conspiracy. "Thank God for that."

This idea that Camellia was at risk with men was an easy one to maintain. Think of her mother.

The one thing Lula and her father were silent about was the fact that they had heard from the colonel who wasn't in the field that heroic day that Owen Jameson was coming home. They heard it two weeks before the marriage.

Crossman remembered Camellia's white blouse with the small cross on her neck, three days before her marriage. Seeing this same blouse and cross tonight, he knew they all had betrayed her.

But that did not stop him from believing she was guilty.

TWO

Owen looked tragically small in the cell—his broad forehead, his head prematurely balding. He was like the high school student she once remembered, the outcast, all over again. He had returned to his former place without even much of a whimper. Bail had been refused because of the train ticket they had found him with.

It would seem that those schoolmarms who had so refuted the books he once read had been proven right. All that mocking of those diligent teachers proved to them their own worth now.

As always, you learn more about the subject you have killed within the hours following his death. Buckler had told him all he had found out: Solomon had been preparing to buy the barbershop and propose to Lula, who lived in a reclusive shell at the back of the house. Each week with his pay in a brown envelope he would head to the bank and meticulously make out his deposit slip in the pedestrian certainty of a happy life. But her father had put an end to that as soon as they heard Owen might be coming home.

"My daughter is not marrying a barber—I'll stake my life on that," he said.

Another fact was that Solomon Hickey had had an abscessed tooth since Christmas, and his pain may have propelled him to stick the comb in Owen.

Owen was sorry, said he would never have opened the barbershop door if he had known, but there was little or nothing he could do now.

It was already growing dark, and the streetlights made the snow glitter—like a frozen engine, the outside had ground to a halt.

Owen was happy to see Camellia, of course. But she had come to tell him something. Something else had just happened today, the seventy-seventh of the haul. This is why the crowd had gathered outside.

"What more could?" he smiled. "The main camp has been burned and four teamsters have run away—only Buckler's old standbys remain."

So she told him.

They needed her help in identifying a body that had been found by Matheson the day before.

"Where was it found?" Owen asked.

"A mile or two down from the cave, washed up on shore," she said. "By Mr. Matheson—but I guess it is all wrecked and they need someone to say who it is."

"It cannot be Reg," Owen said whispering, almost in horror. "It could be anyone—maybe a logger caught up in last years run—or— Who knows, Camellia—but it has to be someone else—"

"I don't know—" she said, her eyes welling up with tears.

"Why can't they tell? It's all for show!" he said, suddenly enraged at how everything was turning.

"I don't know—I have to go down to the morgue—where is it?"

"In—the hospital somewhere, I think."

"Everything is spiraling out of control—why is that?" she asked with sudden calmness. "Even your mother thinks I'm a bad woman now. I married Reggie because he was Will's best friend—and now—they are the first to accuse me of not loving him!"

He thought of what she had just said and realized what an outcast she must have been.

"I'm sorry," he said. Her small dark hat pressed down on her head, a show of that compulsion to understand through ornament something about our own relationship with the deadly world, and inspired him to reach through the bars and lightly touch her cheek.

Yet given any other circumstance he might think just like the town. This puzzled and frightened him.

"Don't worry," he said.

They were silent.

"Then take this back," she said, handing him Saint Jude's medal.

"Why, for Christ's sake?" he whispered in the dim, small corridor, so the sound seemed to echo off the chipped paint and exposed cement. "I'm not a religious man, and I certainly am not a Catholic."

She sat for a moment, not making any motion, looking as if someone had failed her. Seeing this, he put his hands through the bar and took the medal and chain from her hands.

"There—so what do I pray for now?"

"Pray it is not Reggie—as impossible as it seems, pray that Reggie is still alive."

For an hour after she left he had the Saint Jude medal in his hand. When Monroe came back in, he told him of the body. It was amazing that Matheson had found what he had in that current.

"Its like God wanted it so," Monroe said, sniffing as if he suddenly had an open line to God, and sniffed in his likeness.

Owen looked at him without comment but Monroe smiled as he walked quickly by, staring in as he went, his hands lightly touching the bars and speaking more rapidly than he had ever done with almost a wild grin on his face. He was exuberant, carefree, and pent-up emotion now spilled out: "We got old footprints and fingerprints and hair samples, and everything. You should see what we gone and got, Owen. Well—there you have it. You betrayed your family name and killed two men. After the whole town took you in their arms. All this," he said, as he moved rapidly away, "for a piece of French twat—a common cunt from the gutter is all she is."

And then he disappeared and the light went out.

The trouble with having the overhead light out is that in this darkness, three or four rats made their way into his cell each night.

THREE

There is a picture of Camellia Dupuis on the arm of officer-in-training Constable Monroe that same evening. The constable is slightly ahead of her, impeccably groomed, his free arm bent at the elbow to keep the curious back, and she is looking at the camera, wearing that black coat with the fur collar turned up. Though a torn, old coat, it looks new in the picture. That is, the picture makes her look like someone she never was, nor ever attempted to be.

Her dark hair is wavy, her eyes are cast up toward us. The closest you might come to it is the picture of the Black Dahlia—the woman in Los Angeles murdered about the same time. Both are striking women, both have a look of seductive charm, both are walking into a dark they cannot comprehend. This was the picture, then, that would be published alongside the seventeen-year-old picture of herself as a child, during the story of her father. The articles would state—from the Canadian wire service to the BBC—the strange coincidences, and how her adoptive father, who had once thought of becoming a minister, would now have to prosecute her. And because he was a religious man, he did not hesitate or fear the death penalty.

The story was heightened by acknowledging that Owen had been Lula's sweetheart before the war.

GOOD SAMARITAN VICTIM OF LOVE TRIANGLE? the question posed now.

Constable Monroe knew the seriousness of these allegations—that is, that Owen and she had somehow committed a perfect crime, a theory promoted for over a month by Reggie's cousin, who had been added to the list of prosecution witnesses and had come to town on government expense to view the body as well. Monk's theory was the one to take hold—Reggie would be the last person to commit suicide. He must have been lured to his death by Camellia. He had come home to protect her, and had fallen victim to her snare. There was the idea that they had tried to put him in a trunk, and finally threw him into the water alone and still alive.

"Yes, that's it," people said, as if suddenly becoming wise. "Yessir, I can see it now."

The provincial paper ran the picture of Camellia on Monroe's arm and the headline stated: CAMELLIA ON WAY TO VIEW HUSBAND'S BODY—HAVING LEFT THE CELL OF ACCUSED MURDERER OWEN JAMESON.

She had become a single name to the province, and Owen's lover. The headline already indicting both.

This had become a thriller of the town's own making, each person playing a prescribed part. To continue to the end the thriller could not end. It had to continue in its relentless gravity. Monroe kept this picture and showed it around for the rest of his life.

"I'm still your friend," one young woman she knew as a convent girl shouted, and waved slightly her thin hand into the vacant lot, while her boyfriend told her to shut her mouth.

FOUR

The morgue was a room beneath the hospital where the coroner and medical examiner had small glass-partitioned rooms with typewriters and charts and blotters. They were used to it, but it was all new and dreadful to Camellia Dupuis.

There was water on the cement hallway floor, collecting about a plugged drain. Overhead light bulbs were incased in wire mesh. The morgue proper was off to the left, through a heavy leaded door with a huge latch.

Despite steeling herself for this, Camellia needed to be held up by Monroe. The body was on the table in this small cement room that smelled of blood and antiseptic. A sheet covered it. The coroner—Mackey, a transparent and fussy man with fuzzy blond hair and weakened milky eyes—stood beside it, looking at her. Behind him was a large white basin. To one side of that a calendar from May 1939, the month Will Jameson had died. There were other deaths, of course—but the two recent ones were the first murders in town since Mrs. Dupuis.

And it seemed absolutely obvious to them that Camellia, the murderer's daughter, would be caught up in it. All the signs had been there from the time she was a girl—passed over then with reservation to be appraised now. Her peals of laughter at the convent, sitting in detention four hours a week—all the signs never thought about until something like this was done.

Each of these men wondered how she would react. This was a typical point of pride with them. There was no way she could act that wouldn't be deemed culpable if they themselves decided such.

"Well, are we here," Mackey said.

She looked straight ahead as the sheet was taken off.

"You see why we need you here."

She glanced at the body, understood and nodded. It was a man whose face was battered and partially missing. It lay with blackened fingers turned toward her. The silence in the room was profound.

"Can you tell?"

She nodded.

"You can tell it's Reggie Glidden?"

"It is not my Reggie," she whispered.

"Your Reggie. Mr. Monk, his closest relative, said today it is Reggie's body," the coroner said.

"It is not Reggie," she said breathing quickly through her nose, a terrible scent of antiseptic decay.

"It is not Reggie's—I mean, you would still say it wasn't Reggie's—maybe you didn't even know he was going to do it—perhaps—" Crossman said, hoping for an admission where he could snare her and yet still have compassion for the memory of her as an innocent child, "perhaps you did not think he was capable of this?"

"I did not think the town capable of this," she retorted in French, the one thing from her father she had not lost, that for the sake of his memory and her mother's she had held on to throughout the difficult and lowly years.

They kept her another ten minutes, but she said nothing else.

The coroner covered the body, and she was led away. Once beyond the door, Mackey confronted her.

"Tell us why we should believe you," he said, "when Mr. Brower don't."

"I long ago knew truth was not dependent on Mr. Brower," she said. It was the harshest statement she had ever made against him, and caught them by surprise. But there once was a night when Mr. Brower had made a pass at a sixteen-year-old girl, which she never mentioned.

"He brought you up," Mackey said, astounded—wanting more than anything to show that he was a part of her contrite accusers.

She said, "I am aware of that. And I know Reggie is not like that—he is not—circumcised. And you could see where Reggie's left arm had mended—because he broke it baling hay—and his forearms were bigger—and his right arm damaged because they threw pulp sticks at him. His head, too, is bigger. I have said it is not Reggie—you wanted to display this poor man's body to me—for some reason—to shock me into a confession—but it is not him."

"Do you even know what circumcision means?" Mackey asked sharply.

"I know Reggie was not," she said.

"Is Owen circumcised?" Mackey asked. Brand new to the town, he had to instill in others the fact that he was on their side. Never had anyone done this more slavishly.

She turned away from him and looked at Crossman, as if decency should prevail.

"That's enough," Crossman said.

Mackey did not say anything else.

"I want to go home," she said in French.

But there was one other thing that night.

As she left she fainted, and had to be brought to her feet.

She had never fainted before in her life. Of course, she had never been pregnant before either.

FIVE

On the second day after the body was found, Brower was in a bind.

He had an as yet unidentified body. The body, he believed, proved murder—the hit over the head had caused unconsciousness (the timbers beneath the wharf or something else had disfigured the face so identification was impossible)—whereas having the entire body might only establish suicide.

It was better, in fact, for the upcoming trial, to have a body without a face. The town was so outraged, it would be an easy victory. Brower knew this, and like a crocodile to the temperature became morbidly self-righteous. He did not mean to, but he could not fight it. He ate his lunch at his desk out of a brown paper bag. He drank water out of the small fountain down the hall.

The impression the town had was of a betrayal of all he himself had taught this child Dupuis: to be kind, good, and generous to others.

"What's worse," they said, "is he'll have to prosecute her now."

What was more proof was this: The body had no coat, which accommodated the coat, with the blood-stained sleeve, left on the wharf. It had no boots either, but that was a small enough matter.

Then, for a while, Brower was silent. And he said to his assistant: "As for the case with Solomon Hickey, I might be in a bind—"

As for the case with Solomon Hickey; over the last week he discovered two witnesses, a Clinton Dulse and a Maufat McDurmot, on their way home from the hockey rink had passed the barbershop at the very moment. They had both rushed in and tried to stop the dispute, and grabbed Owen when no one else would go near him. Brower was very happy to gain from these men, but he was ultimately disappointed by what they said.

Both said that Solomon Hickey had jabbed a sharp object against Owen Jameson's side (they thought it was the scissors, not the comb) when Owen was about to leave the shop, and you could see how much pain registered on his face.

"He just reacted—just like any one of us would do," Maufat McDurmot said. "And I don't think he meant to hurt nobody."

This is what Owen had already explained to Crossman.

Then there was something else that the prosecutor must think about.

The defense would bring up this wound Owen had suffered in battle as a cause for his outrage.

By the seventy-fourth day of the cut (that is, before Matheson had located a body), Brower was ready to drop all charges. He told Lula that in the morning.

"Thank God—for Solomon's sake—I mean I felt it must have been an accident. A terrible thing that is all."

She smiled, one side of her face cruelly unable to.

Brower went to work with a heavy heart, until the body was found.

He telephoned his daughter that afternoon.

"I think it is far worse than even we had thought," he said.

The town, Lula especially, was suffering through a kind of horror. She decided she should go and see Camellia and offer her help.

But her father forbid her to.

"Not on your life," he said. "She flaunted herself in front of that man. She betrayed you as if you were a fly. She'll never be spoken of again in this house—so leave her to her own designs."

In fact, like Owen, and the rest of the town, Brower was now caught up in the same rumors, spread by the same people, exacting the same price. The rumors had covered him in the same net as it had everyone else, and he was struggling with them just the same as everyone else.

SIX

Owen refused to see anyone—even his lawyer, the bright young Mr. Pillar, recently come to town from Halifax.

"Oh, he'd get someone from Halifax—he is too good fer us," someone said. Yet no one here would take the case.

Pillar came each day at noon, once to show Owen his infant daughter Vera, dressed in a winter rabbit coat—the first birth on the Miramichi in 1947—but Owen did not wish to see him.

"I think we have a good solid case, Mr. Jameson—and I think the prosecution's case is in real jeopardy. I think we have a fair number of witnesses about Solomon, and they have no proof really about Reggie Glidden." Mr. Pillar said all of this as if he assumed that Owen was guilty but it was his job to find some way to get him off. This was the sensation he presented as he spoke. But this sensation itself wasn't entirely truthful—it was a way for the fresh young lawyer to play-act, to pretend that he was dealing with a dangerous murderer. This was the undercurrent of his subtle performance.

"Fine, Tommie—let me know how it goes," Owen said.

Owen refused to see Mary except to ask why she had put Camellia out of the house.

"For you—for you—you were caught up with her—she is a bad girl—and when they see you aren't caught up with her—say, if I give some money to charity and they see you are no longer caught up with her, they will let you go."

He refused to see her also. That is, Camellia. She was pregnant, and the rumor was with his love child. That they had done it in the cave, laughing and reading the letter Lula had written.

This became the paramount reason for the idea of guilt or murder and of their fleeing. Then there was the letter—not the letter Lula had written Owen but the other letter, even more indicative of their plans. The letter Reggie had from Estabrook, trying to hire him away. This was all Estabrook's doing—a way to steal away the best Push in camp. But it was looked upon from a different angle—a different Pythagorean law. The offer of the job must have been because of the concern Reggie naturally had over his men working Good Friday—Estabrook, knowing of this concern, had tried to help a good man out.

"And look what happens—"

Then a sudden inexplicable realization came to Owen, while eating his half-cold plate of stew, while white snow fell one late afternoon and watching a rat squeeze into his cell, hop sideways and disappear into a corner.

It was this: Some part of him was suspicious of Camellia also.

He tried not to be. But they had separated them and were now working on both. His mother had told him that he might be able to strike a deal if he would just give Camellia up, say it was her doing. He suspected this is what they were saying to her as well. In fact, for the last three weeks this is exactly what Sterling was telling her. "Do you want to have that kid in prison?" he would say.

Owen and Camellia were exactly what the town wanted them to be, and Owen had fallen into his role without even so much as a grimace.

He went into the exercise yard only because the jailer needed him to chop wood. The snow fell with dreary regularity. He showered in a separate room, with the nozzle frozen and a small window looking out at the bleak river.

After six at night he was left in darkness, with only one small light over the door. Now and then in the pitch dark someone would come in and throw cold water on him. Then rush out laughing hysterically. He knew by the footsteps it was Monroe.

He sat on his hard bunk soaking until dawn, worrying about the men on the mountain, worrying about the wood, about the new saws arriving at the mill, about the wiring job they needed done.

And now and again he thought about his life—the moment or series of moments which changed it. The folly of stepping down from the train was the worst act of random excess that had ever occurred to his feeble brain.

"Don't let his feet touch the ground!" he remembered them saying. How ironic, now, that this was a comment on hanging.

Had he ever been happy?

Well, of course.

He was happiest when an October sun lingered a moment on his glasses as he walked in an old London Fog coat through the back streets of some European city. He realized that in his loneliness he was at his happiest. Happiness was the moment of acceptance, of all the things said and to be said against your humanity by others not of your stripe; stupefied by you, or envious, or angered, or ashamed—whatever their moment for you, there was a moment in you that would accept it as it was, and come to terms with the universe. It was in the end, joy. If he had strength of character at all.

He knew this when he was sixteen and alone on the steps of the pantry stairs on a still hot June night in 1936 weaving in and out of trancelike melancholy, knowing that Lula did not love him.

He knew it when drunk among the gymnasium boys and girls he swung through his algebraic jungle, and left to the sound of squeaking shoes an hour before the rest.

And when he traveled after the war, the Victoria Cross with its lion and purple ribbon stuck deep within a pocket of his overcoat, rain trumpeting down upon the slate roofs of some city in the north of England, where fog lingered on the cobbles and lights flared and guttered in pubs filled with rough-hewn working girls and men home from war. That is when a moment came, spellbinding, blazing in its joy, the feeling replaced quickly by the dreary pattern of a rain-swept street, and then later that very night the fleeting memory of a childhood love who had not responded to him, and how he had become by one look she gave indifferent to her small tragedies.

When he found himself back among them, among she who had laughed or ignored him, he wanted—envy from her. A childish tit-for-tat, meaningless as the ragtag of human emotions felt by so many for others. Why was that necessary? It was—and he waited for the applause. For a moment then, people wanting to see him replaced the joy of being solitary—and more important, it replaced the joy of being truthful.

Still, in kindness he had set about helping Camellia. He could not do enough for her. She was Reggie's wife. Was that all he felt? No—but he felt it his business and no one else's.

When the gossip fell to her, he fell into the rage against slight that so many proud men have to guard against.

He had decided to live a solitary life. In part it was to prove the prophecy wrong. That is why he had been headed to Montreal on the train. Yet for some godforsaken reason the train was stopped. How silly to stop the train.

Even then, when the men came onto the train to get him, he had believed they were there for someone else. Even when he was being slapped on the back and called a hero, he knew in the flimsy autumn air, the cold storm clouds over his head, it could not last. It could not, yet he himself had run with it as long as it allowed. One would think he was clairvoyant to see it. Not at all—in every look from every person on that platform there was amid the wondrous joy a look of slight recrimination and warning—saying why hadn't this greatness been thrust upon someone they expected it to be—someone more like themselves—

Well, he couldn't say and so here he was.

Now the jailer told him that a huge storm was coming in.

Owen turned his back and stared out the window. The day was pulpy and warm. Finally he sat down on his bunk. He lighted a cigarette and thought. If only he knew what was happening to his men, now that the cutting was more than half through.

"I wish I was there to watch them," Owen said, so the jailer looked up from his magazine.

SEVEN

The sky was low, and all day a breeze warmed Tomkins' face, making him open his coat and stretch into the sun. He stayed out almost an hour after the last of the two sleds went back up the hill, stamping logs with Estabrook's stamp.

There was a smell of tin in the air, prevalent close to the night, and the dreary sound of the wind against his parka, like snow scattering on tarpaper. It was at about four when the wind started to turn a little cold. Tomkins hid the peavey with the wrong stamp, picked up the other one, and started toward the camp.

He was hungry and lonely and heading toward home along the skid road.

The sky had darkened and Tomkins was miles from anywhere, in a sad empty space unknown by ninety-nine percent of humanity. The cold now seeped through his jacket lining, where he kept the rest of his money.

He had been going to pick up a ride with the last two sled, but the two sled roared by in a whiff of winter horse and a clot of snow while he was doing his business in the woods. He had run out to call them but had tripped—and the old horses were gone. There would be another two sled along—Curtis's—but not for two or three hours—well after dark Curtis would make his way back, with a lantern light up near his horses fore shoulders, dangling on a peculiar makeshift rod. It was a way to tell Curtis from all the others. But Tomkins, looking behind him into the desolate emptying of the day, saw nothing. He worried about panthers. For they were still here, in these great lost woods.

His boots were soaking, his fingers raw.

He turned and began to walk on boots almost frozen toward the camp miles away.

He zippered his coat as tight as he could and pulled his hat down tighter upon his bald head.

He remembered all the stings against him, many given by his father, and tried his best to forget them. That is why Stretch always made fun of others whom he deemed inadequate, because his father had made so much fun of him. That is why he called them little men and pipsqueaks, for he himself felt so little in his soul.

As he walked along the brook road, he realized he had never been in the dark before without someone to show him the way.

After a while worry crowded his senses and he began to think he was no longer on the path. He might be in the middle of the field of Jack pine, going in the other direction. If that was the case he might stumble over the second cliff that ran down from Good Friday into the back of Arron Brook. He would be lost in the maze of Jack pine in a second.

He lighted a match to look, but the match went out in the wind, and at any rate showed only his fingers. It was now pitch dark.

He began to call, and stumble forward: "Daddy—"

When he stopped, his voice echoed about him, above him, behind him, and then the wind again began to moan in the trees.

He felt he couldn't make it back to the camp. With this in mind he began clawing the snow with his gloved hands, to burrow a tunnel away from the wind. For now all he wanted was to get down out of the wind. He dug over two feet of dry hard snow, and slipped down under it, looking up at the sky.

He then searched for something to burn. But there was nothing. Only what was left of his bonus, in his pocket. He sat with his knees up, shivering. In a while there was only deathly silence. The wind had stopped, except for the occasional bluster from across the field. Tomkins knew by the taste of the air that the temperature was about to drop below minus thirty, or minus thirty-five. It had been so warm that day that he had sweated, and he had enjoyed the sweat on his back. Now his body felt like ice. He would be dead within two hours.

He could not burn his bonus. Burning his bonus would be worse than death.

Why had he come up here?

He put his money in a little pile in the snow, picked out his last match and looked at it. The snow burned his hands it was so cold, when he piled the money up. Here, surrounded by a billion tons of wood, Stretch Tomkins was about to burn his money, his wide face and wider mouth in a kind of a carpish, elastic grin. But then: "Mr. Tomkins!" he heard. "Mr. Tomkins—for Jameson—Tomkins!"

He paused, and heard it again. Far, far away, but coming closer. He waited, and then it was unmistakable. Like an angel—though Tomkins did not believe in angels.

"I'm here—I'm here!" he roared, grabbing his money. "I'm here—please—good God, I'm here!" He stuffed his money into his pockets with fingers so numb he could not feel them.

Who was here to search for him? Who would it be—who would have come for him—if anyone? He waited ten, fifteen minutes.

And then, walking out of the dark, he saw the tiny, eager, smiling face of Meager Fortune.

When Tomkins had not arrived in the two sled, Meager said they had set out searching.

"Who—"

"Half the camp."

"Really—for me?"

"Yes, of course."

This was not true—most of them simply believed a man should take care of himself. Meager was the one who had worried.

"I'll give you money—here—money for finding me," Tomkins said.

"I don't want your money—and don't parade money, or they will get you into a card game sure as hell."

"They will—who will?"

"Them boys who are the ones to play," Meager said.

So Tomkins stuffed his money away again.

Now Meager had to force him to walk, and so told him of all the times he had been sick, just to keep him moving. Of once when he fell down a shoot into a dam of water, with his parka on. They had to lift him out by crane, a line hooked to his back. And when he was cranked out he was frozen stiff, like an abominable snowman. But, he told Tomkins, not only did he not get sick, but his cigarettes didn't even get wet. Why? Well, because all of his outer clothes had frozen solid and left him snug as a bug inside the ice, and the only thing he could move as they took him to a stove to thaw open his zippers was his eyes.

But that wasn't all, he said.

Why, he lived in a house where the space between the boards allowed you to see the traffic going by on the street, so he could tell who had new cars.

"Try that on for size if you don't think it's cold," he said. And besides that, he had to wake every morning and shovel snow out of his bedroom window, because every night he would have a drift come in. Besides that, the rats would run over his bed, in twos and threes, and he would play a game where he would grab them by the tail and toss them out the window.

"But then again, try an outhouse in January—well, of course, you have tried that—I know—I've seen you in the outhouse many times. Oh, don't worry, Mr. Tomkins, it's just our humanity."

Then he told Tomkins about his family—his little boy, Duncan, and his wife, Evelyn. And he told him the secret he had told no one else except Missy and Butch—that is, that Evelyn and his little boy Duncan had died in a fire when he was in Europe. They had died on June 5, 1944.

"I miss them," he said, and he coughed. "Isn't then that a nice name—Evelyn? I think it's the finest name in the world. I was in Europe, it was June 6—I had not heard they had died—we were pinned down just off the beach, the Germans throwing those fuckin' potato mashers on us. And I get caught—a potato masher gets caught in my jacket—honest! And there I am thinking I'm done for—even more than the time I froze solid—yet out of the blue this lad comes takes the masher and throws it in the air and jumps on me. So I'm saved, Mr. Tomkins, and I said to the lad: 'What's yer name, son?' And he looked at me with the finest eyes and kindest smile I ever knew and said, 'Sir, my name is Evelyn.' And I had never seen him before or after.

"Here—I almost forgot—have some soup—I made it myself—I'm becomin' nothin' if not sort of a half-arsed cook—"

Tomkins drank the soup and kept saying, "Thank you, thank you," whenever Meager told another story.

Meager kept talking, and kept saying: "Come, Mr. Tomkins, come, come."

"I only want my daddy to be proud of me—he was so tough I never measured up," Stretch said.

"Well, what nonsense," Meager answered. "I know your father—you just keep walking and we'll get there and your dad will be proud of you. You don't think he is—well, I will tell you—yes, yes, yes—he always says he is when you aren't there."

They hobbled disjointedly down the road, one voice of humanity to another, both making echoes into the void.

When they came up finally to the last long hill toward the camp, Meager holding Tomkins under the arm, Stretch was a witness to the strangest sight in the world.

Lanterns had been placed at every turn on that long hill down the ravine, burning like glow-worms on the frozen, scattered sled path slick with ice, and up on the two sled—with 175 logs piled high—was Richardson. He was ready to start the first load down at night. That is why Nolan, long ago, wanted space near the foot of the hill, and Gravellier called him crazy.

Tomkins passed the sled by and looked up toward Richardson's scarfed face, the fine horses with black harness as black as bolt air, while scuds of snow blew up against the two sled's long runners and through the harsh and piled timbers, and the little dog Nancy whined waiting for a handout.

Richardson made no sign to Tomkins, but catching him in the corner of his eye, dropped his colored scarf, spit his plug, and whipped the animals down into the void Stretch Tomkins had just escaped.

He heard the sled go down and heard the horses whinny. He watched starkly, shivering, as the back of the sled disappeared beyond snowdrifts toward the bottom turn.

"Is he really doing that, Meager?" Tomkins said, his mouth split open by the cold, and trying to catch his breath.

"Yes, he is," Fortune said. "Trethewey, Nolan, and Curtis will do it too."

They had rebuilt the camp from the battered timber and hung tents about it like sealskin. But at times the wind caught it mournfully, and people would say it was the ghost of Will Jameson watching them.

When Tomkins got into camp, the first thing he did was take off his wet boots and parka—and when he did, the money he had gathered up fell in a hump on the floor. He stroked it up quickly and went to his cot to count it, while a ten-dollar bill fell behind him, and then another. Bartlett picked these up and brought them over, laying them beside Tomkins. The men looked at each other cautiously.

Tomkins looked at them all, and turning away continued to count.

"One hundred, one-twenty, one-forty," he said aloud. And then realizing they were listening, took off his hat, put it on a nail, and began counting again, his lips feverish and the lantern above him glowing on his bald head.

The men went back to eating their stew—saying nothing when Tomkins came to the table.

"Some cold—we had to walk a fair piece tonight—hey Nolan—you shoulda held up for me," Tomkins said, rubbing his hands together and looking at them. "Pass down the stew—will ya—that's the ticket. Meager tells me his house is so old you can see right though the walls—boys, it must be a pretty cold place to take a piece off your wife there, Meager. Her old twat must be cold when you grab at it."

Meager looked at him, his small face looking hurt, but then nodded.

"You're right at that, Mr. Tomkins—you got me a peg."

PART VI

ONE

I was asked if work in the woods ground to a halt because of the trial. It did come to a halt, but it might not have had anything to do with the trial. For instance, at Sloan's on the Tabusintac the buzz saws froze, the chains became embedded in the cedar trees, a man lost his leg by a saw jump, and no real axmen had been hired, for Sloan used inexperienced men to buzz saw to save money. In fact he had fired the best men he had that year, Simon Terri and Daniel Ward. Then the snows came, as deep as any since 1908. It was the same storm that caught the Prince family out in the open, and froze a couple starting out on their honeymoon from the Church of the Great Nativity.

Sloan came to a halt sometime in February and could not start up again until late April, when the roads opened enough to allow the trucks he had hired to get in. He was a visionary who had lost his gamble this year. He cursed and swore everyone up and down, under a spell of depression, and sent men to report to him about the progress on Good Friday, for everyone was interested now in the great cash of wood that had been found there.

Estabrook was at a halt because his entire cut was poor. They had not allowed a scaler near, and the men were worried about working for nothing. The worst of them had taken to going on forays to try and steal other cutters' wood. The Push tried his best to keep their spirits up but finally told them to leave. Estabrook, knowing this to be the case, felt he would be the laughingstock of the province the first year he took over the reins of business from his father.

That is, Sonny Estabrook was the first to realize what became in the next twenty years common opinion, and what I have researched to a stalemate in the last fifteen months. That he, in cruising the large tract of immature Jameson timber after Will's death, was the most likely to have carried the very blight on his boots, into the stand he would challenge the Jamesons for. With the first reports now coming to him, he was just beginning to realize this great irony as the trial began.

"It musta come in on a ship about ten years ago—for it has been seen in Europe and New England," the biologist told him a week before the trial started. "It ruins the cedar, and kills the rest."

At first this did not register in a significant way at all, but then, in a sudden flash, Sonny realized it was none but himself who had carried it in. That is, he and his father had visited the ship *Jensen*, which had been carrying the New England timber, to propose an offer that long ago May. His father did not want to bother with this new proposal before they checked the Jameson tract—but he himself insisted. He thought back over the years to that moment, his smile when his father gave in to him, as fresh as falling blood: "We should see the holds of *Jensen* tomorrow—before we check the tract," Sonny had said. (He had said this because there was a case of Jamaica rum for the first boss who visited.)

He had begun to realize earlier this fall, when the *Jensen* had been to port, a huge diesel-running schooner that had left here just before the snow flew with its weight in dealed up board and its ropes glistening with dangerous ice. He had had a few of the sailors over and they all got drunk. The captain, along with the first mate Conner and the able body Dressler. He made a night of it, with flaming rum pudding at the end.

But now this *Jensen Otter*, long past her prime, convinced him it must have been he himself who had done this deed ten years before. That is, he and his father had walked into the tract of wood with death on their boots.

This time the *Jensen Otter* left at night, sailing out into the Strait on diesel, heading south to the coast of Carolina with board, just before the ice came.

"How could God be so cruel?" Sonny said now, rubbing his hands together in pathetic panic. Not thinking that if he had just let Will's tract go, ten years before at the death and funeral of his friend and adversary, if he had decided that it was a Jameson tract, nothing would have ever happened—no poor wood that a scaler couldn't see, no men out of cut for the year, no under-the-table payment in a ludicrous attempt to get another's wood stamped as his own, no using the scandal as his justification—just as other notaries now did. And yet at this moment, none of this did he see. Only that Owen was a murderer and shouldn't be cutting so far up on Good Friday Mount, because the men were in danger.

But that was not the only point. Somewhere inside him, in his self-justification, was the idea that this would not be a design against him, if he worked hard and took action. And so now he had men like Stretch Tomkins doing what they were doing in order to prove to himself that a moment of unprovable metaphysics was not a source of concern or a slight against him.

Still, as those two camps slowly shut down, more and more men showed up at the trial. That these for the most part were not Jameson's men didn't seem to matter. Jameson's men would not have looked much better. But of course there were Jameson's men out—Lloyd and Colson and Gravellier.

"Men come forward in solidarity," the editorial stated, as if the trial was the reason they were out. And this is the idea that took hold because the papers said so.

This was brought to a pitch by the curly headed woman Owen had seen at the water, who had followed him home after the incident at the barbershop. Cora Auger.

"This has all come because of lack of union—and what kind of man would refuse union to these men? This is what this trial is about, ladies and gentleman. It is about a man named Reginald McDonald Glidden who, if nothing else, supported his men. We are sorry for the Jamesons, that so much has been thrust on the shoulders of inexperience. It may be his revolt against Good Friday that caused Glidden this tragedy."

This editorial was part of the false wholesomeness that so many embraced after such a traumatic experience. Lloyd and Colson now became committee members for the Friends of Solomon Hickey. They held a memorial and pressed for an investigation into why charges weren't laid.

There was a strange turnabout—a sudden registering of the rehabilitation of Will Jameson's memory—and now, in death, that of his best friend and Push Reggie Glidden. "They were real men, who would do whatever they asked their men to, and do it before, not like the lot of owners we have now," the editorial stated.

Sloan and Estabrook were the first to agree—so as to distance themselves from the "owners of today." They talked liberally about the better conditions they were seeking, one of which was the battery-operated radio so the men could listen to *Hockey Night in Canada.*

"I will have the battery-operated radio next year," Sloan said.

"I will have it before this year is out," Estabrook countered.

It was now a case of union and Dan Auger's daughter.

Now, everything Cora had faced, Owen and Camellia would also have to face. If someone told her that by stopping her intractable vendetta a miracle would take place, and she would save someone's very life, she would deny it. For she must now grasp the only thing in life she had longed for—to have the Jamesons suffer as she had when her father Dan Auger had died. And why was this unreasonable?

On a cold day in early February, Sonny Estabrook himself came to see her, telling her that the men needed union and she as Dan Auger's daughter was the voice for it. She knew that Estabrook gave her a donation to say: "Focus on Jameson and not on me."

There was, however, one other thing Cora Auger knew. It had been known by her in the early days of November, because of her position within the hierarchy. It had been kept silent as requested—and so hardly a man of hers knew. Union was coming in 1948 by order of the Forestry Minister himself, for they could not handle a major strike in the woods next year. Demands would be met and pay would be increased.

Therefore, whether she was or was not involved in Jameson's downfall it would not matter a bit to the union. But she still paraded before the courthouse her tribe of derelict men, with signs saying: JUSTICE NOW, NEW TERMS FOR AXMEN. To insinuate her struggle with that of the prosecutor's struggle. And the prosecutor admired this and prepared to mention it in his opening statement.

This made its way across the province, and Cora Auger's name became synonymous with justice for a little.

The idea that Jameson was on trial as much for union as murder was a by-product of the moment. It became in some people's mind a political killing. The idea that rumor could not go in this direction is a ridiculous assumption. It is like saying rumor's main intent was not to misshape events in order to create the most out of scandal, and to quench a thirst and satiate famine. Reggie Glidden, who didn't even care for politics, became in many minds a political martyr by February 5 of that year.

The Jameson cut, which became the most documented cut in New Brunswick history, was snowbound, and the main camp had been burned by a flue fire. Though the men still managed to live there, very few things lifted their spirits.

Five teamsters had gone out, and so had three axmen and a tend team. The pup, Nancy, was sick, and was said to have bleeding paws. They made booties for her paws and kept her well, for the dog was a town whelp and could be nothing more.

The supply depot was snowbound, with the portage road having up to eight-foot drifts on major passes and only four teamsters—Nolan, Richardson, Trethewey, and Curtis—who became the most famous in the province that year worked.

The snow started the night after Stretch Tomkins (a man like ourselves) was rescued, and it did not stop in any significant way for three weeks. But for upward of two weeks beyond that—that is, all during the trial—there was no getting out, and no getting in. A huge block of ice now sat solid in front of them, gray or deep blue it ran ragged for miles. Some angrier than others lashed their horses, put the big animals to the twitch, as if their beasts had not suffered enough and must suffer more just because their owners did. They talked of eating their horses—to the horses themselves. "Ya'd better watch yerselfs or y'all be steak by supper."

The camp was essentially forgotten. Everyone in town thought only of the trial, which the men suffering as great a trial did not know was taking place.

Meager Fortune ran here and there, helping to harness horses with young Gibbs. Bringing the Belgians and Clydes out each morning, he would stand upon a stool to harness them, careful of old Butch's raw back. He would cook meals, wash dishes, clear snow, chaff or water when he was asked, and bundled up like a little beaver would check the lanterns down the run at midnight or make sure the sand was heated when thrown on the ice. Late he would get in from far down on the ice flat, and later still would he get to bed, mumbling his prayers alone in the dark.

Twice he set out to the portager's for word on supplies, only to come back by late night, exhausted, unable to get halfway, driven back by gale-force wind and snow. He felt humbled by this—for he had lived his life in the wilderness and had not been beaten by it. Still, he refused to relent. The men would tease him, of course, about cruelty—even Nolan.

"Don't eat the horses yet—I will find food!"

If the storm would kill them, he would keep them alive. In February he was out in the day with the old rifle Owen had left, to seek game. He brought down a small buck deer, and salted some of the bear meat the axmen had killed. Since the cook himself was ill—and the men didn't want to become such—Meager became their chief provider. He took it upon himself to ration everything, even tea—because, as he said, he was "your own meager fortune."

In fact it can be said that this small, childlike man was Push by February 17. He got up at dawn and went far down the slope looking for signs of moose, and could see for miles snow-bound lakes and rivers and passes. Still, he felt that they could not get out forty miles to the river now—and that these men and boys had to be fed. And he decided to feed them because the portager could not get in.

As for the workers themselves, the skid roads were clogged by high storms and steady gale-force winds off the cliffs, and as the two sleds became heavier the horses came to the morning air strained and sick, sometimes coming through on a downhill up to their haunches in new snow and not able to detect danger in the drifts. Sooner or later a horse would go over. The sleds often turned sideways after the downhill was shoveled, and each teamster had a plan to jump. The sleds themselves, with old iron rails knocked into birch runners, came loose, and had to be adjusted each day with metal and leather bindings. For if a rail came off on that downhill slope, it was death to everyone.

Yet even so, and in spite of all else, Butch and Missy went down the hill in the lead, snow or cold. They were dying, and their teamsters knew it yet could not rest them and prove able for Jameson. In spite of these heroic animals, it was a camp that was doomed, as their master was on trial for his life. The dark smoke puffing up in the middle of the wilderness down to green cuts was a sign. A sign of darkness and a light despair.

All of this plagued Owen Jameson, who could not be there with them. He knew of the storm from the sound of the wind that plagued him day and night in the small jail, open to the wind on three sides, and covered the windows in chinks of frost.

It plagued old Buckler as well, who visited Owen early on the morning of February 24. "The trial is going well," he said.

"So much so, I can see me hang," Owen said.

"I'm up and thinkin'," Buckler said, tears already in his eyes for fear he had brought his own nephew to ruin. "And here is what I am thinkin'," he said. "I am thinkin' I can take Ronald's Young and Gordon and go up myself."

Ronald's Young and Gordon were a team of raw two-year-old Belgians.

"When's the last time you had a team on sled?" Owen asked.

"While go."

"How long?"

"Nineteen twenty-eight," Buckler said. "But it's my mountain."

"No—" Owen answered. "Thank you, but no goddamn way—I'd worry, and I have enough to concentrate on. Besides, if the portager can't get in—no one can."

Buckler turned away, a frail old man who had done the Jameson bidding all his life. Who had honorably worked in a world now changing and could not change with it—and who would be dead in six years.

"But you can do me a favor," Owen said.

His uncle turned and looked at his nephew through the iron bars.

"You can see in the papers in the last three or four months—I don't know—maybe only two months—if someone is missing."

"Who?"

"I don't have a particular clue," Owen said irritably, his leg suddenly paining once more. "I am just saying—someone else must be missing from somewhere—and you have to help me discover who it is. For it is not Reggie Glidden."

Outside he saw Cora Auger walking home in silence, against the great graying snow. It was only now did he discover who she was.

"Why didn't I just go to Montreal," he said.

TWO

The idea that this was not Reggie Glidden's body was absolutely hilarious to the town. That Camellia did not claim it was to some ghoulish, and made people more reticent than ever to trust anything she or Jameson said. Women were the most disparaging, and catcalled at her.

"Yer man will hang now and yer bastard child will end up like you, you evil bitch," women would yell in her direction—after dark, of course. She was alone. She still managed to bake squares for the children, and would wait for them to come down the trails from school on those gusting, furious days. So often they had stopped at the little house, on their way home. But now most of them just passed by, hugging hard to the dry-docked boats like the *Murray One* so as not to step on her property.

"Rachel, it's me—your friend Camellia," she would say.

"Momma tells us all the squares is full of blood." Rachel would start to run, and the children behind her run too.

Buckler did start to look through the newspapers, to search for an article on some missing person. He was so numb with worry and grief he found it hard to turn the pages. He could find no article. So he asked himself, why would a missing man not be reported missing? Why would he have no coat and a coat be found on shore—unless it was Reggie?

"Look what a kiss has done," was all he could say to Miss McCalistar. "Look what a kiss has done—if he didn't kiss her—say, if he didn't see her when he came home and put the big smooch onto her—nothing would have happened. And it was

I who told her to go upstairs and get his bed ready—me, I, I was the one—and then there she was on the stairs, and so the kiss—can you imagine?—I can't imagine."

It seemed so crazy as to be plausible. But then again a kiss had caused much in the world before this. Some kisses were even famous. A kiss, yes—we all need one now and again.

There was no disappearing body, no worried relative in those papers. Buckler enlisted Dr. Hennessey's support and they put up posters of Reggie, and sent appeals to newspapers along with his picture, asking if anyone in the Maritimes had a loved one missing. They waited and waited.

No answer came.

THREE

The Crown wanted to use Camellia as their witness—and interviewed her, telling her that if she complied all charges they might have against her would be dropped, and she could live her life out in peace. That, or her child would be born in prison.

But they decided she was a hostile witness and best to cross-examine, when certain things could come into evidence, because they could not get her to say one thing disparaging about Owen.

Hearing the prosecution was interested in what Camellia had to say, Old Mary was afraid that "that woman" would turn on her son. "She'll ground her boot into his face—that's the kind she is—one heap of a nasty bitch."

Women who wanted to be included in the scandal phoned Mary now, offering support and advice. The advice was to get rid of that "Delilah" who had come into her life. Mary grasped at this like straw, and said: "Yes—why didn't I see her for what she was!" That is, after a lifetime of independent thought she now believed that the way to find freedom for her son was to listen to a dozen women who had themselves never done an independent thing and hugged every word of the scandal in misplaced eroticism. Mary herself did not understand that any prophecy against her sons would use her to its advantage. And so she spiraled into chronic and constant accusation. She forgot that the prophecy would "seem ordinary," just as she had forgotten that everything she had done from the moment he was born—in fact, from the moment her fortune was read—had propelled her forward to this moment. She did not know that others were being propelled forward as well—that Dan Auger's daughter was propelled by her father's death, that Sonny Estabrook was propelled by fear of failure on the massive cut he had taken over.

As far as Owen's trial was concerned, there were many attitudes the defense had to face. The first was the outcry from the press, which constituted a majority opinion now, at seeing so many battered men out of camp in midwinter. And so the press intervened in moral outrage as only the press is able to do.

The second problem for the defense was revenge.

Revenge was needed to expurgate an emotion of disgust, and Brower's basic blinding fundamentalism seemed the right and triumphant course, for he hated adultery almost more than murder.

Brower received the same applause as Owen had just a short few months ago, and felt this adulation in the same way. That it was justified, and his to hold.

"He won't let Camellia off with nothin'," people now said, especially the boys in Jameson's lumberyard who spent half the year in drinking and talk about what it would be like to bed her. "Not after this."

Sterling, Camellia's uncle, saw in Brower the brave defense of his daughter. "That's what he's up to—he's gonna protect Lula and I don't blame him—after all she's been through—can't you imagine what it must be like—can't you imagine having had that stroke and her playboy fiancé off diddlin' a trollop!"

But as February wore on, with no letup in the gales, Lula remained in her room, in her "little desert" as she called it, or spent her happiest days in the hallway listening to records on the giant record player. For the first time she suspected that her father had Camellia married as a sacrifice to her. Perhaps it wasn't even intentional, but her father had always been so protective of her. So Camellia was out of the house. And then Owen came home. In fact, when thinking of it clearly, Lula too must have known this.

So in a way it was all a lie—a fabrication that she, Lula, had willfully partaken in, pretending she did not know.

Lula saw it before her on a bright canvas, like one you see painted in the fall. It was a Botticelli that she could never own, yet created herself. Sometimes our greatest masterpieces are seen by no one but ourselves.

By February 26 Sterling found himself at the police station being questioned about his own niece. He remembered much about her now during those weeks leading up to this. "Oh ya," he said, "I feel terrible I didn't see it before for you guys—but I just loved her so much I coounn believe it—I cooonnt believe she was that much of a tramp and a slut and a bitch and a whore—"

"That's all right, Sterling," Monroe said, "it's a hard, hard thing to believe."

Sterling found out something that day, which he began to spread throughout the town. A bonus for the prosecution. The fantastic revelation that Reggie's suitcase, left in the old warehouse, had Mrs. Jameson's fingerprints on it. For Monroe the trainee spent rumor like lottery winnings, like dust falling from a dry windowsill in an old room. He wanted to impress Sterling with this, to show that he himself was essential to this investigation.

"I knew it, eh," Sterling said. "I knew it—they is all in it and always was all in it, if you ask my opinion—fuckin' rich bastard cunts."

"Don't talk like that in here," Monroe said, using uniform as propriety.

FOUR

The revelation of the fingerprint was standard knowledge by March 1.

Owen had panicked after the murder, gone and told his mother—a momma's boy as he was. Coddled as he was. Sterling was at the apex of his power, with the police having a broad panacea concerning his condition. That is, the police had given him money and would need him to testify—and though he didn't play snitch, this was about a Jameson. And don't you think Cora Auger wouldn't be grateful to him? And Estabrook—why he might hire him—as a consultant. And the more fantastic all of this seemed, the more he bedeviled himself with his importance. And the more he told others, and the more they drank, and the more they said, "She'll get hers," and the more they forgot how they had delighted in Reggie Glidden's shame.

Practical Mary denied that Owen had told her anything about Reggie's suitcase. That is, it was not Owen who had told her—it was old Buckler. It was, in fact, Mary herself who panicked and rushed to the warehouse after dark, to hide what she thought would be compelling evidence of her son's involvement with that terrible "she-devil." So she hid the suitcase in order to fight back.

On March 2, Cora Auger began to petition to have her friend Reggie Glidden buried. Upon hearing this, Mary Jameson phoned Cora and told her she would pay for the funeral.

"We did not take a cent for Daddy," Cora said imperially, "and we will not take a cent for Reggie."

And what Camellia did, made it worse. She upped the offer of a reward to $125 and put a prayer to Saint Jude in the local paper. "I offer prayers to Saint Jude, the saint of impossible causes, to bring my husband safely home."

"Every scoundrel in the world petitions Saint Jude," the editor who took her request said with a predatory smile.

Camellia did not care. She plodded on, certain of all she believed.

A memorial, quick and certain, in the blustering wind, was held in the small union hall that had been the semi-official place of opposition against the lumber barons for twenty-three years. From here men went out to work, and to stop work, to show bravery and disregard for themselves and to help others—to long for a time when the measure of their bravery would be a testament to justice on their behalf. This year the lumber barons had come to the table—and next year union would come. But this did not stop them from gathering and honoring one of theirs.

Looking about—each one of these men had made mockery of Reggie and his wedding, and his fall from grace. Each one of them had tormented him as best they could, to stave off the famine in their own selves. Most of them had thrown the pulp sticks that had battered his arm, furious that he could quell their own great strength while being chained to a pole.

"He was as brave as twenty-seven Owen Jamesons," Sterling said now, "or maybe even twenty-eight. What I told Camellia—brave as twenty-eight Owen Jamesons—and all youse men distrusted him. I use ta say to myself many times, why is everyone around here distrustin' the likes of Reggie Glidden—best man we had here, will tell ya that!"

They all, sitting in dark shirts and Humphrey pants, old twisted boots and leather mitts, agreed as Sterling glared at them, their leader of the epoch. He spoke of his mother. He cried. He spoke of union. He cried.

Yet what did the union coming mean for these men?

For many it would mean very little—little raise in comfort or pay, where in ten years most of them would be replaced by machinery they could not at this moment envision.

For Cora, union meant everything.

For Cora, it meant that her father would be exonerated. In the name of her famous father she had worked tirelessly to bring union to the woodland, and to bring Jameson's to justice. Now everything was at hand. If it was justice, none would mention Will Jameson in the same breath as the great Dan Auger! And Camellia, who had gotten all the attention when she was a girl! Look what was happening to her now!

FIVE

The body was finally to be discharged to a resting place in the public graveyard. And Cora Auger was paying for the burial out of union money. But it so happened that Dr. Hennessey visited the mill and read in the paper what was now happening in town. (Hennessey never bought a paper; he simply read Buckler's once or twice a week.)

"I think many things are wrong with this, don't you?" Hennessey asked.

"Then what can we do?" Buckler replied.

"I have no idea—"

"Just, what if Owen Jameson is not a lunatic and Camellia is right—what if it is another body and Reggie is alive—what if Owen isn't bedding down with her, and what if her child is Reggie's—I know it sounds far-fetched—"

Hennessey put his cold pipe in his mouth, blew on it, and said: "Well, let's go and see this body."

Grudgingly, he was given opportunity.

This put a stop to Cora Auger's kind motion, on the very day the body was to be committed to the ground.

Hennessey came to the morgue with something to eat—a grand plan to be out of there in ten minutes, with a design that the body was Reggie Glidden but it was suicide, that the suicide in the end could not be blamed on one unless on all.

The corpse was brought to the table on a pushcart.

Hennessey bit into his sandwich and looked at the body. It had turned more black and sad, and it said to him, almost from its grave: "Why has this been done?"

And he did not know and could not answer.

It might have been murder—or as he said, it may have happened some time after the fight—that is, a fall from the wharf or somewhere else. Water in the lungs attested to this.

Hennessey looked at the hands and at the bottom ribs, where the blood had thickened and congealed to stone. He pushed the skin back slightly on the side of the skull.

"Ahh—this is where he was hit," he said.

Mackey said nothing.

Hennessey took his fingers and rubbed them over the skull, then looked at them again.

"What boots was he wearin'?"

"I don't know—I never found them—"

"You never found his boots—"

Mackey shook his head.

Hennessey thought, and then said: "He was hit with a hard instrument but probably not by anyone who wanted to kill him. There was water in his lungs, so he drowned—he might have fallen into the water after he had been accidentally hit."

"He was hit so he would drown," Mackey said.

"Near a boom or a pulpyard—having a drink—so a fight among friends over a bottle, perhaps—it is not Glidden—"

"How in hell is it not Glidden?" Mackey asked.

Hennessey looked at him and chomped on his sandwich again, chewing it slowly. He decided to leave, was out the door into the main basement hallway near the laundry room when he decided to return.

"You said it wasn't Reggie Glidden?" Mackey asked.

"No—it isn't Reggie—I think it is someone who has gone missing and isn't missed yet—although he is about the same size and age as Glidden. The hair is red but lighter, isn't it—oh right, you never knew Glidden. In fact, you know nothing about anyone here. Why isn't he missed—that's the peculiarity of the case—he should be missed—or if he is missed we do not know that he is missed. So maybe someone not from here?"

Mackey answered that it was self-evident why he wasn't missed. Because he was found and it was Glidden.

And this statement from the coroner would allow the death penalty case to continue: "Even Hennessey says it is the same size as Glidden, the same height as Glidden, the same weight—and maybe a woodsman too. It is who it is, and that is Reggie Glidden. Nothing in the world can change that."

But Hennessey tried one more thing. He got in touch with the river pilot and asked what ships had gone out in the fall. When he was told, he said: "Perhaps if we can get some information to those ships, something just might come of it."

SIX

In the camp the worry over who the body was or was not meant nothing. It was not heard about. And no one had heard of the men. The wind had not let go in three weeks. Only twenty-two loads had gone down. On certain days between February 26 and March 11, men stayed inside and the food was scarce, for the portager could not get in and did not want to chance it.

Meager was out each morning, sometimes with young Gibbs trailing behind with a set of wire snares. They would bring in pine needles for tea and soup. Meager dug out blocks of ice and took brook trout from the pools. He made the men eat the brook trout raw, heads and all. He felt this would keep the men healthy. At twilight on March 4 he shot a young moose while alone—four miles from camp. He gutted it open, and cut stakes to cool it—though the weather was cold enough, and warm blood soon froze to his fingers so much he had a hard time prying them apart. He put the bloody liver in a bag, and into his sack. Then with his rope he tied the back legs and managed to lift its hindquarters off the ground enough to start the process of taking the hide off from the back hooves forward to the rump, and then little by little hauling the hide down each side with one hand while slicing it away from the heavy white fat with the other. The starkness of the landscape and the sky, the gray naked branches of a thousand hard trees, stated the emptiness of the world, the utter feeling of desolation and coldness that surrounded him. Yet to Meager the world was not only not empty, but filled with possibilities. Trout in the brooks, rabbit in a snare, and a moose down.

The sunlight seemed to dissolve his shadow on the snow as more of the hide was taken down and the animal became whiter, showing its muscled flanks and white insulation fat over solid lengths of red muscle. He cut the head and hide off with an ax, and cut it down the middle in the same fashion, for he did not have a saw. With the carcass now halved it was easier to hang, and he managed this in a big spruce, with blood frozen to the hide and the carcass and his fingers and his face. He now cut a quarter from the first half, and putting it on his back little Meager Fortune, who had been doing this in the deep woods of New Brunswick since he was twelve, made his way back to the camp in the dark, followed by curious moose birds hopping from limb to limb. The wind was pitiless, and it was hard to move—many times he staggered, and once or twice went down to the ground.

He walked under his burden as if carrying a cross, in order to keep men alive and himself go back home to Story town in the spring. He still told people about little Duncan and his wife Evelyn as if they were alive and well and waiting for him to come home.

"Oh yes, I will go back and see them, and hug them," he said. "Duncan will run to me as he always does, his pants high on his ankles and his sneakers untied, and I will lift him up and hug him, oh like a mother loves a child."

This was Meager Fortune, five feet, four inches tall. This was Meager Fortune, who had managed now for a month to keep his men fed and entertained.

When he got to the camp that night, he could hear men coughing long before he reached the door. Our poor Tomkins (a man like ourselves), his long legs as thin as sticks so that the snow seemed to stick more to his pants, was in the corner bunk with his face to the wall, curled up with his legs under him and his bald head half covered. Meager knew a disturbance had taken place.

In fact, Stretch had lost his bonus at poker that afternoon, for the wind was so high on Good Friday that the men had not gone out, and except for the loads they had piled the night before, no sled moved. The air was frozen and the piled sleds dark and foreboding at the top of the skid road, looking down into the night.

Stretch had bet a pair of queens against an ace high, and waited for his one chance to make the money back that he had lost in the fire. But Pitman's final draw included an ace, and our Stretch lost it all. He went outside and kicked the door.

Later he went back to the table and gambled his fine parka, and had now traded it over for a coat with string for button and the smell of spruce and sweat. Meager asked him how he was.

"I got me a sore toe," he complained. The men began to laugh so hilariously at his expense that Stretch started to cry silently.

Meager cooked the moose liver in onions and gave the biggest portion to our Mr. Stretch Tomkins.

And then Tomkins said, quickly, something which he later regretted. "I know something," he smiled. "Meager has a secret—his wife and son are dead—no one knew that, did they—he talks about them just as if they are alive, but he told me, he told me. He has no one in the world to go home to. That's why he stayed here over Christmas—that's why!"

Later he put his face to the wall and wouldn't speak. The cold came again, so his cares remained.

SEVEN

By the second week of the storm on the mountain the trial was in its most important stage.

There was one witness everyone was waiting for. She was called on March 8 as a defense witness. She wore a gray coat and a black dress with white cuffs, a kind of girlish idea of a homemaker—or what was prevalent in this age, the idea of society's homemaker—where the times specified that even the most senior office women were called girls, and thought of as juvenile. She wore a small round hat that turned up at the front, and made her look even more like a girl. Her hands shook when she drank water. She did not look at Owen. She had heard that Owen had betrayed her—and said terrible things about what she wanted from him. She might not believe it, but her own lawyer Miss Fish told her not to have any contact with him now. (That she had hired Miss Fish, the only female lawyer in the province, showed, they believed, her lowly estate.)

Camellia, however, believed she was a witness for the defense. She believed they would ask her what she had already been asked—about her relationship with Owen, how he had helped her, how she had phoned Reggie and told him about the job. How Reggie had said he would come back. All of this to her was so innocent that they would know she and Owen were innocent.

But things had changed. The defense was now scrambling to keep their client alive. Billy Monk had testified that Camellia had demanded Reggie come home or she would divorce him, and that Owen wanted him to change his mind about Estabrook. It was very possible that Monk could have heard the one-sided conversation exactly as he stated.

Therefore Pillar, unbeknown to Owen but known in some fashion by Buckler, treated her like a hostile witness. This had been his plan from the midpoint of the prosecution's case. He had decided to deflect guilt from his own client by accusing the person all thought more guilty or most guilty.

He was after the murderer as well. Camellia had become the principal target of the Jameson family now.

He asked her about growing up. Was it hard, who had taken care of her? What were her cares? What were her ambitions? Were she and Reggie happy?

"Yes," she said.

"Oh—you were happy?"

"Well, he was so kind to me many times."

"And at times he wasn't at all, was he?"

No answer.

"Answer the question," Judge Fyfe instructed.

"Sometimes he was not so kind because he was in pain—"

"Is that why you wanted to kill him?"

"I'm afraid he wanted to kill himself—"

"So you say suicide."

"I say no such thing—he is still alive—"

Owen was staring at the floor; he couldn't look up. It seemed obvious to everyone that he had planned this ambush against her.

Then Pillar came to a point of contention that he knew would alienate everyone, including or especially the prosecution. But he had to ask it—for he had had information about it. It spoke to her motive. He asked her why she had married Reggie.

"I don't understand the question," she said.

"Did you marry him because Mr. Brower asked you—wanted you to be settled?"

"In a small way."

"You had come of age. There was worry about you—because of other things—and people here wanted you settled."

The way outsiders like Pillar and Mackey could take on discussions about the intricacies of a town they did not know, as if they had a unique perception, is one of the grander forms of famine.

But Camellia did answer. "There were many men around and Mr. Brower was worried on my behalf."

"On your behalf or theirs?" someone yelled.

Laughter and sniggering, then the gavel.

"I see—and you decided this was a good thing to do?"

"It was one thing to do," Camellia said. "I married Reggie—and I was proud to. I am married to him, and he will come back and tell you so."

Pause.

"When he treated you badly—did you decide on revenge. For women are often vindictive."

She did not answer this. He turned to another question: Where did her father work before her mother died?

"He worked for Mr. Jameson's father," she said in a whisper.

"By Mr. Jameson, you mean Owen."

"Yes, I do," she said and smiled, "but I am not used to calling him Owen—I always think of him as Mr. Jameson."

"I see—I see— And your father was fired from that job, wasn't he?"

"Yes, he was—"

"Yes, for stealing from the company—did you know that?"

"No, I didn't—but I don't think he did."

"Did you know what happened that day—?"

"I am not sure—I—?"

"He went home early and found your mother gone out—did you know?"

"No," she whispered.

"And he knew where she had gone—to Winch's cave—and he killed your mother that day, didn't he?"

"I—I—don't remember."

"You knew this when you went to work for Mary Jameson—your father, who was hanged, was fired that very day and sent home. That caused a death in your house, two deaths, and you knew this about Winch's cave."

"No, I didn't—I knew I shouldn't go down there because it was where Daddy and Mommy were."

"But you went back."

"I did not—ever."

"The letter from Lula Brower proves you did. Perhaps you were there alone—or with Reggie—"

Silence.

With hardly a breath, he switched topics: "Who wanted Owen home?"

"Well—Mrs. Jameson."

"But it was you, wasn't it, who wanted him off the train?"

"I did suggest it to some of the men—"

"Why did you suggest it—did you suggest it—well—you tell us why."

"To help Mrs. Jameson with the mill."

"Is that the only reason?"

"I was the last in town to know he was on his way home—"

"But did you want him back?"

"Yes—but—"

"Oh, you wanted him back—a hero, a Victoria Cross recipient—you wanted him back."

"Yes—to help Reggie—so Reggie would take his job back and be himself."

"But was Reggie here?"

"No."

"You were here—you were at the house—you were staying at Jameson's during the week—"

She had no idea this was coming, and neither did Owen—though to the end of her life she must have thought that Owen did know. And it must have broken her heart.

"So you felt betrayed not only by the Browers but perhaps by Mr. Jameson too."

"No."

"What else did you know about Owen—you say you knew he saved Reggie Glidden?"

"Yes—I knew that."

"But you would marry Reggie Glidden?"

"Yes—"

"Why, did you love him?"

Camellia didn't answer. The judge instructed her to.

"Did you love him?"

"I don't think so then—but now I—"

Pillar interrupted: "Do you love Owen?"

There was silence.

"Do you love Owen?" Mr. Pillar stated.

"In a way," she whispered, "but he was my friend."

"From the moment he kissed you—isn't that right?"

She didn't answer. Tears started down her face.

"From the moment he kissed you?"

"Before," she whispered, "when he was a boy, just as I would think of anyone being teased and—"

"Do you care for everyone when they kiss you?"

Loud laughter, judge's gavel.

Pillar turned away, adding, "Let's just end with this. Reggie coming back did not destroy Owen's plans—they destroyed yours."

Pillar turned and walked back to the desk where Owen was sitting in a state of helplessness.

"I think we got her," Pillar whispered to him.

After the trial was adjourned for the day Owen was frantic to see her, to explain he'd had no idea the questions his lawyer was about to ask. She didn't come.

EIGHT

The next day Pillar seemed to lose energy. He called few witnesses. One was Sonny Estabrook. He asked about the letter but was never able to refute the prosecution's claim that one of the main reasons for Owen's anger was the fact that Reggie was about to shift jobs. He was about to lose his best Push, who disagreed about men on Good Friday. Reggie had shown Monk this letter and bragged about it, had told Monk what a dangerous place Good Friday was.

The other witness Pillar called was Mary Jameson. The first thing they cleared up was the matter of the fingerprints. Mary had gone down to the warehouse, which she said she periodically did because of Will's memory, seen the old suitcase and put it inside the wall.

"There was nothing intended by it, was there?"

"Of course not," Mary said.

Mary, her hat on sideways and her new suit jacket already looking wrinkled, also told the court that nothing had gone on in her house between Owen and Camellia. That there had been a celebration and the kiss got mixed up. A great uproar occurred, and the judge said he would clear the court.

She said that Owen had been away in the woods, so how would he have known Camellia was enticing her husband to come back—and how would he have known that Reggie Glidden was in town, or how would he have lured Reggie Glidden anywhere when he was not sure how long he would be on Good Friday. If anyone had known, it would be Camellia.

"You didn't see Owen flustered or covered in blood or any of those things?"

"No—never—well, I mean not since he murdered Solomon Hickey—"

This brought an uproar, and even Owen laughed.

The prosecutor countered with this: "Of course you want to blame this on Camellia—it would be nice if you could. You would have it all sewn up. Well, Reggie did wait where Owen wanted him to. And Owen met him there. Reggie wanted to know about his wife. Owen was at the old warehouse—he had been seen there twice. Of course he would say he was going there for no other reason than to look for a place to store board. Of course he would lure Reggie there. Why haven't we seen Reggie, yet seen his bloody coat? And why hasn't live Reggie Glidden come forward to help refute the coroner's assertion that dead Reggie Glidden is still in the morgue?"

Laughter, objection overruled.

That night, alone in the dark, his leg paining so badly he could hardly walk, Owen thought of something utterly fantastic—something that linked this to what was happening in his camp.

At first it was just a flicker—some substance lingering in his thought—but once pressured by his intellect it glowed, and over time glowed again.

He thought of two things. The first was that his men were in danger—in some internecine way beyond the storm. Then, almost asleep, he sat straight up. He got up and dressed and waited until dawn. It was a bitterly cold night. Jail seemed safe.

How had he come to think of this? Well, he was thinking of his hanging. He had been told that there were many who wanted to help build the gallows, Colson and Davies and Lloyd being three. Then he wondered where they would get the wood.

"Hopefully from you," the jailer had told him. "Estabrook won't let a scaler do a rod—people think his wood's bonkers—and Sloan is out."

"You can have my wood—it may as well be stamped Estabrook—"

And then he slept fitfully, woke sweating and thinking of his wood. Then he sat up as if scalded.

If they wanted prophecy, he would give them it.

Someone was going to try and steal his wood, and he would hang unless Reggie Glidden came home, so they must let him out of jail and he must go and find him.

Owen Jameson took the stand at 10:17 on the morning of the 101st day of the haul.

What he had to say his lawyer was not prepared for, nor was the Crown. Nor was his mother, or anyone else. He said they had to let him go because he must do something, and lives were in danger if he did not.

Everyone laughed, but nervously, unsure if this was a madman like people now said.

"What do you have to do?"

"I have to go and check my stamps."

Pillar did not understand this at all, but certain woodsmen laughed.

"I don't understand."

"It is no matter—but lives are now in danger."

"What lives are in danger?"

"I suspect my teamsters are—"

"It's a good time to find out," someone yelled.

Uproar, laughing, clapping, hooting.

"My teamsters are in danger. And I'll tell you this: the body in the morgue might be a Dan or a George but it is not Reggie Glidden."

Hilarious uproar.

"How is that—can you tell us where Reggie is now?"

"I'm not sure."

"But what do you wish us to do?"

"I want you to let me go, and I will help my men get the wood down—stop the culprit from stamping my logs with someone else's stamp and figure out who that poor man in the morgue actually is."

The court was adjourned for an hour. People stood near the door, wanting to get back in as soon as possible. "He's out of his goddamn mind," they said.

Just after one o'clock in the afternoon the trial resumed.

Angus Brower, of the farming Browers, his blondish-red hair over his reddish face, his bow tie just slightly askew, walked to the stand, and then turned his back on Owen before he asked his first question. He spoke very softly. It increased the weight of what he had to say. "Let you go—yes, you would like that, wouldn't you?"

"Of course—and I'd be able to help you solve this."

"Of course you would, and we would all be so grateful to you again—just as we were during the war. You love gratitude, don't you?"

Owen said nothing.

"What you are actually feeling is guilt, isn't it, sir?"

"I suppose I am a little."

"Why?"

"Because—well, because of Camellia and Reggie—who should have been left alone to solve their problems like any married couple."

"But you were willing to go to Montreal with her."

"No, I wasn't—"

"But you gave her money?"

"Yes—"

"You didn't mind compromising her with phone calls and money?"

There was silence for almost a minute.

Chairs squeaked. The prosecutor turned and faced the stand again. He looked nonplused, continued: "Did you like kissing Camellia?"

Pause.

"Did you like kissing her?"

"Well—of course, who wouldn't—but I didn't know who she was."

Loud laughter.

"And you liked putting the VC on her breast, didn't you—that must have been for her husband's benefit, and you told her you would marry her."

"That was a joke—I didn't know who she was—I mean, already married."

"Perhaps she didn't think it a joke?"

"I only wanted to help Reggie."

"Ahhh—helping Reggie—yes, men have been using that ploy for three thousand years, I am sure—and women have been anticipating it—?"

"Not at all."

"Now your lawyer wants to blame it on her."

"I do not wish to."

"No, you know where the guilt lies."

Objection.

"That's why you want to save everyone now—it is your guilt at having destroyed everything one man had and was."

Objection.

"No further questions."

That night, in the dark, upon George Street, Brower walked. The lights were out in the house. Usually most of the lights would be on and supper made. It was physiotherapy day, and usually Lula was more optimistic on these days.

On the veranda he felt something—an anticipation in the cold. The light was out in the hall. But to his surprise he saw his daughter sitting in their living room alone, darkness coming down upon her, the books she so enjoyed as a girl behind her on shelves. These were not the books of Owen Jameson, these were the books of proud young ladies accomplished at winning spelling bees, which their stern daddies had always equated with genius. She knew this now—the books a reprimand not only to her but to him. There was no *Ulysses* here, no Conrad or Hardy, no Brontë either. There were excerpts of tedious novels from the *Ladies' Home Journal*. There was *Picks of 1936*, which never did include Faulkner or Hemingway or Fitzgerald. A book by Steinbeck had made it to the third shelf. There was no George Orwell; there was Pearl S. Buck.

This is who Owen Jameson had thought would be a kindred soul when he was fifteen.

"Can you hear the wind?" she said when he entered. "I have been hearing it—well, all my life now. I should have been prepared for this—you never know when or how 'this' will happen," she said, and she waved her hand toward her face. "Both of us, I suppose, should have been," she smiled. "We would have gotten along much better, I think—without the obligatory search for a husband."

He did not turn on the light. She knew why—he would have to stare straight at her.

She was silent for a moment. Then looking away from him, she asked, or told: "We paraded her about—this is what came of it—I made up stories about her so she wouldn't be liked as well as I was. All your time was given to her—remember that, too, was in the paper. And then there was that night—you think I don't remember—when you tried to go upstairs to her room. She had enough spunk to stop you—well, anyway, this is a continuation. Now we've gone on toward the coup de grâce."

He stood almost petrified, sideways to her, his head turned in her direction.

"What is a continuation of what?" he asked.

"Her destruction. She is innocent and so is he—I know it—she would never ever do anything like this. She couldn't even comprehend it! Just as she couldn't comprehend you going to her room."

"Preposterous," he said, "I went that night to talk to her about her future."

"Well, we gave her one," Lula said.

"You were supposed to be married by now; the woman's a slut—"

And he left her sitting there and went through to the kitchen, cold and dark.

NINE

The next morning the summations began at 9:30.

Owen's lawyer tried every available angle to say the trial was a miscarriage of justice based on completely circumstantial evidence—but Pillar knew that as a young defense lawyer this was the worst case to cut his teeth on, and he had made many mistakes. The first mistake he had made concerning this case was taking it. He hadn't realized the amount of blood that people were after, thinking that Owen, being a war hero, would allow a good deal of sympathy. Now he realized that he was in the middle of some aged blood feud, and had no way out for his client.

The VC was countered by the prevailing tendency, as stated in an editorial, that there was a "necessary evil" in war time that if transferred home became evil. Pillar himself now believed Owen was guilty through an act of hubris so dangerous it inflamed the town. The courageous act he had done was forgotten in light of people now assumed he had. But young Pillar put on a brave front: "If there were mistakes, they are my mistakes" he said, "they are not Owen Jameson's. Any man can go to his own warehouse and any man has a right to defend himself against injury—in fact, any man has a right to make a mistake concerning infatuation—this is all Owen Jameson has done. Why would he come home to this murder—what possible reason could he have? What had he done with this man before? He saved this man who had frozen under fire."

Pillar picked up the Victoria Cross and, without saying a thing, simply held it. This was his pièce de résistance—and he felt it would sway the town.

"What has this man done—but bring honor here?"

He looked at Owen, nodded, and sat down.

The prosecution answered for the whole river, and in a certain way for other winners of the Victoria Cross who were following this case. Angus Brower began: "Who is Owen Jameson—let us begin by asking this. A gentleman; Reggie was not. Educated; Reggie was not. Well spoken; Reggie was not. Well to do; Reggie was not.

"A murderer (here his voice became a whisper); Reggie was not.

"Reggie must have looked up to him, too. That is why he came back to see him. He must have felt he owed this man his life, and he might have decided to come home and go to work. All autumn long Reggie's men were going into the woods—a Trethewey and a Nolan, a Curtis and a Richardson—Reggie knew them, and they respected him. So back he came, (here he whispered) to meet Owen Jameson because he owed him his life.

"What happens as soon as Owen Jameson comes home a hero? Let me tell you what he does. Can I inform you what he does? He cashes in, doesn't he? The Victoria Cross—(here he lifted it up and showed it to the jury, with its purple flag and lion and paws) this—flippantly given to his mistress when he saw her. This was his instant gratification and motivation."

There was a long pause. Angus, visibly moved, had a taste of water and looked out at the dismal sky for a long time through the long churchlike window, holding the glass of water nonchalantly in his hand. Then he turned to the jury again.

"So what about our hero? The defense wants it both ways. They want him to be a hero, and then they say, Well, he is an average man, and has infatuations.

"I will not say that. But I will tell you that something started in deceit never ends well—I will tell you that this 'infatuation' is ever shameful.

"I will tell you it is deceit at the worst.

"They killed a man coming home for Christmas; and why? I will tell you why—she was pregnant and they knew it even then. Pregnant on October 17—the first night he got home. They had to do what they did—the tickets to leave on the train, the money given to her, all a willful disregard of a promise to God at the altar—but there was one brave man who knew, found out, and was watching. This brave man was our God-fearing barber, Solomon Hickey. He tried to put a stop to this error. It cost him too—he too owed a life."

The prosecutor stopped speaking. He stared for a good minute at no one. Until the whole court was uneasy. He then placed the VC down on the table, carefully; was seen to rub his fingers across his robe.

In the jail Owen was suffering from a fever. But this did not dissuade him from realizing that he must escape. Death here was certain. But there was also death coming on the mountain. How this would be done, Owen did not know. But he was now as insane as his mother, thinking that life had a design meant for him.

That night Owen thought of the prophecy. He drifted in and out of sleep, and saw moments that had long tortured him. The idea of Christ on the cross had always troubled him, and how he had made light of it as a youngster with his brother Will. Now it pained him to think back to what he, in frivolity, had said. The idea of blasphemy doesn't start with what you say, but why you say it. Owen said it initially to shock and amuse, but after time it became more than this. It became the common way to mimic others he desired to be like as a young man. The idea of pandering to a certain cynicism he did not feel was justified.

However, the design of the world was far greater than he could ever have imagined. Even in this terrible miscarriage of justice that he would fight to the end, did he see a design in all the faces of all the men and women now deciding his fate. As if any of them could. That is, even he knew they could not begin to decide his fate. And even he had a belief that everything would turn out.

Of course, he now thought, nothing was foretold, you made your own design—and yet this design he had made, to cast his lot out into the world, had brought him home, not because he had failed in the world but because he had succeeded. Is that what the Indian woman had seen thirty-five years ago?

So what would have happened had he failed?

If he had failed in the world, where people wanted and expected him to, then everything would have been fine. He might have come home in an entirely different way—perhaps he would have been a schoolteacher for Peabody. Yes, if he had done so, nothing much would have happened, he might have been the self-contented smirking teacher at a school, hitching his wagon to the star who would become vice-principal.

Or he might have gone on to be a dentist, like Will had wanted him to. He might have extracted that very tooth that had been bothering Solomon Hickey, and been looked at with that whimsical superiority self-deluded Hickey had.

But he had decided to be great—in fact, he had not decided it at all—others had assumed greatness on his part. He had gone to get a man whose rifle froze in the moment of fire, and brought him back to safety—and so they assumed greatness.

Their assumption allowed their adulation, adulation allowed envy, envy spite, spite misery, misery accusation, and accusation guilt. But toward the man he had saved, the emotions ran symmetrically in an opposite direction. Glidden's guilt led back through a maze of stages until adulation came again. Now Glidden was once more the hero he had been in 1938.

Why? Because they themselves felt desperately guilty for having treated Glidden badly, a man who was worth ten of any of them. And so now they had to leave behind the scandal of

Reggie Glidden and attach themselves to the scandal of Owen Jameson, all of it for their own protection. Owen was fifteen all over again, and they had no choice. They had to accuse him. His guilt over Hickey allowed it. Lula's illness allowed it—and allowed her father, so long a fixture in our town, to finally make his own case for a happy life.

In what way was Owen Jameson guilty?

He was guilty of his fame, in a very genuine way. This came because he saw how they reacted to him when he arrived on that platform on that gray October afternoon. They got him drunk and he reveled in their gratitude. After years of scorn, no voice sounded against him. He made the common mistake of thinking that this attitude was the ultimate one, that it could not be changed. Now that he had redefined himself, so had they. Everything would be well. An inner voice that told him something was wrong went unheeded. That is, he did not know that Hickey had a diamond in his pocket for Lula Brower that very moment. When people once again redefined him, Owen could not go back to the way he had been looked upon. As many foolish men do, he demanded respect. He saw this now clearly from his jail cell. Therefore he did the most foolish thing in his life. He opened the barbershop door. If he had not, Solomon Hickey—earning $1500 a year and wanting to marry Lula—would still be alive. This, then, was the sin. It was a very great sin. It was a great godawful sin of pride.

So whether he did or didn't believe, he surely knew what deadly sins were, and what they could become. And so had Saint Jude understood. This was one tangible element in the human psyche they held in common. If he had not been great—or if he had stayed on the train—Lula would not have insisted he honor something she herself didn't want honored when he had left. He saw this now. Both knew this, and both from different sides of the mirror needed to vie for a position neither had held four years earlier, insisting the other see their point of view. When on that cold October night she wore the brooch he bought her on leaving, he knew she was making a frantic pitch not only to him but to and for the town. She was saying: "We must do this—all of them think you belong to me."

She had no one left but her father.

Still, her father could do nothing against him as long as Owen did nothing.

But then Owen's descent began, so very soon. And had he propelled it himself?

All of this he thought about in minute detail. Of course, what was done against him was done in revenge. And he could say now that some women were even worse than the men in wanting him disposed of. He remembered Cora Auger's eyes and shuddered.

And what about Camellia?

The last thought he would have would be of kissing her. But why—what madness must prevent him from not having who he so longed to have?

Both of them knew this and were tragic because of it.

So then if any of this was part of the prophecy, it was a microcosm of man's brief state of inner hell. Could he have married Lula if not for Camellia? At this moment, even he could not say. The jury, however, could. And it was made up of men he went to school with, whom he had played in the fields with—whom he had shunned when they began to shun his family. Now they sat in serious judgment—Butler, Peterson, McGregor, Urquart, Hamilton, and McLean. Their youth already gone, their faces looking placid and sad, they retired to the inner room knowing they needed no inner room to retire to. That at their will the inner room could be conjured up in a glance, a posture against the reclining sun. From

Owen's youth came his dereliction, and their minds being made up, was of course the eagerness of the town to say: "We have put up with the Jamesons enough—we will not put up with this."

It was now the second last week of the cut. And in his pocket Owen had a "reasonable assumption" from the scaler that all things were well with him—a kind of ludicrous greeting to a man about to be hanged, but perfectly compatible with his position as head of Jameson Works. The letter made it to Owen during the storm.

"We have a long draw of wood," the scaler, Claire Mutterly, wrote, "and I have no doubt that I assure you at least eight million board feet—what I have already figured, a prime quality especially in the cedar, hemlock plenty, and good running spruce for sleepers and tracks. It is the men's ability to cut in spite of difficulty that I am proud of. And here they are only nine or ten good men left—but I graciously tell you they are the best of the good men. The weather is still crisp, with a minus fifteen registered today, but the men are in good spirits. I do not know how this wood was not cut out before you came home, I can only tell you I have not witnessed a raw stick bad. Signed, Claire Mutterly, talons of Arron Forks depot, March 15, 1947."

Owen had read that letter over and over. The scaler was taking a chance in his pride and his principal authority to elaborate on the board feet. But Mutterly was a certain man.

TEN

Things continued in the deep woods, with the teams left in.

But then another man made his way to Jameson's camp one night out of the dark on the last day of the trial—that is, about the last week of March 1947. There was a window of respite from the weather, and he managed to get in and out.

They thought it was Innis, but it wasn't. Innis had decided he could not or would not get in from his depot at the talons—a place where four streams into Arron Brook joined. It was a man from Sloan, Blind Andre, who had been fired from his cut after everything halted.

He had walked all the way from the Tabusintac cut in the storm, wearing as many men did then, a Russian fur hat and fur-lined boots. He was disheveled at five-foot-six with a black, full beard and forearms almost twice the size of his biceps. He sat in squat fashion in the corner, his gray coat missing three buttons and tied together with twine, and among every other patchwork of clothing, a silk scarf given to him by his girl who conceived a child every year he was away.

He coughed, took the tattered coat and his hat off, and said: "This is a danger here—so you lads be on guard."

"Why is that?" Richardson asked. He had just come in from laying down his skid load and putting the horses away. His face was haunted, as were those of the other men because they had driven themselves beyond exhaustion now. In this smoky camp they looked every bit like explorers cut away from the herd. Blind Andre had some tea.

"There is a man here sent to steal half your work," Blind Andre said, saluting them as he stirred the sugar in.

"How?" Trethewey said.

Blind Andre said he did not know.

"Who is the man here?" Curtis said.

Blind Andre looked about, passed Tomkins' face with no more than a glance, and said that he didn't know. He said it was a rumor that he took seriously. He said no one could have foreseen what would be happening in the woodlots in this age. That this year 1947 would be a watershed year for the men, and that in ten years—Blind Andre would predict that in ten years not one of these men would be working the way they were today, and many wouldn't have jobs at all.

"So it don't matter what it is we say, do, or don't do—we is up against her—and the world will change for us—forever."

Sloans on the Tabusintac, Andre told them, had a thing called a buzz saw that cut out trees faster then Bartlett, pared trees down faster then Pitman. That in a year or so, these buzz saws would get better and better and faster and faster, and put scores of men out of work, and great roads would be built for trucks and heavy claws that would do the work a hundred men could. The horses would become piddling and meaningless, and the mountains they were on would be bulldozed to nothing—the water table would dry—all they saw would be changed. This great mountain would be nothing in the coming years. The beavers that had made this great stand of cedar would be trapped out of existence, and the world would become one of factories and smoke.

The men sat mute and careful in the way they moved and spoke, as if asking for details carefully would relieve them of the burden of the knowledge being entrusted.

"They'll always need horses," Curtis blurted.

"No they won't, son," Blind Andre said. Though things had frozen up this year, and oil in the trucks had solidified, new years were coming—and no one would look back. Their history would be forgotten. Their smiles in pictures, holding the halters or pots and pans or axes in the shine, would be seen only in museums by men who could not last a day working with them.

The little spruce books they made for their children forgotten.

The songs they wrote about men like Will Jameson and Peter Emberly—now as popular with the men as the Grand Ole Opry—forgotten.

The crazy wheel forgotten.

The two sled rotten and left to wither along roads that would be overgrown, near rivers no longer traveled so arrogant historians would believe they could track the measure of these men by finding a rotted jab pole in the sun.

Curtis, at twenty-two a professional teamster and perhaps the best young teamster in the world, would not be needed. His hands, which bore the traces and marks of the reins, would no longer be needed. His ability to defy death would be considered nothing at all. Not when a truck could do ten times the work in an eighth of the time.

They sat stultified at the possibility that what they did, and why they lived, would no longer be required.

"Why do you think union is coming?" Blind Andre said. "The barons themselves are to be forgotten—all of you together will drown in the new world, and companies will come in to make these trees soft arsewipe for pretty girls. That's why union is coming—in ten years they will have sold out to large companies and made themselves new empires."

They were silent for almost an hour, drinking from a bottle of Captain Morgan rum.

And then, finally, someone spoke.

"We promised to get the wood below—and we will," Richardson said.

"And since the old world is changing so fast—we are all

damned anyway. If nothing we do matters, let's make a stand here," Nolan said.

"We will stay and work," Trethewey said.

The other teamsters agreed.

Tomkins said nothing. It seemed his die was cast. And he was playing Judas. But he had to, for Solomon Hickey had been his only friend.

The next day the men could not work. Tomkins stayed in his bunk. By afternoon, when he woke, he discovered Blind Andre had gone, with Meager leading him out to the top of little Hackett Brook.

The drifts were now as high as the roof, the hovels buried. The only thing he could see from the near hovel was Duff Almighty's tail, and some wet horseshit in the snow.

"Will we die here?" Tomkins said to Meager after he got back that night.

"No," Meager whispered, "I promise for your dad's sake, I will keep you alive here." He said this, and Tomkins shuddered. "You have a fever," he said, "but I will get you tea—and I will put an herb in it to stop your runs."

Each man was down to two cups a day. This would be Stretch Tomkins' fourth. And he had snuck four of the last dozen donuts that had so happily come in a barrel a few months ago.

Tomkins turned his face to the wall and prayed, even though he was an atheist.

"Don't worry, Mr. Tomkins," Meager answered, bringing him over a cup of tea. "Only three more weeks now, and we'll be off cut and home to cause mischief—won't that be a fucker's fun?"

"Well," Tomkins said peevishly, his face to the wall, "how can we be happy on Good Friday?"

Meager smiled, nodded, and patted his shoulder: "Well, sometimes in this old world we only have benefits the boundaries of which are established by my name."

ELEVEN

The storm blew itself out, and the cold hovered and stayed, and then slowly dissipated and the wind died, and the cedar along the ridges was once again being pulled up by rope, horse, and men, their muscles strained and bleeding. The horses once again went into the cut with wild eyes, Butch and Missy and Duff Almighty, and the great Percherons, and each teamster felt as if they had been given a reprieve—or more than this, as if they had been sanctioned by some divinity to recreate the greatest haul of lumber in the world. *Recreate* because they felt it had been done already in olden time.

They worked more furious because they knew the other mills were down. They worked because they knew their lives as teamsters were coming to a close. They cut with bucksaw for the same reason—Pitman and Fraser were on the mountain, and so was Nolan and Trethewey—all for the same purpose. The purpose; well, in five years they would no longer need to use double ax or bucksaw or hitch horse.

The great moon allowed them now to work late into the night, so at times a lonely two sled would be seen way down on the flat after 11 p.m.—not coming back with a load but leaving with one—while the moon bathed down on huge glowing craters of soundless, glittering ice.

Stretch (Tomcat) Tomkins, all six-feet-two of him—so you had to dress him twice to keep him alive once, as the men said—went back to chaffing on the downhill, and Meager went back to cooking, and Gibbs treated the horses to sweets he had hidden, and Bartlett wisely determined which great section would be the last he ever cut.

A fine wind came too, but not too harsh, and lingered in the breath of the men. It was now April 1947—the very last of their world—and yes, forty thousand horses this year in the woods doing the same harsh work as Missy and Butch.

With the white moon on Monday and a bright sky, even the fellers worked after dark, and even the horses themselves believed they would survive. The snow felt warm, and undulated through the glens and valleys of the spruce, and hung on boughs all the way out to Toomey's Quarry. So the men began to sing again the praises of their world.

A's for the axes as youse well know
B's for the boys that can chop 'em down
C's for the cutting about to begin
And D's for the danger that we live in
And there are none so happy as we
No mortal on earth is as happy as we
Hi me hi deary deary hi deary down
Give the shanty boys whiskey and nothing
goes wrong

Tuesday morning the portager came in with a store of provisions, and new socks and boots, and told them that they might not know that Owen Jameson was found guilty but that his order was to get in on the first clear day and bring the men boots.

Innis said this as the first trickle of water ran over the first frozen rock, and the very first scent of earth broke free in a smell of fir bough and spruce. And the great cedar in the shape of a cross that was the inspiration for Good Friday's name, and that was born the very year of the prophecy, was killed by Bartlett's ax.

Innis spoke about the look of the jury—Hamilton, and Urquart, and Butler, Peterson, McLean, McGregor—all honorable men who had a duty to perform and performed it to the best of their ability. All honorable men who had done what people expected them to. Nothing more, nothing less.

"Oh, there were handshakes but not so many—and there were some smiles and jokes, but none too much."

The men decided to work until the end of their contracts. They were down five teamsters and behind thirty loads, and knew they'd be hauling on gravel soon.

On this day Richardson turned his big Clydes and, starting with that large cedar Bartlett had just cut as his first base, went down into the yards and waited upon what would become his championship load. (They needed championship loads now to catch up on their wood.)

These were the largest trees seen here since 1850, when the Cunard line was at its prime, before it was sold to those in England who forged the *Titanic.* And everyone on the river had heard of this great wood—and someone said there would be a photographer here, to show Richardson coming down.

"Take yer time, boys," he said, biting into a cold apple, "this mountain's not going anywhere—and we go downhill fast enough."

The horses stood still in petrified silence, just as the air was blue silent at minus ten, as the two sled was loaded painfully by men who had been loading sled for years. They would take a log on a chain hoist and roll it up on the other logs forming the base, men under it to help the three men above on the sled. If the hoist gave way and the men who strained on the sled couldn't hold the giant timber, it would roll back on the men underneath. Peter Emberly was killed this way, a boy of seventeen. And so too was Curtis's uncle.

As they worked, other horses were channeled around them on the sides of the hill, and hauled their ragged two sleds to other yards, where the same work took place. The smell of horsehide in the wind, the bedeviled smell of human sweat and hair, of snow and the sweet earthen smell of piss.

On Richardson's load, when they had no logs left but tiny ones, Butch was unharnessed and brought down into the shine, to be chained to the devil's mount, bringing the hardiest logs ahead for the two sled. The logs down below were cedar, and heavy and wide. This is what Richardson had dreamed of. The biggest load on a sled hauled since 1933.

So far down in the valley Butch went that Pitman, standing upon a branch of a hemlock he was cutting (for you often had to climb the hemlock to get above the rot), could only see the tips of his seared black ears.

Each log was marked and scaled in the shine before it was brought up, and every log was huge—the diameter of two or three men.

The scaler would be in now until the logs busted free in the water, so sure of his millions of board feet and his bonus of four hundred dollars for the extra time he spent.

The scaler said he had never seen trees this fine in thirty-two years.

"Take yer time, boys," Richardson said, chewing another apple, "I will find better logs and take it down when I have 330. I will not rush my last load—we will be out of here next week and home on a budget of wine and fucking."

Here he grabbed Gibbs, for he had found a broken birch runner and they tore it off, remounted the sled track, and reattached it by heating steel strips and bending them over and along the birch, so it would run smooth along the ice track.

But little Gibbs was unsure about the job—not that it wasn't done well, but that the weight of this load might cause a sled to bound.

Meanwhile Butch, gelding from Missy off Byron's Law, grunted under the weight of each log, so saving Missy they brought Duff Almighty to hook up with another mount, which caused his teamster, Curtis, to say he would give the horse over for a day, as long as Richardson did the same for him, for they were coming to the end of the year and Richardson would be done his haul.

These horses fearlessly strode uphill, disregarding the men guiding them until Butch's huge feet broke the ice at the top of the skid and he came up in a roar of steam and pain, surrounded by glitters of ice and four twigs stuck in his tail.

All this while Richardson sat chewing an apple, and though it was still minus ten, waving his old civil war–shaped hat as if chasing away flies.

"Ya think ya'll live?" Pitman asked.

"No matter," Richardson said, lighting Fraser's well-rolled smoke and thinking of everything he had lost in his entire life, "no matter ever no more." For the McCord girl he had once loved and had not seen in years was no longer his, no matter what.

Far down across the ice flat, almost to Arron Brook proper, Tomkins stamped logs with the illegal and counterfeit stamp. Once in the water with thousands upon thousands of other logs, they would be recognized not as what they were—the fruit of Buckler's mountain—but would be thought of as Estabrook's prize. Tomkins, a man like ourselves, did this because he had not been given a team, because no one had treated him well, and because he had taken a bonus from Sonny to do what he was doing now.

And so he worked. He worked along this old skid road stamping the logs, far away from camp, as dutiful as a squirrel in fall, and did not notice Meager Fortune walking toward him with a Thermos of soup he had made. Meager had made it and decided to bring it to Tomkins because no one else would. And Tomkins was a muncher.

Tomkins had the ability to attract kindness to himself, though he himself never was kind.

"And anyway, he is not a bad lad," Meager thought that morning, neglecting to think of all the things Tomkins had deliberately done to him.

Meager, having been in the woods all his life, thought others were like him. That is, he did not know and never considered that Tomkins wouldn't know he was approaching. Even though he was as silent as a cat, even though he walked half hidden against the side of Arron Brook so you would see him one moment and then not see him for fifteen minutes, he simply thought no one would fail to detect him moving in and out of the old sprag trees and iced-over boulders in April of 1947. As he walked, he was thinking of Duncan and his wife Evelyn and how he loved them. Yes, they were fine people. And if what he had heard was true, that poor Evelyn had loved someone else when he was away, it didn't matter now. He only felt sadness and love when he thought of her.

"Life is hard enough, anyway—and so many of us make mistakes—why, I have made a bunch myself and so why should I say nay to her?" Then he spoke to Evelyn; he said, "If you think you have to wait a long time for me, I believe you will be surprised. I think this world has just about done with old Meager Fortune—for as you know, the new world is here and by the 1950s there will be real fortunes to be made."

He walked up toward Tomkins, smiling and almost ready—almost ready to wave—when he stopped and looked down at a large spruce, with its ragged beeled-back bark and its lumps where the branches came off, and he thought: "This is very strange."

And then thought, "What is Estabrook's timber doing up on Arron Brook side—did he take so much from his cut, he piles it in the freshets next to ours?"

Then he thought: "We have got down all the way to the old Jameson cut." But then looking ahead in the sunlight, seeing the nodding mesmerized head of Tomkins—his elongated shadow seeming to make three people—Meager began to realize something very wrong. Then he thought of what Blind Andre had said. It was suddenly as if he was staring at someone alien with a small nodding head and stiff goatee.

"My God, what has he done to us?" he whispered. "If he is the one to claim our legitimacy, what in God's name will happen?"

Meager turned and walked at an angle down through the yarded trees along a rut road, toward Arron Brook, and sat among some popals and talked to the birds that came around him, sitting at his feet like they had with Saint Francis some years before. If his feeling was right, what was he to do? Meager Fortune, who had caused nothing to befall anyone, really, in his life—whom God had played a great trick on, taking his wife and child away while he was running about killing Germans—this Meager Fortune now had to tell on someone. He had never told on anyone before. What was he to do?

The moose birds flew about him, softly about his knees and arms, and he took out bits of bread to throw at them. He did this for well over an hour. The sun began to disappear behind the wood, slowly and ominously, and he heard the two sled picking up Tomkins and heading back to camp, just as the sun was above some old sprag popals by the river. He got up and, walking up the pathway toward the skid road, seeing his old boot marks, realizing how happy he had been but a brief time ago, he said: "Evelyn, Evelyn, what am I to do—tell me what to say?"

The ground, slightly broken free of winter, was turning hard and cold again. And he turned down Arron Brook in the direction of the last logs Tomkins had stamped. Here he was, our Meager Fortune, wearing dark woolen pants and big heavy-toed boots three sizes too big, with huge buttons up his chest, walking about in the middle of nothing but a channel of wood and rock and ice, looking for a sign of betrayal.

It wasn't hard for Meager to find the Estabrook stamp hidden under long logs right near where Tomkins had done his latest business.

It wasn't difficult either for him to know what a crisis this was now.

"The men—" he thought suddenly, "the men will kill him if I tell he has tried to steal our work. Tomkins has tried to steal our work!"

These great logs—thousands of them now scaled and stamped with a wrong stamp—would simply be pushed into the river without anyone noticing what stamp they had, until they went into the great communal circular boom to be sorted by stamp for each mill.

If he, Meager, did not himself stop it. And if he did stop it—if he did, it would mean—well, it would be the death of Stretch Tomkins.

He held the Thermos of soup that he had made especially for his friend, and tears dazzled his eyes. *Betrayal is such a vicious sin, worse than the cauldron Dante put his sinners in.*

TWELVE

Holy Thursday, 1947.

The jail on a side street, not hampered by light—and an alley in behind. Darkness was coming and Owen was in pain. Still, the idea of being in pain was one he had gotten used to. But he found by about four that afternoon, he was in great discomfort. He lay on his bunk and listened to children playing on the side street. The men who were building the gallows had left. There was supper to be brought and he waited for it. It got darker, the corridor wall flared once in sunshine, then turned gray and dark. Outside, on the roof, there was a shifting of snow.

"Ahh," he thought, "spring will be here."

Finally Monroe came shuffling in with Owen's mashed potatoes, peas and smelts, and weak half-cold tea. He opened the door carefully and went to push it in.

"I have to see Hennessey," Owen said. "Call him."

"Not tonight—I'm goin' home—Clive is out—he comes back, I'll tell him to come look at you—"

"You can't go home while the jailer is out."

"I don't need to babysit you—that was yer problem—babysit too much."

"What if there was a fire—I'd never get out of the cell."

"There was never a fire here—"

"Sure there was."

"Ya, when?"

"October 1825—"

This was the date of the great fire, which burned eight thousand square miles in ten hours. It took, among two hundred others, the life of a woman in jail for having killed her infant.

Monroe looked at him. Owen was sweating, now, though it was not hot. "It'll take too long for Hennessey to get here anyway—I don't know," Monroe said.

"He will come—you phone him."

"No."

"Well, then take me up to the hospital—"

"Oh, you're nothing but a baby."

So Monroe went back into the office grumbling. But he made the call. Hennessey said he would come down after he finished with a patient.

Lula came out of her house that very night, and was seen in town. She walked slowly and painfully into the dark. Exactly why may never be known. Waiting until her father left to go to the curling club at five for the end-of-the-year supper and dance—something she always received an invitation to but could never attend—she had finally decided she did not believe what was being said, for everyone pretended to be saying it on her behalf. And she must hear it from Camellia herself. She would even pay her—bribe Camellia to tell her the truth. That is all Lula Brower wanted in her life. For people to finally tell her what was true, and what was not.

She made her way down the long, sanded street in the gloom. None of the Steadfast Few attended her now. In fact, it took her a half-hour to walk down the stairs in the shadow of fading afternoon and then wait on the porch until certain her father had gone. As Camellia's priest had told her, if a rumor has destroyed others, it has destroyed you—you must correct the rumor to put your soul at ease.

But each step was painful, and every carpeted stair held a memory of childhood temper.

She knew the porch steps were slippery going down, and she knew that it was not a matter of if, but when, she fell, for poor Solomon Hickey who had always loved her was no longer here to take her arm. There were many houses with small dark porches and quiet lights—a cold ground fog had settled, and people passed her, some didn't even know her name.

The reports of Lula's journey have varied over time, and left us with a still scene when all the building fronts and businesses had signs of people you grew up with, and the loitering gray filtered across the plain, unhurried streets among us—she standing for long moments at every pole, to rest, her face in semi-darkness. One of my friends painted this scene, and it hangs in the courthouse as a reminder of that time. It took Lula an hour to make it almost down to Pleasant Street. It was close to 6:30. The shops were closed, and young women who worked in those shops hurried home—it seemed without a care—to lives that would come to fruition in the 1950s. Women who with care and love would raise children who would rebel against everything they held dear or knew. The way of the world.

"Is the doctor coming?" Owen asked at about the same time. There was no sound at all. Monroe, hungry and not wanting jail fare, had gone home for supper as he had threatened to do. The jailer was not yet back. Owen would have been able to make out the light in his apartment if he was. He sat in front of his plate of cold smelts and waited. It was ten minutes later that Hennessey came in. Owen could hear him walking about the desk to get the key from the far side. He heard him come down the three steps, fumble while finding the key to open the heavy door, and come into the cells. Owen was simply sitting there, watching.

"Where is everyone?" Hennessey asked.

"They all of them went someplace," Owen answered.

"Well, you shouldn't be left alone," Hennessey said.

Hennessey did not want to talk about an appeal but he did say he had spoken to the captains of four ships, to see if any sailor was missing.

"Are there?" Owen asked hopefully.

"There is one more we are trying to contact," Hennessey answered.

Owen nodded and said nothing. He stood, winced, and looked at the top of the gallows and shrugged. When Hennessey opened the cell door he just walked in with his bag, as he had done on another occasion. The door was left opened. Monroe, and the jailer too, were out.

It almost had to be spur of the moment, a kind of instantaneous decision that once started couldn't be stopped. Owen watched until the cell door was opened and his friend came in. He told Owen to take his trousers off, so he could look at the leg.

"Snap on the cell light—Monroe forgot," Owen said. Hennessey went back into the corridor to do so, and turned to see Owen running past him. Hennessey tried to stop him—for the sake of the leg—but Owen pushed Hennessey aside and ran, and was gone even before Lula made it to Pleasant Street.

I believe Hennessey glad to see him go, would have been happier had he been able to check the leg and put the man in hospital—and if that had happened, nothing that followed would have.

But Owen could not be reined. He didn't know, nor could anyone foresee or tell him, that as each hour passed his freedom became more certain, if only he had stayed where he was.

Hennessey, it was said, sat on the bunk and had a cigarette and read a bit of Yeats before Monroe came back and reported him gone.

In later years, Monroe said he went home to supper to allow Owen to escape. It was said with hindsight because of who Owen had become. It also allowed him to deflect the idea that any prisoner had escaped on his watch. "Ahh—I knew he was innocent."

But we know that Monroe was one of Jameson's worst enemies, and sounded the alarm sometime after 7:30.

At any rate, the fact that Lula Brower was walking the streets at that moment became the most significant event in my life.

Practical Mary had been a home child, sent over the waters to Canada by a British government that found a way to dispose of and make children as meaningless as wood chips on the sea. She was bought by a farmer down river, and lived there ten years.

Byron, her husband, rescued her from a life of penury and abuse by riding a pure white gelding into the house while the farmer waited for his pudding, and she jumped on the horse's back, yelling, "Fly, Byron, fly," her skirts trailing in the wind and her strong legs across Byron's thighs.

It was said Byron was a greater man than Will Jameson himself, and they took off north along an old dirt road, under an autumn moon, the horse ridden almost to ground before they got away. She found out her brother Buckler had been sent here before her, and had searched for her, for years.

Byron the one who brought them together.

"I know civilization will never, never treat children as disposable again," Byron said, uniting them.

So now that rebellious union tempered by love had come to this. Their empire dying; money in socks, their son to the gallows, and an old lady willing to fight to the death.

Buckler and Mary had talked mutiny for days, one following the other through the great corridors of their ruined house.

"I will die before I let them kill him—gallows being made with our own wood—as barbaric as communism—" Mary said.

So they sat up then planning, writing every detail down, the last great feat of their lives. Buckler had the gelding Ronald's Young, which they were going to hitch to the window bars and tear off. Buckler was going to walk it right through town, Mary carrying the hitch and chains coming behind. They figured the dark would hide all of this. They had Ronald's Young fed so many oats he would kick a whale to death, and in the dooryard that very night.

Owen escaped before their reputations were jeopardized and their sanity questioned in public.

Owen's escape caused panic in those who had arrested, charged, and convicted him. They believed he was hiding behind every bush. Fences skirted many houses in our town, and the little byways and alleys that led to other places sat in a sheen of temporal half-dark, bordered by dense wood.

Monroe was the first out looking for him, sounding the

alarm and blaming the escape on the old jailer who'd not come back.

Owen could hear the shouts even while still in town.

People said that he went to Camellia and kissed her, and asked her to come away with him, for I was his child. But that was a story improvised from the one of how Owen's parents, Byron and Mary, met some forty years previous.

Most felt Owen would flee by train to Montreal and become lost in the multitudinous city, or take a tramp to Europe and wander those old places he loved. People were now quite fearful, and called him a desperate murderer, and wanted him gone, dead or alive.

"Hangin's too good," Sterling said, picking up his 32 Winchester.

"You be careful," Monroe said, "not to shoot someone else."

By midnight, twenty-five men had staked out the tracks, alerted the towns of Bathurst and Campbellton, and waved lanterns at trains in and out of the gloom, walking on sleepers cut out by Jameson men over the last twenty-five years.

Many thought Owen must be off to someplace exotic. Men carried skinning knives and rifles, and assured each other Owen wouldn't live to see dawn.

"I'll get him myself," Sterling said.

But they didn't consider he was a Jameson, and knew the woods well enough. More than that, he remembered how both his father Byron and his brother Will had traveled in it. Oh, they were far greater woodsmen than he, but if he stuck to the same course, made the same turns on roads that even then were no longer evident, he would find himself on the opposite side of the bulkhead of wood left on Arron Stream. That is, a stone's throw from where Meager Fortune had found the Estabrook stamp.

He was headed into the dark night toward Good Friday Mountain. Some brooks were just starting to run, and the great salmon that stayed up under the ice were now backing out to the sea, the coming of winter gone, and each drip of melting ice brought the promise of new lives of short duration.

Owen felt Monroe would kill him if he caught him. They couldn't let Owen find his way back among them. Why? Because of the very prophecy he himself did not believe. He now and again heard Monroe shouting out to the men, not to abandon the direction they were going in, to press on over the snow, to keep their barrels pointed away from each other.

Owen had nothing, not even a coat, and it was early April. Each time he stopped to rest he heard men behind him. Some of these men were men he once ordered into battle. They were the ones he most worried about, they who had been professional soldiers.

His shirt was torn, and the wind was cold on his chest. It was useless now to talk of the pain in his hip.

He heard shots firing in the wind. He stopped just on the outskirts of town and listened, deciding it was not a trained man but perhaps Sterling. He moved through the wood, his shadow cast out along the snow like some monster of Mary Shelley, and found himself in the back pig stall of the math teacher's house in Morrison Lane. The graveyard, with its white monuments, lay to the south, bathed in a gentle breeze, which meant it was only minus two or so. It would warm up tomorrow, and he would be with his men on the last day of the haul. Surely they would be safe now, surely it was too late to have anything go against them.

He thought of them not at work, but in their repose. That was where strong men could be seen.

What would happen then, to these men? They had come through a winter of great hardship, unattended by him or by the greatest Push ever seen in his company, Reggie Glidden. And for much of the winter, through the paralyzing snows, they had been kept alive by little Meager Fortune.

Owen watched the house, and waited for a time to enter. There was no sound, just the small creak of a board.

How had this happened? Why had his great love for this earth—and yes, for the people upon it—been turned to this? What was in man's nature, or his own, to allow it?

"It happened because I loved her," he thought, "and I always will."

But this love was also damned—and that was the secret part of its element. Its very nature, in fact, was for them to be locked in separate cells.

And in a moment of destitution, he knew this.

After a time the moon was white above the clouds, the snow gently rolled between the spacious spruce trees, and he moved through the dark yard, seeing the weathercock point south at the top of the house. It was to him, if not to most in the world, springlike weather, and he could smell in the snow the scent of warm days ahead. He saw golden pine needles lying aground under the first disappearing snow, and it gladdened his heart. It was true he felt alive for the first time since battle. He had heard how men he knew and had fought beside had walked across the ice of the Miramichi in mid-March, water bursting up about their boots, to go to dances, looking in wild and gracious torment for women and fights and oblivion in drink.

He understood why.

Going in the side door now, he searched for a coat.

There was none, and he opened up the kitchen door and searched here, in the black with his hand. Then he snapped on the light with that same hand, maneuvering in wider and wider concentric circles about the wall.

Unfortunately, he was by the very timing of his decision not alone.

The math teacher was awake, figuring some broad geographical locations in his head by the very light of the white moon that peered down into the grubby window of his little house, a solitary house for a solitary man, thinking perhaps of all those elocutions he had heard as a boy in the dusty rooms of McGill when suddenly, with some strange deliberation, a hand came inside and moved about the wall. He watched it with peculiar, fascinated uncertainty as it roamed about, its fingers finding a switch and snapping it on. Then the hand moved again, farther along toward the coat hangers. Then a head poked in, and they stared at each other eye to eye.

"My God, who are you?" the math teacher asked in a kind of wondrous agitation.

"Why, I'm the lad who knows Pythagoras," Owen said.

"Then by my conjecture you will not live another three days."

THIRTEEN

Up in the snowbound cabin, where the men had hauled now for 136 days, a great crisis had just erupted. Meager Fortune had been found with an illicit stamp. Worse, it was Estabrook's stamp. To the men here, Estabrook with his vast holdings, who had put them off the initial cut, was widely viewed as the devil. By his greed, he and he alone had sent them off to purgatory.

The purgatory was this high mountain of logs, where the wind whistled as if off a dock in hell, day and night, so that some of the young boys who were being apprenticed held their hands over their ears half the day. At times, even the experienced men would kick something and yell.

"Let the wind beg off, for fuck sake!"

The great horses sometimes kicked the stalls in the same hope—that the wind would beg off.

But it did not.

This purgatory was made up also of small items the men had brought from their homes, only to make it all the more solitary—a picture or two, or a cup, or a brush that once belonged to a daughter, a plate that had once fed a son—fashioned over the long winter as instruments of slow torture. And torture, in this place, did not let up.

Nor did the sheets of ice or the cold, so the men had fashioned a new wisdom about hell and its great environs. It was a long stretch of ice and snow between the talons of Arron Brook and the upper end of the north branch of Arron Stream. This, they discovered, was where hell was exactly, and had marked it so, on a map, with a circle of red ink and one word in the center: HELL.

Almost no one in the world would be able to find it—it had been, however, discovered by this crew of untamable, hard-living, and generous men.

And now, more hellish, a rogue stamp.

The stamp was found in the most terrible moment, a moment of drink and celebration. Meager Fortune was letting the younger boys hear what Big Ben sounded like. In the midst of this drink and hootenanny on the last night before the last day of the haul—they were drinking raisin beer they had made after Christmas and had stored in a lock underground, so that the youngest boy, a Childs from Millerton, swaggered drunk from wall to bunk and was put to bed by Gibbs at ten—Meager had fashioned a great bell out of a coat hanger and string. Then he instructed the boys thus: "You tie a piece of string on each end of a hanger, wrap the strings about each index finger, put your fingers in your ears, and rock the hanger until it hits against a wooden wall—and there you have it, my pal: Big Ben."

The young boys lined up to try it, while Meager was smiling from ear to ear, when one of the cutters who had drunkenly fallen over Meager's bunk felt under the gray army-issue blanket, hidden well and tucked away, the godawful stamp.

At first he said nothing—but the portent of the disaster was everywhere he looked. All those children lining up to hear Big Ben, and all those men who would bleed to death for their families, in a second, now to be at the last leg of their journey, going home. What did it mean? It could mean that they had only part of the wood they had cut. But the cutter didn't know—so he called in Claire Mutterly and showed it him. They were in the dark near the side of the cabin where they had fermented their beer, and boys were still lining up for cups to drink the dregs. Already a fist fight had been stopped, over one boy telling another in dire confession that though he had seen the other's girlfriend's snatch twice, he had had the fortune to feel it but once. That being taken care of still left the air raw, at this part of the cabin, when Claire Mutterly saw this stamp.

He called Fortune over. But Meager said nothing. He would not say how he had found the stamp or where he had got it from. The argument spread, so that men, laughing and grinning with the celebration going on, slowly stopped, as if some moving current made them struggle. They turned to listen, their silhouettes against the heated wooden walls and their expressions changing to consternation, which in men who have faced death can be terrifying.

"WHERE!" was heard now above the din of men in Humphreys and dark checked shirts, boots with cork and lining, and socks three months worn on feet that had danced on a scaler's pitch against the snowbound ridges.

"Where," was said by others more slowly and with temperate consideration, their smiles now gone, it seemed, forever. The information was spectacular, dazzling, and deadly. Someone had tried to steal their work for Estabrook—and it was of all people little Meager Fortune. And little Meager Fortune sat in a room, surrounded by men, some twice his size, who he had cared about and fed, and walked miles a day to keep alive, and he cautiously smiled kindly, for there was nothing else at the moment he could do.

Tomkins heard the guffaws change to anger while he was outside. Above him the sky was clear and the night was cool. The moon had softened the grand treetops about the cabin, so all seemed tranquil and bathed in light.

He had gone in to see the animals, and had spoken to Pitman about next year, and how he wouldn't be back for a Jameson but would go with Estabrook after twenty-three years.

"Estabrook is the best man," Tomkins said with a sugary smile, "because he knows who I am and what I have done." And this smile then seemed to expand over those trees, and become a part of the light clouds as he spoke. It was poor Tomkins' last smile for a long while.

As he was turning about he heard the arguing—a kind of primitive, hellish thing that his daddy had always protected him from. He walked from the hovel, over the hundred thousand wood chips treaded into the snow, and heard it increase.

He did not know what it was about until he had entered the door, with its colorful beer caps and its drawing of a mermaid, and walked into the inner sanctum of men. Here was Pitman's place, he who had cut out trees that would build the house of a millionaire in Europe. Pitman would never see this house. There was Fraser's bold, small place, he who had done the same and would live another forty-four years after this night and die in Hamilton after telling his grandchildren tales of Good Friday.

"The greatest cut in the history of New Brunswick—and four books written, and I'm in one."

Here was Bartlett whose 171 finest trees would construct a church where two presidents would hear the offering from God, though neither listened to it. Yet he too would die alone, after seeking for years to have his memoirs published.

Tomkins turned to his left along the smoky corridor between the rows of bunks and saw, as if in his worst nightmare, the handle of the Estabrook stamp, which he was sure he had left in the woods near Arron Brook. It was the smoothest, most benign handle one might ever see in one's life, and yet nothing is wrong but thinking makes it so. Thinking had turned this benign object into the one telling point of all disaster.

Meager looked up at Tomkins and said nothing. He simply stared at him. His nose was bloodied and his left arm hung down, because they had hit it with the very peavey stamp they now accused him of using, trying to extract some kind of confession. Tomkins, a man like ourselves, could not believe it—Meager Fortune had not spoken, had not said a word about Stretch's involvement.

Stretch turned and fled, back through the smoky room with clothes stinking and ragged and hanging over poles to dry, and back into the serene night where a moment before the whole world had seemed joyful to him. His body shrunk as he walked, and his long legs wobbled, as if in fear of being hit. He sat on a spruce stump looking down over the valley of snow and sweet moonlight. His shoulders thinned and his body shrunk down like a mushroom as he tried to escape the thought of what he must do.

Of course, he did not think, What must I do? He thought only, How must I act to extricate myself from all of this? How much time before I could reach the depot at talons? Or anyplace else, if I could last in the woods long enough to do so? Who would ever be the one person to lead me there—the one person? Well, the only person would be little Meager Fortune, who was now being tormented by a group of furious men.

"Woe is me," Tomkins said, thinking now of his own life of short duration, "woe is me."

He huddled into himself, corked down lower and lower on the stump as the moon became higher and higher and bathed his ignominious body in more and more benign light. Yes, if only he were as small as Meager Fortune, he could run away. However, little Meager Fortune did not run away from anything or anyone—would not, even if he could.

Only now was Stretch understanding what a horrible part he had played, and who he had sided with in order to play it. And what in fact all his proud vainglory had gained him—nothing at all, not a cent.

This was a breach most serious. It involved Claire Mutterly's report of eight million board feet. That meant Mutterly would never be allowed to scale again. It meant that Bartlett and the five axmen who had stayed, the teamsters and the cook, the apprentice boys so happy go lucky, and the tend teams too, would have worked half the year in this frozen hell for nothing at all. Pittance even less than what they would have. All of this had been fine for Tomkins until he began to realize it. Now that he did, he wanted to hide. He must hide. He had to. He wanted the moon to go away, but it wouldn't. He wanted to take back the stamp and say to Estabrook, How dare you ask me to steal from these men—these men of all men, their trees, the stunted strong who I have laughed at? But he couldn't bring himself to speak, and when Bartlett passed to say do you know what is going on with little Fortune, Stretch squeaked and sat up straight and then shrunk again to a lump.

He himself, his long spidery legs shaking now in his big ridiculous Humphrey pants, wanted to change places with Meager Fortune, but Tomkins' own ill fortune at being a coward prevented him.

"I have to make it right." And he stood up and walked about in a circle and sat on the stump again. "I have to make it right," he said, and he stood up and walked about in a circle in the opposite direction, and sat on the stump again.

Meanwhile, Meager was not saying anything of value.

"Simply because you found it in me bunk, boys, don't mean she's mine—just like someone else's woman, I suppose, if I suppose I ever would be that lucky."

He would look from one to another with curious compassion given the circumstances. They would hit him and he would flinch but he would not yell, and when on a few occasions he got a chance he would throw out a punch that when it connected would send his tormentor back.

"The Germans are better at this," he said, having been in a POW camp for four months in 1945. "Better all around—in fact, if I was gonna be snapped on the head, it'd be by a German—or," he said lazily, to a cutter he knew to be from

Denmark, "or a Dane. They spent most of the war hidden up Hitler's arse. Hey," he said to a French boy, "ya think I could sue fer peace?"

They could get nothing out of him, and the moon came down through the one ragged little window. And once Meager looked, his eye black and his nose broken, and saw Stretch Tomkins looking in at him. He winked.

Beyond that window, out in the shine, without knowing what was happening in the cabin, were teamsters and loaders, making the last loads of the year secure on those old two sleds, their runners buckled by exhaustion. And as high as Richardson's load was, he wanted more—so, therefore, did Nolan, and Trethewey and Curtis wanted theirs to match his. All of them had decided in the hubris of the moment to "snatch" the load.

"I'll snatch yours by ten," Curtis said—and this had now been going on all day and far into the night, with the moonbeams palavering down among them, against the sweet hillocks of snow that still stretched away high and soft through the trees.

The last great trees pulled up out of our great bedeviled mountains.

"The beavers made these trees up here," Old Trethewey said, "and I hear it was Will Jameson hisself brought in the beaver."

"Stole them from Estabrook," Nolan said, spitting his black-as-arse plug.

"So in a way, gave this land to his brother," Curtis said. "And I heard the other land is rotted."

The loads now were almost secure, and it was after ten, and boys were up on the top, putting the last tie-down chains across each one, and checking the great runners underneath.

They would hitch the horses up in the morning and roar downhill, one behind the other, to shouts of enormous freedom, and perhaps a photographer, coming to take a picture to show Miss McCord who she missed out on when she laughed at Richardson for having only one arm.

Poor Richardson did not know that no matter what kind of picture was taken, Miss McCord, who had taught a primary grade, would not see it. She had died three years before.

Richardson's sternness might have come because of this load. But he was in no mood to be trifled with tonight. Not when tomorrow, one load higher than all the others would go down that hill. He could only think now of all the ghosts in the past who had done this, and his name would be just perhaps matched to theirs.

But then Gibbs, his favorite tend team and a boy of not yet seventeen, came over to him and whispered about the trial going on.

"You mean Owen Jameson's trial, therefore?" Richardson asked.

Gibbs explained that it was not Owen's trial he was speaking about—but a makeshift one against Meager Fortune where some of the men said they would hang him because of an Estabrook stamp. An Estabrook stamp. The teamsters looked at each other, and made their way to the cabin by 10:30 that night.

"They already have a rope secured over a beam," Gibbs said, walking behind them. Richardson was the first to arrive, Trethewey behind him. They came in through the crowd, and the crowd parted for them.

"What's this?" Curtis, who came in also, asked.

"He stamped our logs with Estabrook," Claire Mutterly said, "and he'll pay for it, I'll tell you that."

"He was the boy who kept us alive most of the winter," Richardson said. "Why in fuck would he do this?"

"Kept us alive to work for Estabrook," one of the axmen, a Duffy, said.

"Well, if that is true, he'll be cut down when he gets out—we'll take him to court."

"Well, do it tonight," Duffy said.

"Then you come against me and we'll do it tonight," Trethewey said, at which the lad shrunk.

In fact, the teamsters formed a wall about Fortune, who sat there looking from one to the other in bemused isolation.

"Did you stamp?" Richardson asked.

"No sir," Fortune said.

"Who stamped here?" Richardson asked.

He looked about at all the faces, bleak and dirty—and because of the very dirt, somehow serene—and missed one. He looked through the window, past the old thermometer, and saw sitting on the stump of that great cedar Good Friday Mountain had been named for, our Stretch Tomkins "shrunked down," as Bartlett reported in his somewhat overindulgent memoir. Shrunk down and worried, as if on a storm-tossed sea.

"You will not touch our Meager Fortune again," Trethewey said, staring out at the same man. "For it is easy for charlatans to take what little fortune we have."

And they took the rope down.

FOURTEEN

On this same night the ice had broken out of the bay, and the sea was high. The heavy schooner *Jensen*, coming in on diesel with the main sail up and four yards against the wind, was in the Gulf of St. Lawrence on the far northwest side of Prince Edward Island. There were men in the lower berths, and under heavy seas with ice collecting across its ropes, making about nine knots in a gale. The captain had before him two reports, each now requiring a change in his plans and wanting him to come into the strait and bay as early as possible. Or so he had decided that night.

One was a Halifax newspaper sent on request from Newcastle to the ship as it traded along Nova Scotia, which he initially thought nothing about; the other was a picture of a man given to him earlier in the week by his first mate Conner, who had gone in off Prince Edward Island for a chart.

Now, putting these two things together, the captain exclaimed that could they, this old bulking *Jensen*, fitted out with sail and diesel, past her prime by twenty years, be the missing piece in this strange mystery puzzle?

This ship, this strange missing link, was now chugging toward the Miramichi to be born.

Conner, a great young sailor, told him of how things now happening on the Miramichi might have become imbued with a scandal out of all proportion to the cause. The newspaper report asking for information about any missing relative or friend made things urgent, especially with the picture that Conner had handed him as well.

The newspaper asked if anyone was missing a relative or friend—that a body had been found in its bare feet.

And the picture? The picture was of the very man who had signed on with this ship to work, going out off the strait in December, and who had come back with it, and was resting below.

Things were puzzling until the captain reasoned that the man actually missing—the notice that old Buckler in frantic hope had put in all the Maritime papers—might be a man off his ship now unheard of for more than four months.

"If he was up on the sails he would likely have been barefooted and without a coat, even on that night," Conner stated.

The man they now had with them, Conner told him, was this other fellow, the disappeared one, the one the police had probably mistaken their own man, Dressler, for. "Dressler could have fell from the riggin'—that very night we were going out."

That Dressler was not accounted for in the log was a scandal within the ship itself. But no one wanted to admit this, for most of them, captain included, had been drunk coming from Mr. Estabrook's.

The other man, however, was the completely alive and hardworking and common enough seaman Reggie McDonald Glidden, who had taken to the sea well and kept his guts and was fine on the ropes.

So it was in fact nothing more than a simple case of mistaken identity. Glidden had been hired on late at their turn out toward the gulf, because Dressler was gone. And they had taken board down the coast to South Carolina and had come back with cotton bails and electrical fans. This cargo was headed toward Montreal, but a turn would have to be made in the interest of justice.

The captain went below and woke Glidden, and told him what was going on, and asked him to bear with him please, and if he could bear too with the whims of the sea.

"If ice is gone, we can make it to the outside of Sheldrake Island in three days—there Conner will take you in on a skiff, and you will have good enough opportunity to clear this strange matter up."

—

"Tomorrow we will have good enough opportunity to clear this matter up," Trethewey said. And no beating would be allowed of any man caught. They would take him out to the depot at the talons and hand him to the rangers, and not a hair on his head would be harmed.

"For we are to be civilized men," Curtis said.

It was easy enough to know. Tomkins was the prime stamper—therefore, if his stamp was legitimate as he said it was, then the other stamp, the false one, would have had to be stamped over the Jameson stamp. That would be easy enough to see and would have ruined the subterfuge anyway.

"If we see that, then we know it is not Tomkins who used the false stamp," Richardson said.

"There you go," Tomkins said, clapping his pipe on his knee and laughing almost hysterically, "there you go." And he kept nodding his head and spitting, "There you go, there you go—I knew it," and he glared or tried to glare at every one of them.

Then he took his hat off and decided he would hit Meager over the head with it.

"I'll have an apology for this," he kept saying, "I'll have an apology for this—"

Meager simply sat there taking all the hits on the head.

But they stopped Stretch and took his hat away. He kept rubbing his hand across the top of his bald head under the lantern light, looking at each in turn with pursed lips, hoping against hope there was some way to extricate himself and run away.

—

The idea that Owen would come and get my mother and take off was stirring feelings across the lanes and alleyways. It had been since the evening.

Cora Auger was sure the temptress had something to do with it all. She remembered when Camellia's mother died, and her father was hanged—how that had given Camellia more sympathy than Cora ever had later on. How her picture was in the paper more than Cora herself got. She had never been able to understand the fame such scandal generated. Though the scandal around her had given something, it was not enough. And she had loved and honored her father for years. Secretly, she blamed the Jamesons for this lack of scandal. They were able to snuff it out like a wick in church. She had been alone, apprenticed to a seamstress in 1935. She had fought for union on her own, and bled for it too, until Camellia's scandal caught her up. Now, after all these years, the chance to reclaim something for her father was at hand. They would all know Dan Auger had been the greatest woodsman in the world.

"What nincompoops to let him escape," she said puffing on a cigarette, the smoke rising up in the thin air above her reddish brown hair, at eight that night. She sent her men out to look for him.

They came back after a while saying Owen had given them the slip.

"The slip, is it?" Cora Auger said. "Well, go and find him if you want to work for me—find him dead." In fact, Cora Auger was using the same tactic as those she hated once had. She knew what strikes and breaking strikes with lumber barons were like.

"To Glidden's," she said, mud on her new boots and snow on her jeans. She was using her power in union to control the destiny of poor, half-illiterate men.

Four followed her, with much commotion and tired rhetoric, to the isolated house on the windy, open Strawberry Marsh, one-eighth of a mile from the great open dump.

"Owen is in there with that whore!" Sterling kept shouting.

My mother was alone. She had tried to run downstairs and lock the door, but they burst in on her. She ran, but they grabbed her.

"Running, is it?" Sterling said, forcing her to come with him. "I never thought a niece of mine would be like this here."

She was brought into the room. She looked at all the startled, angry faces, angry that she would dare deceive them. Her running had proved she was guilty. There was Colson and Butler and Peterson too, all caught up in the moment.

"Where is he?" Cora shouted, so loud the neighbors heard.

"Where is he?" Sterling said, waving his old Winchester so dangerously that others took it from him.

"Search the house—and don't be shy, take her things!" Colson yelled.

Cora sat in the hard-back rocking chair in the little living room with its one faded plant and its few knick-knacks as they went in and out. She never spoke. Only rocked back and forth with a small squeak, both arms on the armrests waiting, her new boots crossed one over the other in front of her.

One of the men took Camellia's chin in his hand and looked at her, twisting her face sideways. For years afterward he would say he never had. Cora watched this without comment and then exclaimed, "Never mind her, he's meeting her in Montreal—he isn't here!"

And they turned, their faces filled with a kind of delighted hatred, and let her go. She should have stayed just where she was. Again, the world would have been different if she had. But she was disgusted by them and ran after them to shut the door—I have long had dreams where I see this in my mind's eye, as if I am hovering over her head at that moment. Reaching for the door, she fell over the mat one of the men had ruffled and hurled stomach-first from the porch onto the ice. The wind moaned, and no one turned to see or hear her. They had departed and were already near Hanson Street.

She lay in the cold, bleeding from the mouth, for fifteen minutes.

"Everything," she told me later, "seemed to have left me—and I was somewhere far away into the heaven. But then I asked God to please let me come back—for you."

Many nights I wish she hadn't.

She managed to get inside the house, and locked the door. Shaking, she took up her rosary. For over an hour she was sure I was dead.

By 10:07 that night she felt the first sting of labor, crawled on her hands and knees to the bathroom, and locked the door, saying in a weak voice: "You leave me alone."

There was blood down her legs. The baby was going to come far too soon.

No one heard her, and the commotion and the desperate search for her lover continued.

Monroe had not given up, but had gotten lost in the thicket northeast of town, and was not discovered until the next day when he wandered into Buckler's backyard with a troop of disheveled confederates.

Lula Brower suddenly heard that Owen had escaped and saw her father's car go by. Thinking he would be outraged that she was gone, and that he would think she had had something to do with it, she made her way, with her face aching and cold sores on the right side of her mouth, to my mother's house.

Brower himself had been at the curling club for the ice removal dance. Everyone had loved him at that moment, and he was saturated with glad tidings from the people.

Up on deck, Reggie McDonald Glidden felt the cold spray, and watched for lights in the distance that would indicate the mouth of the great desolate bay. Hearing now what was happening, he felt he should have known it would. He felt even more responsible, and more guilty, than when he had left.

He wanted to rush across the water and save his wife, ready to kill anyone who touched her. But he had to endure the swells moving under him without repose, and lashing water over the gunnels and across the deck.

"WHAT HAVE I DONE?" he roared. Only the creak of the sails, the taut of the rope, the wind answered.

PART VII

ONE

It was Holy Thursday night. They stayed up late, playing some cards. Down at the stream they could hear ice cracking and breaking, and knew that soon they would be out on the run, with a massive amount of logs primed for Jameson's mill. They would have bonus and be the heroes of the river this year. And why not—why stay in hell for six months if you can't come out a hero?

Yet if it was true that anyone had stamped their logs with the wrong stamp—even a partial yard—they would be furious.

Tomkins did not know how to escape. Except for most of the night he spoke in a soft and soothing voice to Meager. "Why did you do it?" he asked, just loud enough for others to hear. "You can tell me, Meager—was it because of your wife and children—what was it for, to ruin these men—"

Finally Meager spoke. "Your famine caused this."

"What famine is that?" Tomkins asked.

"The famine in people that rips us all apart. That's what I think," Meager said.

He said he had started to think about this in the war.

"What?" Tomkins snapped.

"That men have rid themselves of God, and are famished, and therefore do terrible things to make such famine go away." Meager's face looked peevish in the light after he spoke, unused to making such pronouncements.

Stretch (Tomcat) Tomkins was silent. At one time he had thought he would be in a great revolution—like the ones they had in places like Spain—and he would be "instrumental" in New Brunswick politics. He had used this idea and this hubris to do something deadly to men he had worked with, and as the night went on, a solid mass of fear crept over him, so for moments he couldn't move his boots, or his legs in his great big Humphreys, or his fingers, or even his ears.

Why had this happened? What had possessed him except the very famine Meager spoke about, which allowed his lying and deceit. Carefully it was crafted to weave about him a web in which fear caused him paralysis.

When Tomkins looked over, Meager was curled up on half a bunk sound asleep. A child with no cares who had, it was reported, escaped from a German POW camp in 1945 and spent a month fighting alongside the Russian army pressing toward Berlin.

The Russians called him Misha and gave him sweets and adopted him as one of their own.

That night, while Meager was asleep, Lynch the axman whispered to Tomkins. "Why have you teased him so badly—is it because he is small?"

"I never did," Tomkins maintained.

"We've all seen you—watched you. But here is something you may or may not know. He," Lynch whispered, "killed seventeen men—four with his bare hands."

Tomkins shuddered suddenly. He himself had not gone overseas because of a pinched kidney.

It was now six a.m. on Good Friday Mountain, and the men would be done and off job and out for Easter Sunday. They would then come back, the best drivers to plunge the wood into the streams and brooks and run them down across Arron Brook, where the danger was, past the talons where Dan Auger had met his end—and then into the sunshine on the Bartibog. Moving onward toward the big circular boom, near the bend in the river where those landings had caused the jam that had taken Will Jameson's life.

If he had just said no to Estabrook at that moment of seduction, every imaginable worry that plagued Tomkins would be gone. But from the first, he couldn't. Meager was right. It had been famine in the soul.

The men had a light breakfast of pancakes and bacon and tea, then went out into the relatively warm air of early morning April, watching as the teams came forward. But what was most sought did not come, the photographer up from Maurice's. All the men wanted him, and all the men waited.

Of course, they had not understood that a photographer needed a guide. They believed because they themselves could come in forty miles, anyone else could as well. They had hitched their horses with as fine a tack as they had left, and made the runners on the two sled shine, and made themselves look presentable for this great day.

The teams now had walked by the hovel, great cedar pressing down every two sled, the horses' bodies already glistening with sweat.

It was Richardson's lead, and he had 323 logs—a great amount to go over this hill. A hill suddenly heavy with spring. Behind him came Trethewey, Nolan, and Curtis.

There are many versions of this story—you yourself have probably heard all about it.

Richardson nor anyone else would go down without a

photographer, which Innis from the depot had assured them was coming, and by letter the photographer had as well. So in common ego, Richardson held up the great Clydes at the top of the camp skid road, looking down into the chunnel of sled tracks, rocks, and clotted dung to the heavy, bowed Bailey Bridge. There was a sheen in the air and a sweetness of early spring—a moment when you think of girls at Easter, the smell of snow and horses, the long timbers along the side of the skid road yarded up with chains. The sound for the first time in months of birds in the early morning.

"We will give it another moment," Richardson said, disappointed, now and then spitting his plug over the side of the logs.

"He was up three stories on those logs," Gibbs reported, for Gibbs and three other men were going to follow down and join after the Bailey in order to be there in case those thousands of logs down on the flats had to be remarked with a Jameson stamp. This is what angered the men more than anything. To them, it was an unthinkable betrayal. The idea that Tomkins was not "one of us" and had stolen the great efforts off Buckler's mountain was inconceivable.

Men muttered as they looked at him, and he was relieved only when they looked away. He knew what it was like to be condemned and to see the gallows being built with Jameson wood. In fact, he knew this now in his heart as well as Owen Jameson would ever know it. He knew now what it was like to be an outcast as Reggie Glidden had been. Who had teased Glidden about Camellia the most—talking about her unfaithfulness? It was poor Tomkins; he did this only to please Gravellier, whose eyes would always light up.

Now he needed a way out. A way to set things straight. And it came. Then and there—and for all time. If this had happened five minutes later, no tragedy would have occurred. Yet it happened, just as it was supposed to.

There was a speck in the distance holding hard to the side of little Arron Stream. It moved first like an animal, far away, a buck against the horizon or a small spring bear. But then its form took shape in the glimmer of the sun, and all the men were watching him as he came closer. That is, the men on the bank—the other teamsters couldn't see him yet. Except for Richardson, in the lead.

"Yes, there he is now," Richardson said, "the photographer is coming." Richardson nodded, put the reins under the front bindings, and climbed down off the rig and started to walk away. Some said he was going in to put on a clean shirt. That was ridiculous—all the shirts were tatters, hanging on poles with the camp doors left open, the smell of bacon grease and snow.

He stepped off to relieve himself, was another theory. He could have done that from the top of the sled. Someone said he was going to get his scarf that he wore all winter and tie it to his neck. That is a possibility.

One reason might be that he needed to check the rivets he and Gibbs had put on the runners—that the sled felt bowed on that side, and one of the rivets had snapped. Late the night before they had used the English wheel to bend another sliver of metal against that birch runner, and maybe he sensed it loose.

It may have been that. For he did look and walk away—perhaps to go to the hovel to find something to change it over.

Gibbs said it was inexplicable, why he stepped down. But he felt the photographer was still far away and would have to set up. The others, however, did not see this; they were ready to go when Richardson went.

No one will know why Richardson stepped down.

My feeling, somewhat romanticized, is that he suddenly decided he didn't want his picture taken after all—fame to please or worry a girl who had turned her back on him. The McCord girl, who he did not know had died of pleurisy long sad winters ago.

So the men held up their last great loads, all over two hundred logs. Richardson walked by Tomkins, and glanced over at him as he stepped about the hard snow in the spring weather. They glanced at each other just a second. In their looks at that moment was complete understanding of one another's essential natures. Yet Richardson kept moving.

Bartlett's diary is exhaustive in how all of this happened, but I do not think it any better than what I will say. Tomkins wanted a chance to escape ignominy that his lifetime of scandal had caused. And he stepped up, looked about, and decided to steal Richardson's championship load. This was exactly where his days of famine had led him. He climbed the same side of the sled that Richardson had just exited, and made his way to the top.

Butch, the great gelding on the right nearest the embankment on the way down, looked back at this man and gave a head toss as if he suddenly understood there would be death.

TWO

I was born two months premature, in a small house's bathroom on a side lane, near the marshes on Good Friday morning, 1947, at about that exact moment.

Lula Brower was in attendance. Why had she come that night before? My mother always said an angel of the Lord had sent her—or Mom would have bled to death, because no one expected the child this soon.

Why didn't my mother get to the hospital? Lula herself did not think my mother could be moved, and my mother did not want to leave.

"I am not going anywhere—if I move I will kill the child—" She was so certain of this, Lula concurred.

"The angel of the Lord told her to be with me," my mother said. "And that's why you are here."

Lula did her best, but she was positive I was stillborn. She lay me down on the floor and cried. Then I did.

They said I would not live; if I lived, I would not walk; if I walked, I would not run. That I would not speak or learn. That I would never attend school, let alone university.

Nor could they then determine, by this premature birth, whose son I really was.

Timing might make it impossible to know.

Camellia never forgave herself her trip, and so coddled me a while. Not knowing that when this happens a child will either smother or fight. No one realized at that moment how well I could fight.

I began to cry, and the Clydes on a mountain forty-four miles away were whipped forward simultaneously.

THREE

Tomkins pulled the whip and struck out at the animals far beneath him. The first thing he did not understand is that neither Richardson nor Curtis nor Trethewey nor Nolan ever in their lives touched the animals with the whip, but only cracked it above him.

He snapped the ten-foot-long whip down across the burnt back of Butch, and bringing it back across them again allowed the tip of this whip to hit Missy's right eye.

They were gone but his hold on the reins made their heads crank as they left, and Tomkins felt his stomach in his mouth. The great timbers began to groan in their chains and the animals were suddenly turned halfway blind by Tomkins wiping them down furiously one moment and hauling them back another.

It took everything he had to keep from falling forward into the animals themselves.

The others behind the Clydes had not seen Tomkins replace Richardson on the sled (Tomkins having lost his fine parka to Pitman was one reason), all of them watching for each other to leave. When the Clydes went, they went too, as they had all winter, thinking the photo would be taken, and would be published in the papers for them to give their loved ones—all this great wood coming off the mountain at the same time!

Yet Tomkins' inability had caused his horses to stumble, so that Nolan's Miss Maggie Wade and Mr. Stewart were almost running Tomkins off the downhill by the time they got to the first turn. Behind Nolan, Curtis; behind Curtis, Trethewey with the Percherons. All of them now dancing toward the bottom. How long did this take? I think about thirty-five seconds. My airways were being unclogged while the lives of the four greatest teamsters in the history of our river were coming to an end.

Richardson had turned as soon as he saw the Clydes move. "HEY!" he roared, and ran along the bank.

He managed to jump from the cliff near the Percherons' hovel to the sled as it straightened after the first turn. It was his duty to do so—the team had been entrusted to him, and were Jameson Clydes. It would be the last thing he ever attempted. His physical disability finally betrayed him.

He tried to put out his left arm, which no longer existed, to grab the bit of pole at the back of the load, and stumbled. As he fell, his right hand grabbed a cedar, and he strained to lift himself up. But the sled bounced and he fell under Miss Maggie Wade and was spit out behind the sled, laying on his side, his colored jacket like a bit of fall foliage, his body crushed.

Tomkins had no idea Richardson had given his life to try to stop the runaway. He was bouncing two feet off the cedars and falling to and fro as the sled came to the last turn. There, his eyes frantic, he saw Meager Fortune, who had been down on the flats helping with the last chaff, waving the horses to turn. It was useless. The whip had opened up a sore on Butch's back, had half-blinded old half-blind Missy, and Stretch's heaviness on the reins caused Butch to bolt.

Nothing would stop Butch from trying to escape the load that had taken three days to pile. All Butch's memories, whatever they were—to do too much and do it well, of coming from the devil's mount to the sled, of working beyond exhaustion through the horror of this mountain—came to a moment in April when he may very well have decided to do exactly what he wanted—to kill the bastard who had whipped him across the back.

Meager had to jump out of the way as the load started to spill to the left, which meant that Miss Maggie Wade was the first horse to be crushed. A great sickening snap was heard, and Tomkins jumped the load while the horses ran straight past the turn and into the dammed brook that would have been let loose in two days. Huge thousand-pound timbers bounced in the air thirty feet, and the animals were gone into the water.

There was almost eight feet of water, and Missy and Butch stumbled into it headfirst. Behind them, Nolan was obliterated by their dropping load, his chest crushed; he tried to keep breathing, and did for a few moments. Behind him, Curtis fell under the feet of Duff Almighty—at twenty-two years old, carrying 320 logs, he died in a second.

Then Curtis's load, snapping its chains, went straight backward like battering rams when the bindings broke, and killed the Percheron Cole Younger, and almost decapitated Mr. Trethewey.

All of this was over in a moment, so those men at the top of the run who had been laughing and jousting with these men a few minutes ago, now looked down in muted astonishment, and then cold horror. Logs like straw strewn down the half mile of hill—men running toward the destruction hoping to help. Of the two animals in the water, Butch was drowning while Missy kept her brown nose above the ice. Looking down at Butch, Meager could see his eyes staring back up out of the water, out of the furious and uncompromising spring blackness. Yet each time he tried to lift himself up, he sank down and struggled into the black soup like darkness. There his life, great and bold and wondrous, trembled away from him.

"Ah boy," Meager said crying, "ah my boy."

Missy, however, was still breathing.

Meager called for a pole and two men and Gibbs and Bartlett came. Meager, grabbing the pole from Bartlett, jumped through the ice. He thrust the pole under Missy's front legs and yelled at Gibbs to cut the animal away from Butch, already dead, and help him lift the pole up. He stood on drowned Butch's back to get this done.

With this done, the animal's head came up a bit. Meager told Bartlett to jump on the lower end of Missy's rump and for Gibbs to hold her nose closed. The animal became frantic and, with pressure hauling up on her front legs and someone standing on her back so her back legs could feet the muck, she found her way ahead, breaking the ice, all the way to the shallow end, where she thrust onto the bank causing Gibbs, who had her bindings, a shattered arm. She ran off into the thicket kicking the broken two sled, with its new runner dragging behind it.

Missy was the only animal to survive that day.

Then this man, they assumed the photographer, ran up the bank as others still came down, trying to help who he could. But there was no one to help. The four teamsters were dead. Certain of the horses tried to raze themselves up, as if felled by cannon.

Down on the flat, Stretch Tomkins, who had suffered a sprained finger, his hat off and his bald head shining in the early morning, almost as slick as the shine Fraser and Pitman had made through the wood, looked back amazed at what he was witnessing. Then he sauntered back, strangely relieved that the idea of the stamp was forgotten.

"It weren't my fault," he said to the man he thought must be the photographer.

"Why wasn't it your fault?" the man asked deathly quietly.

It was Owen Jameson. He was wearing the old math teacher's coat and boots.

Tomkins shuddered, his lips quivered, and he smiled.

Meager kept going from one to the other, trying to hold people in his arms, but there was no sense in it. Even after an hour, when the sensibilities of the men became reasoned enough to know a great godawful tragedy had occurred, Fortune was still sitting beside Curtis holding his hand, even as one of the men came down from the camp and shot Duff Almighty.

Tomkins stood in mute and civil anguish while what had happened was reported to Owen. Owen said nothing. Looking back at Nolan, laying under ten tons of logs, one arm still outstretched, there was nothing in the world to say.

"These were to be the last loads," Bartlett said.

Owen told Gibbs to find men and punch out to the depot, to report this to police and the hospital, and find five more stamps and come in and stamp the logs back again, to Jameson on the great Bartibog.

"What do you want done with Tomkins?" young Gibbs asked. The men were ready to kill him. The strange fact was that Owen being there prevented this.

"Let him go," Owen said to the men holding him, "he can be found later."

As soon as that was said, Stretch Tomkins, a man like ourselves, began to run away.

Owen could not be worried about that now. He had all the men try to free those battered bodies from the lumber that had enslaved them. Moving a ton of cedar to see the head of Miss Maggie Wade; moving another to see the back hooves of Mr. Stewart caught in the traces, bound by the decisions of men they had never understood.

It was as a loving gesture that Nolan's arm was reaching out to help his horses, that Richardson had jumped over the precipice in a final effort to save the Clydes, and that at the last moment Trethewey tried to turn his animals to safety rather than jumping to freedom himself, the letter from the wife who had disowned him still in the pocket of his coat. Curtis lay near Duff Almighty, the reins wrapped about his gloved hand, as they had been all winter long.

The greatest teamster in the world at twenty-two, who had wanted to go to Hollywood and be in a picture show.

Owen would not stop working even though the men told him to rest. He forced some of the younger cutters away so they would not see it, and took over the job of clearing the lanes. He had torn muscles in both arms, and his left leg had swelled already to almost twice its size.

The wood was strewn down half a mile and gouged deep into the cold earth. It would be lumber still used someday to build houses of meek, disgruntled men, those already spoiled and coming into a new age who would in my class in 1973 dismiss these men as nothing.

Three men to a log, and peaveys rolled this wood to the side, to see the sad, astonished, and private agony of once great lives.

FOUR

In the hospital my heart stopped four times as those peaveys were rolling those logs. People said it would be much better if I died, being as I was the love child of a disgusting union. Camellia needed a transfusion and people were so upset with her (thinking she'd orchestrated Owen's escape) they milled about but did not give it. Until Hennessey himself walked into the crowd, stopped a woman who he knew had the same blood type as my mother, and took her inside.

"You don't mind doing this, do you, dear?" he said, grabbing her by the arm and leading her up the long stairs in his powerful grip. "She is a human being after all."

The transfusion was given or my mother would have been dead in ten minutes. And the woman's name—Cora Auger. She had found her way to the hospital, secretly hoping for my mother's death. So it was help unencumbered by joy.

"No matter," my mother said, "it was Saint Jude who was helping us that day."

It wasn't until later that Hennessey heard of the tragedy. He left for the mountain with Buckler. There they saw Owen Jameson. As soon as Hennessey looked his way he said, "Get him to the cabin and get his pants cut open."

And as soon as Owen heard this he said, "I will kill the first man who touches me—Dr. Hennessey, sir, you know that to be true."

And no one touched him. He told them he was staying under his own care until the run was over—then, if they wanted, they could take him in again.

So by three o'clock the bodies were freed, pronounced dead, taken to the shelter of the camp, and placed on bunks and wrapped in blankets.

It was then that Owen did for them the same as was done for Will; a great vigil took place within that smoky, desolate room, with sky birds singing again. There was a reading from the bible, a psalm of David: "Yea, though I walk through the valley of the shadow of death, I will fear no evil."

There was silence otherwise. A complete soundlessness as men stood about, not even whispering.

Little things amazed people. Richardson's picture that he had of himself with two arms, thought lost in the fire in January, was sitting on the floor near his bunk. There was no way to know how it came to be there.

Curtis's cup, which people were sure had been empty, was full of hot tea when they got back to the room, as if he had just poured it.

No one would say he hadn't.

At six o'clock Saturday night, with lanterns showing the way in the evening light, the bodies were brought out to the sled of Gordon and Ronald's Young and, with the Belgians dressed with plumes, taken away. By now it seemed as if the whole world was alive with their deaths.

By the next morning, still in spring rain, the rivers had swollen and broken free.

"It will be an early drive this year after such a winter, I do suppose," Pitman said.

It came in an instant then, spring.

The logs were restamped by Fortune, by Bartlett and Gibbs, with Owen Jameson not sleeping and overseeing it all. Why, for the money had to go to the widows or families of these men, even if his business was doomed. This is what he pronounced.

So men from the other camps came over the next few days to help the run down. They cut the logs free of their chains, and rode them out along the rapids, dark swells of high tormented water, across the Arron Brook talons, where to fall was to die, and into the great river. Men like MacLeod and Curry stepped on those logs, cursed at them, and at anyone who would take a freshet from their piles, on timbers so fast and slick you would think they must all have God on their shoulders—all these men: Underhill, MacLeod, Curry, and Curtis's brother. All the way down the river, from streams flowing against the budding trees, the snow still six feet deep in places in the woods and the raw birds singing, to Arron Brook with its danger, and on to Bartibog, where his brother died—none did a better job on the river, they said, than Owen Jameson. He was up day and night, went back to help the men get the stragglers and landings, made sure the food was hot on those cold days. All the while his lungs filled with fluid from the wound he had taken in the war that had turned septic by the punch of the comb. He unwrapped it on the third night to look—took a hot piece of stove wood and tried to lance it. But he did not sleep. He took out Camellia's picture, which he had taken from his house, and stared at it most of the night. He had loved her as a child, and had not known. Someone once told me if Hennessey had not had to get back to make sure I lived, he would have stayed to make sure Owen did. It is not an easy thing to force a man to live with.

"There will be no rest until tomorrow," was all Owen said.

On the fourth day he worked too hard, and stood on a hemlock in the bracing river. But then his fever hit. And he came in and lay down on the spot he and Will had stayed the day they stole the beaver. No one said a thing. Once again he had Camellia's picture in his hand.

His leg was gangrenous, and raw poison was spreading into his chest.

He looked strangely angered by his incapacity—as if people had played some enormous trick on him. They gathered about him staring in strange, almost affixed wonder.

He was, after all, only twenty-six years old. He had, he thought, survived the war.

"Just the age of Keats," he smiled at Simon Terri.

Unfortunately, most of the men didn't understand. Some

of them thought he was a murderer, but even those now had sympathy fill their hearts.

They made a place for him below Toomey's Quarry. That is, half a mile from where Will had broken the cedar free.

"I must get up," he said.

"No no," MacLeod said, "you never mind that now, boy."

Meager Fortune tried to give him rum-laced broth. Owen was going away from them and they knew it. He, the most solitary of men, tried to clutch someone's hand.

They decided to keep his death a secret until the run was over. Half the province was still looking for him.

Little Meager Fortune said he would bring him out, planted on the center of one of Richardson's fullest cedars. Fortune rode it down, with Owen before him clothed in white linen from Brennan's farmhouse, Fortune speaking at certain intervals to his son and his wife.

"Why do you want me to stay here," he said, tears in his eyes, "this old world. Why can't I go home to you?"

By the evening of the fourth day of the run, a thousand logs were seen by women watching for their men, a thousand more—and then ten thousand after that. It was incomprehensible that four teamsters had done so much, they thought of them now as spirits, they thought of them now, and forever, as ghosts.

Men who became legends in spite of all that was held against them while they did what they now were legends for doing. They were spoken about in whispers.

"I remember when he lost his arm," one said about Richardson. "'I don't need 'er,' he said; he said, 'I do as much with one arm as any a you boys do with two.'"

Until that moment, none remembered Richardson ever

having said that. Now a man would take his life in his hands to refute it.

Trethewey had knocked ten men out in one fight. His wife, they said, had come home, and was here for the funeral. They always loved each other—you could tell by her letters.

Nolan, a man they had dismissed for being washed up, old and silly, they now said was overall the greatest of the teamsters. All of them had done what they could. All of them had stayed with their horses.

They would go and build a monument to them on Good Friday Mountain.

FIVE

The news spread of Owen's death. It seemed a chapter was over. The sordid business, as Sterling called it, was done.

And then, quite shamelessly, a man walked in from the old Curry Wharf, at about nine in the morning of the fifth day after the deaths.

He stopped at Flynn's store to buy cigarettes. The woman shook as she waited on him. He looked into the corner by the old pot-bellied stove with its two extra homemade reflectors and smiled at Old Flynn, brother of the mathematics teacher, but Flynn was staring at the floor shaking. The man said, "Good day," and went across the street and along the old dirt road in behind Strawberry Marsh. Sometimes he stopped people, asking questions as innocently as a child, and then, cigarette in his mouth, kept moving.

"My good God," men and women said, looking out the windows of their houses into the great April wind.

They believed he was Lazarus. In fact, at first they didn't believe it was him at all.

It was this man they had mocked when alive and made monolithic when dead. Reggie McDonald Glidden.

Finally they gathered about him near the post office, and what was unusual became usual, what was unheard of became commonplace. He had come home.

He was told in spitting gestures from outraged people, all of what had happened in the last five months.

Some wanted to touch him—some wanted to know if he was real, wanted to see the wound on his head, for they couldn't believe he was alive.

"I am completely in the dark," he said, "about all you are saying now."

By four that afternoon all charges against Owen Jameson were dropped. Mary Jameson was at the station to pick up his books.

"Things fall apart—the center cannot hold," was written on the back of a page. For the rest of her life Mary would tell her friends Owen had written it.

Crossman turned toward the filing cabinet as she left, and stayed in that position for an hour or more, looking out at Owen's friends as they dismantled the gallows.

At first, few seemed to care that this had happened. It was simply a mistake, and people should get over it and get on with their lives, for there was much work to do.

Owen died from the wound in the war. That was not unusual.

Yet over the next week, the knowledge of the miscarriage of justice spread, so that ten papers covered the story and people became flabbergasted at it all across our country. And then from Cora Auger to Gravellier to those on the jury, people literally ran away and hid. Suddenly they couldn't stand to look each other's way. They blamed Crossman for not taking care of Jameson's wound.

"How dare he not take care of the wound of a VC winner?"

Recriminations started against Judge Fyfe, and Butler, McLean, Urquart, Hamilton, and others. Mackey the coroner was sent packing back to London. Sterling stood at the crossroads near Camellia's house, guarding it, he said, for her.

"God, I hear it was nothin' but a big jessless lark," he said. He kept walking about town trying to shake people's hands.

For days the streets of our town were empty. For the next two weeks, no local paper was printed. The truth itself had vanished.

Everyone was speechless, as if their souls had suffered when the sustenance they had taken for their famine disappeared.

The *Jensen Otter* came in to Will Jameson's wharf, and over time a great load of wood was taken, three-quarters of the money from that year given over to the widows and the families of the men. It essentially broke the back of Jameson industry.

The body was exhumed, double-checked, found out easily—by the marks on his bare feet from climbing the yards, and the clothing from England—to be the able-bodied seaman Dressler, and given to the captain of the *Jensen* and buried at sea.

He was a man who had climbed the yards when drunk, was knocked by a pulley when trying to scamper down, and fell. From his picture later published, people could see he was almost the same age and size as our Reggie. Therefore, the paper said in its editorial of half-apology, it was a mitigation.

Mary Jameson and Buckler bought a new 1947 Chevrolet and drove about town every day. Though their hearts were not in it. It was the last car they would ever buy.

Mary's friends all came back to the great kitchen, saying something should be done against those who perpetrated all of this. For days there was talk of Estabrook and Bots, Sloan and others—how they had all conspired. How they would all end badly—how they used false public opinion to further their own ambition.

This was true—but I suppose no worse than the untruths said about Owen or Camellia.

Owen's Victoria Cross was returned to Mary.

Meeting Reggie Glidden on a windy day in May, when seagulls were full in the sky, little Cora Auger, her plump legs in heavy jeans, turned and said from a distance, while backing into the future she no longer held dear: "I gave her my blood."

Yet over time there was the idea that this had been done by Reggie on purpose, to hang Jameson because of what was suspected to have been an illicit romance. Because he himself was impotent, and my mother had a proof of crime in her belly.

I was the stumbling block to reason. I was in an incubator for weeks and half-blind until I was ten. I had a crippled left hand, and all of this pointed to some secret liaison. My life was set at the moment of her fall to be something other than what she had ever planned. In a way, I was proof of her infidelity—like some wounded bastard in the back end of a Shakespeare play, the one they pointed to as divination.

There wasn't much I could say about it.

The idea grew that Reggie knew, being impotent, she had had me by Owen.

This rumor began to spread against Reggie, sometime that June. It lingered over the wavy lilacs and the red-winged blackbirds on the cliffs. In part, I think it was understandable. He had tricked them all by not giving them the right to defame him in public. He had left on a ship to start his life anew.

He had come back, however, to save his friend.

The conflagration once again spread out willy-nilly to houses of people who hardly knew the participants and yet wanted scandal for themselves, to fill up the famine in their lives.

The idea of Reggie's elaborate memorial at the union hall was most distressing now. Yet he said nothing, and did his best to protect his wife and me from any defaming that might arise.

Amid speculation of a call to be debarred, Brower resigned on July 5. Coming from the bank, the first person he saw was Mary Jameson, arriving with a certified check for the lumber, ready to take out cash and give bonus. There were tears in her eyes. She had lost so much.

He tried to smile, but his great dignity came unhinged. People now said he was an outsider, not one of ours. How dare he try a man who had won the Victoria Cross? They remembered him dancing too close with Mrs. Mackey as her little husband tittered in the corner.

Unfortunately, the one who fared the worst was Lula. Scathing things were said; she was called whore and worse as she walked our streets, and was seen but rarely.

To everyone she had started the rumors that had killed

Solomon Hickey. And that itself had killed the greatest man who ever came from town, Owen Jameson.

There was even a group formed, called The Friends of Owen.

On July 10, in the midst of summer heat, Lula was seen out at the restaurant with her father to celebrate her twenty-fifth birthday. Her hair was blond and lay flat upon her head. Her face and skin were deathly white now. She walked in with her cane and on her father's arm. The celebration had been planned for a long while. Now it had whittled down through the bric-a-brac of shifting loyalties, and a ten-place setting on that hot evening was reduced to two.

There was bravery shown by both Browers because of this, or in spite of it all.

They were alone, sitting at a table with the silverware glittering under the light. No one came to wait upon them. She looked shallow and small in her new dress with Owen's small brooch pinned on her breast. She smiled at nothing as she looked about.

They tried to signal the waitress, but no one came. Finally, old Buckler, tottering and half-drunk, who had dined in a room by himself as he'd done once a week for years, saw their predicament and insisted they be treated with respect. He insisted and stayed until they were.

He left without them knowing that he had done so.

In late August, Tomkins went to Estabrook asking him for bonus, telling him of the trouble they were in. For the investigation of the stamp was in full bloom. He was disheveled, he had lost weight, his eyes were downcast, and he trembled as he spoke.

"Everything is blowing up on us," he said.

But Estabrook knew this by now. He knew he must get rid of his witness, his confidant, his partner. He, in fact, told Tomkins to go away for good.

Tomkins was given money and left on the very train they believed Jameson had wanted to take, to the very same place, Montreal, where Tomkins had a sister who worked in an office on Ste-Catherine Street.

The police were waiting for him when he got there, with his new hat and coat and a letter of recommendation.

But except for a fine, Bots and Estabrook were considered men above reproach.

And it was put behind them.

I was asked when they first met afterward, Camellia and Reggie.

They met at the hospital, where I was. It was said that seeing her husband, she fainted. And poor Reggie took this as a sign that I was not his child, not as a sign that she believed a miracle had occurred. She believed, and always did, that her prayers had kept him alive. Her sanctity during the trial, her lighting candles beneath the porcelain Virgin Mary.

"You see," she kept telling people, "you see?"

She was as hysterical as a child over this, and loved everyone. She kissed nurses and doctors and anyone who came to see her.

Until she found out that Owen Jameson had died.

SIX

When I was little, Reggie, working as Push for Jameson, was consistently gone. He would keep the legend alive, no matter if it destroyed who he was.

For he felt the bullet had killed the man who had saved his life. If only he had gone in as Push when they wanted him to, if only he could have realized what a selfish thing he had done to the man who had carried him to safety. But he had not realized. And therefore he suffered. He would take the suffering of both greatness and scandal onto himself. And as he did so, he transformed into the truly great man he became.

He left us at times during his summer layoff, and would go on terrible drunks. So we were never rich. But he did his best to keep the Jameson business going, and was always sober by fall. Farther and farther from any safety net, he would cruise the great north counties with a compass and a horse. He never listened to those who told him a new age had come, that it was now hopeless. He found the great northern county barren and filled with newer and newer machines.

"No," he would say, "there are trees to cut and men to cut them and that's all we need."

He had few to be Push for now. But he was the one old Buckler and Mary relied on. Still, they were worried about him disappearing for a month at a time in the woods, appearing as a shadow against some pile of cold railing logs near their house on an October evening, spreading his map against the flare of the porch light, with Saturn visible in the northern sky.

"How many men do you think I can get?" he would say.

But they wouldn't know—for the men had drifted away, and other companies had come along.

"Never you mind—I will get the men," he would say.

But the men told Mary he drove them too hard, and complained of his consistently doing something dangerous. So the men became fewer—and fewer still.

And yet he worked.

"If they have tractors, I have horses; if they have trucks, I have sleds; if they have buzz saw, I have ax—if they have jimmies, I have peaveys—I need no more," he told my mother.

Even when they were being shoved off track and could not find ground to cruise. He did it not only for Owen Jameson, or Will, but for us as well.

"I want you to be proud of me," he said, "even if no one else ain't."

I was proud of him. I never knew if that was enough.

Still, there was one thing he did not reconcile.

She begged him to realize I was his son even if others would not.

He only smiled and nodded at her.

Then after a run of time, like wind scattering leaves in a dooryard, came the long agony of Mary and Buckler—to fire a man they loved to keep him from killing himself. Yet Camellia went to Buckler often, and petitioned Reggie be hired on again in the fall. She did this without him knowing. She would stand in the muted hallway of the house where Owen and she had met, pleading with the dignity she never lost.

Sometimes old Mary's and her eyes didn't even meet as they spoke.

They did not want to hire Reggie, because he was destroying his great body, the asset men who have so little so often give.

"He will die on his job and I can't have that," Mary would say each time Camellia came begging, many times with me by the hand. But the job was given. What could they do? They would be out of business without him—and secretly kept it going past its time, just for him.

Other companies finding a thousand acres to tear from our soil. Reggie finding a hundred.

What a figure of laughter he made himself, coming out into the dazzling sunshine on those winter days with Ronald's Young on sled, while huge trucks passed him by going to lands he no longer could reach. Ronald's Young brave hearted and not diminished by the truck splashing mud against its proud, buckled harness.

They said Reggie was so strong he once carried a man on snowshoes seven miles to get to Dr. Hennessey in a storm. No one, however, managed to carry his burden.

One day he came home with a picture of a cottage he said he was going to buy us.

Another day he came home with a picture of Camellia he had found at Bartibog near Toomey's Quarry. Where Owen had died.

It had lasted all this time under some moss. When Reggie had sat down for tea, he'd seen something and lifted it up from an inch under the dirt.

He'd stared at it in quiet, serene wonderment for an hour. How beautiful she really was. Then brought the men to their feet, and said, "Me boys we have a long way to go."

Reggie never said a thing about the picture after. He only brought it home and gave it back to Camellia.

So Reggie worked as a walking boss and a landings supervisor and main Push in the camp up at Rolfe's turn where they cut for the next two years, the world increasingly crowding them—new implements of cutting pushing their small stakes further and further away.

Then one night in the cold February wind, Buckler appeared at our door. I think my mother by now was ashamed of where she lived and began trying to clean up. There was the idea that you entered into the past when you entered our house—but other houses on the river carried this stigma too, holding too long to something they needed, that the world in all its furious entitlement had long let go.

He came with a reprimand. He told her Reggie was taking too many chances on the ice. He had not done this before.

"It is hard on the men, and dangerous to the horses," Buckler said. He looked at me a moment and did not smile.

His face was drawn; he was very, very thin, almost bony. None in town said a word against the Jamesons now. Buckler was the uncle of the great Owen Jameson. Greater, they said, than Will himself.

"He will not put the men in danger," Camellia said.

"Not intentionally, no—but you must realize he puts himself in danger—he strode Auger's hole with Ronald's Young."

This was where Dan Auger had fallen in the shifting ice—it was perhaps the most dangerous place to trek out a horse.

Camellia did not answer for a long moment. Then she said: "Let him have his danger please, just one more year."

I remember Reggie now as he looked, his great broad face covered in graying beard and his hair tousled, his thumbs as big as some men's wrists he sat in the chair by himself smiling at everyone.

It was 1952 and I was five years old. He had come out for my birthday, though there had been terrible weather.

He went back into the camp the next morning, for he said he had a job to do. I believe it was my birthday that made him drink for the first time, on the job. Or that the illness of my mother, which I always remember as vague and indeterminate, had reoccurred—and he in his big, stumbling, childlike manner did not know what to do.

He was solitary, strong as a bull, and thirty-five years of age. He never mentioned me to my mother and never spoke of her or Owen except in kindness.

"He was a great lad, that Owen Jameson," he once said to me.

"How was he so great?" I asked.

"Read books," he said.

He knew his position in life had given him the most difficult task toward courage. For my mother and I, he struggled toward the light.

He was my father.

At the door before he left, she patted his shoulder, as she would pat a schoolboy in the morning. Then reprimanded him for not having his leather mittens.

"Go on now," she said when she turned her cheek to brush away his kiss, "or you'll be late for the drive."

He winked at me.

The reports are scattered in the testimony of men long since gone.

At Arron's Falls that spring below the talons. From Rolfe's turn the logs were harder to manage, and the drive was trouble. The fact that old Buckler himself had to come in and tell his Push not to drive the men straight down but take two days or more, and be easy on the water, told of everyone's unease.

"I can't keep you working yourself to death just because of my feelings for—"

But he did not go on. The men were solemn. Reggie only shrugged. "I will do it to cause them the least amount of pain," he said. Not knowing he had just quoted Keats at almost the very place Owen had mentioned the poet five years before.

He smiled and went out, looked at the sour sky pelting rain, and the wood already in the little Hackett Brook, as he tucked his shirt into his pants.

"We will do it today, boys, and please our boss," he said, "and please the God my wife still believes in."

And the men started to slip the dark, peeled yards into the water.

"A's fer the axes," Reggie said, "B's for the boys—"

For some reason he felt the logs beneath him slippery and easily submerged, while those behind him seemed to rise in the swells. The last time he remembered this was at Will Jameson's death, the jam on the great river.

It was only seven miles to the falls, but you came to the falls not straight like you did from Arron Brook but at a right angle, 230 yards above—it would be hard to keep them from jamming going over. That is why men had petitioned Reggie for a road above, to bring in the trucks at that point. But Reggie Glidden was stubbornly against this modernization. He felt it would put many drivers out of work.

It could have happened just as it was stated. None has ever found out.

The first of the run was fine—with the extra chute of water from sluices the men had built on Arron Brook and from the snow runoff they had dammed, the logs plummeted over and kept going with the help of peaveys.

Until about two that afternoon, on a cold windy day, when a huge cedar, a limb still upon it, came into the turn sideways and went over the falls before they could turn it right. There it stayed, and the logs piled upon it.

"A road would have been the thing," one of the men said to Reggie.

"Never mind that now," Reggie said. "It is not a big problem. See if the peaveys will work on it—take your crew and go to the other side and try to loosen the jam above."

But the peaveys did not work, though the men gave it their all, calling on each other to "push and be damned."

The logs were not cleared, and now backed up all the way to the turn.

Reggie studied the water, could see deeper into it than most.

"If I jump-start that fucker there," he said, pointing down over the falls to the submerged cedar, "we will have out by suppertime."

It was twenty feet down over this cliff. Wet and cold, a shorebird had come up this far to nest, and kept its place even as the men worked around it. On the shale side were the letters *BJ*—for Byron Jameson, who had lived out here one winter on his own, cutting with one horse and a double-bitted ax.

Reggie, of course, knew all of this, knew all about bravery except how to answer when people said he didn't have it.

He asked for rope, and with a rope about his chest was lowered down with a peavey, to pry the main log loose and let the rest come down the falls. He did this for honor, though a road would have been better, and for loyalty to the Jameson name.

The trouble with doing this is once the logs start, you have to be pulled to safety in a second by men atop the cliff, in a vital pull to keep you out of the way of those logs coming down over your neck.

The men, a Matheson and a Curry and a Joyce, held on to this rope and teased Reggie a bit as he moved over these logs.

"She's all as wet as a varr skid," he said.

"Or a good woman," another answered.

"Ah, a good woman," he said.

The men were silent after.

Reggie kicked at one log, pried at another, and said: "It *would* be the day I quit drinking."

"You quit drinking?"

"Yes," he smiled, "I will die a free man now."

He found the cedar—and how the limb had braced it against a rock.

"Ah, this is easy now," he said. "I have the problem solved, me dunces—" And he moved about as the rope tangled above him.

"Don't go over any farther," Matheson cautioned, "or it'll be a hard pull to get you back."

But Reggie could only solve it from the far side, down near the bottom of the falls.

So he paid no attention to the warning. He jabbed his pole down, and with every bit of strength in his tired muscled body he felt the cedar move.

"Watch it now—here she blows!" he roared.

Just then the logs began to come.

Some say his rope was too fast by a tangle, when they tried to haul him up, and he was too far from their cliff.

One man, the diver who had looked for him, Harrison Matheson, risked his life reaching down to grab him. But it was no use at all.

Little Meager Fortune came to the door that night to tell us.

"They was all my friends," he said, tears running freely down his face, his coat opened to the wind, his chest half bare.

So they had become equals once again: Reggie, Will, and Owen.

SEVEN

My mother knew she had broken Reggie's heart. And this time he left for good to set her free. She had never told him she loved him. Until after he died. Then tears burning in her eyes, she said it almost every day, sometimes looking out onto an empty street.

We say no so often to those who admire us too much.

I heard a Shaver song not too long ago, and I thought of Reggie and my mother:

You're going to want to hold me
Just like I always told you—
You're going to miss me when I'm gone

How often had he reached out for her only to have her turn away? Afterward, at night, I often saw her looking toward the door for him to come home just once more, to call his name.

The town, too, was sorry. The funeral was large. People speculated Camellia would marry someone very rich.

Reggie's statue was placed on Good Friday Mountain along with the teamsters.

He had gone back to the fold the only way he knew how.

"I like the sea," he told me on the day of my birthday, when he drove me about town in his old truck before he left for the drive, "but I belong to the woods."

That is all he said. Except, "Would you like a chocolate bar?"

It was the only thing I remember that he bought me. He patted my head. My eyes half blind, I looked up at him. I believe it was the only time he ever touched me.

"If you think that is good—I got something good," I said, trembling all over as I sat there.

"Ya, what?"

"I love you," I said.

I don't remember what he answered. I never saw him again.

He was the last Push for Jameson. They sold out the next year, parts cannibalized and their holdings restructured. Some said they went bankrupt. One night I saw Sterling rushing past us with a truckload of pilfered wood, a smile on his face.

After a time, on long ago summer nights, my mom would go to the Pines dances, and sit alone, and listen to the music of Harold Savage and the Savage Boys, as they fiddled and stomped out the last of an age that was ending. She loved music. She was solitary, mostly alone. Sometimes I would see her walking along our lane, coming home alone with a small present for me in her pocket, once a mouth organ that I learned to play, or bits of colored glass she carried to give the girls who played hopscotch.

We lived on a military pension. She could be talked into buying anything—always saying she would pay for it later. But of course she never had enough money.

At times I remember when collectors were at the door, men vastly experienced at scrounging. We would hide upstairs so we wouldn't have to pay, her arm about me and holding her nose, trying not to giggle. A child to the end.

She bought me a record player so I could listen to Gene Vincent: "Be-bop-a-lula, she's my baby."

When I was nine she came home from the Pines with a man I had never seen before. He was sitting at the kitchen table and spoke like a woodsman for Sloan. He had in his time hated and fought both Reggie and Will. My mom did not know this.

I remember seeing the tip of his cigarette as he flicked the ashes into the cuffs of his green pants.

It was May, and I could smell fresh mud and grass. I was alone for a time, awake in my bed. He had a loud voice, serious and cross. She was trying to explain something. But I could hardly see because of my eyes.

"I love May nights," she said. And, "I never finished school—someday I'd like to."

I listened to this melancholy enthusiasm and drifted in and out of sleep.

Then the lower hallway light came on. There was a song on the radio. I think it was Hank. I think it was "Your Cheatin' Heart."

I cannot hear that song now without breaking a radio. Strange, how much I love Hank Williams.

She was so fragile. After a while he was cursing and then called her something and slammed the door.

I got out of bed. She was lying in the living room, vomit in her hair, her skirt pushed up. Her underwear torn off. The man whoever he was, had gone. There were photos on the table. Most were of she and me and dad, she had been showing him.

"I'll help," I said.

I ran to the only person I knew—far away. Lula opened the door.

Time had changed her as well. The suffering had changed us all.

"A man beat her up," I said.

Lula left with me in her black sedan.

It was as if Lula was now of a different world and time, and we were in a past that had already ended. She had married Peabody, the high school principal, after her father had died. Peabody, they said, married her for the money. I will never know.

She went to meetings where they spoke of "preserving our natural heritage."

She wore her hair back, which made her forehead broad and white. Sometimes she and Peabody went to Florida at Christmas to visit his brother.

So the fiddle music of Harold Savage and the Savage Boys had all but stopped.

Lula told her to go to the police. But Mommy couldn't. Who among them would believe her? It was to her the most terrible thing she had ever done, asking someone to come into her house.

She tried to put the pictures away, but her hands were shaking.

She asked Lula to forgive her.

"Don't be absurd," Lula said.

And then at the door, Lula, once the most self-serving of girls, kissed my mother's cheek and whispered: "He loved you—he always did—and you loved him."

It may sound absurd but which one, Reggie or Owen, did my mother have to be reassured about?

Someone phoned my mother to ask her what she was doing, and who she thought she was, and don't think she hadn't heard about her shenanigans years ago and her bastard crippled kid. Well, as if they didn't know!

Then men started to phone her.

The phone would ring—late at night.

She never went again to listen to music.

Sometimes I stood in the hallway all by myself as dark was coming on, saying, "Oh boy," because she cried and I didn't know what to do.

She was sure that she had a disease.

In 1968 I found out the man was Huey Gravellier. I took my father's 303 and went searching for him. I walked right to the wharf with it over my shoulder. Before I got there, I was tackled, charged by police and the weapon taken from me.

"Yer gonna end up like yer fuggin' granddaddy," Monroe said.

Meager Fortune died in 1970—on a sunny afternoon in April. He was in his barn painting a small skiff he used to ride the rapids in.

He is buried beside Duncan and Evelyn.

Stretch Tomkins is still alive, and as far as I know has written a first-hand account of Good Friday Mountain. "I blame the bosses," he wrote.

He and Cora Auger are pals and go out to bingo and cards together—now almost in their eighties, they are figures in our town.

There is a monument to those teamsters now, looking out over Good Friday Mountain. It is visible from all the roads built near it over the last fifty years. And I am now fifty and go to one of a half-dozen places to see this monument—usually in the fall, when the light from the sky is just right. Statues of Reggie and Will and Owen have been placed there too. It is such a little tribute to them, really.

The woods are muted and stilled and broken and bulldozed away, by machinery none of these men could have foreseen. Nor could they have foreseen our great skyscraper mills that turn our logs into soft toilet paper for softer arses. Our companies owned by other countries.

They could not have foreseen that this monument to tenacity and courage and goodness would be the cause of such disruptive anger over the years. That some mining company would claim this tract and want to take the monuments down, while in the 1980s certain frivolous young men would joke about these men and their horses while drinking in a bar. Or that hunting parties would fire out shots against the granite hides of Missy and Butch.

So these men who died, faithful to Buckler's mountain, over time became again part of a scandal. Another scandal started because of our famine. To fill up our souls with the trinkets of life, instead of with life itself.

On the roads at times, almost at dark, I meet the tractor trailers bringing the logs out—those great trucks carrying twenty times the wood of those sleds that were once so cared for by Curtis and Richardson. What in the world would they think? Their sled wouldn't be as high as one of the tires of those trucks I meet along the myriad roads. Yet they had given their life for it all.

When she got sick later that winter, Camellia begged me not to tell people—for she didn't want them to know she had a disease. She told me to go get her ginger ale. So for days and days I came home from school in the dark afternoon, with icy fog over our river and men across the street at the oil tanks and girls walking home with bookbags across their backs, all stretching toward the sunless future in our lives.

I would sometimes sit into the night at the table listening to the heater glumly, like a sick animal, turn on and off. Her fall had half crippled me, and left me blind in an eye. I suppose at that time I couldn't conceive of life without her. My poor mother—I was the only stigmata she ever had.

I would stand in abject desolation wanting to know if she wanted soup. For hours I would stand silently in the dark.

She was left alone with me, their living proof—in a way, I was her worst enemy. And she cared for me to the end.

I sought oblivion in the dark and left the lights out as I walked in our little house, so street lights flared across the windows and lighted walls like an omen.

Sometimes I would stare blankly at the TV, which we had bought and which had been taken away and brought back twice in the last year—still owing fourteen dollars. Or I would stand at the bottom of the stairs and look up. So when she rose to her feet, in the scattered hope of children I would believe she was fine.

But one day I came home, the light falling under the old oaks in the park and Antonio's barbershop being torn away, and found she wasn't all right. I ran to Foran's and asked for a taxi.

I got her to the hospital and sat in the waiting room, without a coat, in big black boots, with snow whispering across the solid golden-tinged field where Owen made his way into the woods that night in 1947.

For a while she had a room with three other people, and then two, and then she was alone at the back of the hospital.

So I was nine when my mother went away from me. But it was no terrible disgrace she died of. It was cancer.

She had treatment, primitive in the 1950s—and they took a breast and then another. Some nights late, I could see her searching for the card that a friend had sent.

Sometimes, not often, she would talk about when she was a little girl. One Christmas her father and mother bought her nail polish in a small jar. She kept it always.

I told a friend I had once, a man from university with his ponytail and beads, about the fingernail polish. But he had trained himself to be curiously unmoved. I am sure he thought it was all sentimental. He was of the same opinion as Graham Greene, that cruel men cry in theaters. That is true. But crueler men don't.

I buried the polish with her. I didn't tell anyone I had. I tried to be the man my father was.

In the hospital I found out something I have never mentioned to anyone until now. I was listening in almost dumb despair at the door of the waiting room. I had brought my bookbag from school because the teacher, Miss Gilks, had told me to.

I sat in a chair as nurses spoke in the dying light of afternoon.

The doctor, one nurse told the other, had found this tumor in her when she was pregnant with me. He suggested she remove it.

"And what will happen to my baby if I do?" she had said.

"It will die."

"Then I will not do it—never."

The bustling nurses so filled with energy on the last day of my mother's life, smelling of the faint iodine that covered up smaller wounds.

"Though she come now and again, they couldn't do nothing about it—after that."

"And look what she got," another nurse said, "a cripple no good fer nothing at all."

I looked at my bookbag a long time, until it was dark and there was a whistle from the mill, and I could no longer see my name written on the bookbag strap, and the chocolate given to me by the orderly had melted away in my mitten.

Some days I take a backpack and walk all the way to Good Friday, imagining those sleds and the horses—the tack and harness, the boldness of the loads—seeing Pitman, Fraser, and Gibbs, seeing Bartlett, Nolan, and Curtis, Trethewey and Richardson, and Meager Fortune, all in their prime once more. They are hilarious at supper, or playing cards about a stove.

Once I found a peavey stamp in the snow. It was a Jameson stamp left behind when the wood was remarked over to Buckler, when all the timbers were unleashed.

Bullets fired from boyish hunters far away have littered Butch's flanks, and the carved-out two sled is covered with curses, and down in the dark toward the stream there is nothing anymore, and no logs wait.

The mountain has long ago been bulldozed back by the mining company looking for ore. There, in its silent tractor ruts, I found the buckle from Nolan's harness. And on the far slope, the remains of the devil's mount sticking out of the snow, like a top-heavy mushroom.

I sketched them all one night. Butch with his head half turned on the downhill run, and the Percheron, Cole Younger. I was going to keep it forever—but I was only fourteen then and, like Owen with Camellia's picture, I cannot find now where I set it down.

There are still those places in our life, swallows in the air and brooks sounding like children when darkness is coming, filled with the memories of young women far up on rivers picking out berries in the trembling grasses.

But the world has moved on, and they are unknown.

Over time, I discovered Owen Jameson was right. Those who someday would tell the story would no longer be ourselves.

I was treated very well by Lula—I was like her own child, so in the end I called her my mother. But she died many years ago. Still, people didn't know where to place me or what to say or who the hell I was. So I never spoke to anyone about who I was. Not since the day Camellia died.

I bore the physical injury so many of these real men who mocked me on the street have run from most of their lives. Camellia had given it to me in that fall. It was my bonus given on the very day those men died. My heritage I bore for them.

I bore it fifty years.

Often, though, I just wandered from one place to the other, all across our river, drinking Jameson whiskey down until at forty-five the doctor told me he wondered how I was still alive. No liver could take it, he said.

"Well, we'll have to wait and see," I answered.

He told me that alcoholics didn't know they were ill.

"They and everyone else," I said.

I live in my mother's house at Strawberry Marsh. I have a dog named Jeb Stuart. I was given every one of Owen Jameson's books.

When DNA testing became common, a doctor asked if I wanted to find out who I was.

"Come close and I'll whisper," I said, "I already know."

Unlike poor Reggie, I had no choice in the matter. I could never be in the middle of the pack.

Now, whenever I look out my upstairs windows, I can see the new generation traveling on their skateboards off those old pipes at the side of the mill Will Jameson once owned. They teeter and move like princes in the wind, their shirts behind them, and maneuver across the cold railings in this desolate broken lot, thirty feet above the ground. They are the out-of-work children of out-of-work fathers whose grandfathers worked in the long ago. They are as tough as stone and as kind as a day is long.

Their names are Underhill and Nolan and Curtis and Curry and MacLeod. And they move like their forefathers before them, as if in their primitive hearts a fortune was at stake.

Meager fortune, to be sure.

Just before I turned fifty, I was sent Owen Jameson's Victoria Cross.

Someone felt I should have it before they settled the estate.

As I told you at the beginning of this story, I walked up to see the great Jameson house once more before it was torn down, the huge lot sold off for smaller prefab houses manufactured in Germany.

Too many pictures of men and streams and wood, and too many failed memories.

So I turned away in the night. And going down through the graveyard found the place where my mother is buried, quite near Reggie.

There would be no more famine for her now.

Her famine is over.

And the rest?

All is cut out, muted, torn away.

ACKNOWLEDGEMENTS

I would like to thank my editor, Maya Mavjee, and her assistant, Martha Leonard. Special thanks to my agent, Anne McDermid, and my wife, Peggy.

The author is indebted to the historian Don McKay and his book on Lumbering, and to Louise Manny's *Songs of the Miramichi.*

www.vintage-books.co.uk